Getting Life

Getting Life

by Julie Shaw Cole

The Advocado Press

2000

Published by the Advocado Press, P.O. Box 145, Louisville, KY 40201

FIRST EDITION

Cover and book designed by Barrett Shaw
Cover art by "Emily"

Library of Congress Catalog Card Number: 00-107280

ISBN: 0-9627064-8-5

For Ramona

Chapter 1

*T*hat light hits the side of the red roof at a different time each afternoon. I sit in the same place by the window every day. This window is on the other side of the street from that red roof. And I watch the light change just slightly each day, brushing back the shingles into shade, like gray paint rubbed into red.

There are pictures I remember in a book, churches, all alike, yet all different. There is one fat old soft chair. I am propped up on folded clothes and an old raggy pillow. Aunt Jo puts that book in my lap and leaves me to go do what she does. It might have been the only book we had, probably Uncle Nate's. He would try to make pictures kinda like the ones in the book. He would paint on old window shades from garbage cans he rooted through when he did hauling work. At times Aunt Jo'd scream, "Go, and take her with you!" and I'd get strapped on pillows up in Uncle Nate's big truck seat and off we'd go down alleys looking. I loved it so, sitting up in that old truck, bouncing down alleys lined with cans offering interesting junk. Nate would finger cracked mirrors, study broken shelves, and stack tons of cardboard boxes. But he especially treasured those canvas window shades.

In the light of the back window he'd set up some wooden props and put a board on that, easy; at least I think he said easy. I guess 'cause it made it easy for him to stand there in the light of the window to paint the pictures. I would watch as the light moved across the room and onto the board with the tacked-on window shade. Uncle Nate put a can with a few brushes and a strong smell in it on the smoking table. He squeezed buttery wads of color from small tubes he kept in a box high in the closet. I

1

watched as he moved the brushes in the light and made shapes on the old stained shades. He didn't mind that I watched. He didn't know that I wished very hard to be able to make such shapes and colors and lights move about like that. He didn't know that I wished that I could change the pages in the book. But when I lucked into the pictures of the churches all on two big pages, I could watch them changing in their light. It took a long while before I realized that it was the same church, but in different light, at different times of the day. I just hadn't expected that.

Here on Two-South, light makes new pictures of the roof and trees, never the same, day after day, season after season. Then the light slips off the red roof and the trees go black against the sky.

"Time for your supper, Emily, and you'd better eat it tonight, or it'll be bed rest for you for three days!" With a jerk I feel myself yanked backwards, then a turn and jerk forward toward the elevator doors down the hall. Never sure when the jerks will come. I can guess when the light gets to a certain point, but it changes every day and the jerks are nowhere near as predictable.

The elevator sinks out from under me. Another jerk as it stops and out the doors with a quick swerve to the left. My stomach turns, my head spins, and the dizziness overwhelms me. I could sink forward but the velcro straps hold tight to my shoulders. Then the smells hit, onion, burnt chocolate, corn, and the sickly sour sweetness of cabbage. It's just as well I didn't eat the lunch or it would be down my front and on the towel over my knees. It seems there's hardly any time between breakfast at 8:00, lunch at 11:00, and dinner at 5:00, and then a long time with nothing.

I wish I could eat in my room or in the sun room. If I could just sit quietly before I eat to avoid the awful sick from being jerked around. And if I could only escape those horrible kitchen smells. If I could choose when and what I eat. But it all comes at me so fast. I feel like everything in me is pushing back, "Back up, go away, keep out of me!"

"Here, Emily, you just quit that gagging." She rubs my dribbly mouth with the towel. "You wait here with George and Marie and I'll bring you your tray."

The table comes at me, and my knuckles scrape, my knees bump, and finally all the movement stops. My stomach churns, my head rolls back on the chair edge, and my eyes close against the hard fluorescent light grids glaring from the ceiling.

A moment of peace is dashed as Marie starts her babbling. "Ooh onn ook oh owl, Onnee." I open my eyes, slowly attempting a roll in her direction. George chimes in, his deep crisp voice pushing at me. "She says she thinks you don't look so well, Em."

How the hell does he know what she says, and who cares? She nods at me and grimaces congenially. I begin an eye roll in George's direction and then back to blink twice at Marie.

Jerk! I jump as the pressure on my knees is eased and a napkin appears under my chin. Trays arrive from behind me. The aide takes the large orange lids off the trays and stacks them on the empty table. George maneuvers his splint fork until it slips into the slot on his wrist brace. Marie clutches her strange swinging spoon and they begin.

I dread this so. The ordeal of food begins with the aide leaning her cigaretty face into mine.

"Honey, you ready to eat now?"

I notice my right hand drifting toward her face. Somewhere inside me a conflict begins, wishing to make contact, fearing the consequences.

George watches wrestling on Saturday nights. Sometimes I join him. He jabs and grunts, taking great pleasure in the minimal movements. He laughs loud as the big-bodied men crash and fall in a brutish tango. I enjoy the dance and sometimes slip down in my chair against the velcros and my arms wave like I'd like them to. I laugh with George till I cry.

My left hand hits my face as the right one drifts away from Nancy, the aide. I want to yell from the hurt.

"Now stop that wriggling and pay attention to your meal. Looks real good now, so c'mon."

A spoon with some unknown yellow thing on it comes at my face. She expects me to pop open like a baby bird and gratefully accept any crud that she pushes at me. I'd like to smell it first,

3

please. And then a tiny sample. I'd like to reserve judgment on that item. Let me inspect this more closely, if you don't mind. She does.

I know she means well, but she's rushed and has several more feeders like me to get to. I'd just as soon she'd not bother with me, but no one believes I could get enough in on my own. Maybe I couldn't. But I'd be willing to try.

"C'mon now, honey, open up. Gina said you'd be on bed rest if you don't get your food down. Now you know you don't wanna get stuck in that bed for three days!"

No, I am not sure that I know that. What bothers me most about bed rest is the loss of my window with its changing light. And sores. Out of sight, out of mind. When the aides don't see you in the hall underfoot, in their way, you are gone. So if I get stuck in bed for long, sores can get started on my back or heels. Like George, he's a quad, wrestling accident when he was 19. He can't move himself below the shoulders and hasn't much control of his arms. He uses splints to hold and grab things. But if those aides aren't sharp and move him at least twice in the night, he'll start to break down real quick. Pressure sores and skin breakdown are secret and bad. You can't feel where the blood ain't going and the sore starts deep down near your bone where the blood has quit because of the same pressure all the time. I've got kinda light red-headed skin, and when the aides forget to rinse me at bed bath I get a rash right away. And with "bed rest" (cold storage, George calls it), even if I try to wiggle when I'm awake my bony points get red. The thin tissues under the skin starve for blood, when the pressure cuts off the tiny veins and such, like broken straws. Judy and George both said that the places die inside, all secret deep down. By the time you know it, you are in deep trouble. Sometimes I feel like one big pressure sore, circulation cut off, secretly dying inside.

The good side to "bed rest" is less hassle in the halls. I just go into my quiet place and dream. That's better than what I see and hear anyway.

"C'mon, open up now. I haven't got all night with you! There's others want to eat, too, you know!"

I've been dreaming. I pushed her too far.

Jerk. "Wake up now!" Push.

In the food comes. I choke, coughing, trying to clear my throat. Oh, God. I haven't really eaten anything and my throat spasms out of control. I can't stop coughing. Marie fusses at Nancy.

"Not ath Anthy, Noo ukkin, Onnee!"

George chimes in, "She's saying you should stop that, stop harrassing, stop buggin' Emily!"

"You just keep shut, George, and mind your own dinner. I'm not so crazy about feeding her and I don't think you'd be too crazy about bed rest either."

George doesn't usually jump in on the defense like that. He keeps a low profile. He knows the danger of wave making. But there's times that our just being alive makes waves around these folks. By being, we get in their way and make hassle.

Well, she has managed to stuff that spoon in my mouth. It's full of a musty corny mush and I try to swallow slowly to keep from coughing up again. Why is everything I get mushed up, baby food?

Sometimes George's cousins bring him a box of snacks. What he can keep away from the aides he will share with me when we watch TV together. I treasure the hard crunch of thin wheat crackers against my teeth. Even more I love the salty cheesy hard-then-mushy cheeto feeling in my mouth. And my very favorites are the chocolate-covered raisins. Ummmmm, I love the dark rich pleasure and then the bitey sweet rubbery little raisins.

One night Mira, the new aide, peeled George an orange and put sections on his tray. The smell of orange rinds filled the room. The Rock and Stone Cold Steve Austin were sweating and grunting on the tube, but I lolled on TV Florida beaches and floated through magazine-picture orange groves full of fragrance. Mira left, and George stealthily bit half of a section poised neatly in his splint fork, then he put the other half to my lips. I quickly slurped in the treat. It was heaven, super sweet tart juice and chewy pulp.

5

Juice squeezed through my teeth and tears through my half-closed eyelids. I enjoyed that for weeks.

How can they make canned fruit taste so much like cans, all bitter and metallic? Mashed up apples like so much dust.

Oh! Uck. What is that? Nancy has shoved something new between my teeth. It's soft, lumpy, and smells of burnt beans. I try to swallow, but the shock of the bitter taste makes me burp and I lose it and more down my front.

"Oh, Emy, can't you ever learn to pay attention and eat? But here you are spittin' it up again like a filthy baby."

I'd love to shriek, "Nancy, do you ever have to eat this ground glop? And why is it always mushed up? Why can't I crunch the corn, feel the beans all fresh and round?"

I remember Aunt Jo's tomatoes. Late July she'd get so many fresh bright tomatoes. The Averys grew too many in their yard, and we enjoyed the overflow. I'd sit and watch the light from the window roll across those shiny red hot fruits. They gleamed like rubies, light flashing off like TV laser rays. Aunt Jo chopped some and put a bowl on my high chair. She didn't care from then on what I did. She put my chair on old papers spread on the floor. I'd get my face close to the tart juicy bits and watch my hand move near, inch by inch. It was a race to see if my hand or my face would reach the bowl first. I think Aunt Jo would have liked my hand to win, but usually the old face came in first. The pleasure of sucking in those tomato juicy nibbles made defeat into victory. I didn't mind juice in my nose. It smelled and tasted like sunshine felt and I'd laugh and sputter and chew.

I used to try to use my hands like that and often had some luck. Now I don't even feel like trying. When I first moved here, the aides would slap my hands when I finally got them onto something I wanted. They would slap them because I often turned over what I reached for. They didn't want to have to clean up a mess. And they wouldn't put old newspapers down like Aunt Jo did. They'd just slap. This cut something off in me. I gave up wanting to try to control things. I stopped reaching and succeeding. But my attempts to accomplish can never be like theirs. I can never reach what they consider their level, and I hate their anger when I try. Their actions are so easy, so successful. My efforts are a struggle and end up in chaos, to their way of seeing it. They hate me for causing them to put forth more effort. I feel trapped by their world, controlled. I can never be like them and we all know it and they don't hesitate to let me know it forever.

Now there's another spoon knocking on my teeth.

"Emy, pay attention and eat this, hurry up!"

She leans in the direction of another aide, Mira, who is wheeling someone toward the door.

"I get so tired of trying to get her to eat. I can't understand why she won't open up. She's gotta be hungry, there ain't nothin' to her."

I hate to be talked about like this. Sure ruins my meal. Another spoon surges at me; this time the muskiness tastes of chicken and cold starch and smells of weeds. Four bites into this meal and I'm ready for bed.

On TV one night there was a show about astronauts. It was a science show for kids or something. I really liked it; I still do try to see it when I can. They go places and talk about stuff that I've never heard about. This one night they were talking about how astronauts do on their spaceships. They were eating things out of bags and tubes, mushing them around to mix them. They were laughing and talking about how a B.L.T. tastes from a bag. I laughed and waved vaguely at Marie. She joined in and got the connection. "Onnee ons hu be a arwo not."

George picked up the joke and said, "Yeah, you wouldn't have to get used to the food. And with what they pay those folk you gotta know its gonna taste better than that goop here."

Then he laughed at the idea of weightlessness, but his face changed with the thought of floating free. Each of us went into our own thoughts of being weightless, no longer fighting the tyranny of gravity. I went to sleep that night dreaming of the imagined pleasure of no longer fighting meaningless muscles, of floating from place to place at my choice, with the merest nudge to propel me. Since then, I often carry that dream to my window to float in it out over the rooftops.

Ehh, a jerk. I hear Gina's tinny voice from behind. "She eating anything, Nancy?"

"Naw, she's mostly spitting up and gagging, and then sneaks in a bite or two. Lord, I don't know how to get her to eat. She's only weighing in at 85 pounds and I doubt we're getting in 600 calories a day even when someone remembers her snack and shake."

How pleasant to be analysed so thoroughly over dinner. I notice George putting his head down so his ever-present cap visor shades his face. He hates the constant pressure the aides and nurses, especially Gina, put on us about food, sleep time, radios, wheel tracks, bath requests, you name it. It is a constant war. It wears all of us down with the tense monotony.

I like to hang around with George when I can. He is smart and knows lots of things. He likes to watch school shows on TV and he writes in little books. He says he wants a diploma someday. He writes with a pen stuck in his wrist splint making each letter careful and nice. I never got to learn letters. Wish I could. A guy just moved in upstairs, and he just uses a paper of letters to talk. I'd like to do that, if I just knew how. I watch the letters on Sesame Street when I don't get laughed out of the Lounge. I can say them all in my head. But then the aides turn on their soaps. And what can I do with letters in my head?

"Open up, damn it. You quit this dreaming and eat. I got other stuff to do!"

She's yelled so loud that I startle and hit the spoon.

"Oh shit, Emy, now look what you've done."

George looks up sharply at Nancy, slips his fork off, and quickly backs his chair from the table and turns out to the hall. My heart sinks as I hear the elevator door open and the whine of his chair as he boards and is gone. Marie glares and tips her head back in Nancy's direction. She begins her backward shuffle, sluff, sluffing her slippers down the hall, rolling toward the Lounge.

And now I am alone at the table with Nancy, and Gina hovers, pushing old people out the doors toward the elevator, one by one, to load them on in groups of four. Nancy stares at me coldly and begins to push spoons at me one by one.

Chapter 2

Somehow I've managed to get up to my floor without losing all that crud. and making more people upset. I am in the line outside the hall bathroom. There are five other women in the line ahead of me. If I sign to go to the joint bathroom in my own room, I have to wait for the aide to notice that I need to go before she will come down to the room. Frankly, the aides have all they can do right now; they can't be running around checking rooms. They are feeding on the floor, cleaning up the bed people, doing early evening meds, getting rollies ready for any possible evening doings, and three aides called in sick. So my only hope of using the pot is to get into the very conspicuous line of ladies in need. Gina pushed me up here 'cause I made my pee sign after dinner.

There is only one aide working this john. There is only one stall wide enough for chairs. Three out of the five of us waiting are in chairs. The pot by my room is too small to get a wheelchair in. If I go in there it is because the aide carries me in. There are only two aides who are strong enough, and I still get embarrassed when Jerry is taking me in.

The older ladies in our joint pot are usually camping in there. I don't see Edna transferred in there often. She usually uses a bedside commode or the ever-present pan.

The aides most often transfer me to use this communal pot. Granted, there ain't much of me to haul around, but they manage to yank parts of me every day that I wasn't aware of before. You would think that after a while they would develop some kind of consistent method of jerking people around, but it is always new and different. I guess it keeps us from getting too bored.

George watches some goofy foreign stuff on that station with Sesame Street. He was watching some comedy thing one night a while back that made no sense whatsoever. George was rolling and howling to beat the band, but I couldn't understand them much better than I can Marie. Anyway they were going to torture this old lady with pillows and they threatened to put her in the "Comfy Chair."

"Yes, it's the Comfy Chair for you, har har!"

Now I really laughed at that part. I know the torture of the comfy chair.

Marlane's on pot watch. She pulls us in the john three at a time, if there are two walkers and a wheeler. The semi-walkers, using canes or walkers, are helped into the small stalls. Genevieve is crying. She is lost and doesn't know where she is. She never will. Wails float over the stall as Marlane scoots my chair up to the stall door. I guess that I can be grateful that I can't eat that gunk they serve because I am light enough for Marlane to heft up under my shoulders and swing me up and around and onto the pot. I lean clumsily onto her as she fumbles with my elastic waistband.

"I don't know why they don't just go on and put you on a catheter, girl, 'cause it'd sure ease my back a whole lot."

Them's fighting words, Marlane, and don't bring it up again. I'd like to hit her up the side of the head, and I can't. Lady! don't think you can take away my last semblance of human dignity. This is one thing I can control.

Aunt Jo spent twelve years potty training me. Twelve years of sitting just at a certain time of day, training me to respond physically to her own rhythms. Of a morning, Jo would go, and then she'd sit me on the pot and tie an apron – halter style – around my shoulders and onto the tank to keep me upright. Off she'd go to do what she did, and I'd wait for nature to call. Eventually, when I was about eleven and a half, nature began to coincide with Aunt Jo, and I only had to wear diapers at night. Even now I wear protection at night. The aides aren't anywhere as predictable as Aunt Jo. But they will not take this tiny bit of control away from me!

11

When I first got here the nurse on the top recommended I be put on a Foley, a catheter they put inside you. How humiliating, I felt, and how disappointing to Nature and to Aunt Jo, who knew nothing of catheters and leg bags and all that crap. She just knew that people used the pot and babies used diapers and so I was a baby to her till I was twelve.

Not long after I got here, a nasty bout with pneumonia laid me very low. Most of the staff here decided I wasn't long for this one. They put a Foley in me then, for the duration of the disease – much to the satisfaction of the top nurse, I am sure. My chest got better, but I got a super bladder infection. They yanked the Foley and put me in diapers until I proved to them that I could go the regular way, as long as someone paid attention to my signals. That was always the kicker. When no one noticed my signs, it was always my fault if I had an accident.

I know that catheters and paraphernalia like that are not the end of the world; I mean George and some of the others don't complain about their bags and such. But nothing really works in their plumbing, so they have to use the catheters and have a bowel program. But I still have this little bit of control left, Marlane, and you and all the wild horses are not going to take it away from me. Forget it.

Marlane has leaned me back on the tank and is hovering over me waiting for me to relax. That would happen a lot faster if she would just mosey on down the line and deal with someone else, like poor Genevieve, lost and wailing. A watched pot never gets peed into, Marlane, move on. I wonder how well she'd go if someone was staring at her. Particularly if her bladder was into spasm in the best of circumstances. Marlane, Genevieve just wet all over the floor of her stall. Go check on her, and maybe nature can make her customary visit to me while you are gone. I stare at Marlane, and try to catch her attention to the pee which is seeping under the stall wall toward us. Look! Marlane! Go!

There's a groan and a loud thump and a shriek. Genevieve has slipped in the pee and fallen. My chair plummets outward as Marlane tears through the stall door to the rescue. She's gone and the stall swings shut. I startle, but I'm fairly balanced and I don't slip down somehow. I can take a deep breath and let go. The ruckus around me is loud and scary. But I am relatively safe here in my stall and feel secure and can relax. I can let the chaos fade around me and steal the silence inside. In the distance I hear the slam of the door as the aides rush in with the gurney. With quick movements they lift and slide Genevieve onto the gurney and bang the doors until they are all out. Rose and Myrtle are moving slowly from the sinks, tap-shoving their walkers with extra care on the wet floor. They make quiet comment between them about Genevieve's condition.

"It didn't look good!"

"Whad ya say, dear?"

"I says it don't look good for Genevieve."

"How's that?"

"Now, stop and look at me when I'm trying to say to you."

"I don't need to, dear, I hear you just fine."

And they gradually get the door open between them. I can hear rushing and fussing in the halls. Creating quite a stir. Rose and Myrtle tug and manage the door between them and their walkers, and then there's quiet. I have found a little lucky solace of my own.

Sometime later, maybe twenty, thirty minutes, maybe more, I am abruptly brought back to the present by a door slamming against my chair which has rolled across the bathroom.

"Emily, you here?"

I make a noise in reply.

"Emily, where are you!?"

I noise louder. She has Myrtle's problem.

The doors slams shut. The voice fades saying, "I didn't see her, Marlane, and I don't know where she coulda' got to."

I can't help but chuckle. Didn't she notice the chair she slammed the door against? Now I realize that I have gotten cold and a bit stiff from leaning on the porcelain plumbing all this time in this funny position. I'll be glad to get back to my window and the setting sun. Way down the hall I hear Marlane.

"Lord, I left that child setting in there. Where could she be?"

"Well, I donno, you gotta look around."

I gotta admit, this has been pleasant. When I was doing all that potty training, sometimes Uncle Nate would read to me out of his big book of pictures. I didn't understand much about the French stuff, words which were names of people who painted those pictures that I liked. But I loved to hear Uncle Nate's quiet kindly voice and I'd dream about the places that he spoke of, like Paris, France. There were paintings of ladies on chairs, and dancing, and with children out in beautiful fields or near lakes. There were flowers that whirled and twisted, or that shimmered like lights as if the painter had grabbed sunbeams and rubbed them squeaking onto the picture. Then there were the churches which changed in the light.

"Em-i-lee, where the hell are you?"

The door has slammed open. I try to make my sound. The stall door crashes open, my body spasms and I startle so badly that I go stiff and slide off the commode with my leg stuck jerking underneath me. My slacks are all crumpled and twisted under me, too. Marlane grabs me up before I hit bottom but my right arm gets caught in the opening at the end of the seat. Well, this is what they mean by a rude awakening.

Marlane wrenches me off the floor till my leg untwists and makes a nasty snapping sound. I feel suddenly very cold. There is a sinking inside me and a strange numbness. Then a raw ugly screeching pain rushes up my leg and into my brain. I make ugly yelps with the hurt and tears pour down.

"Well, just quit that bawling, the nerve of you; we've been looking and calling and worrying our heads off and you just sitting in here all this time probably laughing at us."

Through the pain I am stunned. Why the hell's she blaming me? She was the one at fault, leaving me here all alone. I want to scream, what the hell was I supposed to do, come out jumping and apologising? If I had any strength and wasn't hurting so bad, I'd front end you, lady, and then I'd total your ass. But all I can do is scream and noise my head off and so that is what I am going to do now. But I want so bad to swing at her and tear her hair off. I want to slam my head up against the wall till I bleed.

"Emily Mason, shut up! Shut up now!" she shrieks at me.

Everything in me flails and rips, and she grabs me and squeezes until I can't breathe.

"Now stay quiet till I get your chair."

I am lying on that jerky leg and I can't believe how it hurts. She gets up and grabs my chair and pulls it to the stall door. Then she yanks me up from the floor, swings me around, and plunks me bare-assed onto the chair arm. It's cold. It's hard. She missed.

"Oh, damn!" she crabs.

I guess this is my fault, too, huh? Like it was my fault you left me here? And it was my fault you got hell from Gina Potter about losing a patient? And now it's my fault that you trimmed my rear and did God knows what to my leg and arm.

She grabs up my slacks and yanks them up as she slides me into the chair seat. With another shove she backs my chair, straps my velcro shoulder supports, slams open the door and speeds me down the hall, cussing under her breath the whole way.

Chapter 3

I am finally in the Lounge, where at least it is a bit warmer than in the john. It is a fair room with a couple of tables for cards and to eat at, and some old chairs and a TV on an old chest. My chair and I are stuck in the left side of the room where I can't see TV if I wanted to. There are a few folk watching from the other side, and a couple of old guys leaning into snores on the sofa.

Now that I am still, my body is setting up a howl. There are places hurting that I didn't know anything about before. My ankle and leg are really yelling. My left leg is starting to swell and throb. I can't help the sobs. They are coming from way down inside where I have no say over things.

Someone suddenly jerks my chair from behind. I gasp. Gina mock whines, "Why, Emy, what could be the matter with you? Poor thing, you feel left out?"

Her sarcasm barely penetrates the pain.

"Now stop that sniveling, Emily. You will upset everyone in the Lounge, and we are all here to have a good time."

I glance through the fog of tears at the whole gang good timin' it like crazy to the rhythm of Mr. Kneble's snores and the theme music of the soaps. Gina grabs my nose with a kleenex.

"Now, Emily, cool it, or you'll have every old lady on this floor upset. Blow!"

I blow obligingly and all the pain rushes at me like a crowd. I am going to faint. I do.

When I come to, I am still in the same place. I guess Gina in all her medical skill thought I had fallen asleep. The pain is steadily worsening, and the leg is filling my usually loose slacks. I try to concentrate on the TV sounds. The old ladies on the other side are now looking at Jeopardy. I can't even think to understand the questions. I recognize the pad-pad of Marie's slippers coming up behind me. Her chair backs next to mine and she takes my arm, the one without the big bruise. She mutters, "Oh, Onnee, ohta nattah?"

I am not really sure what she is saying, but I fall apart at the kindness in her tone of voice. I think of Uncle Nate stumping over to me when I'd fall off a chair, and he'd pick me up in his big smoky arms, and hold me till I didn't need to cry anymore. If Aunt Jo caught him, she'd yell, "Put that baby down, you gonna ruin her holding her all of the time, so just stop it!"

But he'd find a place where we'd be by ourselves and just sit and hold me on his lap. Sometimes we'd rock in the big chair. The crying felt good then, and Nate never said, "There, there, big girls don't cry." He knew better.

The memory opens more floodgates and I just cry with everything in me. Gina interrupts from across the room.

"Marie, tell her to shut up and stop that whining."

I can barely see the look Marie flashes at Gina. Marie moves behind my chair and with tiny shuffles she pad-pads out of the Lounge with me in tow.

We move along the hallway in our chairs, back to back, shuffling along at Marie's top speed until we reach the bank of windows on Two-South. She knows me well enough to know this is my hangout.

Marie's not too bad a person. I just hate to hear her try to talk. And her constant country music gets to be a bore, oozing out of the little radio on her lap. It's like Aunt Jo and Elvis and Tennessee Ernie. What a wierd combination. But Marie likes Waylon and Willie and Wynonna, not to mention Garth. They wail out all the sadness of lost loves and abandonment on the little jam box. The sun is long gone and my red roof is gray as it gets darker. So I just close my eyes and try to close out the mournful songs, but I can really hear their pain inside my own. And I try to dream of other times and places that haven't been and likely won't ever be.

17

A jerk, and my chair yanks me out of a pained peace and I am propelled away from Marie's music and down toward the elevator doors. Surely not another food encounter. What time is it anyway?

"Emily, Gina said I had to get you ready to go down now."

Down? Down where? Whoa. I want to yell no, but a noise blurts out of me formless and without meaning for her. Here is another space of the day where they have me totally at their mercy. Shit. Mira's quiet voice breaks into my muffled rage. What right has she?

"Emily, just relax. It can't be as bad as all that."

I feel myself slipping down in my chair. I wiggle against the velcro restraints and the monstrous pain until I feel my right foot's toes touch the floor between the foot pedals. One more random flail and I'll make contact. Mmfh! Damn, now I've bashed my head on the side of the chair. My left leg screams, but I feel my right slipper on the floor. The rubber sole grips, hard.

"Emy, you stop this, now! You could get hurt."

Get hurt? Get real, lady! I feel my foot firmly planted against the cold hard floor, and relish the pressure against her pushing. It feels firm and solid, and I slip down to the limits of the velcro using the hurt to stay put.

Gina appears way at the end of the corridor. She approaches like a white flag flying. Mira calls, "Gina, Emily won't let me take her up the hall."

"What did you say? What? Won't let you?" Gina barks, and my chair jerks back with Mira's jump. My right foot catches under the foot rest as Gina faces Mira down behind me.

"You'd better shape up, Mira," she hisses. "Your attitude needs a lot of work."

They come 'round the front of the chair and rip open the velcros and grab me front and back and haul me up. My caught foots scrapes badly on the pedal. Now with everything else, it feels like my foot is on fire. I cannot take anymore and I am going to scream until I run out of breath and die. Oh, there go my hands and legs, as if parts of me are taking off on their own, and I am left behind, a torso and pains and not much else.

Gina's face is directly in mine, eyes like ice cubes with flies frozen in them, getting bigger as she closes in for the kill.

"Emy Mason, get a hold on yourself! It is bed rest for you for three days. You have just let this whole episode get out of hand and I am sick of it. What in God's name has gotten into you, girl. Now shut your yap and go to bed!"

Breathing is becoming a problem. At this point I wish I had a push stick like Marie so that I could reach the elevator buttons. The door would open and there would be no car there and I could back me and the chair right down into that dark hole. I could enjoy the sensation of weightless floating down, down into sweet nowhere. Wouldn't last long and couldn't hurt any more than I do now. But the buttons and stick might as well be on the moon. Ah, to be on the moon, almost weightless, floating.

Suddenly the real elevator doors open, and there are lights and the car. And Gina whips my chair around and we slam over the inch of crack and on and up.

I am sitting near my room on Three-West, home again. Behind me a yell.

"S'Em scheduled for shower?" Please, God, no!

"Tomorrow night."

"Yeah, but chart says bed rest next two days." My sentence seems lessened by a day.

"I don't care what her chart says, I ain't got no room to shower her on my list for tonight. She'll have to do tomorrow."

When it gets like this, I feel for the prisoners on death row. The chair jerks, she mutters, "Damn, damn," and we head for home. Home. A hospital bed, a two-drawer bedstand, six inches of closet space, and rare access to a john for four. And the TV of course, which Edna pays for and controls. Her hands work, her head doesn't. I think.

I remember Shrine hospital. I am maybe nine or ten. I don't really know why I am there. Aunt Jo says, "The doctors will straighten you out, honey. You just do exactly what they tell you."

Those doctors are all hands on me pushing and tugging and

looking. I feel like Gumby, but no back talk. They say I can't talk.

They have this nurse named Mrs. Flanner who comes in. "Emy, we are going up now!"

Up! Up where? What for. What am I going to do that she announces so cheerily. I remember that I watch as Flanner and an orderly put me on a gurney and off we go to wherever they have in mind. Here's another elevator. A nickel for every mystery ride on elevators could buy my freedom. Bump, off the elevator, the lights of the hall roll over me and edges of faces float by.

They make a sharp turn into a room, green all around and a huge dome of light dangles in the middle. I see the tops of cabinets and funny-looking machines. What do we do here? I am terrified and start to cry. People in masks crowd around my head, and one with a head all wrapped in white comes at me with a huge needle. Every part of me moves to lunge away in the direction she isn't. What is this horror show with its white-wrapped spacemen? One grapples with me from the other side. They hold me down together and the needly one makes her attack and goes for the kill. I noise and struggle. A thing goes over my face. Muffled voices call out, "Emy, this won't hurt, don't worry, it'll be OK."

They lie, it hurts, and what is happening that I shouldn't have to worry about? With the mask-thing over my face they continue," Don't be afraid, breathe in slow and deep, sweetie, and you will go to sleep."

Oh, no! This is it. This is the big one. That's what Uncle Nate said about Rita Avery's dog next door. "Don't worry, Emyem. They'll just give the old guy some sleeping gas and he'll be off to doggy heaven." And I never saw Tipper again. Old Tipper, who had been my friend and guard when Jo would leave me on an old beach towel in the yard. They just killed him. I can't hold my breath any longer. My lungs fill for the last time with a terrible sucking gasp and a buzzing starts in my head and all the white-wrapped aliens dance aswirl down a tiny tube of light into nothing.

Unlike Tipper, I do wake up again. I come to, feeling their lies all over my body. I hurt everywhere and can move nothing to ease it. No! Something has eaten me alive. A huge white worm. From my toes to my shoulders it has devoured me. I begin to focus through the pain and heat and an unwrapped nurse comes in.

"Emy, are you awake?" I noise at her and cry which hurts more making more tears, a vicious circle.

"Now, don't cry, honey. That won't make it any better."

Perhaps nothing will ever make it any better. This realized, I feel a deep awful sensation overwhelming me, like an insatiable void opening up deep inside me, and I begin to fall, tumbling into that emptiness. A tremendous racking shaking passes through all of me as I continue the descent. As if to have something to hang onto, to break the fall, a clear cry thrusts out of me. As I sink I hear this piercing wail and try to grab its strength for survival.

"Emy!" she rushes into my view, "Stop that terrible sound. You want to wake the dead?"

Yes, that's it. That is where I am going. I'm falling down to wake the dead, to go to them and find out if it was like this for them.

"Emy!!"

Smack!

Her hand stings my face, distracting me from my mission to Limbo. Now, I am stuck here in this present void, half eaten by a hard white worm and hurting.

"Now, Emy, you are not hurting all that much."

Yeah? What do you know? Liar.

Since then, that year in the white worm case, the ache in my spine and hips and knees has never gone away. I dread being handled and moved and tossed. I am so small and light that they plop me like a pillow on my bed. Off with the snaps and velcro; yank down my slacks. That invariably sets me into spasms, pulling my legs together. My knees try to cross and badly stress the surgically repositioned and plated hips. And why was it all done?

"They have rebuilt your hip bones, Emy." Aunt Jo's face floats through the druggy haze. The nurses had come again with needles after my aborted trip to hell.

"When we get you home we'll start you to walking. It's gonna be great when you can walk like your cousins."

Why should I have to do that. They live in another town. Besides I ain't never walked before so I don't know that it's worth this hell.

I've been content to sit, in my stroller chair, on the sofa, in the little yard. Nothing I ever reached for had ever connected with my hands. This was all I knew. Things just sort of go by me, just out of reach. I am used to it. Why does Aunt Jo want to change this now? She wants me to walk like her? But when she walks, her arms and legs move together in rhythm to her steps, swaying lightly, easily. I knew in my pain-fog that all the white worms in the world couldn't mold my body into something that moved in swaying rhythms. Each limb is in independent operation mode. Messages I send with my mind are generally disregarded and often totally sabotaged.

No, Aunt Jo. I don't think that I will be walking like my cousins, or you, ever. No matter how important it is to you.

The pain brings me back to now. While Gina rolls me onto the bed, I watch where my leg has swollen from the fall on the toilet. It hurts deep down like old bad memories. My backside feels raw. Whatever is there now will really be in good shape after two days in bed. I try noising at Gina to get her to notice the bruises and swelling.

"Stop that noise, Emy. You are hitting the sack early tonight, no argument."

The dim light in the room does not support my side of the argument, and Gina plows into her work with no notice of my attempted signals.

Now comes the blouse; roll me right; roll me left. There's a finger in my eye. It's mine. She snaps off my bra. Even through the pain I sense the perpetual itch on my back. Laundry soaps, metal clasps, the fake leather on my chair, the velcro straps, all contribute to a perpetual rash. I can never get relief. No one knows of this constant discomfort.

Uncle Nate would scratch my back, maybe unconsciously, as we'd sit on the sofa watching wrestling. I'd be kinda draped over his lap or against his shoulder, and his gentle touch moved lightly on my back. The year of the worm cast left my skin like onion-skin paper, flaky and dry. Nate would gently scritch-scratch down my back to the waist cuff on my brace. I doubt he thought much about it. He just did it.

Gina props me up like a rag doll. "I sure don't know why I fuss at you to eat, you're easy to dress 'cause you are so light."

Flippable, flexible. Maybe I even bounce.

"Doing Edna is such a hassle," she hisses into my ear, so poor senseless Edna doesn't hear.

"I just hate that damn Hoyer lift!"

I often watch as they tug poor stocky Edna, pump, pump, pump, up into the hydraulic lift, her head lolling on the little attached support. Her hands hang flaccid beside her when she's in the lift. It is like she totally has given up control, sold it all to the Hoyer. Yet those same hands can change TV stations, feed her face, and rummage through my closet and dresser when she's wanting something. In the lift she's like a helpless baby.

Gina always sees me as a baby. She's ignoring my crying now, like a hassled mother changing a colicky baby, hoping that the end result will be a more content baby. Each turn, flip, jerk, aggravates the pain in my leg, behind, and arm. Gown now on, up go the rails, out goes the dim light.

Edna, long in bed, is now watching the dangling TV with men jumping out of cars, chasing others down an alley. I cannot deal with the pain of the men shot down in the alley. I can't get beyond my own.

I seem to have dozed a bit, such a relief, when the lights go on loudly and the graveyard nurse barges in.

"You asleep, Emy?"

Not now, dummy.

"Gina said you were a nasty girl tonight and making trouble. We called Dr. Pescula and asked for a TY.3 for you."

23

For being nasty and making trouble, I get a pill. The pill is for them, not me. They obviously have no idea what I am enduring. They only want to have an undisturbed shift.

A little cup appears under my nose and the bed head raises a bit. I work my mouth to reach the little pill. This is not often successful, but I want that little bear badly tonight. It's just hours too late. The abrupt awakening enlivened every ache and my behind and leg are screaming. She props me for a strawful of water. With more mouthwork the nasty thing gradually makes for my throat, leaving its bitter trail behind. It'll stick in my throat and burp bitter all night to add to the fun. But enough may get down to ease the sharpest edges.

Chapter 4

A bell rings over the whole building at 7:15 a.m. The morning shift are just starting their day. Edna wakes at 5:00 a.m. and turns on the TV, so the bell isn't cock's crow for me. I've probably had two to three hours sleep from the Tylenol. But as the aches sharpen with awareness and begin to creep back through all of me there is little hope of return to sleep.

I will wait here till the a.m. aide, Judy, comes in. If I smile at her maybe she will look at my arm and leg. The clock ticks and the farm report drones on, barrows and gilts up, feeder pigs; what the hell are barrows and gilts anyway? The weather, "cool, pleasant, and dry this fine autumn day," announces the cool, pleasant, and dry weather man. But no Judy when the bell goes off. Finally at 7:45, as the news lady bubbles cheerily over me, Judy strides sturdily into the room.

"Mornin', girls! Up and at 'em."

I try to catch Judy's eyes, but she bustles about the room pulling out clothes for us and getting a basin and towels to do baths. Surely then she will see the bruises.

"I see you are writ up for bed rest, Ms. Emy. So we'll just get old Edna up and at 'em so's she can head down for breakfast."

Lord, that makes it another hour anyway. I want to scream at Bryant Gumbel's placid face and Judy's big fanny as she hooks up Edna's Hoyer lift.

The Edna bed bath seems astonishingly meticulous today. I slide into an ugly memory dream of the hospital and nurses floating in and out of my awareness, as the pain seems to fill the room like a pressure, coating the walls with a slippery screamy slime. It

25

pushes at me like the room is filling with worms, or hot spaghetti. The pressure squeezes at me, suffocating me in the ropiness of it. I wonder how Edna and Judy still fit into the space.

The deliberateness of Judy's movements never seemed so obvious or so insistent. I try to focus on the TV, but the bland morning people are sucked into the purple whirlpool of squeezing pain.

Finally Edna is rolled out into the hall to await the breakfast "train" which will fill the hall with chairs and walkers and their attached people. When the danger point is reached these folks will be gradually shoved on the two elevators and shoved off on the Dining Hall floor. Those who can manage to fill their own faces at this hour of the day are the privileged few. The feedees stay in their rooms where harried aides will eventually get to them with mushy eggs, and hardly hot cereals.

Judy moseys back into my room and yanks down the side rails and throws down my covers. I now see the source of the purple screams. My leg is twice its usual size and has blossomed into a bouquet of blues, greens and purples.

"Lord 'a mercy, girl! What have you done to yourself?"

Sure, Judy, I just ran out in the night and jumped under a car; no, I jammed my leg under a moving elevator; oh, no, I fell off my steed Lightning, the NightMare, while doing battle with the Black Knight.

So much for the silent quick come-back. I just noise at her while flailing my color coordinated arm in her general direction. She looks disgusted and tears out the door toward the nurses station. She's gotta cover her ample ass and report this right away.

Judy and the day floor super, Ms. Neeley, are back in minutes. Judy looks mad.

"What happened here, Ms. Neeley? Nobody at shift staffing said anything about injuries or medications for Emily."

Her voice is protectively brusque.

Ms. Neeley is holding a clipboard, perusing it with a very concerned expression. She hands it to Judy and begins to poke at my arm and leg.

"Is this the extent of the injury, Judy?"

"I don't know. When I pulled back her covers, I was so shocked, I came right for you without touching her."

That's to protect herself, as if I could do anything about suing this joint.

"Yes, good. But there isn't anything about injury on her chart. They did order a Tylenol 3 and a two-day bed rest, but that is all that's irregular."

I try to catch Neeley's eyes, but no chance. She goes on about her work like a mortician. Up go my arms and gown and over I go so they can hear the tune on the other side. I hear a sudden intake of breath, probably Neeley.

"Yes, a number of contusions and discolored areas, with excessive redness and a major laceration just over the right trochanter. This is just disgusting. That night crew must do everything in the dark."

Judy is looking at the chart. I see her puzzling at it out of the corner of my eye which isn't fully stuck in the pillow.

"I don't wonder she was restless in the night. I'd 'a probably killed somebody if it had been me."

Gosh, maybe she understands. I often forget these girls are people, too. Mostly they act like pain-producing robots, or prison guards.

"Give her a thorough wash, disinfect the lacerations, and I'll order ice packs. I'll give Pesky a call when he gets here. He'll want to do a writeup right away.

They left, fussing and fuming, blaming the other shifts and generally fretting. I sometimes think that there are contests and rivalries between shifts, just to cause enough uproar to keep things interesting. This situation could be very entertaining for some time. It may even top the soaps for conversation topics.

Judy comes back and I get a fair bath, plus more intense pain, especially in my leg. When she rolls me on my left side everything in me spasms, and there go my arms waving and slapping in aimless revenge at me.

"Stop all that, Emy. I can't finish with all your jerking. It can't be helping you much either.

What is it like to stop moving on command? Judy, that is not something that I can do. I want to shriek. I make feeble screechings which further irritate Judy. Her washcloth is rough and raggy, and she roughly returns the irritation by rubbing bruises on my back. Vicious.

After all her scrubbing, I feel I am in a pool of pain-born sweat.

"Now your chart says bed rest, so I'll put you on your ice packs and you can watch TV."

Ah, the hot and cold treatment. From hot and sweaty, I am shocked into the intense cold of the iced compresses. I get rolled on my left side, and the St. Vitus dance starts all over again. The useless jerks take me over and the pain intensifies terribly. It feels as if it's filling the room again. It takes over me, then Edna, and Judy, then out to the halls felling each person it meets, shattering their wills. The power of the pain fills me and it sends my loose arm out into the air with tremendous force where it contacts Judy's big chest causing both of us to reel back. She looks at me with hurt horror on her face. I just jerk about on the freezing packs..

"Emily Mason, have you gone mad!?"

She's clutching herself with both arms, wincing and tearing up. Tears begin to drip down as she says, "I don't think you realize what you have done! Striking staff is a matter for the Staff Council and the Advisory Board. You could get in big trouble!"

Get in big trouble? What do you call this? I try to ignore her as she rages on. She even catches Edna's attention, as she tries to hear her post-breakfast soaps. I just rest on lumps of ice, relieved to be off of my left side. It is like relief you get when they stop beating you. The pain takes too long to go away, and you know it's bound to start up again.

Sometimes when she'd been drinking a lot Aunt Jo would just wander around and scream. Uncle Nate would take the rage for a while, but as soon as she started in throwing things, he'd leave and I'd know I was in for it. Sometimes she'd jerk my chair and I'd fall out and she'd roll the chair over me again and again. At times she'd get a brush or a heavy spoon and swing at me for a while. Being a sitting duck, I must have given her a lot of satisfaction. Or maybe my inability to fight back was frustrating to her. But then she'd pass out and I'd pass out. For real different reasons.

One time I remember Uncle Nate coming back in and picking me up. There was even less of me then. We walked out the door, he walking in his lulling limpy way for a long time. I could doze till we reached the clinic in Marston, just up the road. Nate would cry as the nurse checked me over. I wondered if she hurt him, too. Aunt Jo, I mean. I remember one time the nurse had to sew places up on me. Then he picked me up and held me till the stings went away. That was the one thing good about the body-eating worm. There was a lot less of me Aunt Jo could get at.

I guess Judy's stormed out to get help. I know she is going to hold this against me. It matters not that I have no control of these arms. She plans to take this personally. They always do.

For a long time Regis floats over my head, his audience applauding every stupid little remark. I wonder if I could get that kinda support if I could walk and talk and look glamorous. Regis fades away and Maury Povich intrudes on my pained napping.

Suddenly a dietary aide pops in with a tray. Breakfast? I notice the Noon News overhead, with chuckling anchors making the stories so pleasant, palatable. I don't remember breakfast. She puts the tray on my bed table and slides it vaguely in my direction. If Judy gets out of her swivet at me, I may get to eat some. That might be nice. No disgusting lunchroom stench. But I fade out as the soaps drone on. I am too tired and sore to stay conscious.

The light in the hall tells me that it is late afternoon. There is a bustle of voices and steps in the hall which wake me. Gina and Dr. Pescula blow in, clipboards at the ready.

"Well then, when did all this start?" he asks briskly, scanning the board.

"Yesterday, when Genevieve fell in the bathroom, Marlane, a new aide, was doing transfers and she got rattled and caught up in Genevieve's emergency and left with the gurney. Emily was on the pot at the time and Marlane accuses her of hiding there."

That was said with a fair amount of sarcasm and raised eyebrows on both their parts.

"So she went back looking for her after the mess was taken care of and Emily was missed on the floor. She couldn't find her."

Yeah, where was I going to hide? Dr. Pescula looked at me skeptically, then at Gina, then at the chart. Pretty unlikely, eh, Doc?

"That doesn't begin to explain lacerations and bruises."

"Well, Doctor, Marlane said she went back to check again and found Emily in the first stall. She cleaned her and transferred her and took her to the Lounge. Later she brought her up to bed."

Gina, you forgot the best parts, like the cracking sound my leg made during the transfer, and the close encounters with the toilet seat and chair arm. And that it was you, not Marlane, who brought me to bed.

"Here, I'll look her over," he grumbles and tosses the clipboard at her.

"Her behavior has been just abominable lately. Why just this morning she was yelling and screaming and took a pop at Judy Swade on the shoulder."

"Is Ms. Swade doing OK now?"

He shoots a nasty squint in her direction and proceeds to poke and pull around my leg while noises squeak out of me uncontrolled. As he lifts my leg he notices the flat melted ice packs.

"What are these doing here?"

"Oh, we've been making cold applications."

He gives her a wry look, while holding the limp tepid bag like a dead puppy.

"Um-hmm, I see."

There was one shock application at 8:00 a.m. and I don't believe I've eaten today either, Doc. Does this bother you? This is my version and you will likely never hear it.

He continues moving my leg causing pain waves to roll repeatedly over me. I noise uncontrollably and tears just wash out and down my cheeks. He eases me back into a decent position and puts a pillow between my legs, relieving the adductor tension. He smiles and turns, shoving Gina toward the door. I don't recall being spoken to.

I can hear them outside. You know dummies like me can't talk, or be spoken to, so therefore we cannot hear. So he tells Gina, "Ms. Potter, that woman has a possible multiple fracture and a sprained elbow and her back is covered with contusions and an incipient decubitus is starting on her rear and you have no indication on her chart how this all may have transpired. I want to see your floor staff in my office STAT!"

I wonder what will happen now? They leave and I see no one else until Mira brings Edna to bed. I watch them swinging about until Edna seems clean and comfortable. Just before shift change Mira brings me a Tylenol. By then I am almost used to the torment. Who cares. I can doze in and out, and no night staff comes in.

Chapter 5

*E*arly next morning Judy rambles in to fix up Edna for her "family day." Particular attention is paid to clothes and hair. That makes less of Edna to deal with as she'll have lunch with her niece in town. Judy rolls Edna gleefully into the hall.

Judy doesn't come back until Regis floats over me again. She has a gurney and the orderly, Jerry. She pulls a hospital gown from the drawer and tucks it around me after a quick wash-over. They slide me onto a fresh sheet half, roll me to the left, agh, then unfold the sheet, magically lifting me onto the gurney. Judy grabs the drab green blanket and tosses it over me. Out we go.

I begin to stiffen as heads and lights float by fast. Where to now? The front elevator? The front entrance? An ambulance? Whoa! Isn't anyone going to consult me about this? Maybe I don't want to go anywhere in your ambulance. Wait!!

Jerry looks down at me as he shoves the folding gurney onto the ambulance.

"You'll be fine, little lady. They just gonna check your leg."

That is the first clear direct message I've gotten since I fell.

Thank you, Jerry. I would like to wave at him in thanks, but I just make strained giggle noises and grunt when the pain meets a bump. Jerry secures the velcro straps on the gurney. Judy jumps in at the end of the driveway and sits near my head, looking nervous, like she's the one with the bad leg. New bumps in the road are all outlined in pain. I imagine my leg filling the interior of the ambulance, squeezing and shoving me into a corner.

"We're nearly there, Em."

Judy shifts her bulk uncomfortably as her knees cramp in the small space. I can see hurt in her eyes, a tiny mirror of my own. There is no siren, no emergency. The ambulance waits at lights. No particular rush.

❖   ❖   ❖

I wake to sounds of soft voices, air-conditioning rumbles, clinkings of ice, and rubbered footsteps. I don't remember anything since the ambulance. Must have fainted. The fuzziness fades and I feel a sense of bloating fullness and in a rush everything in me, and that can't be much, jumps out of my mouth. It doesn't go far as I am on my back and can't move anything. There is a heaviness below my waist and, as I begin to gasp for air through the nasty mess in my throat, I realize a horrible memory. The white worm is eating me again and I barf again and choke.

"That woman is aspirating!" I hear called from above me and a person rushes up to the gurney and flips me and the weight over. I feel my mouth drain and the person pushes me hard in the stomach from behind and up all comes again. And then I can breathe.

Arms go around me once more and I am up in the air as a new gurney rolls toward me. That person leaves me on my stomach and a nurse wipes my neck with a blessedly cold cloth. They are quiet and the fuzziness takes over.

I wake slowly in a pleasantly bright room. The eternal TV hangs a soap over my head. I don't know where I am but I know the worm has returned. My right leg doesn't seem to be eaten this time. I send a move message to it and as usual it does its own thing. The message to the left leg is met by a dull ache and no more. The consuming pain is gone, eaten by half a worm. Better than none!

Again I wake. There are three people: Dr. Pescula and another man and a woman.

"Hello, Emily, this is Dr. Harmon and Dr. West. They are going to take care of you while you are here at the hospital."

Oh, so I am in the hospital. First I heard. How long is my stay? Stay of execution? And who gave you permission to do all of this stuff; oh, not that I am not very grateful. Here's one from the soaps. "Oh, Doctor will I be able to walk?" Answer that one. But Dr. Pesky ignores my noise and blinks and the two men leave. The woman stays.

"Excuse me, Ms. Mason. Would you mind if I check your injuries?"

After a noise and blink she gently pokes at my bruises. She asks permission! Then she pulls up a chair and sits. The soap draping over us must have caught her attention.

No, it's not that, because she scans the ever-present chart, then looks at me and smiles. Smiles! There are suddenly tears running down my face and I can't control my throat and, like the vomit earlier, I feel a huge rush of feeling swelling up and out of me in sobs and cries. I am so embarrassed. She takes my hand and tissues off my face. No questions, no chat, no there-there shit. She just quietly wipes my face as all this whatever drains out of me. I shake with racking sobs; I can't remember when I've cried like this. Finally the deep gulps for air slow down, so I can lie and just breathe. She's still there.

"Ms. Mason."

She asks for Aunt Jo again. No, she's looking right at me. She means me. No one has ever called me Ms. Mason, a grown up Ms. Mason.

"Ms. Mason, may we talk? I realize you are tired and need rest, but I thought you'd like to know what's happened with you."

Would I, sister, you bet! I suddenly feel very strange and cold. She's been sent to tell me I am a goner. Nobody's ever paid this kind of attention to me before. No, lady, I don't want to hear it. Go away. I try to turn my head away.

"Ms. Mason, would you prefer that I come after you've rested?"

What, to delay telling me goodbye? I stare at her with one of my killing looks.

"Ms. Mason, I realize you must feel very angry about all this. I have to tell you that your leg was badly broken. Since you don't get much chance to put weight on your bones, they are fragile.

Dr. Harmon set your leg and applied the cast. The anesthetic that helped you sleep also made you nauseated. But you are doing very well now and on the way to complete recovery. I predict that you will be back in your chair and home in a week.

As I realize that I am not dying after all the tears come again. She has tapped a ground spring in me and I ruin a lot more tissues.

I cannot remember anyone else, other than Nate, ever explaining anything to me. Maybe she is crazy like Nate? But can you be crazy and be a doctor going through all that school?

I remember once being in the lounge when George's brother came to visit him. I heard him yelling at George, "But why in God's name did you let them do this to you? Them doctors are just crazy as you are to let them cut you up like this. I just can't believe this. It is too horrible!"

"Lenny, I just wanted to be able to move about on my own. They said it would let me sit again. My legs had gone bad what with the contractures, and the bedsores, and the ruined circulation. They wouldn't let me sit up with the legs so bad. "

"But George, they was your legs. You'll never walk again now, never. Them asshole medicos have done you in for good."

"I was never gonna walk anyway, you fool. When are you going to wake up and see that I am a gimp, a cripple, a hopeless basket case. A C-4,5 quad does not walk again. I took the chance with the surgery to get some control. It was my only chance to really live, to get out of this dump. So you wake up and smell the light and get the hell off my mutilated ass. It's ugly but it's all I've got."

I had never heard George yell in anger, and only rarely did he yell in pain. I was shocked. I thought a long time about what he said to his brother.

So who is crazy? What does that really mean? This crazy lady, is she for real? I'm not sure I can believe her.

"Ms. Mason, I am Ellen West. I'd be just as glad if you called me Ellen."

If I did what?

"I hate to keep pestering you but I would like to ask you a few questions, if you aren't too tired. Dr. P. said you use one blink for yes and two short blinks for no. Is that right?"

My eyes and noises scream a rich yes.

"Thank you. If I might ask a couple of quick ones for the files, then if I may return tomorrow for more?"

I squeeze out a clear yes.

"Thanks. To verify some notes, are you . . ."

Why is this woman asking me these things? They always ask the aide or orderly. She thinks I know about me. I do. But no one else ever seems to think that, or asks me.

"Thirty-four years old?'

A long squeeze and accompanying noise.

"Have you lived at South Pines sixteen years?"

I guess. I'm not sure. I musta been 17 or 18 when Jo died. First Nate, then Jo just kinda hung on for three or so years. None of them good. She just wasted away. In the end she was there in one cot, I in the other. I watched her fade. I was so hungry and scared. She'd probably been gone a day or two when Rita came round to look in and found her dead and me nearly. Now I am drifting again and this doctor is paying me attention. She's crazy.

"I am sorry if that question upset you, Ms. Mason."

"I blink two times to cover, but I am upset, and tears ooze through blinks.

"Ms. Mason, has anyone ever taught you to read, use letters, or a symbol board, you know, with pictures on it to point to?"

I blink two shorts. I wish I could tell her about my Sesame Street dreams, and TV tag. Nobody, lady, has ever given a shit what I thought outside of Nate, and maybe George. The only thing I'm ever asked, "You need to pee?" And they only ask that to avoid a clean-up job.

"I get the impression that you have a lot to tell. What do you say we get together again soon. Maybe I could introduce you to some people that I know."

Another blink and she off-handedly tissues off the tears.

"May I see you tomorrow at 10:00 a.m. sharp?"

Sure, honey, I'm free then, but I do have luncheon and cards at noon and a concert at 2:00, so no dawdling. She stands and swings her tall self around the door with a high sign and a wave.

Chapter 6

Next morning I am awake with the shift change, and eager for clean up. This is the first day in years I remember being excited about waking up. The achy leg is almost a relief from the painful days before, and that crazy lady really talked with me, and she is coming back. Feels like cold ginger ale popping about in me and I'm a bit light in the head.

Breakfast is heavenly. This is the first meal I've eaten here. They've put stuff in my veins till now. My unrestrained arms are getting some feeling back since they took out the needles. No one must have told the food people about the mush rule. I have a real poached egg and crisp buttery toast. There are fresh orange and grapefruit pieces in a bowl. There's apple juice and a milk shake and all with a straw.

The aide is patient with me. Crispy bits of toast fight my teeth and dance around my tongue. The soft tasty egg mixes all in for easy swallows. The aide asks me if I like it. She asks me! I blink a long yeah and make an eggy smile.

"That's good. Take your time. Enjoy."

The fruit in its fresh sweetness makes me think of George and I wish I could share it with him. The rich cold shake fills me up so full I need to scooch back to give my stomach room.

"Well, there you are, all done. Let's clean up, then you can rest till the doctors come."

As we "talk" there is a pang in me that I have not sensed since Uncle Nate died. With his horrible deep coughs I would wish that I could cough for him as I sat by his bed. I wanted to ease the hurt. When the coughs would quiet he'd look at me and we'd talk.

"Emy, honey, you gonna take good care of Aunt Jo for me, ain't ya?

I'd blink long and try to noise and nod.

"Emy now, don't you let 'em put you away, honey. You learn to read now. We started your ABC's and you got your book, so you can do it. You ain't no dummy, and don't let Jo make you believe that you are. She always wanted you to be the dummy so she could feel better than you. That's 'cause she was never treated too good either. I took her in after that pig husband of hers beat her near dead and she needed to hide from him. I guess we none of us knew any better about being beaten. Our pa was always after our ma and us with his belt.

"Then when your ma died, and I took you, Jo grouched for a long time cause she was jealous, but now she's trying to do right by you. Don't forget that. Oh, why didn't I teach you earlier? I'm a damn fool. Time goes by s'damn fast. You was just a baby no time ago and here you are 14."

We had our last few talks together. Jo didn't sit with Nate much near the end. She was hurting too bad, I guess. If he'da taught me letters, maybe I could have had another chance. But even if I could have spelled my thoughts to people, where could I have gone to live, other than a place like South Pines?

"Ms. Mason?"

A knock at the partly open door. Someone knocking for me? Why not just barge in? I noise at the call to say, "Come in, please." Not a bad try, not clear as Marie. God, I hate to sound like Marie. But I do. Only worse. I hate to hear her talk. She sounds like I could. Aunt Jo always said, "Don't make those disgusting dummy noises, Emy. They are so horrible, like an animal."

So I don't, unless I can't help it.

She smiles as she comes in, that tall doctor, and moves over to the orange stuffed chair near my bed. "May I use your chair?"

My chair? What a laugh. I blink long and try to direct my eyes at the chair, like polite people on foreign TV. "May I?" "Please do," Mrs. Mumbles mutters, casting her gaze at the plush chair behind the tea table full of cakes and silver. But just noises here.

Dr. West doesn't seem to notice the disgusting sounds. She doesn't screw up her face and look offended. She looks at me even better than TV ladies at tea.

"Ms. Mason, can I get personal?"

My eyes drift from where I wished they'd go, but I blink a long one at her and grunt.

"Are you doing OK at South Pines? Do you like life there ?"

She is looking quite sincere. My eyes wander and I feel an urge to laugh uncontrollably.

"Do you get to do any interesting things?"

Blink, blink.

"Is anyone there arranging activities, involving folks in stuff to do?"

Blink, blink. Unless you count roof-watching and Marie's jam box interesting things to do. Well, there is down-hall slalom, for sport, or the weight events, like clean and jerk. And there are the soaps, both on- and-off screen. It gets old. Do you like bingo? Once a week, quarter a win. Not a bad way to meet people. They try. They're very trying. Once George started a Video Club, but when the VCR broke after four weeks, four films, it was never fixed.

Blink, blink, what can I say?

"Do you think you'd like to be doing more things?"

Blink, and noise.

"Before you go home, would you mind having some assessments done by the clinic people downstairs? It would give you an idea of what you might get more involved in."

I guess she saw my puzzled look. I blinked within it.

"I also have some friends who are involved in a place called an independent living center. I am not sure that I can get them over here before you go home, but would you be interested to hear what they have to say?"

I think, perhaps, but how is that blinked. I guess, lady, that a friend of yours couldn't be too bad, if they are like you, or are you an illusion?

"Do you feel well enough for a ride downstairs? Would you object?"

My head rolls away, because I really want to look to see if she is there. Did she ask if I objected? Two blinks, a noise, and let's go.

"Fine. Excuse me just a moment."

Oops. Gone. See it was all just a fantasy.

Then she just as suddenly reappears. With her is Dr. Harmon and an orderly. Harmon looks at my leg and feels near the top of the wormy cast.

"How's this feeling inside, Ms. Mason? Not too much pain?"

As he continues his examination I give quick blinks and make a smile in his general direction. He gets the message and grins.

"She's yours, West."

Harmon leaves in a rush and the orderly and Dr. West move my chair close for a transfer. She sits me up while the orderly maneuvers the chair closer. She holds firmly but gently and her perfume or something makes me feel dizzy.

"Are you feeling faint? We can wait another day. No rush."

Two blinks, I don't want to wait. I don't know what she is planning but its gotta be better than soaps.

"Mike, could you run to the box just left of the station and get some cola or juice? Blood sugar boost, here."

She sits with me leaning against her till the orderly brings a drink and a cookie pack. I sip in my usual snarf, gulf, cough manner. Mike unwraps the soft cookies and puts bits of them in my mouth. It's a real treat and we have some laughs. And sure enough I get a peppy feeling and we make the transfer into the chair with the footrest propped for the cast.

We wheel out the door and down the green shiny hall, Dr. West walking next to my chair, steering with one hand and chatting.

"I hope you don't mind. I took the liberty of setting these appointments so you could have them before you leave. I figured that would save you the hassle of having to come back for them. And somehow, by miracles, there were openings, in optometry and audiology, so we have a busy day if you feel up to it."

I blink and grunt a bit. We fairly whiz to the elevators, passing carts, aides, nurses, and patients moving through the halls.

The elevator sinks out from under the chair and I watch the dial as we drop ten floors. I make a note to try to get near a window when I get back up. I've never been that high up before. Think of the sights and lights going on way up there.

We turn right and zoom past glass-fronted doors with words on them. Some are slightly open and I just glimpse people sitting inside waiting, waiting. I begin to feel a bit tense. I recall waiting rooms and Nate, and hurting and wanting not to. I hear Nate's low voice trying to help the hurts.

We open one of the glass doors and Dr. West leans into a window in the wall of the room. A hidden voice indicates still another door to pass.

I wait for Dr. West among the waiters, and a child with glasses and a patch over her eye stares at me with the other one. Her braids swing as she turns to her mother.

"Mommy, why does that lady sit all twisted?"

Her mother turns red and jerks the child near to her and hisses into her ear. Dr. West notices and turns from the window.

"Ms. Mason has a condition called cerebral palsy. Her muscles work differently from yours, like the muscles in your eye which are getting training now to work better with the other one. For various reasons our brains might not get all the right messages to all the right muscles. So they act differently from what you might expect."

The child smiles and touches her glasses. She smiles at me warily and curls close to her mother.

The inner door opens, so we head down a narrow corridor and turn into the door of a tiny room with a big black machine hanging down.

"That machine just checks your vision. It only looks weird."

Another white-coated lady steps in.

"Hi, Ellen, is this your little friend?"

"This, Barb, is Ms. Mason."

I detect a little hard tone in Dr. West's voice.

"Dr. Walker is an eye doctor and she will look into your eyes and check them for you."

Yes, I'm afraid. No one has mentioned whether this will hurt or not. Before, when they said it wouldn't, it usually did. It's hard to trust these people.

I get drops in my eyes. No hurt. After a bit, Dr. Walker looks in with a bright light. Then I get to look in the machine at little pictures and big ones and things on the wall and little cards. Lots of blinks and grunts. A black spoon over one eye, then the other. More grunts. It is kind of fun. Dr. Walker asks me if I can see better, not better, over and over as I try to focus on the shapes. I frankly find the whole thing a bit of a blur.

"I'll send you a report in a day or two." Dr. Walker talks to Dr. West.

"Her left-eye vision is fair, possibly correctable, but . . ."

"Excuse me, Barb, Ms. Mason needs to know this, not me."

There is a momentary exchange between their eyes that I catch in spite of my rather blurry vision. It makes me a bit uneasy. I feel a twinge of nausea.

"Excuse me. Your left-eye vision is fairly good, but you have little use of your right eye due to untreated amblyopeia. You could see to read, but probably not for extended periods of time. Right now, I think a left-lens correction might do you a little good, but not unless you do a fair amount of reading."

She seems a bit curt and looks at Dr. West with an edge to her glance.

"Well, Ms. Mason, you have the same problem as the little girl out front, but she is young enough that it can be corrected to a certain extent. You are seeing pretty well with what is still working."

Dr. West smiles and thanks Dr. Walker, and we leave without dawdling. I get a feeling that Dr. Walker was relieved.

"Do you want to go on with this?" Dr. West asks as we wheel out the clouded glass door. There is a pinch of darkness in her voice which makes me wonder if she is asking me or herself.

I blink yes, and I gotta admit I am enjoying this attention. We roll toward the elevator and Dr. West greets various people we pass. One lady stops for a minute to ask a question and Dr. West introduces me. The woman doesn't look at me as she nods vaguely in my direction and continues talking to Dr. West. As they ended their chat, the woman waves a hand in my general direction and says, "Well, Ellen I guess you'd better get your little charge back to bed now."

As we roll away, Dr. West apologizes for her adding, "She's a nice person, but sometimes is a bit of a twit."

Oh, Doc. I wish you could know all of the twits inhabiting my world.

Before we get to the elevator, we reach a central hall I haven't noticed before. Same glass doors and letters, until we arrive at a small office with a very small person. He comes right out and shakes my hand, looking at me at eye level. I am shocked. His moustache gives him the age his size denies him. I feel him looking into what I am thinking of him.

"Ms. Mason, this is Mr. Hanson. He is an audiologist and will be testing your hearing today."

I guess I look as startled as I can look. I know I am making fretting noises. Mr. Hanson smiles at Dr. West and goes back to another room.

"I hate to ask you this, but is there something bothering you?"

I squirm randomly, trying to avoid her glance. I can't. I see she is amused.

"Could it be bothering you that Mr. Hanson isn't what you expected? That his size and differences are not what you are used to?" she smiles, and her eyebrows do a little dance.

I feel a shock like icy water on my face. Hanson is back and I feel their eyes, and I roll my head to get away from them. Hanson chuckles and rolls his eyes, turning to go over to a desk. I notice leg braces under his slacks, which explain his stiff rolling gait. I can almost hear the Aunt Jo in me saying, "How can they let a crippled midget run a hospital office?" I can't believe my own thoughts. But I have never seen a different sort of person able to do any more than sweep, or do dishes, like Teddy at the home.

Dr. West rolls me into a booth with an open door twice as

thick as usual. She says I'll be in here for the tests and sits next to me after closing the big door with a heavy thunk. It seems deadly quiet. I can hear us breathing. I think of all the times I'd have enjoyed this kind of quiet in my life. At the home there is a constant drone of noise. Even in the dead of night an aide may have on a radio or several rooms may have TVs on. There is a sticky muzak that plays over all the other sounds, and in summer there are huge droning fans at the ends of the halls pushing what little room-conditioned air there is around the place.

We watch as Mr. Hanson climbs onto a high stool and reaches for the controls before him. His voice comes at us warmly through a speaker just above the glass window. His voice sounds tall then. It's confusing. He asks Dr. West to put the headphones on my head when I am ready. I blink my readiness as she asks with her eyes. The voice now comes directly into my ears. It is like Mr. Hanson is sitting in my head, somewhere in the center. Weird.

"Ms. Mason, Dr. West says that a single good blink is your yes response."

I blink in reply.

"So if you don't mind, would you give me a blink if you hear a tone in your headphones."

He plays a tone in the center of my head. I guess it is in the headphones. I blink.

After a few more instructions, like signals for each side which we develop after some trial and error, we get rolling. He obviously knows what he is doing, and I am having some laughs at the whole process. At the end he says he is going to give me a sound treat while he adjusts some knobs and dials. Suddenly somewhere deep in my head and coming from everywhere I hear the most breathtaking sounds I have ever experienced. It is music like George listens to sometimes on the Sesame Street station. But it feels like it is coming from inside me, around me, and everywhere outside of me. I am overwhelmed and shiver with the beauty.

Dr. West looks concerned. "You OK, Ms. Mason?"

I blink a long yes, squeezing tears out of my eyes. They roll down my face as the sounds move through me like magic waves. I feel carried off and away. I blink yes again, wishing this could last forever. But a few minutes later the music ends and Mr. Hanson signals that we can take off the headphones and come out. Dr. West offers a tissue and asks again how I am. I wish I could tell her how that made me feel and ask her how it could happen again.

We roll out of the little booth and Mr. Hanson comes 'round to shake my hand goodbye. He's a nice guy with a warm gentle face and rich brown eyes. I smile at them, inwardly ashamed at my earlier feelings. I have had to learn the hard way how people react. How I have reacted. I'm put off by gimps like me. I guess we aren't like most people. But everybody is different. I wonder why people like me or Mr. Hanson are considered so much more different? And why am I so bothered? I ought to be used to it.

I can remember before we got the chair at the rummage sale, that Nate would strap me in the basket at the grocery. Me and a sack of potatoes, cruising around the aisles. Women and kids would pass by. The women looked away. The kids often stared into the basket. Did they wonder why a kid near their age was so lazy, or why Nate would let such a big kid ride? Bolder ones would ask. "Hey mister, why's your kid all bunched up in that basket? Don't she got legs? Don't she talk? Whyuntcha make her walk? Huh, mister?"

Nate usually smiled and told them that I couldn't walk or talk like them. They would often then back away and stare from a distance. I would see them watching as they moved to other aisles. I would see them in a glimpse as they passed the end of the aisle and looked again and then hurriedly moved on. The difference seemed so big, so worrying to them.

I want now to change this thought subject, as it is making me achy. I want instead to cling to the music sounds which just poured through me. I also notice that I am very hungry, and considering those possibilities is very amusing.

Dr. West rolls me back onto the elevator and up we go. I can feel pushed into my chair and bounced up as we reach our floor near the top. As we get off she pushes my chair over to the huge window across the hall. I remember wanting to see from up here. The window reaches all the way to the floor. I am floored. I had no idea that so much could be seen at once – the big buildings in town and the cars so far away and people scurrying about like bugs. I am amazed. I wish desperately that I could ask her if I could come watch the sundown here. But I can't figure a way to get that across to her.

Back in my room is a real lunch. Vegetable soup and thin sliced chicken on a sandwich with a tomato. Oh, a tomato! The aide who helps is polite and gives me plenty of time, but I could see that this is new for her and she is rather uncomfortable. Perhaps like I was with Mr. Hanson.

After lunch I get put into bed and gladly take a nap. I wake up to a lot of noise and commotion in the room. It seems dark. I can't believe the nurses haven't brought me any dinner or anything. I must have been more tired than I knew.

Now someone else is being moved into my room. The clock on the TV has a 3 on it. Could it be that late, or that early? The person being moved in requires a lot of assistance. People mill in and out behind the curtain for a long time. When things quiet down, the drape is partially drawn and there seems to be a young woman lying there in a big white worm cast. I really feel sorry for her. But I am soon asleep again.

In the morning I wake really hungry, quite achy, but actually feeling better. The drape is pulled around the other bed. I hear tense voices, against one which seems whiny and shrill. After what sounds like arguing, a nurse shoves the curtain around and I startle and jump. She glares at me and stalks out.

I see the aide finishing cleaning the new girl's face. The girl snaps at her in a squeaky angry way.

"Stop that now! Go away! I didn't choose to be here. I don't want to be here. I want out now!"

The aide tries quiet consolations.

"If you'd let yourself relax, you'd get better a whole lot faster."

"Don't kid me, bitch! I ain't gonna get no better. You get

shoved out a window, and you won't have no legs to use neither. I'll never get better'n I'll never walk again. You can't understand that with your fat legs still working under you scooting you around. I can't believe this, I can't. It just can't be true!"

She is getting really hysterical and the aide vainly tries to calm her. They neither notice my attempts to crane about to see them better. The aide finishes her work, then after trying to console the woman, throws up her hands and quietly steals out of the room. The woman never looks my way, but I can just see her and she is very young and thin, and mostly angry.

After a tasty, if gloomy, breakfast, Dr. Harmon brings his tired but sweetly amused face in to check my cast and leg. The nurse helps him turn me to look at the sores on my back and hips.

"We are going to get you up in a minute because you don't need to be lying on this red butt all day. Are you feeling better?"

I blink no, and then laugh at them. He gets the joke and laughs right with me. I feel thrilled. Someone's got my joke! Nobody since Nate has ever cared if I could laugh or make a joke. I feel giggly and confused by Harmon's attention and my feelings about his tired toothy grin. I can't stop giggling, even as he heads over to the next bed.

"Ms. Reiner, how are you?"

I side glimpse a sharp movement. I'm suddenly less giggly, and the mood in the room chills down rapidly. Dr. Harmon continues to try making conversation with the back of the woman's head.

"Ms. Reiner, unless we can establish what is going on with you we can't be of help to you."

"Tough shit!"

That's all she says for the whole day.

Dr. West comes by for me around 10 on the number clock.

"Would you mind one more trip round the old hospital?"

Hardly, I blink; I would be relieved not to be in this atmosphere of despair and gloom.

We head out toward the elevator. Dr. West gives me a chance to check out the great window while she makes a quick phone

48

call at the nurses' station and pushes for the elevator. The cars below are creeping in the bright morning light. I can tell the days are getting shorter with the nearing of winter. Shadows from the tall buildings break the bright reflections on car tops, so they go in and out of shine, flashing on and off.

Dr. West comes by and we head for the open elevator.

"I have set up a psychology evaluation, like the ears and eyes check. This would let you know if you do have some of the skills you would need for reading. Besides, it is kind of fun, and I think you might like Dr. Harper. She has a great sense of humor."

Off the elevator we turn left and down a long hall. There are big double doors that Dr. West opens with a shove on a metal plate near the side. She shows me how that is done. She stops to see if I have enough arm strength to shove the plate. I concentrate on my elbow moving in that direction. With a somewhat indirect slam I manage to get the plate moved and the doors swing open. We share a triumphant smile and head through the doors onto an enclosed sort of bridge. We are going into another building. Down a brightly colored hall and back on the elevator. What a hike.

"Hello, welcome to my parlor."

As Dr. West opens the door with the glass window with writing on it, I see a small lady sitting in a little scooter or cart-like thing. She is thin and has dark hair and glasses and a big smile. Her speech is slow and a bit jerky.

"C'mon back to my lair. You must be Emily Mason. Ellen has told me a lot about you. I am Anna Harper."

Dr. Harper's office is full of pictures stuck all over the walls. Near her desk are shelves full of books. She has a table on the other side, and we head for that. She brings over a large box from her desk. She easily maneuvers the cart near my place at the table. We begin to play games with little blocks with black and white shapes on them. There are pictures and questions. She asks me lists of numbers, and asks if I can remember them enough to point to which numbers I heard on a big paper on the table. My pointing is as usual more random than not. But I can manage to rub my hand over the ones she says after a while. She seems OK with the time I take. It is all a lot of fun, though I am not too good at the parts where I have to move stuff around.

"Emily, I will send Dr. West a written report about all that we did today, because it will take me some time to sort out your scores on the activities. I can tell you now that I see no reason for you not to work on letters and begin to learn to read. It is a lot harder when you are grown up, but with a lot of work and determination, you could do it!

"I hope this was fun for you. I really enjoyed meeting you. Dr. West and I have some friends that we wonder if you would like to meet. A lot of these friends use chairs to get around, like you and me. They might have some ideas of things you could do with them. OK? Hope to see you again."

Here is another gimp like me out living like the normals. How did she not get stuck in a place like South Pines? Of course she can talk, but so can other chair people who get stuck in places. What is the difference?

Dr. West heads me back to my room. I hand signal and noise to her to see if I can get left near the window. It is near sunset and I really want to see it from way up here. She understands and mentions to the nurses that I am going to be out near the window, so that they will come get me in time for dinner. What a treat to watch the stripes of light pouring through the big buildings from the other direction. The cars still glint and flash but from a new angle. A burst of orange light hits the dark glossy windows of the tallest building making the whole top of it catch fire. It lights the two just across from it with a tremendous glow. What a light show! What a break!

I don't see Dr. West for the next couple of days, but things continue hopping in my room, so there is no time for boredom. Ms. Reiner, the name I know her by, manages to roll off her bed in a terrible twist and screams constantly and wildly as they get her onto a gurney with a heavy collar on her neck and wheel her out in a terrible rush. Later they wheel back a contraption like nothing I've ever seen. The nurses call it "Striker." In it she is flipped like a fish in a skillet, wheeled in a giant circle. Ms. Reiner isn't moving anything.

Apparently when she fell she broke an area in her spine which had been badly bruised and injured when she fell from the window. She really screams and carries on and everyone rushes in and out of the curtained partition for a long time. When the curtain is back momentarily, all I can see is tubes and wires and the edge of the big wheel.

A social worker comes in to try to talk with her. Reiner screams and shrieks at her.

"I am only trying to get an idea of what caused your fall."

"You stupid bitch, what can you know? You talk like it was a what, not a who. That shithead was drunk as usual and he was beating on me as usual. He slammed me, I fell against the window, it broke, I fell out and the ground came up and slammed me good. Finished the job for him."

"Why hadn't you reported that your friend was abusing you."

The social worker bends over her yellow pad while asking this question. It is a dumb question and she looks like she knows it.

Reiner replies with a barrage of blue that fairly lights up the room. A passing nurse rushes in and demands that Reiner tone down the talk and just gets spat at for her trouble. The social worker packs her case and leaves. I never see her again.

Who could Reiner tell? If she was trapped in the house with someone who was bigger and crazy, what could she do? But I guess she could walk then. Could she have run away? Could she have gone far away? I never could.

It is morning again. The aide gives me a smooth and relatively pain-free bath. She says, as she pulls down my knit top and tugs up my elastic-waisted skirt, "You are really doing well. You'll be going home again pretty soon."

A small sensation starts in my stomach and begins to grow slowly. It feels like an uneasable ache, like when your legs feel jumpy and restless, crampy, at night. You wish you could unscrew them and hang them out to relax. The sensation reaches my mind and says, "You have to go 'home.'" Home, what is that?

Since Nate is gone there is no home. That place, South Pines, that's not a home. That is an endurance test. I realize that I'll lose this new real connection with people. I'll lose this real food. I'll lose Dr. West, and the aides who really seem concerned and fairly interested. The frost begins to set in. From my center outward it creeps in until I am shaking with cold.

Dr. West comes in after lunch and shares some cake off my tray. I have a bite, and she has a nibble. She chats a bit with me.

"Ms. Mason, you don't need to be here any more. They will send you home tomorrow."

I blink twice and attempt to turn away. The frost seems to be encasing me in its icy shell. She catches my glance before the tears solidify to ice.

"The hospital is no place to stay, and you will do fine at home."

That's what you think, sister. How do you think I got here. For her benefit I blink twice. I can feel my head sinking and my arms randomly reaching to nothing. She looks down too, and seems a bit strained. She changes the subject.

"Your test results are in and your hearing is fine."

So what else is new. It is other people who have assumed that I couldn't hear all these years. People who talked to me as if I were deaf, or a baby, or just couldn't comprehend their wonderful words of wisdom. I would like to have said to all of them, "Quit shouting, or quit talking about me as if I were not here."

She continues, "Your vision is fairly good, but you are having some trouble with focus."

My unfocused eyes blink.

"There are corrections that can help that a bit, so if you would like to deal with that later we will."

That gives me hope. I may be seeing Dr. West again. But why must I go back to where they don't hear or see me? Isn't there anywhere else like this where I could be treated more like a human?

"And Dr. Harper said that even though the tests you did with her were never set up for people with speech or movement problems, what she was able to do with you makes her think that you might be able to learn to read. It will go slowly, but she feels you ought to persist with it."

How can I persist with something that I haven't the foggiest notion how to begin? If I go back to South Pines I'll just fade back into the woodwork and vegetate. Oh, I wish she wouldn't send me back there now, not after what I have seen.

She can't hear my thoughts so she gets up to go.

"I'll be back tomorrow to help you get your things together."

Chapter 7

*H*ere I am on this gurney again, in the ambulance with Jerry touching my arm reassuringly.

"Did you have a nice vacation, Emy?"

Yes, I blink. And wild horses and you are taking me back to that place.

Dr. West came in early and waved at me during my wash-up. She goes over to talk to, no, at Ms. Reiner. I couldn't hear words. Reiner hasn't spoken since that social worker had left three nights before. I couldn't imagine what Dr. West could say to open her up, but I heard sobs, and then quiet again. Dr. West's face is unusually dark when she comes around the curtain. She brightens when she sees me looking at her. She comes close.

"Ms. Mason, I believe I noticed you were upset about going home when we chatted. You became quite pale. I don't know what your situation is like there, but from your expression I would venture to say that you are not keenly anticipating your return. You aren't crazy to be heading back, in other words."

I blink once, long. She gets that dark look again.

"You do realize that you must go back there now, because there is no other place for you right now. I am going to be keeping tabs on your situation. I may not be able to visit you a lot because of my awful schedule here, but I have talked to my friends who might try to contact you if you would like that. I'll send you a letter about them and . . ."

I blink and flail and grunt to interrupt. How can I get across to her that a letter doesn't get to me since I don't read. It could

54

be intercepted and used against me. She seems to get my drift and shakes her head.

"Ah, a letter. If you can't read it, it could be a problem for you?"

I blink my relief.

"Would it be better if my friends just call on you for a casual visit?"

After my blink she assures me that her friends would come and that they would let me know that it was she who sent them.

So I am heading back at least assured that there will be a visit, sometime. Maybe even Dr. West. Sometime. Maybe.

❖❖❖

A bump! My arms wake and jerk. I open my eyes to dim morning light. Judy is bumping around the room colliding with furniture in the narrow spaces. I drift back to sleep, knowing Edna's getting her wash and I have time to doze. But Judy is in a chatty mood. She's talking to herself, 'cause Edna doesn't know what's coming down.

"You OK today, Ednie, honey? You gotta special day coming up today? You got someone coming to visit? Well, we will dress you up real nice for them."

I wonder what thoughts are going through Edna's mind. The non-expression on her face shows nothing now. She doesn't talk much. What comes out isn't straight. What must it be like to have been a talker, and then to lose it? Then there are Judys who talk all the time about nothing. It ain't fair. Why should she get to waste so many words while Edna and I don't have enough to get our points across? Listen to me feeling sorry for old hateful Edna who will probably have a visitor today. Or who am I feeling sorry for? I've been back a month. No visits, no changes.

Judy shoves Edna down the hall to the elevator. I can hear Judy cheerily bug the folks waiting to descend to breakfast, who will then wait to have it served, then wait if they have to be fed, then wait for the pot, then go wait in the Lounges all day in case somebody drops by to visit.

We all get the spit-and-polish treatment the day before official visit days like Sundays, holidays. Carrie crams people into her little two-seat parlor. Its a renovated closet.

Anyway, when she could, and I could afford it, Carrie'd kind of hack off my fuzz into an easy wash-and-wear cap. I could never let my hair grow out, even when some state license people came in and wouldn't let Carrie cut hair for a while at the nursing home. The aides won't allow my hair to grow out. They just hack bits of it off in the shower. Too much fuss. They don't want to have to fool with it. So there's never been much point in trying to get appointments with Carrie. The nurse will set one up if she thinks you are gross, and the aides have been negligent, and you are likely to have a visitor. I don't think I have had a visitor, except maybe the social worker for a while after Aunt Jo died. But I have to admit, I've been hoping since I left the hospital.

After a wordy bath, Judy rolls me to the elevator and I sit waiting with twelve others. Might be a few minutes, an hour, who knows. The doors eventually open and an aide steps off and runs up the hall. The doors shut. Doors open. A truck of insulated trays rolls off, a tall man behind, pushing. Doors shut. Doors open. A CMT with a medication cart rolls out, doors shut.

Finally a floor orderly hits the call button and the doors open once again. Three ladies are wheeled in, doors shut. They sink to their destination. The light moves up, doors reopen. The orderly wheels Edna, old Genevieve, and me onto the elevator. We reach first floor, he shoves us out the door. Another wait as he ascends for another batch. We sit accumulating in the hall as doors open and shut. Four more trips. Hall gridlock. The orderly disappears.

Eventually a dietary aide notices the growing nest of wheels and begins shoving us two by two toward the Dining Hall. The independent rollies and the walkers are already waiting there. The aides get trays and we are poked, jerked, and napkined or bibbed into place. The eaters start opening trays and making faces. The feeders will wait over rapidly chilling sludge until someone can find time.

A new morning aide comes over to sit next to me. She starts shoving this amazingly putrid stuff into my mouth. Some of it makes it, most doesn't. She gripes when I dribble. It tastes awful, like scorched and sweetened wallpaper paste. I hate sweet cereal.

When she deems my meal complete, I get wrenched back and around and out the door to the downstairs Lounge. It's a favorite warehousing area.

"Now you just sit there and don't bother anybody," she admonishes me.

I spend the next hours trying to devise ways that I could bother somebody. Creative botheration. I guess I could giggle insanely and constantly for a very long time. Or I could breathe very loudly. I might sit and shriek over and over. That one is done a lot on the Skilled wing. Or I could just sit and pee on the floor. That bothers folks a lot. This is boring. I tried all those things when I was first sent here. Before that sometimes they got a rise out of Aunt Jo. Mostly they got me beatings. Maybe I figured that a beating is better than being ignored completely. Maybe that is what Reiner figured, too. Where will she end up? Probably in a dump like this where she'll be ignored even more, and get a lot angrier. Kinda like Madge.

But here they ignore me completely, or put me on bed rest, enforced ignoring. Or is it just ignorance. I quit the elective peeing first because the nurses were hot to put me on the Foley. I realized I was giving them an excuse. I went through an unproductive phase of throwing whatever I could get my hands on. They saw to it that I couldn't get my hands on anything. I tried scratching my arms when I could get a purchase on them. The aides hate unnecessary blood. They put thick cotton mitts on my hands and velcroed them to the arms of the chair. That ended that. No matter what I tried to get their attention, nothing was noticed, only squelched. I gave up.

I hate this Lounge. The windows are way up over our heads so the only thing to look at is the broken TV or each other.

Someone comes in. A lady in an old worn chesterfield coat, like Jo's. She has a fuzzy hat, gray hair, white gloves, and red galoshes which may have once matched nearly red trim on the coat. She clucks and fusses with Mr. Kneble and leads him out and down the hall. Must be a long-lost sister or friend. His wife and sister-in-law are dead.

One by one, visitors arrive, some with little bags of goodies, others with reluctant grandchildren in tow.

"Come here, Jimbo. Come say hi to Uncle Ernie."

Shy, uncomfortable, and visibly repulsed, the children edge up to Ernie Padgett's chair and mutter "Hi" to his unhearing ears. Quietly, so as not to be noticed, they ease out to play in the little courtyard away from age and fears.

It's about the same each time. George's brother comes and they toodle through the halls, talking quietly. Marie and I sit in the Lounge. She has family but they don't get along with her and rarely visit. I saw them once sitting rigid across from Marie. Everything Marie said, the woman would say, "What was that, Oscar?"

Oscar would say, "God, Erm, I don't know. Would you just shut up."

Marie would endure their presence and questions and try to answer yes and no until she was relieved of their company. She always looked exhausted after those visiting days.

Edna's sister comes with her grandniece. The niece is a big woman and can transfer Edna into her own car. In her way Edna seems to know she will have a good time.

One visiting day a few weeks later, a small woman with a cane walks into the room. She asks the aide a question. They gesture toward my corner. I do what I can to see who is near me. Yet the woman walks slowly toward my chair. My heart pounds.

"Excuse me, Ms. Mason? How do you do? My name is Sarah Cohen."

I am startled to see a stranger address me by name. She is a small pretty woman with dark hair and eyes. Something is different about her eyes and smile. I can't tell her age. Her expression is young, but her face is wise and mature.

"Ellen West asked if I'd drop by to meet you."

I notice the difference. Her smile is genuine, not plastered on for effect. Her speech is a tiny bit different, not from around here.

"I hope you're doing better, Ellen told us about your leg. I trust it mends well!"

She nudges me with her smile. She has to be a friend of West's to believe she can carry on a conversation with me. I am blinking at her questions, but I miss a few. She doesn't seem put off by this. Most of the people here get really mad, even nasty, when you don't respond to every stupid probing question. No conversation, mind you, just nasty personal questions, embarrassing ones. I watch the others cringe in the halls under the barrage. "Marie have you had your B.M. today?" yelled down the hall. "Oh, Em, are you on your period again?" asked in a tone of enraged desperation, like I could stop it at her convenience. I shrivel, but I am used to it. I see Marie and others just turn their heads as if to pretend that they are not there. Marie is a dignified lady. Just because her speech is difficult and her movements unlike theirs doesn't give them permission to be wholesale rude.

I bet you'd never just go out on the street, or in a friend's home or in a restaurant and holler out, "Honey, you gotta catch your pee. I gotta record it for your program."

Even the doctors and nurses on the soaps never ask the patients how their stools were right there on the TV.

Or, "George, you really got a bad odor!" announced in the Dining Hall where all your friends can hear. Institutional life doesn't make one immune to embarrassment. We'd like privacy about personal things, too.

But I feel that this Sarah Cohen isn't like that. I can tell right away. She sits next to me on a chair so she can look me right in my wandering eyes.

"Ms. Mason, Dr. West told me that you didn't seem to want to come back."

Now, that's personal. But somehow I don't mind blinking.

"If I just list a bunch of problems that other people I know have had in homes like this, could you blink at the ones that bug you ?"

I can't believe this woman. But she rattles off a bunch of the usual stuff I live with and I blink like mad. Then she tells me that she and West studied stuff together at a Rehab Hospital. And then she tells me about her job at what she calls an independent living center. Seems to be a kind of coming-together place for gimps. Now, that is hard to believe, but I have to say I am fascinated by this lady.

"Most of us who work and volunteer and do stuff at Access to Life have disabilities of some kind."

Well, why am I here and you there? I wanted to ask. But she can talk and walk. Makes all the difference. But then George can talk, and he gets around fairly well in his chair. Why is he here?

I listen for quite a while, then she asks if she can visit again and maybe bring along a few friends. Needless to say, I'm not going to argue her out of it.

"Is there a time that's best for you?"

If I could, I'd be snide and say, "I'll have my girl look into that and get back with you," like on Dallas or something. But what does it matter. I blink a yes because the powers that be have preferred visiting times. Keeps down on the zoo atmosphere at feeding and changing times. I'd rather have visits not on expected visit days, when the parade rests all day in the Lounge, waiting like birds on the wire. Cohen patiently runs through the days and times she has available, and I blink when she reaches a good time for me.

"Next Tuesday at 10:00 a.m., that's OK for you too?"

We make our goodbyes and she moves slowly to the door with her cane. I begin to realize how amazed I am that this has happened.

Chapter 8

*T*he next Tuesday, Judy gets me up before Edna.

"What's this about you having visitors on a Tuesday? You gettin' kinda uppity, ain't you?"

What is uppity about having the first visitor in at least fifteen years? And what could be your problem, Judy, with me having a visitor on Tuesday? And how come everyone in the building knows that I will have a visitor? Was it on the morning news? I guess Ms. Cohen must have told somebody, so there'd not be any big surprises.

She gets out one of my better blouses. It even matches the slacks color that she's chosen. I usually get what's grabbed. Often subs or temps will put me in Edna's stuff. I get swallowed in a doubleknit flowered shell which drips off my shoulders all day. But here is Judy really trying.

"We don't want your company to think you ain't got good taste, do we?"

Oh, I know better. Your outfit here doesn't want visitors to think we ain't treated like regular folk.

After breakfast someone shoves me up to the lounge to wait. There is a clock but I am still not too sure about telling time. One stick is nearly on the ten, so maybe it is nearly ten.

Not too long after the clock stick hits the ten, I hear the tap of a cane and two motor chairs. The first in is a woman with long dark hair. She is driving her chair with her hand in a splint, like George. She is pretty but her body is very curved and leans to one side. She has on red shoes and rose colored slacks. Behind her swerves a man who is very thin and has curly graying hair. I am struck by his eyes, bright blue and searching.

"Hi, Ms. Mason. Or can we be less formal now, and I be Sarah and you be Emily?"

I blink a laughing yes, and try to look at the new people with interest.

"I would like to introduce Sherry Kemper, and this is Andrew Duncan."

Sherry says hi, but Andrew makes a noise like Marie. I probably wince at it, because I feel him look right through me, not angrily, but searching. I shiver a bit as Sarah takes a chair next to mine. Sherry shifts her weight carefully.

"We are also from the Access to Life Center. I guess I am Sarah's boss."

They all laugh, and I wonder what kind of loonies I'm getting in with. They don't know who's boss?

"Andrew is on our board and is a peer counselor, and causes a fair amount of other grief as well."

He positively leers at Sarah and she shrinks back in mock defense. Then they shape up again. Oh, brother.

"C'mon, guys, let's not give Emily a bad impression. She is probably wondering what kind of crazies we are," Sarah admonishes.

She's right on target. That is just what I am thinking. But I can't quite describe how I feel about these people. I am inside their jokes and laughter, not on the outside looking in. Part of me feels right at home with them even though we've just met. But their talk comes fast and is confusing.

"Please slow us down if we are saying too much too fast, Emily, but Ellen called right after you got out of the hospital, and we all decided to give you time to settle back in before we'd come over to see what it was Ellen and Anna were so concerned about.

"Ellen told us that she got the impression that you weren't really happy here at South Pines. She said just a little about how you seemed afraid to come back from the hospital."

The guy named Andrew is watching Sarah as she talks, then he looks at me as if to see if I am listening. He scoots around in his chair to reach his backpack. Slowly with effort he gets the leather latches opened and shuffles through what looks like papers and books. He pulls a thick shiny piece of paper out of his pack. With foot shoves he scoots back to sit straight in his chair and holds the shiny paper, which has letters on it, in his lap. He kinda tosses his head at Sarah when she is at a stopping point. Long, gray, pulled-back hair flips out from under a tied-'round blue bandanna.

"What do you say, Andrew?"

He starts by making those Marie noises and fills in the blanks by spelling out words for Sarah to read from the shiny white card. I don't know if I really want to sit though this. I feel a bit sinky in my chair and need to yawn real bad.

"Yoh dow ahvw tuh be ih a pways akh ihs. Yoh ahvw – paper spelled, options, said by Sarah – tuh omuvh ouw onh own."

Then Sarah kinda translates what he's said. It isn't like I can't understand him. But it's like with Marie; I just have a feeling I don't want to. And when he finishes a sentence he looks right into me waiting for an answer, even if he didn't ask a question.

"Andrew may be jumping the gun a bit here, but he is right. There are more options for living for people with disabilities. And that is one of the things we talk about at the Center."

Sarah looks a bit mock mean at Andrew, as if he stole her thunder.

"People are gradually realizing that having a disability does-n't shut you out of of life. We all want to live the way we choose, just as much as anybody else."

Sherry leans into this with energy. I am still not sure what the heck they are talking about. I'm living my life. And who chooses much about how they live? I am sure most of the people who work here at South Pines might choose not to if they could. A lot of them gripe enough about it. They gripe about how they live when they aren't here. So who's choosing?

"We meet at the Center to talk about a lot of things that have to do with having a disability, like getting and using chairs and communicators, or finding out how to get around town, or even finding a new place to live. I just recently found a new place myself, and it was a lot easier because of things I learned and people I knew from the A.L. Center."

Sherry's chair is across from me now as she nudges nearer while talking.

"Weh htawk bow lyaw, ahn mahging hpeopow jhanjh lyawz soh hpeopow don en oup en pwayses lyhyk yhis hshitheow." He spells the last word out quite unnecessarily. I'm not sure I like having my home called a shithole, even if it is one. And I am not sure I like his snobby attitude. Who's'e think he is? I really gotta yawn. Whew, feeling kinda wiped out suddenly. My eyelids drop, then I open them to another chair whining into the lounge. It's George.

"Oh, excuse me," he barges in. "Who are your friends, Emy?"

I pop my eyes open again and look at the visitors.

"Hi, I'm Sarah Cohen from the Access to Life Center, and this is our director, Sherry Kemper, and this is Andrew Duncan, a member of our board."

"Well, what the hell's an Access to Life Center? Oh, sorry, I don't mean to intrude, but I am a friend of Emy's and I am insufferably nosy. What has she done?"

There is something going on here with George. He's being sarcastic, on guard, and I guess protective. He natters on while moving his chair slightly between mine and Andrew Duncan's.

"Name's George Danton. Emy doesn't often have visitors, and any friend of Emy's is a friend of mine."

There is just a touch of a hard glint lurking in his dark eyes in the ebony shadows under his visor. It is directed mostly at Andrew Duncan, who is a startling contrast with his gray bandannaed hair and pale blue eyes.

The atmosphere warms up pretty fast as the group begins to field the humor thrown through the initial hard balls. They begin to answer George's probing questions and I find it easier to listen this time to Sherry's description.

"Access to Life is an independent living center. That's a long name for the place we gather. Our main reason to get together is to show each other new ways to live – y'know, Emily, the options we were talking about earlier. We might want to live out in communities like anyone else. We also want to get other people to see that we can do these things. A lot of people aren't comfortable with us. We'd like to help them to understand about people with disabilities as we live with them in our towns and neighborhoods."

Andrew Duncan chimes in, "Whe ginz wan wuh ahn ee on wanz." It is all noises to me. I would like to split. I am really put off by his jerking growling sound, and his eyes.

"So we 'gimps' want what anyone wants. That doesn't entitle us to get it."

George knows what Duncan's saying, just like with Marie.

"I got no legs, I got no feeling neck down, so how's I'm supposed to get out and get a job and buy a house and live like your anyone? Who's going to feed me and wash my ass and take care of my sores? Who out there is going to feel entitled to that?"

While it is obvious that the folks are blown back a bit by George's pissing tone, they are equal to it. They talk Greek about stuff like attendants, and SSI, and community access, and accessible transport. And George is right in there swinging. This is not unlike Saturday night fights. I'm beginning to enjoy it. Duncan can swing 'em back at George as fast as George can throw 'em.

"OK, Uncle. Shit, folks, you got a lot to tell us, but how on earth could you believe that somebody like little Emy here is going to be able to get out and get a job and live in her own place? I hate to poop this party, but this cannot apply to her. Find another tree."

Duncan maneuvers his chair in line with George.

"Harah, daak foh me. Ah wannn ii gleeh."

Sarah begins to echo right along with Duncan, and follows the harder words as he spells them on a little sheet of letters on his lap.

"You may believe that this is the only life there is for you, Mr. Danton, but I'd like for you to just give us some time and a chance to hear us out. What we have to say to you and Emily may not be right for you, but it can't hurt to hear. If nothing else ever comes of our visit, we've made a friend. And from what Emily told us, she has no outside friends, right?"

I blink as he talks, agreeing, but afraid. I can't help it. I've never been talked about like this. Oh I've long and often been talked about in third person while I am there, defenseless. Such as, "She's not had a B.M. in three days; what do you suggest?" "Try the Fleet, but not till tomorrow. She never eats anyway." That is so pleasant, as you sit there unable to state your case. But this guy is talking about things that could be new and better for me. And it is scary. And George is scared for me, I think. Sarah starts talking for herself.

"Mr. Danton, I hear your concern. Dr. West asked us to come here to get to know Emily. She got the impression Emily wasn't really comfortable here. We can offer her a bit more, maybe not a new home, but new friends, and new things to do. Isn't that a bit better?"

"Ms. Cohen. Have you ever lived in an institution, like a nursing home?"

"No."

"Of course Ms. Mason is not comfortable here. No one is or ever will be. If you have a few hours I'd love to tell you what a hell hole this place can be. But I'd have to do it on the sly, because I could really get it from the staff if they found out about my dissatisfaction. Dissatisfaction, shit!"

George's expression darkens. He looks at me, then looks away toward the window, in the middle distance somewhere. The silence grows thick. Everyone waits, appreciating the necessary pause.

Then he turns rather majestically and glowers at me.

"Emy, you making plans to leave?"

I blink twice very fast.

"Then why are they here?" he asks accusingly. I close my eyes. I'm not sure why they are here. I am also scared of them, but I like listening to them. I also like fairy stories and impossible tall tales. I'm beginning to feel really angry at George, and I'm not sure why. I wish he'd go away and leave me with my tale bearers. I open my eyes just as George gets ready to throw out more caustic questions. Andrew jumps in and I find myself understanding as he says, "We were invited here by Emily. But our interest is not just in Emily. We are here for anyone who wants to know of other ways to live."

That took a while. His speech is slow and round and has few hard sounds, consonants, they say on G.E.D. on TV. But I am beginning to see shaped sounds in my mind and how I can understand him with them. As he goes on I find I see more and more, and I am captured by his tall tale.

"I used to live in my aunt's basement. I figured to spend my whole life there. But there was a bad fire in the house and frankly I used the panic effect to move out."

Occasionally, when a word isn't working, Andrew pushes out his spell card and Sarah says the word for him. He looks intensely at each of us to gauge whether the sounds are making sense.

"My aunt tried to make me stay. She was afraid to lose the $280 in rent that she got out of my $407 of SSI. She often complained about how much I could eat up that money."

We all had to laugh at that because Andrew would have been lost in a high wind. He was obviously a heavy eater, like me.

"Anyway, her kids are grown and Uncle is still working, so it wasn't like she needed the money real bad. She found ways to use it, like her bingo addiction."

The words continue to drawl and mush around, but I can hear the sense of it. It is like his intention to speak makes much of our understanding possible. We are glued to our seats waiting for the next words. I feel confused by my fascination and an accompanying sicky feeling in my stomach about the way the words connect to memories. It feels like I ate too fast and can't digest.

The group is laughing at Andrew's aunt's bingo problem, but I am having trouble seeing the humor in being trapped in a fire-hazard basement while someone else squanders your livelihood on gambling. The sicky gets worse. It feels close to home.

"So, Mr. Danton, I chose a new life. Got a place of my own, with a ramp. I manage my own money. I get what I need to deal with my mobility problems."

I watch his long finger making mobility into a word for Sarah to say and feel as if something is pressing on me. He looks over at me and I feel a keen pressure from his eyes as if trying to get into and through me. I slip a bit further down in my chair and I get my head turned and wedged between the arm rest and the back support. This often happens and gives me a nasty crick, and the aides never spot the problem. But as Sarah says some Andrew words, she looks quickly at him and then at me.

"Ms. Mason, would you like a scoot up? You look a bit uncomfortable."

This startles me and I slide a bit more as I blink reluctantly. I steel myself for the jerks on my arms. Sarah moves behind my chair and grasps the elastic of my slacks and with a light and easy tug and a nudge to my head the velcros ease their bite and it's over. No pain. Much gain. I am straight and comfortable. I'd like this lady to stay; give her a job. And she's got a brace and a cane. I blink and grunt in gratitude.

Now George and Andrew are really going at it. They talk a long long time. I certainly can't get all of it. They talk money, and doors, and curbs, and ramps, and buses, and places to live, and work. Some of their talk is angry, and some defiant. But as they begin to leave, George asks when they plan to come back.

"We can come back in two weeks at this same time if it is convenient for you," Sarah offers gently, after the heated row cools a bit.

I blink when George says, "These are your guests, Emily. Tell them when to come."

They nod agreement, and Sarah notes this in her little book. Chairs whine down the hall, and they are gone.

As George turns to go he says, "Emy, we gotta talk tomorrow. Meet me at your window on Two-South after lunch."

I blink and he heads out.

68

Chapter 9

Since my cast is off I'm back at my window as often as I can get a shove here. Breakfast was such shit. I'll find a way to hide in an obvious place in order to miss lunch. It is so consistently bad. Some days it is a lot easier to hide than others. A few minutes ago Myrtle lost her balance going to the lunch room. In all the hustle to get her up and out and checked for breaks and bruises, I get turned in my chair facing away from the door to the lunch room. That's all it takes. Everyone decides that everyone else has already wined and dined me and so I get left leaving. Its great when things like that happen. I can laugh for hours.

When she finishes picking over her tray Marie finds me near the door. So she shuffle drags me down the hall and up the elevator to the window for look-out time. Marie isn't aware of my meeting with George. I hope she will stay to talk with him. I'm not sure what else to do. I need her as a buffer, although I don't know how I'll get my points across. I wonder what he is going to want to say?

While we wait I notice a window open in the house with the red roof. It is just a little peaked gable. I believe I see a person moving inside. There is just a shadow in its own space, changing and moving things around. I watch as if from the corner of an attic room as the person makes her place different, moving things, hanging shapes, changing furniture, all her own. Then she leans out the window, grabs the latch, and closes off that little world to me.

"Emily!"

It's George, roll-whining toward me.

"That bunch yesterday. They upsetting you?"

I blink twice defensively, then pause, then blink once.

"Oo hey, wahz hgoon on? Wah hbpunh?" Marie tries to break in to ask.

"Excuse me, Marie, this is between Em and me, OK?"

She backs her chair away from the window a bit, but just out of firing range, and waits to find out the news.

"You needn't be worrying about having to go away from here. They can't throw you out. You always got a place here as long as you stay."

He pauses and looks out the window at the red roof. He looks down on his desktop at his stack of books and water pitcher. His hand shifts from one side to the other of the papers and magazines, and he looks out the window again.

"Emy, you really unhappy here ?"

Since my head has drifted further to the west I notice Marie is watching our conversation with wide eyes and a confused expression. Her confusion mirrors my own state of mind.

I wonder how I can tell him that I think I am unhappy but I can't really know because what else is there or what else have I known, and what would an improvement be like. But when I hear the tall tale people, these other gimps, talk about their work! I mean work, like in offices, helping people, doing neat stuff, going places. That all makes me want to cry and to laugh.

"Aw, Emy, I don't mean to upset you, but those people are crazy if they think people like us can live any different. We can't do for ourselves, so we just gotta put up with whatever's left. Left of their time, attention. And that ain't much. And you can rest assured that it ain't gonna get no better out there. It's bound to be worse. It's their world, the noncrips. It's fast and furious and they expect you to keep up and compete, even for the most basic things, food, a place to stay, work. You can't be like them. You can't ever, so stop having crazy notions."

I am shaking. I've not felt quite like this ever before. Perhaps times when Jo'd get really drunk and go after me and Nate with them damn sharp-heeled shoes. I'd want to scream out. Now, I want to scream, go! Go, George, get out'a my way. Even if I can never go, I want these people to come here. I want to hear gimp fantasy tales. I want visitors. I want to see new people. You cannot understand this. You have family, friends. I have nothing. Nothing! Back off!

I want to say that but all that happens is noises and jerks and parts of me flying all around in various directions. The noises are trying to sound like, Oh no! No no!

"OK, Emy! I get the drift. But don't you come running to me when you are out there abandoned, stranded, and forgotten. Just don't even think about I told you so!"

His words of warning fade off as does his chair whine. I'm left all crumpled in my chair with parts of me in all the wrong places. I am sweat drippy and the air conditioner is cheerily blowing more winter onto this dreary scene. I hate George. I hate everyone. I hear Marie's shuffle, her slippers slick on the stony floor.

"Onnee, wah hid Gawj hay dos hfings uh uthet ou?"

I look at Marie as my eyes drift in her direction, and realize that I have made sense of what she said. Emy, why did George say those things that upset you? She is not that hard to hear. It is like a puzzle in the lounge where the old men fill in the colored pieces. I have just never bothered to connect the pieces, 'cause I hate the sounds so. Like my sounds that Aunt Jo said, "Never, never, never make those horrible animal noises. It's disgusting!"

"Id Gawj wan ose peeul go way? Ot cub bag?"

Did George want those people go away, not come back? It's clear. I noise a "Noh" back at Marie. She jerks back in her chair, head back and startled, as my eyes drift past her expression, catching the major changes.

"Oh, Onnee, ou gan tawg!" she almost growls.

"Noh!" I noise in resistance.

"Oh, Onnee, ah ner noo ou gan tawg, oh noh!"

Well, I can't. Not really. And I certainly can't now, as I find myself breathing much too fast. Marie shuffle shoves my chair toward the nurses' station.

❖❖❖

71

I wake hot, sweaty, muscles all tensed. It was a nightmare. There is this huge white husky dog, at first just a-barking in the distance, then coming closer, closer. I am scrambling over rocky hills. I sense surprise at this but cannot take time for the wonder as the dog comes closer. I almost feel hot sticky pantings near my feet and find myself climbing up onto the roof of a house, shinnying up the shingles. Yet the dog follows, its steamy breath pouring out as it begins to talk!

"Don't run, don't run," it barks.

"Stop that, stop that now," it howls to my scuttling heels. I see an open gable window down the red roof. I try to climb down the gable peak to the window ledge. As I just touch it, a black hand stretches out and pulls the window closed. I am trapped as the dog reaches me. "Noh, noh!"

"Stop that, now, stop, Emy! You hear me? You gonna hurt yourself on these bedrails!"

But I can't stop crying and shaking. Judy gives me a rough bath. She seems upset and her anger rubs me raw with the raggy towel. She mutters exasperated noises while yanking on my unmatching clothes and dumps me in the chair and shoves me out the door.

I hear her doing Edna as I lurk outside the door. Her movements are sharp, but her voice seems calmer. Tears keep dripping and drooling off me. Edna comes rolling out the door and Judy behind her grabs my face and nearly peels it off with the rasp-like wash rag.

"Just stop that damn crying now, Emy! There just ain't no call for it."

How can I just stop? I can't figure out how I started.

I am still shaking as Leena shoves oatmeal at my mouth. It just can't all get in and big lumps get caught under my tongue. Leena throws up her hands and throws in the towel, in my lap, after further rasping off my oated face. She jerks the chair back and swings me out the door and into the hall. Everyone's in a great mood. Might as well be state inspection day.

Then I realize it is Tuesday, my visit day. George didn't say for sure he was coming but, as she rolls past me into the hall, Marie asks to come visit. As I blink she laughs and brings her hands together in quiet applause.

❖❖❖

At 10:00 a.m. Marie has dragged us to the Lounge for our wait. I hear George's wheels whiningly pacing the hall. Then the elevator doors open to more chair dronings. Cohen and Duncan and a tall dark lady with tiny short iron color hair and big shiny earrings turn into the Lounge with George not far behind, but hesitating near the door.

"Emily, good to see you!" Sarah starts the conversation.

"Ueh!" I noise. I work at leaning in Marie's direction.

"Eh-eee," I noise near Marie. Sarah smiles and shakes Marie's hand.

"Thank you for coming. I'm not sure I caught Emily's name for you. Could you help me with it again, Emily?"

My mouth starts working on its own time and my eyes drift out of bounds, but I muster a new sound. "Nhe-ee."

Sarah watches intently. "Nellie?"

I blink no.

"Mary?" Blink. Half blink.

"Oh, Marie?"

"Ueh!" I noise while blinking yes. I breathe hard with the surprise of being understood.

"Marie, it is very good to meet you," says Sarah, but Marie is sitting gape-mouthed looking at me. Then she abruptly acknowledges Sarah's greeting and jerks back to stare sharply at me. It hits me. She feels cheated by my sudden speech. But how could I ever explain to her about the animal noises and Jo and my terror at my talk attempts?

"And I'd like to introduce Denia Blane who does a lot of independent living training, and housing preparation."

The tall lady smiles and makes movements with her hands as she talks. I notice that above the dangly earrings are skin-colored things hooked into her ears. Mr. Kneble has things like that, and so do several people. I think they help you hear.

73

"I would be happy to answer any questions about what goes on at the Center, or anything else you want to ask." Her hands gracefully gesture along with her words.

"Sister, whatcha doing with those pretty hands?" George is still near the door but not so far away that he isn't part of the group.

"I am signing. I am hearing impaired, and when I first meet people I sign as a polite way for any other Deaf or hearing-impaired people to immediately join in the conversation with me. If no one signs back, then I assume everyone hears. I do tend to sign for emphasis, like if I get really mad. So you just better watch yourself."

George obviously appreciates the flirt and touches the edge of his ball cap gallantly at Denia.

I feel Andrew Duncan roll next to me.

"I have something I'd like to show you," he mouths slowly and with care. There's a big desk-like board on his chair. He flips a switch on the side with a hit-or-miss flail, and the board lights up. There are squares all over it with letters and numbers and stuff in them. Andrew smiles and asks if I know letters. My head drifts the wrong way, but I try to noise, "Eh, Deh, Tch, Deh, Eh, Pft, Deh, Hsh, then I break down, giggling. I know the letters from Sesame Street, but I am not sure I can tell them apart or what to do with them if I did. Andrew laughs with me.

"You do seem to know letters, but can you read?"

My arms flail aimlessly, expressing the energy I wish I could use to read. "Noh!"

"I am sure you could learn," he continues. He moves his hand jerkily over the board and hits a button. A strange tinny voice declares, *"Hello, I am Andrew Duncan. How are you?"*

"That's the voice I use with strangers."

"Its funny how strangers would rather hear that squeaky mechanical thing than take the time to hear what Andrew is saying," Sarah comments, glancing around as George creeps closer to where we are sitting.

"This device is called an Express 3," Andrew says, "and people can use it to talk to unready able-bodied types, TABs. That is temporarily able-bodied people who aren't ready to believe that we aren't so different from them."

George nudges a bit closer, trying to appear unobtrusive. Andrew shows us more tricks with his machine.

"But that is what it is. Its a trick machine which makes it a bit easier for others, but it gets in my way. It's like another barrier set up between me and others. They want this distance, to protect them from me. They don't want to hear my animal noises and mutterings."

As they laugh together my insides all freeze. I hear him say this, out loud. I look at George and Marie, and inside I hear Jo and feel the back of her hand on my head, "Never let me hear you make those horrible noises in public, you brat." And somewhere a dog barks furious and insistent.

❖❖❖

Marie and I wait for the dinner jerks at our window. Willie Nelson mourns softly under her arm as we watch the progress of the sun.

"Os peeul aw niz."

I blink at her. George whirrs up beside us.

"I still can't figure their need to come here."

I picture myself turning sharply to stare him down, but my head drifts otherwise. So I fuss, "Eh ah ah ens, Awg." I repeat several times for emphasis and hope for understanding.

George looks out the window and grunts. We get quiet as the CMT and her cart roll by, and then two aides on break. Their rubber soles pad out of hearing.

"Friends, that's what you're saying? You may think they're friends, Emy, but you have a good home here and they are trying to spoil that."

This is worrisome. George has been in and out of this place and he may know what a "good home" with friends and relatives might be like. I've been here since a dog's age and don't know anything but this and Aunt Jo.

"You'll be sorry if you let those folks fool you and jerk you

75

outta here. What'll you do? Where you going? Get real, Emy. This is all there is, and them gimp girls, and that ghost-faced hippie and his high-class hand-dancin' bitch ain't gonna change that, hear?"

I won't go to George's room for TV for a while. If Mira pushes me in that direction after Sunday dinner, I noise disapproval till she gets the picture and leaves me at my window.

"You and your honey on the outs?" Mira grins knowingly at me. I try to pull an angry face and I flail about a bit.

"Well, that's your business, but you are gonna miss wrestling out here."

No, Mira, I'm doing plenty of wrestling nowadays.

❖❖❖

One afternoon I am stuck in the hall just around from the nurses' station. I hear Gina and Mira talking and strain to hear them over the big fan.

"Yeah, she was living in the Bethel Grove home, and doing fine, and these people come in having meetings for nearly a year. Then one day she up an' leaves."

"God, how could she? She's a respirator patient!"

"Hell, I don't know. She moved into some high-rise with aides going in and out couple times a day. In about a year she's back in the hospital. They said they didn't think she'd make it. She's still at UMC."

"Well that's what she gets for going against medical advice."

"Yeah! The visiting doc at Bethel told my sister's friend, Sully, who is first shift super, that there was no way he'd authorize discharge for such an involved patient."

"I should say not! Have you met those weird people been hanging around George?"

"No, what are they like?"

"Well, they are all crippled themselves."

"How do they all get here?"

"I don't know. Maybe in cabs, or on buses? You know, some of 'em can't even talk and one is deaf and fingerspells. Whatever can their families be thinking to just let them go out and about like that?"

"Well, I can't see how people can be so thoughtless and stupid."

"And why do they keep coming here? I don't even think George much likes them, yet they continue to show up."

The longer I listen, the tighter my guts get. Maybe George is right. How awful to get pneumonia and maybe not make it. The nurses and aides blame that lady's family, and the A.L. people's families. I ain't even got a family they could blame. Out there who would give me a bath, or transfer me, or give me food? All that the A.L. people and Dr. West said to me begins to sink through me down to my feet, like lead weights.

I am thinking about these people and their notions as Mira grabs my chair and shoves me down for a shower. She is in a hurry, tossing me about as my clothes come off. She throws a big towel around me and off we go in the plastic shower chair.

"Mira, don't dawdle with Emily. You have several more scheduled showers this evening."

Mira mutters furiously as we tear down the hall to the bath. She jerks my chair through the door. She sticks me in a shower stall and then turns the water on. Of course it is bitter cold and I jerk forward in the chair. She has turned to get shampoo off the shelf and unhindered I slide out and bang my chin on the tiled lip of the shower. The big towel, which she had forgotten to take off has cushioned my fall enough that only my mouth is the worse for wear.

"Dammit, Emily, what the hell are you doing on the floor?"

The breast stroke, I guess. She isn't going to see that this is her fault. It will be spread around that I threw myself onto the tiles. The water is still pouring on me in its frigid glory. I am not enjoying this shower. But as she picks me up and dumps me back in the chair it comes clear to me about this idea of blame. The lady that died was blamed for her own death because she changed the way she lived. The family was blamed for letting her change, and not stopping her. No one would blame her caretakers who may not have known how to handle her respirator. No one would blame the nurses who didn't show the caretakers how to do it right. It was the lady's fault for wanting a better life. So I sit here bleeding in my plastic chair with the now tepid water pouring over me, and shampoo suds running in my eyes. I know who would be blamed if I wanted to change my life. I have to consider this carefully.

A week later the A.L. people come, but I don't motion to go down. George rolls by my room later and taunts, "Your buddies were here asking about you."

I do what I can to look away from him. He rolls on.

"They left!" he chuckles as he fades down the hall. A cold air settles over me. Another World drones over me, Rachel scheming for survival. I feel like an empty bag crumpling in on itself.

Chapter 10

I've been practicing something by my window. I slide down in my chair until the velcro's just starting to cut into my armpits, and my foot sticks out over the pedal on the right. If I don't think about it, my foot will eventually slip off and drop to the floor. If I'm really lucky and no over-eager aide comes by to readjust my position and put my feet back, without asking, I can get a purchase on the floor and scoot a bit. I had known about this from desperate moves I've made to brake my chair as a protest to being moved away from where I wanted to be. But then it had been accidental panic. It recently hit me that I could use this skill, like Marie, to my advantage. I could use it not to stop, but to get going. I could go whenever and wherever I want to in the building. But I'm starting slowly; don't want to draw anyone's attention to this. I don't know what they might do.

My chair is too big. It belonged to someone who died before I got here. They strap me in so I won't fall out. There are bigger chairs but I really need a junior size. I could really reach the floor then.

I wait for quiet moments. No one in the hall. I try to forget that I am trying to do something specific with a body part. I've taken to wiggling hard while they position me in the morning. That gives me more velcro stretch. I could only toe touch at first, but now I wiggle enough to get most of that angel-tread sole to meet the road.

I start at the left side of the long window and scoot, scoot slowly, but surely, with a few useless slips, to the right side. I can hardly describe the wild sense of freedom this gave me the first time I made the trip. Jerry, the orderly who had left me at the left side of the window, returned later and looked at me suspiciously. I was sunk in my chair and shaking with excitement, but I had managed to retrieve my foot before he found me. He looked puzzled as he jerked me up to reposition me in the chair.

This matter of getting around by myself has really got me thinking. I see the motor chairs that Andrew, Sherry, and George have. I want to know how you get one, what they cost, how to drive one. I'll ask George.

The next evening I endure Mira's teasing as I motion for a move to George's room. "Can't stay away from your honey, huh?"

It's wrestling night. The Rock and Stone Cold at it again. That's a good enough excuse to try to mend a fence with George. He looks up as we wheel in, but doesn't smile. He gazes back at the clown on the TV hawking some slice-o-matic "It peels, it grates, it juliennes!!!" like his life depended on it. I guess maybe it does, in a way. With George occupied, I take my time to wriggle my sole to floor and inch over to his chair. Doesn't take long in the ridiculously cramped room. Larry's bed is too close to George's, so the chair sits at the foot of his bed. It has to be moved to get into the dresser, or open the window, or do anything near his bed. They move his bed over by Larry to transfer George into his chair. Larry doesn't seem to notice anything. The aides crab about it all the time. "Damn bulky buggy! Chuck that elephant, George, and give us some working space."

I ease up to the chair and try to tap my loose foot on his foot pedals. George is propped in the bed still caught up in the initial throws of the wrestlers. I tap harder. That is a real feat involving ignoring my foot while focusing energy in that general direction.

"Whatcha doin', girl?"

"Nyahr, Awj. Ouh ed nyahr?"

I feel icky making the grunty squeaky sounds, but my desire to understand the wherefores of chairs electric overcomes my embarrassment.

"Naw, nothing's wrong with my chair, Em. I'm just down

nursing a butt sore."

I could see this could take a while.

"Ohn. Ouh ed nyahr?"

If he could hear my mind screaming, "How the hell'd you get this sucker, George?" I'm making gumbly mush of this but I'll be damned if I'll quit. I'd love to get closer to the chair to demonstrate, but I'm foot pedal to pedal and there is no room to maneuver. Wrestlers grunt and fall and moan in my left ear; I grunt and moan but no fall. Velcros say no.

Jerk!! That one sure took me aback!

"Girl! You in the way! Who's stuck you here?"

George glances down to see me shoved out the door and Larry wheeled in on the gurney from his whirlpool bath. Larry is ninety-three and has not spoken in six of the eight years he has lived here. His family comes regularly and fusses and feeds him and he's dressed and sat up and taken for hall rides. A good roomie for George. He is utterly quiet and no bother. Several Larrys live here.

The flurry of activity is over. Nancy and Mira leave. I have to start from scratch. The slow sinking into the vest. The diffused focus on the foot. I begin the tedious pull into the room again. The wrestlers cover my grunting entrance. Ten minutes later I continue the attempt to ask George.

"Nyahr, Awj, ouh ed nyahr?"

"How'd you get back in here, Em?"

The wrestlers had covered for me. George had missed the whole process. I continue to tug at the floor and try to get closer to the chair and the bed. George is now watching me wriggle, shove, grunt.

"You got fleas, girl? Or have you just gone off? Lord, look at her go! My God, Emily I had no idea you could get around like that! You just been goldbricking all these years? Holy cow, look at her go!"

George sounds as excited as I feel. The wrestlers thump and shove and so do I. I almost ram his chair and blurt out, "Oud dje nyhar?"

"You asking about my chair?"

I blinked and gurgled, "Ehn. Oud dje eth eth?"

After I run that one past him a few times, he picks up the gist and says,"You are wanting to know how I got my chair?"

I'm so glad he understands. I'm just whipped, and I settle down to hear his tale.

"I got the chair in '80. Our church members all got together and had a big box supper, a raffle, and a fish fry down on the lake. They raised enough to start a fund, in '80. For two years they raised more money and got some business sponsors to agree to pledge support for maintenance for fifteen years. Chairs are supposed to be replaced every five to eight years. These nice folk couldn't do that. I've had this bear for fifteen years, and my maintenance money has run out. It cost them $1845, slightly used, in 1980. It won't go on much longer. It's running on miracles now."

I can't believe I've been understood and got a very complete answer to a question I've asked. But the answer confirms my old sense of hopelessness in the midst of this rush of hope.

"Em, you upset about something?"

I must be red. It feels so impossible. This glimpse of freedom gained by my foot shoves is squelched by the absurdity of any further changes. I just grunt and flail and noise.

"Em, you want me to ring for an aide?"

George is just trying to be nice, but I could think of nothing I'd want less. I ooze further down and begin a noising backward shove shove. I shove, then, jerk!! Mira yanks me out the door and de-drools my face with my little towel, then jerks me up in the chair and shakes me a bit.

"Emily Mason, get a hold of yourself. Just because you got something against George doesn't mean you have the right to upset everyone on this hall. Now shut up and pull yourself together. You've been on your high horse ever since you came back from that hospital."

She pops into George's room again.

"George, I am sorry she's acting so weird. I won't bring her back in here again."

I barely hear George say,"You didn't bring her in here."

She just continues right on over him, "Do you need to roll over? You are bound to be done on that side." I was relieved that she had not heard his comment. I wasn't ready for them to know what I could do. Besides, Mira is getting just like the other aides. Push shove jerk. But I'm ready for bed when she comes back out into the hall to head me that way.

Three days later I am paged to the first floor lounge at 10:00 a.m. I'm certainly not expecting anyone but then I remember the A.L. people. I guess George didn't frighten them after all. I debate whether to go down, since I really have felt very hopeless these past days. Marie shuffles by and nudges me.

"Ou wanna go dow? Ah dake ou. Ah go wiff ou?"

Well, I hate to disappoint Marie. So I blink and we crabdance to the elevator. Marie hasn't found out about my foot, so I let her drive.

We crab off the elevator and head to the Lounge. I still feel the urge to leave, but decide not to dampen Marie's excitement. We back into the lounge. Marie turns my chair to see Andrew and Sarah talking near the window.

Andrew buzzes over to us and Sarah says," We missed you at our last visit. But we had a nice chat with George and Marie."

Those finks. They never let on that Marie was there that day. I look daggers at Marie and she ignores me in favor of Andrew, who is heading her way. So I shriek. Andrew jumps and startles, like I would. Your wiring off, Andy? I want to yell at Marie, too. But I just start to fuss. I can hear another chair whine.

"Hi, George. Maybe you could help Emily tell us what is upsetting her."

I thought these people were my friends, but it is obvious that they have been commandeered by George and Marie. I might as well leave. I begin to scrunch down in my chair as best I can while they hold their conversation.

"George, do you know why Emily is upset?"

"Em, will you calm down. The other night she was in my room for wrestling and asked me how I'd gotten my chair. I told her how my church had worked for a couple years to get it, and that it was too old to be running. Then you went off, right, Em?"

I just manage to reach the floor and begin my shoves. I gain momentum and start to back toward the door. They are quiet for a few seconds, then Marie bursts out, "Onh, Onnee, Ah nah no ouh awked."

"Keep your eyes open, Marie. Em and her friends may have lots of surprises in store for us," George says.

That did it. I am going to cut out and leave these finks to their little meeting. They don't need me.

"Emily, what has upset you about George's chair?"

Andrew wheels around me to look in my face as I try to shove past him. I can't get past his chair.

"Do you want a chair like George's, like mine?"

I blink yes and the tears start again. "Ob eth, noh eeh enneh nyahy."

Yes, it feels hopeless, no way Emy could have such a chair. After I repeat this a few times and Sarah dries my face the group begins to see what I am getting at.

Andrew looks up at Sarah. "How do we explain this?"

Sarah shrugs and stands to move her unwheeled chair closer to mine.

"Emily, the way the funding is set up now, there is no way I know that you could get a chair like that unless it is given to you, like George's was, or you buy it yourself."

Everyone as one snickers cynically. I see nothing funny. It is just too absurd. They all know I have no family, no church, and certainly no income. I flail in Andrew's general direction.

"Oh ejd nyahr, Ehdu?"

"I'll wager that she's asking how Andrew got his," George translates. I blink to back up his success. Andrew begins slowly with Sarah filling in missing sounds when needed. He explains how he went from shoving himself around in his manual model to getting electric wheels. He moved out. Andrew had lived with some members of his family all of his life until just a few years ago. A bit of me fades out as he tells again of his aunt's house, the basement, the fire, his aunt's bingo, and how she'd waste the

84

money he paid her for rent. I tune back in as his neighbor, Jeff, sees the flames in the kitchen from his porch, and tears open the cellar door in time to carry Andrew out. He speaks of the hospital where after being checked for smoke inhalation he refuses to go back home. He's transferred to Psychiatric, and then to Rehabilitation for evaluation. His aunt threatens to sue the hospital for stealing her nephew, but it's probably for her bingo money that she feels the loss.

At the Rehab, Andrew gets a motor chair and an Express 3, Andrew's computerized letterboard that talks. The Rehab refers him to the Access to Life Center. The peer counselors help Andrew find an accessible apartment and a home health agency. Their aides come to Andrew's home daily to do with him things he does better with help, like dressing, bathing, fixing food. The case worker and Andrew decide what services he can use and set a schedule for him. When the aides come to work, Andrew talks them through the schedule and directs what they do. The agency checks for physical and occupational therapy needs and that is where the chair comes in.

"If the agency feels that you can benefit by using a motorized chair, they'll apply to Medicaid to try to get one for you," Sarah continued.

"Unh edh ajd?" I noise in George's general direction.

"You asking what's Medicaid, right, Em? She's blinking that she wants to know more about Medicaid."

"We'd all like to know more about Medicaid, Emily." Sarah laughs.

They talk a while about boring stuff, but I try to understand, as I could tell it would be very important boring stuff. They say that Medicaid is a "health coverage system" for people receiving government benefits, like Supplemental Security Income. When you go to the doctor, if that doctor takes Medicaid, then your bills are paid for that visit. Your home health agency bills are paid if your doctor wants you to get an aide to come in, or an occupational therapist to tell you better ways to do stuff. If the OT says you need equipment to do stuff better, that may be where the motorized chair comes in.

"You see, you have to be living out with a family or on your own to get Medicaid coverage for your chair. As long as you live in a facility, you have to put up with the equipment that they give you," explains Sarah.

"And that is substandard at best! They don't expect that you'll need to be mobile here," growls Andrew, looking down his nose at my outsize vehicle.

"Onh nyahr nyouw."

"If I've got you right, Em, you are right, no chair now." George looks as dejected as I feel.

Andrew derbles out a question, "Would you like to try a motor chair?"

I blink, but can't figure how this could happen. Andrew wheels his chair next to mine with an unwheeled one next to him. He scoots forward in his chair and with a swing jerk he spins on one foot in a clever if ungraceful transfer into the stuffed chair. He wave pats at his chair seat while looking pointedly at me. Sarah gets up and slowly walks to the hall motioning to a passing aide.

"Could you help me transfer Ms. Mason into this chair?"

The aide looks at her like she's crazy. But she reluctantly hauls me up, pivots, and dumps me into Andrew's chair. She wastes no time taking off down the hall.

The chair is high and the cushions so soft and easy. I am astonished at how comfortable I feel. Even though it is still a bit wide for me, I feel right in a chair for the first time ever. Sarah takes my velcros off my junker and puts them on this chair so that I can sit up right. Then she fastens the seat belt, just like in a car.

"Now, Emily, how is the grasp of your right hand?"

I have no idea what she wants. She gently takes my hand and holds it and moves it around.

"Emily, can you hold my hand?"

The others chuckle as Sarah continues to manipulate my hand till I am able to grip on to hers.

"Now you move my hand."

I am puzzled about all this but figure she knows what she's doing. I focus away from my hand like I do when I want my foot to shove, and it jerks and nudges against Sarah's. She uses her other hand to push a little button on the box below the arm rest.

"The chair is on low power, Emily, so if you can take the little joy stick and nudge it like you did my hand, you'll be on your way."

Again I focus away from my hand. I take a big breath and sense my hand about to bump the stick. Whump, bump. The chair moves. I shriek. What a sensation. I get the feel of bumping the stick and the movement of the chair. I'm just lurching along inch by inch but it's fabulous. I've never been in control of power before. It's like the first time my foot had hit the floor with purpose. It's heady and scary and grand. I laugh and cry as the chair jiggle hops across the floor. I'm so high that I don't notice the wall coming at me, or the aide running in my direction. We all collide at once. The aide yells, Andrew collapses laughing on his chair, and Sarah tries to console the aide, whose leg might get a bruise. I'm still on the moon and giggling, but I've managed to get my arm caught under the arm rest which keeps it safely away from the joy stick. I can see why it's called that. Marie shuffles solicitiously in my direction, but I don't see George. Maybe he left during the crash.

After dinner I foot scoot down the hall all the way to George's room. I don't care who sees. I feel like a steam shovel rolling massively down the hall. Gina leans over the counter at the nurses' station and watches most of my journey. As I passed she snickers, "Get a horse." I shoot my tongue at her as best I can and pull a horribler face at her. But I hear her commenting to the pool aide as I go on, "I never saw her do that. What has come over that girl?"

It takes a while, but I finally reach George's room. His lights are down, but the TV is running.

"Nyaj?" I gurgle.

"What you want, Em?" His voice sounds strained, pushed.

"Ouh oh ay?" I churn at him.

"I'm just tired, Em, really tired. And I'm worried, about you. You acted totally nuts around those people today. I was so embarrassed for you that I had to split. I'm sorry but I couldn't watch those uppity gimps making fun of you like that."

I gurgle at him, amazed. I can't believe how he saw what had happened.

"They laughed at you till they were sick. It was disgusting."

"Nah, Nyaj, Nah nah!"

I can't really make him understand how I'd felt. He doesn't know about how Sarah and Andrew stayed a long time and explained the chair to me so I would understand the steering and the stick. Sarah assured me that if I really couldn't control the stick with my right hand that other types and positions of switches would probably work for me. She said there were foot switches, and headbands, and even puff-and-sip switches which are mouth controlled. But she had said that she thought I could learn to use a joy stick with lots of practice.

"Have you ever played a video game?"

Andrew laughed at my confused blink. He was really wired.

"Have you seen on TV games played with little sticks or buttons used to move figures on a TV screen? People use these little sticks to control the game figures and win the game."

I blinked out of habit. I'd seen those on TV but I couldn't see the fun in them until I had jerked that chair around by myself.

George has a chair. Why would he resent my being able to get a chair and move around like he can? I can't figure this out.

I quietly leave George's room, and relive the day as I move toward my room.

Chapter 11

*I*t is dawn. Another unannounced state inspection day. The graveyard girls get the movables up and at 'em really early, around 5:00 a.m. Now they see me as sort of a movable. It has its advantages. For the first time I can go to sit at my window and see the light as the sun comes up. I watch it move the other way on the house roof. The street is just getting going. Lights come on in this and that house. One car is puffing to warm itself up. It feels round and right to see the sun seep up over the trees like that. And bonus time, I probably won't be noticed by the aides, and won't have to eat that breakfast crap. I sit back and take in the already emerging din of radios, TVs, aides and residents fussing or pleading with each other. I'm sort of tucked behind a potted thing so I doubt if anyone sees me here. I hear a conversation starting at the station. The sound travels down this hall and hits this wall strangely. The talkers are Judy and her new shadow, Brenda. Judy tells her what to do all of the time.

"Brenda? Have you been watching Mason lately?"

"No, M'am, should I be?"

"No, goose, she's not your bed. I just mean have you noticed how uppity she is since she broke her leg?"

"I'm not sure what you mean, uppity," Brenda whines defensively. She couldn't know. She doesn't have an uppity molecule in her body.

"I mean she is getting irritatingly self determined. She always was a stubborn little bitch, but now she's taken to going where she wants and doing whatever she's got in her mind. It's really getting on my nerves."

"Well, Judy, maybe she's just finding herself," winced Brenda.

"Dammit, one of these days she may find herself out on the curb thumbing a ride, if she keeps up these irritations!"

They trudge up to the next room and I hear the airy thump of sheets lobbed into a laundry cart. I no longer hear them. I must admit it intrigues me how Judy could have seen me as a stubborn bitch, when the only way I've ever been able to resist her pushes and shoves was by closing my mouth to her spoon attacks. And that rarely worked. I feel a chill moving off the window. A cloud blocks the new rise of the sun. Red sky at morning, I've had my warning.

I'm beginning to realize that there is so much more to this than just learning how to get around. I am really scared. I'd like to ask George if those biddies have the power to really get me put out of here. God, what would I do out on the street? I can see myself one-foot shuffling down the road with my slippers on in the cold wind and snow with only a shawl and a cup of pencils to sell to strangers. Could George be right not to trust people like Andrew and Sarah? Is it dangerous to be talking with them?

After some laborious foot-power motion I negotiate the corner just before George's door. I will try to get him to understand what I need to know.

"Nawj! Nawj!"

I roll slowly into his room, back first. Hoping that he is in his bed, I wait for his answer, and wish he wasn't in his bed. It's the sores again. He's had another surgery to cut and clean a really bad place. Poor old butt.

"What's eatin' you, Emy?"

I manage to maneuver my chair to a point where we can see faces, but I can only guess how I'll get my points across.

"Unh, Nawj?"

"Emy, you look scared. What is the problem?"

"Ehhszzz, unh ehszz!"

"Ez? Uh, nobody here called Ez, I know of.

"Ehhszz." I noise again, trying to make bath-like motions that probably look like a bad day on Soul Train.

"Ehzz, hmmm. Ess? No. Oh! AIDS? AIDS?"

"Es, Nawj!!" I blink and noise yeses. He's understood!

"Now, Emy, I know that's a worrisome subject. But the people here all use gloves and are careful with needles and such. In a place like this there ain't gonna be no guarantees. I mean, with all the blood I've gotten over the past fifteen years, its a miracle I ain't HIV positive. Hell, who knows, maybe I am and don't know it."

He looks at the ceiling during this recap of the assembly talk for the residents' council. Then he suddenly stares pointedly over the rails at me.

"Oh! Emy. No! You ain't been hurt again, have you? Somebody doing stuff they ain't got no business doing? Oh, shit, girl, you gotta tell. Who can we trust? Oh no!"

It takes me a while to get the gist of his distress, and then I realize what he's saying. I have to find a way to ease his mind. That kinda stuff ain't been in my cards for a while. I've pretty much managed to forget those troubles for a few years. In fact I had forgotten about most all of it, until one night when Marie was telling me some of her troubles. What she said woke up some old bears in me I'd have rather let lie.

First there was Jo's cousin Sam who moved in with us a couple years before Nate died. I was only left with him five or six times. Geez, I had no idea what he was up to. Only knew that I was scared silly and if I noised he hurt me more. Then there was an orderly here they called Rawly who hung around in the darker corners of the basement at night. Somehow I got pushed down there by him a few times, before somebody squealed on him, somebody better able to let people know what was going on. There were apparently several of us on his schedule, and he only messed up when he tried his tricks with a talky.

Only way I figured out what was going on with those two thugs was remembering nights when Nate had been gone to visit folks and Jo often brought a man home from the bar. If she thought I was sleeping, she made no bones about busying herself with her friend right in the other cot. Early on when I was kinda little, I saw a man on her doing hurtful-looking stuff and I noised and shrieked. She popped up in a sheet and put me in the kitchen on a bunch of blankets piled up. I could hear them going right on doing so I figure she was OK about the whole strangeness. Well, I was not OK about Sam, or Rawly, or that other weirdo with the belts. I don't wanna think about that anymore.

How am I going to ease George's mind? Ah! Here comes Mira.

"Ehhszz, ehhsz, Nawj!" I noise as Mira dumps George's tray by his bed. She may eventually get back to feed it to him, but she is out as fast as she was in.

"Oh, Emy! Gawd, that's a relief. Them aides. Yes. OK. What about them?"

"Ouh, ouwh?"

"Is somebody hurting you, Emy? Are some of the girls getting kinky?"

"Onh. Ouh? Ouh?"

Combinations of blinks and attempts at moving about in the chair keep George's attention. I toe myself to the door jerkily and my head and arm move more to the left. Then I back up again, noising, "Ngo, ouh!"

"Ah, are you saying the aids are bugging you about your new ways of gettin' around by yourself? Gawd, that's dumb."

He's getting close, and I blink and hope he sees it as my head is now clear to the left and my neck stiff with tension.

"It seems they'd be grateful that you were on your own more now."

My head snaps around and throws me off balance, probably to emphasize my agreement.

"Who's griping the most?"

"Oohwee."

"Was that Judy?"

I blink and try to toe the chair more towards George's view.

"Judy does me some mornings when Ethel's not on this wing. Mind if I kinda poke her for the information? Just kinda casual, you know?"

I blink twice as my head continues its persistent leftward journey. I am disappointed that he hasn't understood my fears of being thrown out, but maybe I will ask again soon. George asks me to join him in G.E.D. on TV. The subject this morning is math. Way over my head, but I won't have to think and be afraid for an hour.

❖❖❖

It seems a short time before Leena barges in with trays for George and Larry. They are both feeders today. Larry gets propped up and the semiliquid sop is shoved briskly at him. Larry hasn't spoken in years, so he is only able to grimace in response as the spoons tip into and scrape under his mouth. Larry frightens me because in him I see how I could be. It could be easy to give in and get that way. Granted, he is very old and very disabled, but I am at least 34, and not much less disabled. Leena fusses and mutters about Larry's leaks and it makes me want to gag just watching. But I am trying to not be noticed so she won't think of me and make me go down to eat lunch. Then she rasps off Larry's face and moves around the bed to attack George with dogs and kraut. She sees me and scowls.

"You still here? You'd better get on down and get your lunch. You wanna starve?"

It's probably better than the alternative, and certainly a better fate than what you do to Larry.

She rolls George's bed table up to his shoulders and raises his bed-head. I peer into his tray to see hot dogs, sauerkraut, mashed potatoes, and some orange glop.

"Go on, Emily, get out of my way," Leena barks.

"See you later, Emy. You'd better get a bite," George mutters sympathetically as Leena prepares her assault.

I maneuver out the door with some difficulty due to the squeeze between Leena, the bed table, and George's chair. Out in the hall I dodge hot carts with stacked trays of sour smells, and the C.M.T.'s wagon as she makes mealtime meds calls. Just about everybody takes meds of some kind here. When I'm more trouble than they want, they give me a muscle relaxer. George gets lots of things for regulating his systems and dealing with pain, but he's really pissed when they give me the relaxers. He says I don't need them, and they are doping me for their sakes. Like the wanderers and the oldies, it is easier for them to be on the pills and mostly sleeping than to have to watch or entertain them. I tend to keep a low profile so they forget to dole it out to me. Anyway, now I got to find a place to hide till lunch is over. The idea of pureed hot dog and kraut is puke city.

❖❖❖

There is a page scratching at me over the inadequate speakers telling me to go to the Lounge. I shuffle to the elevator and wait with a couple others till an aide comes by to open it for us. I attempt a two-fingered wave to indicate my floor. A few are rolled off on two so I luck out in the rush, and scoot off to the Lounge on my own.

I am frankly startled to see Andrew Duncan sitting alone across the room. As I back toward him I am finding it not so easy to breathe.

"Emily," he grunts, "I came back to see you because you looked off the wall yesterday."

He noises, no, speaks very slowly and deliberately with broad hollowed sounds. I understand most of what he says, with some surprise. As he asks if we can talk about it, I am wondering how I will hold up my end of the conversation. I am finding that looking at him makes me breathe different, and I feel shaky.

"Emily, when I first thought about moving out on my own a lot of weird shit started coming down. Little shit. Sarah can't share this stuff. She's been too independent most of her life to know.

I grunt acknowledgement and feel even shakier. He needles me with those pale blue eyes.

"I almost felt like two people, one who wanted out real bad, one who had no need to move on. The second one was really scared. Well, so was the first one. I needed for my family to see me as more than the eternal crippled kid. *I* needed to see me as more than the gimp in the back room. Does this shit make sense?"

He is sitting on the edge of his chair gesturing with slow and expansive movements. I can feel the energy and I wonder why it is directed at me. I blink. He continues telling about the sneaky ways that his family used to keep him at home in the basement, a source of steady, though not much, money.

"I had met a guy when they sent me to Rehab after the shrinks tossed me out for lack of crazies. Did Sarah tell you about the suicide attempt? I just quit eating. The shrinks told me I didn't want to kill myself, I wanted a change. Right. Anyway, about this guy. He was living out and paying only half of what the folks were screwing me for. He had a guy staying with him who did cooking and clean-up, personal stuff. He paid that guy with some of his SSI money and later got on a program that pays him. They let me move in."

He talks for a long time about the nitty-gritty particulars and problems of living with two new people in a two-room apartment. No worse than me and Edna crunched up in one room. But I can see there would be a lot to learn about survival that I haven't the foggiest notions about.

"You want to learn to read?" He startled me with this change of topic.

I blinked and he told me how he learned on his own with help from some family and a short-lived tutor program and lots of persistence.

"I ain't no scholar, or speed-reader, but I can use reading to learn and most of all to spell out things with my letterboard for folks slow to hear. Kids now can go to school. Kids like we were. But folks have to watch that real teaching goes on, not just babysitting."

He goes on. Part of me is fascinated. I am baffled at the weird feelings this makes in me. Another part is trying to get me to leave the room in a big hurry. This is tense. Ah, shit, there goes the nose.

"Emily, I am sorry. I've upset you. I don't mean to."

He draws his chair closer and puts his hand over mine. His head leans toward mine and there are those awful eyes. I wish I had a speedy motor chair, I could make a fast break.

"I'm sorry. I'm throwing too much at you too quick. Sarah always says that I jump the gun on people."

He seems distressed, though not at a loss for words. I am torn by liking his hand on mine and a desperate wish that he'd disappear.

"Look, it's nearly your dinner time. I'll just mosey on and maybe we can get together with the gang another day, huh?"

I try a muffled noise and a flooded blink. He pulls out a blue bandanna, twin to the red one wound around his hair, and gently if jerkily he dries off my face, grins, pockets the bandanna, and swoops crazily out the lounge door.

I listen to the squeaks and hum till I hear the elevator door close. Still more tears. Still feeling weird and shaky, scared to death and excited all at once. I just want to sit here and try to cope with all this.

Jerk! I fly against the chair back.

"Your boyfriend gone, Em? Did he get you all worked up?"

A cheap tissue is thrust at my nose and eyes. Mira twists my nose.

"Blow, honey!"

Agh, how gross. You blow, honey. Blow off somewhere far away. As soon as she gets over her need to prune my skin I'm out of there.

"You better get yourself down to dinner now!"

Her voice fades as I turtle-scoot toward my windows. None of that excuse for food for me. Some barf on a spoon. No way.

Chapter 12

I've had two quiet weeks. I find that I spend more time listen-ing to the aides talk, bicker, and do their stuff. A lot of eaves-dropping. I guess I started it when I thought they might find a way to get rid of me. I needed to find out what they were saying. I don't think I ever paid that much attention to them before. They are for the most part good-hearted souls. Sure, there are bad eggs in every dozen, but that could be how they live. Like Aunt Jo. I'm really only beginning to understand about Jo as I listen to these women, and even Jerry and some of the orderlies.

Anyway, these aides complain constantly. Their lives must be a stream of struggle and constant pain. They rarely talk about what they do for fun. And when they do try to have fun, that often ends up in pain. Like Mira and her boyfriend. They go out of a night for laughs and it ends up with him drunk as a skunk and her with a couple in as well, and he beats the daylights out of her on the curb in front of their building. Somebody calls the cops, and there's their evening of fun.

It was like that some other times when Jo brought men home. One time Nate came back just in time. A big red-headed guy with a moustache started in on Jo and she was not pleased. She told him to beat it, so he did. The screaming and hollering could wake those poor, often-disturbed dead. And in runs Nate with a really big stick all set to wear this ape out. We were all pretty worn out before the blessedly nosy neighbor called the cops. They came in, boom! guns drawn and all. The big guy got hauled off, as did Nate and Jo. I was left unnoticed in the corner I had luckily been pushed into during one of my encounters with the stick. The neighbor, Miss Rita Avery, came in an hour later, after a call from Jo, and washed off the blood and put me to bed.

It would seem that with four usable limbs and a voice, life could be rather pleasant, but you wouldn't know it from these folk. They talk so darkly about their lives, and hardly ever speak of dreams. I know they don't like their work. That is why they call in sick so often, or just don't show up, then don't come in for a year or so, and then reapply, and get hired again. What do they do during that year? Have babies, do motel housekeeping, wait tables, try to get on at factories. That is what they tell each other when they come back. They sound like the stories on TV but without the money and good jobs. That must be why they like the soaps and watch them so avidly. Misery loves company. Look at me!

But I would like to piece their worlds together from the puzzle snatches they offer in their conversations. Could I fit into such a world? It sounds too horribly hard right now.

Mira sometimes talks about things at mealtimes. I notice that when I show up she's even been asking me things.

"Emily, now we know you can understand us, so I want you to answer me."

I guess they never realized I was on to them all those years. They were never sure I got the gist. Uncle Nate always knew. He'd paint and talk to me a little about his own growing up. It wasn't too great, since his pa, my grandpa, drank and hit on the kids a lot. I had the notion, from what he said, that that was how he got that bad leg, or maybe he talked about the army and getting hurt in Korea. Anyway, Jo and Nate were two of nine kids. My ma was between them in age, and when she was killed in the wreck, I was two and Nate took me in, as he had Jo, too, just months before. She was pissed, I gathered from him, as he'd shape colors and light on the window-shade canvas. She didn't want to have to wipe up after no shitty kid, particularly Retta's sickly crazy no-good baby.

Would life out be like that, again? We lived in a three-room joke, with a toilet and shower in a closet. One room was the living room and Nate's place to sleep. It had a worn-out pull-out sofa and a chest of drawers with a lamp on it, a closet where he kept his stuff, a little smoking table and a window. The second room was a kitchen with a table and sink and a two-burner hot plate on the sink counter and a little fridge and one cabinet. The last room was Jo's, with a small bed and a little dresser, and I had a little army cot in the corner, which was close to the floor. Nate would wind me up in a bedroll at night so I would be less likely to flail myself out. When I did, I didn't have far to fall.

Nights Jo came home alone she'd stagger in about three. I'd hear sharp-heeled clumpings in the dark and occasionally got hit as she kicked shoes off in any direction. Next morning she'd be sick and mad and scream at me if I'd messed the bed or needed anything. I gave up trying to talk, not just 'cause she hated the sounds, but 'cause when I'd try to state my side, my side just got bruised.

Is this what the aides live like? Is that what life is like out there? All hitting, drinking, screaming about money, or sex? Do I want to leave here, where at least if I'm hit it usually gets reported if they get caught, and nobody stays here long if they get caught drinking?

I don't understand about drinking. Jo made me drink with her a couple times.

"C'mon baby, you get snocked with me and we'll have a good old time and watch the stories and cry together."

She'd have a gulp and then put the glass to my mouth and hold my head still. It was horrible and burning. I'd gasp and down my windpipe went stinging fire. I'd gag and cough up whatever had recently gone down. She'd throw the glass at the wall and hit me with a towel.

"Clean that up, bitch!" she'd yell. "Gawd, I am tired of you and your fuckin' messes!"

I don't know how long I sat once with the towel hooked over my head, the barf-fumes rising up under it making me gag and puke all the more. I made moves to try to get it off. I really wanted to be able to clean it off, what a laugh. Jo had disappeared, I guess she hit the sack. I fell asleep eventually in all that muck still be-toweled. I woke with Nate cleaning me off in the dark. There were shouts and loud crashes from Jo's room before she stomped out, late for work.

Is that how the independent living people live independently? Who'd want it? But Andrew described his life with his aunt as better than mine had been, and he decided he had to get out of that to something he wanted more. He didn't tell me if what he went to was better. Not really. Maybe I should listen to George and trust less of what these people say. I plan to listen in to a lot more from a lot more people.

There is a page for me to the Lounge. As I dodge my way through the logjam of chairs and carts in the hallway Marie catches up.

"Onnee, an ah ngo wi you?"

She is caught behind two hall sleepers, deftly moving one out of the way. By the time I reach the elevator she has caught up and shoves the buttons with her stick.

"Beez, Onnee, Ah onna ngo. Ah lak Ah El bee pul!"

Marie knows too well that no one on this planet would be here for me but the A.L people.

Off the elevator, we crab toward the Lounge. There is no one there we know. We look suspiciously at each other. An older woman approaches us.

"Which one of you ladies is Emily Mason?"

I noise at her.

"Ms. Mason, I am from the Adult Protection Agency. Nelda Legrand."

She waves her hand near mine, attempting quick contact.

"We received a report a few months ago describing your having sustained an undocumented injury and it is necessary for us to make a thorough follow-up report."

Marie quietly crabs out of the area and goes to turn on a TV on the other side of the room. I see real disappointment in her face. That's set me to wondering as this woman natters on in her own private language about whatever it is she's talking about.

She suddenly grabs my hand and asks loudly, "Can you answer my questions? Do you understand?"

I blink yes and no, and wonder if she has any idea what that means. So I try noising, yes, and no. She looks baffled.

"Maybe I am confusing you. Can you answer my questions?"

"Ehhs," I noise as clearly as I can.

"Fine. We can go on. These questions must be answered accurately for your continued safety."

She natters on and on again and I notice Marie glancing at me edgily. My head continues its leftward drift away from this lady.

"Ms. Mason, previous to this injury for which you were hospitalized were you ever hospitalized or treated as out-patient for a similar occurrence."

What the heck? I try to look at her but the head is on its own trip.

"Ms. Mason, were you ever injured this way before?"

Before what I wonder? Before being here? "Ehhs," I try to noise at her.

"You have been thus injured before?"

How are you thus injured? I've been injured all kinds of ways. So I noise again, "Ehhs."

"While you were here at South Pines?"

"Ehhs," I noise remembering the guy in the basement and those occasions. Who is this dame? She didn't show up with her secret language after those memorable incidents, or the times that weird girl kept popping people who couldn't talk 'cause she figured she could pop us with her fist, no problem.

"When you were injured here, each time did someone wilfully strike you?"

"Ehhs, nah."

"Sometimes yes, sometimes no? Did anyone deliberately hit you?"

You can bet the poppin' fresh girl knew she was gonna before she'd let us have it. I saw her lay one on poor Sammy one day probably because he was crying, lost inside himself, couldn't ever find a way out. He often cried. She often popped him up the side of the head, until they finally caught her. They never knew about the rest of us that she'd labor on and off.

"Ehhs, nah?"

"Again sometimes yes, sometimes no?"

"Ehhs."

"More often yes?"

"Ehhs."

"This is not reported?"

I startle her as I let out one of my jerky shrieky laughs. It catches Marie's ear too, and she starts shuffling away from the tube and quietly lurks toward us.

"I can assume that your laugh means it is not reported?"

"Ehhs, nah?"

"Perhaps that it is not reported more than it is reported?"

"Ehhs."

"Would you judge your injuries ever to be the result of neglect?"

Marie laughs with me this time. We're getting on a roll. I am afraid this is befuddling the Protection lady. But she persists.

"Was the injury in question, that put you in the hospital, a result of a direct intended blow?"

"Nah."

"Then was it an incident of neglect, in your opinion?"

As I say yes and no, Marie chimes in with yes. The lady points out that she wants my opinion. Marie says that I might go easy on the aides. The lady seems to understand what she is saying. Marie says that before I talked the aides often just let me stay in one place for hours and rarely checked if I needed anything. She is on a roll for sure. The lady seems to be picking it up.

"So Ms. Mason, do you believe that your injury was caused by someone not paying attention to you when you really needed it?"

"Ehhs," I conclude after thinking that most of the time most of the non-talkers are not paid attention to. There is so much to do for the talkers who can make their needs known that the aides never catch up with them. I can see how it is hard to do it all for the others, too. There are never enough aides, ever.

"Now, Ms. Mason, this report says you sustained injuries such as a broken leg, a severe laceration on your lower lumbar area requiring stitches, lacerations and contusions on your legs and one arm, and a sprained wrist. Is this correct?"

Marie gasps and looks at me in something like horror. I couldn't tell her if it was correct, I just know it all hurt like hell. I try to make a shrugging movement and mostly sort of fall to one side.

"I won't keep you much longer, ladies, but I need to ask you, Ms. Mason, if you sustained these types of injuries previous to your residence at South Pines?

Have to think a minute about what she is saying, but I believe she means did I get popped around before I moved here. So I noise yes.

"Are the people you were living with then still involved in your care?"

"Nah, nah," and weren't much then either, save for Nate when he could be.

"Ehh aw dead," Marie bobs in quickly. She seems to have a satisfied look on her face about this, like she might have helped accomplish this condition, or perhaps would have liked to.

After a few more repetitions of those questions, the lady left us. We wove our way back through the chairs and ice carts and housekeeping wagons and meds carts. Marie backs into the weekly dog who yelps and scoots fearfully into Mr. Kneble's room. Poor cute little guy, he's gotta learn about avoiding wheels. At least he's quit wetting on them. Does it less than the rest of us. We reach our usual spot and out comes Marie's boomer and its mournful sounds of country love-lost. We get real settled in to watch the sun move and there is another page to the Lounge.

"Noaw da sa Ah El pee pul!" Marie fairly chortles with anticipation.

We begin our journey through the obstacle course again. Mr. Kneble blocks Marie's way and she tries to move him to one side, but he grabs her arm and begs her to look out the window with him to see if she can spot his missing people.

"They have all gone there, and seventy-five. I must have

done, all, all around there. Do you see? All around there. And I haven't been able."

Here this poor guy can talk, but not to any of us where it makes sense. Marie gently tugs her arm out of Mr. Kneble's iron grip, pats his worn old hand and says, "Bye." He stays at the window, hands clutching and shaking, tears streaming down his face. He wonders who he is and why. And where they all went.

We reach the lounge after considerable effort. Backing our chairs into the room, Marie and I crabwalk around and there is Andrew. I feel a jolt and my unexpectedly squeamish stomach churns emptily about.

"Hey, Emily, Marie! Good to see you both again. I just got back from a big action in Lake City. Twenty of us were arrested for surrounding buses at city bus stops and making them stop for good."

Marie looks half puzzled, half dazzled, as if she was Robin Hood's girlfriend, and he was just in from a hard day in the forest. I saw that movie with George on a video. Pretty neat.

"Oh, Anrwu, yoh ahve a goh toh djael?"

"Well, we got hauled onto medical lift-vans and stuck in a school gym overnight. The judge came to us to arraign us next morning. I get the idea that the courthouse isn't totally accessible. Neither is the schoolhouse. The johns were a real bitch for most of the gang to use. Luckily we have a big support group there and they stayed the night with us after the judge gave them permission."

I have a hard time comprehending why anyone wants to go so far away just to get arrested and thrown in any kind of jail. Hell, Jo could do it right here. For some reason the cops would pick her up when she met guys she was gonna bring home. I never understood why except that it made Nate furious and he made sidelong comments about "the money that bitch hustles" and how it all made him sick. They never explained why she was arrested. Now Andrew is trying to explain why he goes to get arrested. Doesn't sound like a much worse reason than Jo's. He tries to get on a bus, or stop a bus, so they arrest him. What is this country coming to? You can't bring home friends for a night, and you can't ride the bus. I think I am missing some things here. Besides I was on a bus once, and that was nothing to write home about. It was a bouncy bumpy ride and I wanted to barf the whole time. So for this, this nut goes to jail. The more I hear about that world out there, the less interested I feel.

I wish I didn't want to hear what Andrew is saying. I am afraid of what he tells us about that life, but I want to know more. I am afraid of what I feel as I watch him tell about it. His eyes worry me.

"Anyway the others couldn't make it over to chat today, so I thought I'd come by and tell you a little about the stuff they don't bring up much. There is a real push to keep gimps like us on the bottom of things. You really don't notice it until you can back away long enough to see what is going on. You need to talk to other crips who can see these things, so that you can start to see them, too. That's a good reason to start coming down to the Center, even if they soft-peddle this part of the idea."

Marie sits ga-ga watching old Andrew perform for her. I guess I know why she wants to visit with the Ah El people. I don't want to think about it.

"The only way we can get how crips are treated changed is to make people change. That is why actions like stopping the buses work. It makes people have to change something, at least long enough that they can back up and see what people are doing to other people. It makes them think!"

"Ehs, mahin peepul phink, hats goohd."

Marie's gotta pipe in and play his game. She polishes his hat for him as he tips it her way. What a show. How long's this gonna go on?

"Well, ladies, I can see by the old clock on the wall that I will wear out my welcome if I continue on. Until we meet again, 'parting is such sweet sorrow.'"

Whew, what a load of hype. Marie follows him down to the elevator, but I just stay here to get back some sanity.

Later I'm watching the sun wipe over the roof across the street. I can shut out the myriad voices of aides, TV's, radios, residents in distress, the P.A.: "201 needs assistance, 201 needs assistance!" "Would Mrs. Carver please call line 5, Mrs. Carver, line 5!" They always repeat, repeat. But none of this pertains to me, so I will wipe the sounds as the sun wipes the roof, left quiet and gray.

That gives me thinking time. What is the difference between outside and here? Could there be any advantages if outside is what Jo and Nate and the aides live? But Andrew describes his life: travel, new people, different places, even jail. I get very excited, but I feel really scared. Is it what he tells us, or that he tells us? It's not how he tells us! What is so appealing here? Damn his eyes!

Chapter 13

*T*ime begins to have an interesting quality here. I guess I just started really noticing. Lately I find myself paying attention to clocks. There seem to be two kinds. There are round ones with circles and numbers and sticks that George calls hands. Where the little stick points I can guess the hour, but I ain't got the knack for the big ones yet. The other kind show up on people's night tables. They have rolly numbers or little light-up numbers. They say just the very time it is, and I gotta know that because Andrew and some of the A.L. people are coming most weeks on Tuesday at 10:00 a.m. and I watch school with George most mornings at 9:00 a.m..

Edna has a clock on her night stand. I turned her clock to face my bed. She doesn't know where she is, or who, so why know when? I just rolled over to her stand and let the old arm fly. Magically it turned just enough. Leena'd say, "That was meant to be," because she thinks everything happens for a reason.

I can't quite see what I'm learning from George's shows, but I guess I am supposed to watch them "for a reason." I am noticing how letters and numbers work better now. When I can catch Sesame Street, there are things about mixing letters and numbers that I can figure, and they make sense to me. Buh – i – guh, big. I like the monsters that dance the whole time they sing the sounds. Sometimes I'll just spend time in the hall dancing and working at making the sounds with the tune in my head. The other day Judy walked by during one of my workouts.

"Girl, you having a convulsion? That's all we need!" She seemed a little disappointed when I blinked a no and continued on with my wiggle dance and "song."

Today Judy was on the spot and I'm up and out at 8:00 a.m. It's Tuesday so I'll skip breakfast as usual. Never a breakfast in bed, yeah! The "upstairs" assume that I go down to eat. The "downstairs" believe I eat upstairs.

Andrew is bringing friends. I found a window where I can watch the bus stop. Andrew comes on the regular bus and is sometimes late. Then I get really tense. I watch the longest hand on the clock. Sometimes Andrew's friends drive, or come on Metrovan, which also stops at the bus stop.

Here's a bus. The door opens and the lift is there. A round small red-headed woman rides down the lift. Her hair is short, her heavy jacket is blue and red. The lift jerks untrustworthily back into position.

This time Andrew rides down. I try to ignore a tense shaky feeling creeping over me. I look away, to the clock. I look back fast. He's down and rolling in his loony western jacket and that silly bandanna around the curly hair. He talks a lot to the round lady, but she seems not to listen directly to him. They roll toward the door.

I begin my journey before the page. I might not have to deal with Marie in tow that way. The elevator takes forever. It may be locking up for lunch deliveries. My toe taps the floor. Door opens, I am in luck. Brenda is going down too, so I wiggle my one finger in her general vicinity. The button is pushed and the terribly slow journey continues. Brenda gives me a good shove off at my floor and I get momentum for the lounge trip. I hear the page, as I round the corner, with a few more hard pushes. Marie swings around the corner ahead of me. She can really move fast when she wants to.

Andrew greets us with a smile and moves my chair to face him and his friend, while Marie jockeys hurriedly for position.

"Hey, Em, Marie, this is Micky Kruze. Mick used to live in the complex near Bob and me, but I'll let her tell."

My reluctant head hesitates to leave the vicinity of Andrew as Micky Kruze begins her clipped hollow-sounding speech. At times her tone seems tense and strained. She rarely looks at me as I can rarely look right at her. When I can I notice that she seems closed and tight in her posture. She moves only one arm in occasional sharp stabs to make her point. Her speech is clearer than Andrew's or Marie's.

"Emily, Marie, if I may, they all call me Micky, or Mick, Andrew said you might want to hear about when I got sprung from a dump like this. He said you may not want to split, but thought you might want to hear a horse's-mouth account of my adventures. I do peer support stuff at the A.L.C. now, so this all fits in."

Andrew watches her, and our reactions to her. We watch him watching us, and we listen.

"I lived at Birch Hills after my grandmother died there. She had told me we had to move there because no one anywhere would welcome chair users, and she had just gone to a chair."

She drones on a bit about Birch Hills and the flies on the food and other stuff, and Andrew doesn't seem a bit bored, so I try not to be bored, too.

"Anyway this lady, Ms. Arliss from the A.R.C., wanted to know if I'd like to meet her A.L.C. friends."

Hmmm, this sounds familiar. Is this some kinda cult like on TV, that sucks lonely people into obeying some cult leader, Andrew? I saw that on a show once, people convinced and led out of their old lives. And these people sound culty sometimes.

"I said, what could it hurt? So they came and told me about their lives, and a few other birds joined us for weekly meetings. They talked about not being able to find houses they could get into, or streets they could go down in their chairs. They told about problems getting into the doctor's office, and not being able to go shopping or get into stores. They told us what a house could look like, and how easily you could move your chair around in it. This was all fairy stories to us. Wasn't even a usable john at B.H. Heft that bod, tote that pail."

Andrew casts the occasional wry look at her, and we maintain our interest, because she does talk about our lives. She's been here, and knows.

"I can only start to touch on things you need to know about if you do want to move into a different sort of place. I guess Andrew told you about attendants from agencies. Did he tell you about the program where you can hire your own attendant?"

"Anwru tohk abow ahdz in his apawhmen." Marie chimes in with excitement.

Andrew nods at Micky, and she starts up again.

"That program is just a few years old and there is not a lot of money from the state supporting it. We need for people to let lawmakers know that it is an important service. You know, the nursing-home lobbyists would like to keep the lawmakers in their pockets, so they can get all that money."

She said the last in a loud whisper as if to keep it from the aides going up and down the hall. I am wondering what do these people live on. Who pays their bills? They talk about hiring aides, and apartments, but they haven't said how they pay for it all.

Marie's been gazing at Andrew like the silent-screen vamp at the sheik. It's a bit embarrassing. Micky talks right around them and I wonder what Marie's hearing.

"If you guys have other friends here who want to know more about life out there, tell them to join us on Tuesdays."

Somehow I feel funny about that, culty again. I don't know why I feel tense about this. I feel there is so much more to know, more than I care to, and I'm not sure I want to.

"You may wonder why I did move out of B.H. I do myself on occasion. But I always wanted a little space all my own to fix up my way. All my B.H. roomies were possessive irritating types. Couldn't hang or place a thing to suit them.

She tells just a little about her life at B.H., which is good, because this we know about. It sounds just like life at S.P. with a few little differences.

"But even though I grew to hate the way I lived at B.H., it all seemed too impossible to live out, alone, and it very nearly is."

Here come the real war stories. I notice Andrew looking a bit irritated at Micky. Since she isn't looking at him, like Marie is, he huffs and clears his throat. Their eyes meet.

"Duncan, you may picture yourself as some lone crusader, but people should know the ugly truth from the beginning, and then work and decide from there."

She practically snarls. This is getting less boring.

"Yes, Duncan. We gotta tell them. The able-bodied world is the enemy camp. We are the enemy, they the powers-that-be. Ladies, it is a richer and better place to be but it's an A-B world and they intend to keep it that way. They don't want to know that they could be seeing life from a permanent seat in just a split second."

Marie's early gray hair seems tight-pulled back and her eyes are round and staring. Andrew is pulled inward and facing away.

"Wa d ya mean, Nick? Ey don ike seen us?"

"No, Marie, they actually don't but it's because our obvious differences don't fit their neat world view. Perfect is the way they think everyone should be. They believe in the illusion that they will continue to get better and better. And they impose this delusion willy-nilly. Broken people go into big Rehab hospitals to be made "more like us," and can't be. So people like you and me are seen as failures to be shipped to gomer cities like this where people who don't get better and better are stored outa sight till they disappear completely. Otherwise we might reflect badly on the doctor's trade and the whole damned illusion."

"Mick?"

"Duncan, these women have a right to know it all up front. I've hardly begun. You can't just open doors and march people out into a hostile world and expect them to have a ghost's chance of survival."

She switches on her chair and throws it into high and out the door, whoosh, only fading on reaching the far elevators.

Marie looks open-mouthed at her crestfallen idol. This is the first time he's looked anything but cocky. He hangs his head and then gazes out the window.

"Yeah, ladies, it's a jungle out there. Micky's right. Able-bodied people don't like us around, except on their terms. We are OK on telethons, where they can send their money and feel better about being nearly perfect, but they don't want to have to hang around with us. Why do you think I have to fight like some kind of crazy to get a ride on the bus that they just get on every morning without even thinking? Why do I have to ask some stranger for help up a three-inch curb? It's a major glitch in the culture, and it's been going on as long as I can tell. They are so uncomfortable with us around that they'll do nearly anything to keep us in the back rooms and institutions just to keep us out of sight. They are the enemy.

"But we are part of that enemy. We are so used to things being this way that we want to believe in our failure, our hopeless helplessness, our dependence, as much as the A-B's do. Everybody and us want us to stay in our place. They don't like us to get out to explore their fake jungle!"

He jerks his chair around and darts out. Then he pops back and with that impish grin says, "Can we still come back and play?"

Marie, of course, says sure, do come back! So he and his fellow warrior escape, leaving us, limp wounded bodies, behind. A wave of awful starts in my toes and worms its way all through me till it shoots out my head in a sudden wrench of deep jolting dry heaves. Marie startles in her chair.

I feel like I've exploded inside some kinda sealed-up closet. I want out, but I know that there's no way out. So everything in me is coming out instead. What the hell's going on?

Brenda, who Marie fetches, yanks my chair out of the Lounge and to the john where she scrubs my face and makes me pee, like a two year old. Shit!

Chapter 14

About two weeks later I decide that I have to see for myself what Micky is talking about in these Tuesday harangues. I want to see gimps in the world, doing, being, with the world gazing, judging, and gimps moving right along anyway. I decide to ask about buses.

With George's help I'm getting the round clocks down, and 9:45 a.m. finds me bus waiting at the window. I spy the bus rounding the corner and toe-race for the Lounge, held up only by the uninhabited elevator. Luckily two aides board and I wave my finger. Off I go and right to the Lounge. Sarah, Micky, and a new guy await us. No Andrew. No, I don't feel sinky, no. No!

Marie doodles in, gazing disappointedly around a few minutes later as I try to get my point across about the bus. It is not going well, but the new guy is a good listener. He is leg short, and he uses crutches. He has a broad kind face and dark eyes and beard. Sarah introduces him as a peer counselor, Wayne Baker. After a bout with charades from me, bus noises and horn sounds, and my usual irritating noising, they all make guesses about my chosen subject matter.

"Can I assume you have a question about vehicles?" Sarah asks.

I blink and sound, "duzth ibe," in Marie's direction. She looks quite horrified, to add to her disappointed look.

"Oh, Onnee, ou don wanna buth, no buth wide! Anwru say ith a yun-goh ow dere! Dey awr ookin ah uhs, an hate uhs. Ou don wann goh!"

Wayne laughs, "Duncan been scaring you guys?"

Micky looks sharply at him. "Can it, Baker. I've just been truth-telling. That can't hurt."

He laughs again. "What kinda Halloween stories Micky and Duncan been laying on you guys?"

"Emily, what did you want to ask about the bus?"

Sarah's quiet voice settles every one as we begin to get to my question. After some explanations about how the buses work around here, Wayne asks, "Emily, have you ever had a letter or symbol board?"

I noise and blink no, and look at Sarah.

"No one has ever taught Emily letters, but we could put together a picture and word board to get her going on sight recognition."

After they left, I felt a good deal taller. Sarah had promised bus ID applications. She explained that to ride the gimp bus you have to sign your life away, filling out bunches of forms. Then you need to get the doctor to certify that you are a gimp, no matter how obvious that might be. Wayne talked about three buses. One bus you order a week ahead and it gets you at the door. Priority, doctor's appointments. Well, that's what they think most of us gimps do for fun. The second bus gets you at the stop, and you order it the day before. The last is just the regular bus, when it has a little chair symbol on the lift door. Before they had lifts Andrew liked to chain himself to these buses. Kinky. But it works. Now we can all get on them, well, some of the time. Maybe businesses next, or new houses.

Wayne's says he's going to find me a picture/word board, and maybe a volunteer to help me with my letters.

A few days later, about 3:15 p.m. on the hall clock I get a page and hit the next occupied elevator down. I'd been watching Sesame Street on Mr. Kneble's tube. He doesn't care what's on, likes companionship, and the aides all had soaps on everywhere else. Anyway I left Mr. Kneble and Grover rescuing the kid at the bus stop who doesn't need rescuing. I am in the Lounge and so is Wayne.

"Here it is, your picture board!"

His face is quite bright as he clips the large plastic board onto my chair arms with velcro clips. It makes a nice lapboard. Then he looks at me like a Santa elf.

"Well, Emily, what works?"

"Unh?"

"Well, you gotta have some way to show what on the board you want. Do your hands move where you want, ever?"

I guess he can see the tears filling as I realize that I'd have little chance of pointing at anything when and where I wanted. It's all a crap shoot. I could use my good foot but then how'd I get around. Besides, who's gonna read me off the floor?

"Now, Em, never say die! We'll lick this sucker yet, you bet."

He pulls out a clean tissue and gives me a very comfortable face wipe, unlike the clean-and-jerk of the snot-grabbing aides. He is patient and waits with me as I regain my cool.

"I can't really get inside to understand your frustration and anger but I can see how it is bothering you. We aren't going to give in this easily."

After a final wipe he looks at me and smiles. "How's your head?"

Well, it's kinda drifting south now, but it is the best one I've got.

"Emily, can you control your head movement even a tiny bit?"

I concentrate in his direction and make the big effort to get my head to go that way. It slowly does, but not exactly right.

"Great!"

He pulls out a thing like a hair band with a little net on it and stretches it.

"Like a new spring hat?"

I blink yes and he pops the band around my head. Then he pulls out a pen-like thing and pushes a switch on it. It is like a tiny flash light. He flashes it into my eyes to show me and then clips it on the head band just next to my right eye.

Now, here's the trick. If you can get your head to look at the word picture, your friend can see which picture or letter you are saying, because the light shines on it."

I must look as astonished as I feel. He laughs right out at me. "Try it!"

It seems so obvious. I look over the whole board. There are bunches of little pictures arranged in boxes of related things, and one box with letters and some words. There is a heart with a word in it. It starts with L. I bet it is love. I watch the light move as my head moves. I never remember my head being so cooperative. It's usual random float has turned into a purposeful part of me. I watch the light creep jerkily past pictures, as if separate from any action on my part. It finally reaches the heart. I let it sit there wavering. Wayne looks at the light and then puts his face where I can see it without moving my light.

"You love it, right?"

We both break into hysterical laughter. Mira passing in the hall, comes into the lounge to see what's wrong.

"Is she all right?" she asks Wayne.

"Hell, lady, I don't know!" he laughs at her. "Why don't you ask her?"

We continue the guffaws and giggles, me gasping for air between eruptions of noise. Mira stalks out in a huff. I guess we have hurt her feelings, but I'm laughing too hard to care.

We spend over an hour testing the light and laughing. I'm glad Wayne likes pocket-pack tissues. I find out new ways to say a lot of things and Wayne tells me to make speech sounds when I can, and use the board to help get the idea across.

"When you learn to read enough to use the letter board, you'll want to talk more, and use the letters to explain the harder words, and spell out the real boogers. There's a lot of words folks have a hard time hearing. And granted, there will be a lot who will refuse to listen to you at all. Watch Andrew sometimes. Check out where he uses his board, and with whom he usually tries talking."

I spend most of the afternoon playing with my hat and board. By bedtime I am really good solid tired from so much fun. Wayne had told me as he was leaving that he is still looking for a tutor volunteer. At his seminary where he is studying, they have ministry-in-community people who get credit for volunteer work. Later in bed, I fall asleep praying for just that kind of minister to show up.

I am rolling down the hall and I feel my chair come to a stop. I look up and see a tall man with strange luminous eyes who beckons me to go with him. We roll down the halls to the door and out into an open meadow. We are talking together all this time, like old friends. We head across the field and then into a large old building. There are books everywhere, millions going up to high ceilings almost unseeable. Nothing like this I've ever seen before. The strange-eyed man beckons and smiles leading me down halls of books going in circles. We reach a center place with halls like wheel spokes radiating out from the middle of the huge room. The man stands with me in the center and swings his arm in a wide gesture.

"This can all be yours now!"

A tremendous light bursts in from the circular window above us and the man above me smiles and becomes a part of the brightness.

My eyes open to Judy flinging the drapes apart letting in the sunlight with a promise of early spring.

I am frustrated as Judy finishes dressing me. She's never seen my light or headband or board. She can't know to put them on me. I feel as if the shining strange-eyed man has gone and will never return. My board, tucked in the corner behind the dresser, calls me. I want to scream.

Marie! She saw me with my board. She might be able to help me lift it or could get someone to help us. I scuttle off to find her, probably in the dining room. She is not one to skip meals, even though you can't see the results on her.

After some elevator negotiations and delays, and misinterpreted signs and noises, I reach the dining room just as Marie is heading out.

"Unh uh tuh, unh un tuh!"

I try to cajole her into grasping my message and coming up to my room. She's quick and picks up that I want her to go with me.

"Weeo, Ah ain gah nuh'n tuh duh. Ohwn ngo whi ya, Onnee."

So we maneuver between hot trays and meds carts to the elevator. Marie pops the elevator controls with her trusty stick. We head to my room where I wish the light man of my dream was waiting. Marie remembers the gear, and in spite of her doubts about the merits of such contraptions manages to get the little hat a bit askew on my head and the light stuck into the side. She fumbles with the penlight a while until she is able to hit the switch. From the slightly screwy location I can move the light to reach things. I point it at the board in the corner.

"Onnee, Ou on't awn't nuch. Hah!"

Marie squeezes into the corner and backs around so she can reach the board. She struggles to pull it from behind the dresser. Light for Wayne is a burden for Marie. Mira, the night aide, had likely thought I'd never need that thing.

"Oudy, Oudy?"

Marie sees Judy coming down the hall out of the corner of her eye. She catches her just in time, asking her to lift the board onto my chair arms. Judy huffs and does it reluctantly. I manage to hit the light onto the Thank you card as she finishes. She looks at it, and at me, and smiles in a funny way I haven't seen before. I leave it for Marie to see, and then switch to the love heart. Marie laughs, and we toddle out for a day at the windows, practicing the light and listening to country.

Chapter 15

I suspect the aides hate my board and light. They avoid putting it on for me, and I still have to drag Marie up to help me with it and to get an aide to help her. It is silly, because it would take Judy two minutes or less to set the whole thing up for me after she dresses me. I don't like to feel this way, but little things make me think they resent my changing from a veg to a wheelie. Well, I love it, so they are going to have to get used to it. I want to show it all to George as a coming-home surprise. He has been in the hospital with surgery on those damn pressure sores for a couple of weeks.

This morning Judy sneaks out before doing my board, on the pretense of having to take out linens for Edna. I run into the hall after her but my foot moseys are no equal to the roundly efficient moves of Judy. I drag around looking for someone to coerce into lighting and boarding my chair. It must be inspection day, or board of directors visiting day the way everyone is tearing around so busily. I spy Jerry, the orderly, zooming in my direction and swing my chair into his path.

"Whoa there, Emy, what are you trying to do, you 'bout took off my toes and a couple other things, there!"

Well, I got his attention. "Oad, phweth, oad?"

I feebly make graspings on his greens and try to lead him into my room.

"Naw, Emy, I can't come make whoopie with you now, I gotta catch up. Inspection day tomorrow."

I wonder how they know that. Inspection is supposed to be a big surprise. It never is here. Spit and polish and nothing normal. But I can't let Jerry go so easily.

"Pweth, pweth, oad oad!" I fairly shriek at him. I can't take the tension and start to puff and wheeze. And damned if Nurse Neeley isn't just now strutting by.

"Mr. Donald, I assume you are attending to your assigned tasks?"

"Yes, Ms. Neeley, I am doing just that."

Off he goes, abashed, and here I am with my red face and Neeley staring down at me. I want to grab her skirt and pull.

"Ms. Mason, is it really necessary for you to clutter the hall with your emotional upheavals and spectacular displays like this, disrupting the duties of the aides? I would appreciate if you would go to your room and quit making a spectacle of yourself."

Maybe being a veg is better. I want to pound this bitch. Disruptive, spectacular displays. You ain't seen nothin'! So I increase the volume, the rage, and the drama. I try in vain to reach her dress to yank it and rip it. Jerk, there goes my chair. I've pushed her too far, now she'll push me too far. Time out. Neeley's last resort. Then there will be a new medication ordered for me. We zoom down the hall to the linen closet. Door opens. In I go. Yeah, lady, stuff me in here with all the other linens and towels. They muffle the sounds. This way I can be safely forgotten.

I used to accept these occasional trips to lockup as a necessary part of my personal growth, or lack thereof. Now I know what they are for. Outta sight, outta mind. But it makes for a great opportunity to get one's yips out. I do, royally. I haven't had such a good shrieking rage-out in years. I learned from Jo, a pro. South Pines sucked it out of me. It is coming back.

When Jo'd start in on me, shoes, dishes, knives, furniture flying, I had no defense but what might be called my voice. So I'd let lose when I could. I might be gazing and wailing in one direction and a sudden cup would smash against my head and shatter on the chair arm. As long as I was conscious, I'd keep shrieking in hopes Nate or a neighbor would hear. A knock at the door and Jo'd push back her hair and open to the chain.

"Any trouble, Ms. Mason?"

"No, Mr. Avery, just watching the stories. You know how they get."

"No, can't say's I do, Ms. Mason. Don't go in for that kinda thing."

Just as well for him he didn't. The soaps never got that bad. I'd wonder if her breath would knock him back before he stepped on his way. But I'd always pay for the interruption. Another cup, maybe a fork.

"Ol' man Avery oughta mind his own life and keep his shitty face outta mine," she'd storm and throw more until she slept again.

And so must I have because I wake up still in the dark which smells of the ironer and disinfectant. There is a faint glow from below the door crack behind me. It must be evening. Ha, Neeley has left me here and didn't tell the shift change. They will either miss me at bed check tonight or will find me at linen distribution in the early morning.

Must be a bit after 11:00 p.m. shift change as the door opens.

"Who the hell is this?" the voice booms into my back, as I spasm enough to knock me out of the chair. Good thing for seat belts.

Jerk, back flies the chair and Mavis spins me around to gape in my face. "Gawd, girl, whatever possessed you to hide in here?"

Explanation impossible, I make my pee sign 'cause I gotta go really bad. Maybe I should have backed up against the door and made noises, but I know how many people go past this door at the end of the hall. Futile at best.

Mavis gives me a good jerk in the direction of the "rest" room, what a laugh. She continues her tirade as I try to relax the old spasming bladder, straining against its instinctive need to empty.

"How the hell do you get into these messes, Mason? You are really getting to be a troublemaker. You have got to shape up and act right. Your negative behaviors are being noted and there will be ways to get you to stop. I will see to it."

A hundred or more new jerks and jabs, and a big pill, and I

am safely in bed on my side, easing red bony spots aggravated by a day of immobility in my chair. I wonder what Mavis has in mind. What are they planning, other than more pills, to keep me in my place? Who is she going to see to this with? Am I in danger here, and also out there?

Marie waits at my door early the next day, Tuesday. She's hopeful for an eyeful of Duncan. But she'll help me put on my board and beanie; I can't complain. As we juggle and jerk it all in place, Marie indulges in a chat.

"Onnee, a cupa peepuh ah tawk to wanna go meed a Ah El peepuh."

No problem, Marie, I don't own them. I want to say that, but I can't. Such a streak of meanness lurks in your thought, I say to myself, wanting to let Marie know that I know she just wants to show off her new beau to the girls.

"Onnee, Gawj comin, too."

Rats, I won't have gotten to surprise him with my board. I wanted to do that, 'cause we could have some great jokes with it. Well, later.

We start our trek downward to the Lounge. If we stake out the area the "ladies-aide" bunch won't go in there and turn on and up the tube so we can't hear ourselves talk. It's hard enough with so many of us weird talkers.

At 10 minutes to 10, by the big clock, a few more rollers come in. I am surprised and pleased to see George, because even with Marie's assurance, I doubted his recent surgery would be healed enough to warrant sitting up for long. After George comes Teddy Bower. I can't fathom what he'd want to know about independence. He's not quite on board, according to my sources. His oddly squinched face and close-set slanty eyes seem always ready for a senseless laugh, but little more.

In rolls Madge Stark. Only here a few months, since a year at the Rehab after a bad car wreck. She uses her hands with splints. There's always a cigarette stuck in one splint any time I look at her. And if you look at her and she notices, she glares at you.

At a couple past 10 a new group comes in led by Wayne Baker

on his sticks. Following him is a walking lady with sharp green eyes, a long straight nose, and a quick smile. Andrew brings up the rear in his usual zip-jerk manner. My head drifting west catches Marie's look. Yeesh.

Wayne M.C.s the group.

"I guess all coming are here? Let's go around for quick intros for the benefit of newcomers."

"I'm George Danton, 39, lived here twenty years or so since my injury. Not sure why I'm here today, probably hopeless curiosity."

"Ah'm Mah wee Wha h. Been hew nah-tee eighty two. Ladeez don teow age. Ah wan know bout Ah El Cennah."

Like hell, I find myself muttering. But then maybe she does. What am I so bitchy about?

"I'm Andrew Duncan. I talk like Marie, but slower. Please be patient with me and my letter board. I'm a peer counselor at the A.L. Center, an advocate (spelled on the board with the smiley lady's help) of sorts, and a pain in the transport system's royal ass. I'm here to cause strife and answer questions, and a lady doesn't tell her age."

That quip is accompanied by a toss of bandannaed gray curls and a blatant grin at Marie. She goes as white as her name. She might die of palpitations. No such luck. The line comes to me.

I proudly point my light at my name letters on the board, and the numbers 3 and 4 while I noise vague attempts at these words. I catch Wayne's expression out of the corner of my eye. He is pleased for me. I am pleased for me. We go on round the circle.

"I'm Madge Stark, C 4-5 quad, and useless bitch. I'm 28 and no lady, and I'm sicker'n puke of this hellhole. I came to see if there really were any other options to this slow death."

"I'm Casey Oakley. I study at the seminary with Wayne. I volunteer at the Center with publications, and I hope to spend some time reading with Ms. Mason here."

Oh, here she is. Wayne came through. I like her eyes, and I cast my light in their direction as well as I can muster. With time I catch them and direct the light to my Thank you card on the board. She sees it and oddly sticks up three fingers and swings them from her right to left shoulder. I wonder what that's about. Back to the ring game.

"Hi. I'm Ted Bower. I live here and work in the kitchen. I am 35 and I like nature and movies and I can't read could I please sit with you and Emy, Ms. Oakley? I'd sure like to try!"

"If it's OK with Ms. Mason, I'd be delighted."

I am surprised at his interest. I had no idea he was this together. People acted like he was some kind of dummy. At Ms. Oakley's glance I poke my light at "OK" on my board. I blink yes.

Wayne sums up the introductions with his statement that he is a 27-year-old seminarian who will be glad to meet with any of us for as long as we care to get together.

It is an interesting meeting. I don't understand a whole lot; there is a lot to think about. Madge asks blunt fast questions.

"If I want to move out of this dump, where can I go? They tell me I gotta have 24-hour care and that this is it."

"Yeah, you'd have to find an accessible place, get good attendants, and be able to live on whatever income you have and your insurance."

"Baker, you are unreal. This is a crock. I guess I am supposed to go knocking on doors to find one with a ramp, set up a damn nursing agency, and develop dynamite steel buns to boot. What a shit-pile."

She joylessly bumps her joystick to turn her chair to leave. Wayne starts up again.

"With that kind of patience, and forbearance, you are right, this 'hellhole's' your only option. You won't even listen long enough to see that there might be a chance."

"Yeah, what chance?" she shrieks as she starts heading out the door. Wayne sits silently, the room thickens with tension.

"Yeah, what chance? Huh? Tell me!"

I get the distinct impression that she wants to be begged back in. Wayne doesn't bite. She huffs loudly like a low scream, and wheels up the hall.

"You all probably know that you can get up to fourteen hours a week of attendant help paid by Medicaid. If you are lucky enough to get to the top of the waiting list you can get up to 40 paid hours from the PCA program fund. It's sometimes possible to set up a live-in arrangement in exchange for roommate privileges."

While Wayne goes over these and a couple of other possible options, I hear Madge's chair creeping up to the lounge door. She isn't going to miss a word. He doesn't even bat an eye as she nudges slowly back into her place in the circle.

"Anybody see if I dropped my cigarettes?" She pops this in at a lull in Wayne's story about aides. He goes right on as she shuffles her arms about her chair looking over the sides for the lost cigarettes.

"I can't find the damn fags. What's it matter, I can't get the shitting things lit half the time. Nobody will bother."

She is muttering loud and clear so that anything Wayne says is cancelled out by her noise. Finally she blurts out a new tirade at Wayne.

"You know, Baker, this is all too fucking complicated for anyone to cope with or understand. You college types are so full of great fucking ideas. I guess I am supposed to be some kind of slave-driver, or straw-boss, getting these girls to step and fetch for me every minute. You have no idea how awful it is to have to ask for everything you need every second. It's horrible to have to rely on anyone with their attitudes and shit. You can't know. You've got two arms, and you can walk, even if it's with sticks. You don't have to beg every minute!"

Madge's tears are a real surprise to us. We've never seen her any way but bitchy.

"Ms. Stark, could you take a little time and talk with me after this? We are just about to end here."

Madge, looking distraught, shakes her head no, then she turns her chair as if to leave, turns it back and, eyes closed, she nods yes, and goes over to the TV area. The rest of us file out and go our own ways.

Ms. Oakley walks behind me toward the elevator.

"Ms. Mason, can we set up a time to meet about reading?"

Teddy turns back from the elevator and waits for us as we move ahead. We miss the elevator as Ms. Oakley pulls out a brown book and pen. We three set up a Thursday meeting.

Chapter 16

The weeks are moving faster. Too much going on to spend much time at my window. That's OK. When I do get the chance to stop, the light moves just like it always did. It's only me that is moving so much faster.

I had a funny dream the other night. I tried to tell Marie, but she didn't quite catch it all. I was running down a street full tilt. I realized that I was running and was shocked and tripped and fell. Then I felt myself safely rolling in my chair. There were cars coming fast. I was in the middle of a street. I panicked. My chair suddenly was being pulled backwards. I felt myself on a sidewalk and behind me Wayne and Andrew were silently moving on up the street and then they seemed to be big birds and flew away.

Thursday has rushed up towards me. I finish what was their excuse for lunch double quick and head up to see if I can find anyone to help me with my board and beanie without getting linen-closeted for the day. I run into Teddy Bower in the hall and get him to follow me up to my room. Hah! Imagine me saying run! Ted is quite good at putting on my board and beanie with the little instruction I can offer, mostly pokes and grunts. We have some laughs at misplacements and bumps, then head to the lobby together. He seems as excited as I am.

Casey walks in promptly at 3:00. It is so different living by clock hours rather than meals and bedtimes. I like it.

In the lounge Casey sits on one side of my board, Ted on the other. We learn to sing the alphabet song with her, noising each in our own voices. Ted seems to know the letters as well as I. Sesame Street again. We have good laughs as Casey tests us on letter identification using my letter board. She watches and listens as I sound a letter and then point it out on my board. Ted does the same and we take turns till we have them all down.

"Ms. Mason, remember to practice these every day, pointing, and saying them. Doing it all at once, pointing, saying, looking, will make it all stick that much faster so that next time we can begin sounding out whole words.

I use my light to hit the B. I make a B-like noise. Then I hit the I, and vowel out that sound. Then I light the G. "Bhuih gueh."

"Yay, yeah, that's the idea. Do you see how Ms. Mason sounded out BIG? That's the way to do this. That is really great! Don't forget the pre-G.E.D. reading class on the Sesame Street Channel, and Sesame Street, too. The reading class is at . . ."

She pokes through her purse to pull out the ever-ready brown calendar book. She really lives by that thing.

"Yeah, it is at 1:00 p.m. Wednesday and 11:00 a.m. Saturday. I'll make a note of this, tape it to your board, and then you will have to read it to remember it."

Teddy looks a bit abashed. "Isn't Sesame Street for babies?"

"Well, I have a five-year-old niece who watches every day with her mom. Her mom loves it. I watch with them when I can. I like Kermit and Grover, but I also see people like Stevie Wonder and Robin Williams and Itzak Perlman and Hootie and the Blowfish, and lots of other people I enjoy. It is strictly up to you, Mr. Bower. But it will help with letter recognition, and numbers, too."

"I see. You can call me Ted. That's O.K."

"Fine, Ted. You call me Casey!"

We set up another class in a week. Casey says we'll meet more often in the summer when classes break up at the Seminary. She explains that a seminary is a college for ministers and people who do other ministries, too, like social work or counseling. I'm not entirely sure what that minister means. I guess I think of ministers like the ones that come to do chapel most Sundays. I go down sometimes to hear them talk, now that I can get around. Some of them tell good stories from the Bible and others just mouth about doing bad and never get to the point about what doing bad is. So I am always wondering if I am doing bad, because I don't know any different.

Anyway, here is this Casey, and I wonder if she is going to be a preacher. She is so soft-spoken, I find it hard to believe she could get up and yell and carry on like some of those guys. Amen!

I meet Ted at 1:00 in the Lounge and we stake out the tube before the aides can change the channel. It is great to have Ted as a backup. We flip on Sesame as Nancy strolls in with pop and chips and her smokes. She announces her break to Mira heading down the hall to a bell and sails over to flip the channel. Ted jumps up.

"No, no, Nancy. Our teacher told us to watch this for reading."

"You got rooms, ain't ya?"

I start to cough.

"Nancy, I beg your pardon, but my TV's broke and Edna's got stories on in Emily's room."

I uselessly point my beanie light on Yes. Ted goes up to turn the TV over.

"Don't touch that! I gotta see what happens. I don't want to be interrupted."

Ted looks at her with uncharacteristic daggers and then at me. He stamps his foot loudly and harrumphs at Nancy. She ignores him. He takes off out the door in a controlled rage. For a few minutes I can pick out his rarely raised voice very raised down at the station. I hear two sets of footsteps. One sounds like Gina Potter. I remember a movie George and I watched while our short-lived Video Club existed. It was about lots of guys in a mental hospital. It was wilder at times, but there was a lot like this home, especially the main nurse. Her name sounded like Hatchet or Ratchet or something. She was so like Gina. Stiff tight face. It could break like stretched cellophane over a dish if you poked too hard. I dread her squishing sounding shoes approaching. She whitely swirls into the lounge.

"Nancy, I am afraid you will have to go to the Staff Smoker for break if you want to see this show. Teddy's teacher made a specific request that he watch his program for reading class. You can't deprive him of that. This is his home, not yours."

She spins back out on her heel and is gone. I am stunned by the unusual defense. Nancy grumbles herself slowly out of the chair and flips the channel during an ad. She gives a maiming stare and mutters out of the room, something sounding like "teaching dummies to read, bullshit" exuding from under her breath.

I have to say that I am pleased at Ted's spunk. I never knew him to have any before. But as he adjusts the picture Nancy deliberately left blurry, I find myself drawing a whole new picture of Ted Bower.

The TV picture clears and a curly-haired smiling man is seated with a group of kids, one in a chair like mine. Well, not like mine; the kid's chair fits her. I notice the man has on leg braces like Micky. He is talking with the kids and then begins to play a fiddle. I am struck by the music. It goes right through me. It isn't like Marie's country, and not like rock or hymns. Just a little bit, but so beautiful I get teary.

Ted and I get together between sessions with Casey. He gets out of kitchen at 7:00 p.m. so we head to the little lounge off the Activity Room. George comes when he is still up and helps us. When the card games are done, Grandma Sample comes over and sounds out my word board with me. The board has plastic inserts which slip in over other charts; some have symbols, some letters, some words. Sometimes Grandma Sample will let Ted and me read her the easy books Casey brings us. Ted is so excited. He could have been reading all these years if someone had just noticed him. Grandma is patient with me as I write sentences for her to read with my beanie and board. It is tedious for her to watch as I make the light slowly hit home on chosen words or letters. Then she must remember each piece until they all make up a sentence. I love her for her calm and patience.

❖❖❖

It is Saturday, and the weatherperson on Edna's tube said it would be a warm one. I am dressed and ready, and Judy even took time to put my beanie and board on me. I am always surprised when that happens, since I have a sneaky feeling that most of the aides are resentful of my board. Doesn't make sense, but they often make snotty and uncalled-for comments, especially since the incident of Ted and the lounge TV.

Anyway, here I am, having indicated to the upstairs folk that I would dine down, and to the downstairs folk that I couldn't hold another bite, having dined in my room, I head to the door. A temp comes by. I catch her eye with my light and spell, "Wan out," really fast. I'd been practicing upstairs while waiting for an elevator friend. She looks at me, then out on the patio where Grandma Sample is already stoking the neighborhood birds for their day.

"OK, I guess so. Are you supposed to go out?"

I'd never considered this. By whose orders? I figure if I can convince someone that I could go out, then I am out of here. So I light up the Yes on my board and get ready to hit the door. But Jerry is coming down the hall.

"What's up, Emy?" he asks a bit suspiciously.

"NUT IN MUSH!" I spell out laboriously while they wait.

"Huh, they put nuts in the cereal this morning? That sounds pretty tasty. Did you have a hard time eating it?"

I know I must be looking at him weirdly. So I respell, "NUT-TIN MUSH."

"Oh, I see, you ain't doing nutting much. Yeah, right. I'm onto you now. That's good. Yeah."

He fades on down the hall after an appreciative survey of the nice-looking temp. I make my play again.

"OUT NOW?"

"Yeah, OK."

She pushes the door for me. What a joy! I scoot out into the fresh air and sunshine.

I've gotta think that a year ago I'd have never even given a thought to getting outside, and certainly not on my own. I foot-scoot across the patio absolutely exhilarated. If I could sing and dance I'd do a "Hills are alive" thing like the movie. No hills, but who cares? This is great. I can scoot on my own. I can tell others what I want with my board. This is such a rush. I head over to where Grandma Sample is breading and seeding the bird world.

"Why, hello, Emily. Out early today, aren't you?"

She doesn't miss a seed and crumb toss as I slowly approach her, partly not to bother the birds, partly because I can't go any faster.

"I don't recall seeing you out here this time before? Is this something new for you?"

I scoot next to her and light my board with, "YES. NEW."

We watch the birds quietly. She tells me which ones are which. I see the difference really for the first time. Well I always knew about the red ones with the hats on, like baseball teams. George has a hat with one on it. I've noticed the ones with the orange chests, robins. But now I see little brown ones with black hats, and dark brown with speckles, and there is a bright blue one with a hat. Grandma's favorites are soft gray, always two of them.

Out of the corner of my eye I see an aide wheel two ladies out, wrestling with the door each time. At our last meeting, Wayne asked us why our building didn't have automatic doors. What's that, was my reaction.

"Oh, you know, like at grocery stores, sometimes drug stores. So folks with carts can get in and out. It's funny how its OK to wheel out a cart full of food, but not a chair full of person."

I've only been a few times to a grocery store that I remember. I couldn't imagine what it would be like to not have to wait for someone to open a door for me. I couldn't tell him what I was thinking. Too many words. But Madge blasted him with some.

"You've never had to live like this, in a prison. Gotta keep the gimps, gomers, and loonies from cluttering the streets. If some of these poor loonies got out and didn't know where or who they were, it'd be hell to pay for this hole. They gotta keep us locked up so we don't scare the normals."

She's right, I think. If Mr. Kneble got out, for instance, awful.

He gets hopelessly lost in his own wing and just sits and cries. Maybe people out there wouldn't understand about him and might hurt him if he couldn't make any sense.

I scoot over to the patio gate. I notice a locked latch on it. So even if I can come out onto the patio, that's as far as it goes. I'm not like Mr. Kneble. I can make sense. But would the people out there be patient with me and my board long enough for me to get my point across? Or would I be as unsafe as Mr. Kneble? Maybe Micky is right. It is their world and we don't have any rights to it.

❖❖❖

I am a little late to the Tuesday at 11:00 a.m. meeting. Casey called this morning and told George to expect lunch, pizza and cokes to celebrate the start of summer. Wasn't it just Easter, with bulbs up around the patio, and new birds for Grandma Sample to show me? What do they say about time flying, and I never saw the wings so clearly before now.

We decide to meet on the patio to get the early summer breeze. It's started out a June day with that gentle breeze feeling coming through the few open windows. It blows through my hair like the soft paws of the therapy kitten who tangles in my curls when Anita holds her up for me to see. And as I nudge out to the patio I see Marie, Wayne, Madge, Teddy, George, Sarah, Andrew, Micky Kruze, Denia Blane, Sherry Kemper, and at the other end of the circle, Dr. West, and Dr. Harper, of all people. Then out the door I just scooted from comes Casey, Ms. Neeley, and Judy shoving a tray cart. Then everyone starts singing, for God's sake, "Happy birthday, dear Emily, happy birthday to you!"

"It's June 12, Emily, your birthday. Since this is a special one, the folks from the A.L. Center all wanted to be here with your friends to celebrate."

The contents of the tray are lifted by Judy and Casey and carried over to my chair. I've seen cakes with candles on TV a lot and in magazines, and they have one each month for the older folks in the Dining Hall, which I tend to avoid. But this cake, candle tops lit and blowing in the breeze, is mine. I can read the letters on the top, "Emily, Happy 35th Birthday." The cake is white and glistens all sugary in the sunlight. Yellow and pink roses echo the ones on the climbers over the patio wall. The candles are yellow and pink, and oddly so are my slacks and sweatshirt. Yeah, Judy was real insistent on what I wore this morning.

"Blow it out," yells Andrew.

I guess I look funny as I try to move my head his way, away from the cake, while still keeping my eyes on the cake. As I look at his eyes really smiling at me, with his big silly grin, it really hits me that 35 years have gone by for me and this is the first time anyone ever gave a shit. This will be the first cake I've ever blown, but I may blow it because as my eyes drift around the crowd, trying to get back to the cake for the task at hand, I see all of their smiles and the hit reaches home. As I try to take the preparatory breath for the big blow, it comes out a deep gut-wrenching sob jerking out of my chest and onto my face. I figure I could just drown the candles, but I really don't want to spoil this for these dear people who had taken this time to celebrate with me.

My mother had been a Witness, and she didn't truck with celebration occasions, and Nate didn't do that sort of thing either. Jo wouldn't have even if she was the apparent party animal, because she didn't truck with anything regarding me beyond food and shelter.

Casey and the gang give me time to explode and then she dabs at me with her ever-present puffs.

"Take your time, Emily. I guess we startled you a bit with all our raucous singing, if you can call it that."

Everyone laughs and she dabs me again. Take my time. Which means I take their time, and yet they have been so willing to share their time. Why?

A few more wipes and then I feel I can tackle the task. Judy steadies the cake on my letterboard and I begin to direct my head in the correct area for maximum blow efficiency. Yeah. After several fairly well-aimed drafts two candles go out on the drawn "35" made of candles. So I pull in a big one for the next puff. Out go ten as two seem to light up again. While I ready the next breeze, three re-light. Six go out. I wait, eyeing the crowd. Lots of canary feathers lying about as these cats stuff the laughs. What is going on? This I haven't seen before. All the candles are burning, as if I'd made no effort. I blow a mighty wind. All candles and part of a rose are affected. No fire. I lean back in triumph gazing at the guests. They burst into hilarity as I look down on a brightly burning 35.

"They are joke candles, Emily. They are supposed to relight. I am afraid they were Andrew's idea, so you can take it out on him."

Andrew wheels around to my chair and puts his hand on my arm as Casey takes the cake to the table.

"With your permission," he spells permission on my board, "I would like to start the birthday honors."

As I nod, not knowing what this means, he leans over to give me a bear hug and a kiss on the cheek. What a rush! As I get my position back he smiles and leaves a package on my board. Others then come over as we move to the table and there are more hugs and packages. I am dizzy.

We have pizza and cokes. Casey is sitting next to me and she cuts the cheesy spicy pizza into little squares for me to chew. I chew and chew and work every last bit of the wonderful tomatoey zippy taste out of the crust. The sparkly sweet coke provides a startling contrast to the salty tart pizza tastes.

Casey and I open the gifts, while the group oohs and ahs appropriately. More tears, more tissues, more hugs. Andrew has given me bus tickets, and a Publitran application form. Marie has lent me her jam box for a week. That is a terrible sacrifice for her. How will she play her favorite country tapes? Madge gives me a tiny pink flamingo pin in a little gold box. More tears as Casey puts it on my shirt. Madge hardly knows me. Casey, Jerry, Ms. Neeley, they all give me books all my own. The one from Casey is about art and painting. Sarah, Denia, and Sherry, Dr. West, and Dr. Harper give me tapes. Ah, that is why Marie's gift makes sense. One is about the independent living center and the movement that started it. Another is about relaxing and has soft music with it. The third is a story about a lady named Gaby, who writes books

135

and has cerebral palsy. The last one is personal accounts of people going through the independent-living process. Marie sparkles because she was in on these gifts. Micky and Wayne give me bus schedules and a city map, and Wayne promises to ride with me if I need him to when I first start to go to the Center. Finally I open the gift from Teddy and George. It is a tape of the cute curly fiddle player. George has taped a concert he heard on TV because Teddy told him how much I liked him on Sesame Street. They tell me his name is Perlman.

We finish with gooey cake, chocolate with the white frosting and sugary roses, and coffee or tea. I have orange tea which smells like it sounds. I wouldn't in a million years have imagined such a feast and such friends.

❖❖❖

It is late afternoon and Marie and I have sneaked up to our favorite window. With such a heady day behind us we plan to hear some of the tapes. She wants the independent living tape, but I am on such a high I beg for the Perlman tape. She loads it, "Since it is your birthday."

The music starts and lifts me up and out of the chair, out over the rooftops. I let it flow through me and tears just roll out freely. I sometimes hear music like this when I visit with George and we watch it on TV. Now it seems to be moving through me like all of the feelings I have felt today carrying me in a hot air balloon with the wind.

"You nawt lyke ah hape, Onnee?" Marie wonders as it finishes and I am still dripping tears.

I beanie a quick,"Love it," to her. She looks perplexed, but wipes my face and asks for the independent living tape. It starts and we listen hard to the voices on the tape telling their stories of moving out and how they manage to get care and fend for themselves. It feels scary. But we listen quietly.

"My name is Melissa and I have lived in a nursing home since my mom died when I was eight. My dad was always on the road with his job, so he couldn't keep me. I have C.P. and I can talk fairly well, but my arms and legs don't work well, so I use a chair.

136

I had therapy and several surgeries before Mom died, but since I was in the Home I had no therapy of any kind. While at Mercy Home, I attended a picnic when I was 26, and met a lady from the Association for Retarded Citizens. I don't believe I am retarded, but a lot of people think people with C.P. are, especially those living in institutions. Well, I am certainly educationally and socially retarded, delayed, you name it. I never went to school. The only young people at Mercy besides me were Billy, a really retarded boy, and Janasue, who had C.P. and didn't talk at all. So there was no one to talk to. But I learned a lot by listening to the old folks. They were so lonely and had lots of good stories to tell. But I was still lonely.

Anyway this lady told me about the A.L. Center and the P.A.I.L. group so I got interested, and I got real scared. P.A.I.L. meant 'people awaiting independent living,' and I wasn't so sure I was."

The tape rolls its story into my ears and I can really feel the fear of this girl right in me. I understand better why the group I'm with makes me feel all mixed up and strange. The tape girl goes on.

"I went with this lady on the lift van. She showed me how to get on and off and it wasn't too hard, except when the lift shakes and it scares me. I need help on and off the lift in my manual chair. We got to the center in time for P.A.I.L. to start and the group invited me to sit in with them. I heard more war tales and began to really lose nerve.

"Later at home I thought about the pros and cons. Outside I could get a motor chair to get me places on my own. I could get on a waiting list to have a place of my own with a bedroom, a kitchenette, and bath. Sounds good, maybe too good. The hitch is getting adequate personal care. Finding people to work for me, people who will listen. The aides won't listen to me half the time. Why should I believe that anyone else will?

"I stayed in the P.A.I.L. group for two years, learning all I could about management of people and time, taking care of my money, about food and shopping, and how to have fun and friends. Few people realize how hard it is to find friends who won't be afraid of your disability. A lot of us with disabilities are taught as children to avoid people like ourselves. Our able families often deny our disabilities and pretend we will grow up and be 'better,' meaning like them. So we don't grow up having friends like ourselves, and we think that people like us are bad and to be avoided. So we must also be bad and avoided. It's kind of permanently confusing.

"At P.A.I.L. the group leaders, especially Sarah and Wayne, were good teachers and took things slowly and answered all our questions. They let us talk about our bad feelings about ourselves and others, and about our fears. They never cut corners or minced words. We knew from day one how very hard this all would be."

An odd birthday gift. Makes me feel more scared and baffled. How do I slide from the joy of that delicious party to this leaden feeling of hopelessness. I can't see how I could do like Melissa. The fear isn't like the daily weight of possibility, possibly being locked in a closet, or having to eat slop, or being dropped in the bathroom. It is an open fear like being on the edge of a bottomless cliff, getting ready to roll off without ever knowing if there is a stopping place. The hope is the scary part. Knowing that there might be a remote chance, and wanting it to work too much.

Marie slowly flips the cartridge in her box and turns on the tape again.

"During those two years we met lots of interesting people and learned about places in town that offered things we might need. There were people who could help us with money and our benefits. There were home-health and respite care aides and nurses who came to talk about their programs. We learned about transportation and how there had been improvements, but lately things were slipping back to the old ways and we would probably have to get out and fight again to make the system work for us.

"People came in to teach us to cook. The microwave part was great. One lady worked a long time with us on how to really listen to people and watch their responses. She showed us good ways to work with others in cooperation. She let us realize that there are people who are very prejudiced against people with disabilities, and helped us with ways to deal with them. She talked about how to manage our time and the time that people worked for us. She . . ."

My head starts to hurt. I signal Marie to stop the jambox. She looks reluctant but moves her finger to the stop button and gives a sharp push. She looks crossly at me as I board-write "NO MORE NOW." But I notice that she is not wanting more, either. She looks tired and stretched as we mosey toward the elevator and the Russian roulette of dinner.

The usual unsettling rush-jerk monotony of bed prep puts me in an agitated frame of mine. I wish I could hear more of that tape. I wish I'd never heard of word of it.

I begin to dream a persistent dream of life like on TV. Going where I want, when I want. Talking freely with people. Meeting someone to hold and love. This is all so distressing, I try to put it out of my head. I think about what I do have. I have Marie and George, nice friends. I have treats now and then, like that fantastic birthday. I have memories of Nate, and others.

I need to be realistic about my dreams. I crank at my absurd TV notions of life. I could never drive a car, that's so silly. But I can meet new people, and I'll learn to get my point across better. There's hope there. I doubt I'll ever have a special friend, but I have made new friends and can make more. I've got to hang on to these dreams, but make them realistic. I can look back a year ago to me as a window veg living like a rag doll full of rage and not knowing any better, yet hating it in an accepting way. That was my life.

New doors can be terrible things.

Jo is coming into the house and I am sitting in a high chair in a corner. She rushes at me with a shoe and I scream, "No! Never again!" She turns and runs out. Another woman comes in and says Jo would be back after she washes it all off. The woman takes me out of the high chair and sits me on the sofa. The dog rushes in and scares me and I jump back onto the high chair in one leap. The woman shushes the dog and puts me back on the sofa. I get up and go look out the door. I am stunned by the beauty outside of the door and begin to walk out. I then remember that I can't walk and turn to hear Judy say, "You slept through the farm report, Em. How are you gonna get through the day without knowing the pork-belly futures?"

Well, damned if I know.

Chapter 17

*I*t is July 3rd. The day before Independence Day, and I go to my first meeting at the A.L. Center. Yes, I have finished the tape. It gets much worse before it gets better. Not sure if it ever really gets better.

Melissa recounts horror stories about all-night sessions in her chair; roaches all over her first apartment walking freely over her during the night. She tells of thieving attendants, complaining neighbors who come in and borrow without telling her, and case workers who never work. I could go on. She does.

I figure it this way. Why not take advantage of the social aspect of these classes. Even if I never move out, I've made some nice friends. Sarah Cohen said that there were other group members living in nursing homes who may never move out. She said there are no rules at the center about this. People meet to share experiences and information and to work together for change. Where people live is not important except to each person. This sounds OK to me.

Jerry waits with me at the bus stop. He had to unlock the patio gate so we could scoot down the street to the stop. The van is late. We wait for over ten minutes.

"Maybe I should go in and call?" Jerry asks. I spell "WAIT" on my board.

"Yeah, you're right. These things are chronically late." He frowns down the street at the oncoming cars. No van.

Another five minutes and here it comes. The driver throws open the door dangerously close to where we stand. As he lets down the lift it jerks to a stop well above the pavement. The driver jumps out and grabs the switch on a long cord. He kicks the lift and pushes the switch. He grins at us as the primitive maintenance method works.

This part I hate. I've only done it once before, and I'll never get used to it. Jerry rolls me on, my back to the van door. I try to hold my breath to stop all my moving parts. Jerry's hand is on my left arm rest, the driver has my chair handles from behind. I should feel safe. I don't. The lift lurches and shakes. I can feel my chair pull forward, even with the brakes secure. Ching-rattle. The lift quits midway. I could fall forward or backward. The driver jerks the lift and Jerry grabs my chair. The driver jumps around me down to the ground. The van drifts like a boat at dock. I am queasy. The driver crawls under the lift, pliers in hand.

"Ratchet's stuck here. I'll have her loose in a second. This bear's been acting up pretty regular lately."

So why's it still on the road?

Micky had told a story about how she and Andrew left a meeting once and it took them two hours and five broken buses to go nine blocks to get home. Andrew said, "Hell, we shoulda just rolled it, the buses be damned!" But he is so adamant that people be able to use public transport that he'd wait for hours to prove his point.

"If they don't see us out here using these buses they'll find some way to say there is no market for the service, and they'll lobby to have it cut out of their budgets again. We gotta show them we will ride!"

The driver continues jerking and pounding at the lift underneath me. I have a 10:00 a.m. meeting. The bus is scheduled for 9:30 a.m. He arrives at 9:55. The lift breaks, and he mangles it for twenty minutes. It is now 10:20 and I am very late for my meeting. I am just about to ask Jerry to get me off this thing when there is a loud pop, a horrible bone shaking jerk and a drop. After I am soaked in a cold sweat, the lift slowly finishes the three-foot journey up. I beat you, Andrew. I went three feet in twenty-five minutes.

"You still want to go, Emy?" Jerry gently touches my arm as I ready for the final stage of lockdown. I point my light to yes. Hell, nothing worse than this could happen. Jerry waves bye as the driver pushes the door shut button and I am secure in the locks. I am still shaking all over. Maybe I should have gone with someone the first time.

The driver reports the late pick-up on his radio. His tone makes me feel like I am to blame for the delay. That steams me.

He tears away from the curb and the wild ride starts. You haven't lived if you haven't done the wheelchair-sideways-in-a-runaway-van ride. You feel totally insecure as you sit perpendicular to the heading of the van. Every bump is magnified by the fact that the chair is only minimally locked to the floor by the big metal catches loose on the back wheels and the loopy seat belt which offers little support. Yeah, the wild ride, something in a cartoon movie on TV about "The Wild Ride of Toad Hall" with critters, like rats and a badger and a wild crazed toad driving a real old car frantically till it crashed.

What happens next is so sudden that I'm not really sure I recall it accurately. We round a curve. I can't see anything but a stone wall on the right of the van. I feel the chair pulling to the left. There is a sudden shattering tearing crunch. My chair is thrown to the floor to the right. The left lock-down is wrenched out and my right wheel seems to have just crumpled. I don't remember anything else for a bit. Then I hear sirens. My eyes just open and I can see through a fuzz and an ache. I realize I can't move at all and I am on my right side with the seat belt slightly strangling me.

"She is apparently conscious. A bruise on the right of her head and face, likely from impact on the floor. Likely more bruising all the way down."

Radio noises come from various directions. I hear several voices.

"Heart rate 120, BP, 110 over 80. No shock, she'll do fine."

"He's caught under the wheel. Impact there not serious. Suspected compound fracture of left leg. Bleeding. Pulse 110, BP 90 over 60, likely shock. STAT hospital run."

There are loud crunches. Worse than the lift before. They must be pulling out chunks of the van. We must have swung wide in that curve and someone else swung tight.

"Hospital run on the woman to check for internal injuries."

I wait after the sirens fade and a large woman holds my hand and towels my head with a cool cloth. Another siren and a group hops in and frees me quickly. I'm soon on a stretcher with things on my neck and straps all over. More sirens. I can only think where is my light board and my light beanie? How can I talk to these people? How can I get another chair? I'd had that one since I was 18 and now it is gone. They will keep me in bed forever now and I'll never talk again. I can't help but cry as I realize my losses. The large woman looks down at me and tries to console. She must think I'm hurting. Maybe I am. But my loss is hurting me more. Shit. First attempt I get to act free, and I get the shaft on all of it. Shit shit shit.

"It won't be long, M'am. You'd do better just to stay quiet."

She is trying to be nice. I will hold this for later.

Hospital lights, cold X-ray tables, white coats and more ambulances later, I am at home and Marlane is putting me to bed.

"That'll teach you, girl. You oughta keep in your place. Goin' off on some dumb bus to a meeting you have no business going to. Hard way to learn."

She is a hard teacher as she scrubs over aggravated bruises. I'd like to deck her, chew her head off. I can only fret through her mauling and wonder what would possess her to talk so stupid.

Gina comes in with a Tylenol from Dr. Pescula. I ache as much in my heart as my side. Got anything for that, Gina? I can't ask with no board or light.

More dreams. Nate and Jo are fighting about whether I can go out the door. I sneak out. Jo soon tears out after me in a flaming red dress and feather boa. She grabs my chair and shakes it.

"You may think you can sneak out on me but you never will. You will always be what you are. A horrible dummy." I cry and continue on down the road. And I am in a boat with Nate and a white husky dog in the back. We are rushing over rapids. It is cold and scary and exciting, but then we go under and water rushes at me and I can't get my breath.

My eyes pop open full of the ice water that Judy has knocked off my bed stand onto me. She makes apologetic noises at me and scoops ice off of my gown. She moves me to the dry side for a bath. At least the washcloth is warm.

Post bath and dressed, bruises and all, Judy dumps me in a huge outsize chair and velcros me in all sorts of places as I sit swallowed in the seat, totally unsupported. I realize with horror that there is no way I can scoot down to reach the floor in this huge monstrosity. I pull and tug and sink and with my butt practically off the chair I still can't get a purchase on the floor. Judy grabs my pants waist.

"Don't wriggle so, you'll slide right out. Now sit still. Mr. VanMeter died last month and his family donated his chair. You should be so thankful, after you go out and wreck yours, that you have anything to sit in."

She stalks off with wet linens and I am stranded here with Edna and the soaps. Mr. VanMeter was six foot four and probably weighed three hundred pounds. I simply cannot believe how bizarre this is, that they think this is a fine chair for me. A hideous cold sensation creeps up from my dangling toes. Newborn panic begins to bubble up inside of me. I must be the horrible dummy. I can't move myself for the first time in months. I push and jerk at random against the secure straps. I am really confined to the wheelchair now. But every muscle is dancing a tarantella of terror and I feel the panting start. A real panic begins, and a low growling moan starts deep inside me.

Jerk, that old familiar sensation. I'd almost forgotten. I am propelled from behind.

"I guess you ain't gonna get around much anymore," Leena drawls in my ear like an executioner gloating with his axe. We are half way to the elevator before I know what's hit me.

Down to the dining room, and I am dumped in front of a plate of oatmeal and a sipper of juice. I sit and stare at congealing oats and warming juice for twenty minutes. I can't reach the table. Leena saunters back. She begins shoving her pasty mass in a spoon at my face. Some goes in, some goes down. She is rough as she sticks the spoon further back against my teeth. I feel like choking. Oats ooze shirtwards as I vainly try to swallow the excess. I know I look like shit on a bad day. To escape I make my pee sign. Leena doesn't know it and just scrubs me to her satisfaction and shoves me out the door. I pray for a familiar face. The hall is strangely silent. Thirty minutes later Judy wanders by on her way to break. I may break too, any second. The urgency in my bladder is beyond critical. I wave my pee sign at her. Nobody's used to it anymore. They got accustomed to the light board.

"Uny, eee, eee, hweez!"

"Oh, Hi, Emy. See ya later." She waves and smiles and heads for her long-awaited cigarette. I begin to cry with the pain and the despair. I might as well be on Mars. It hits me very deeply that if I don't make the effort to get out again this will be my life forever. I can't hold that grief anymore. Everything lets go. I sob and I trickle all at once. I've never felt so helpless and hopeless. I want to die. Not like before. I really want to live but cannot see how. But I can never be the veg in the window again.

I startle and jerk as the PA yelps above me.

"Emily Mason, visitors in the Lounge. Visitors in the Lounge, Emily Mason."

I can't believe it. There is nothing I can do. I couldn't deal with the horrible humiliation of them seeing this, the real me. The piss-puddler in the basement hallway. I start making screamy noises.

Of all people, out pops Judy. Her break is long over, yet she's still down here.

"Didn't you just have a page, Em? Ain't you going?"

That licks it. I just open up and scream at her and the tears fly hard and fast. She comes over and sees the wet floor and smells the telltale odor.

"Well, Em, why would a nice girl like you pee on the floor?"

I shriek over and over.

"What brought on such a state, girl? What ever got into you

that you gotta foul yourself in the hall. Give it up. Shape up!"

I want to kill her. I want to roll over her in a steam roller and completely smash and destroy her and everybody else in this hell hole. I want to mangle and mutilate them all.

She calls housekeeping to clean the hall. She then calls the desk to tell the Lounge that there's been an unavoidable delay. Shit, this was all totally avoidable, totally!

She hauls me upstairs in a huff and cleans and redresses me and then shoves me over to the Lounge. She pushes me in to where Andrew and Wayne are waiting. I am red faced and shaking still and am embarrassed to let them see me. Wayne pulls something out from behind his chair. It is my board and light. I break down again with relief and misery all muddled together. He puts board and light where they belong.

"Did you think it was lost?"

Yes, I point, still crying. I put the light on Thank you and then spell "SO MUSH." Wayne smiles and glances at Andrew.

"Is this supposed to be your chair? I've seen roast turkeys trussed up more comfortably."

Andrew always has to make a joke. I point to Yes, and spell "SAD."

"You got it, more like pathetic, or maybe disgusting."

Wayne laughs at Andrew's spelled jibe. Andrew explains that I have no recourse in the home. This is it. He tells about the two years it took Micky to pay off the price of a junker motor chair which she'd cadged from some guy while she was in the nursing home. With her $25 a month allowance she made payments that left her with no money for personal items. She got good at borrowing soap and making her Salvation Army toothpaste and shampoo last a very long time.

"See, Medicaid figures that what they contribute covers her stay including any equipment. It doesn't bother them that the equipment sucks. Folks at home can get medically approved stuff, because Medicaid figures they don't have access to it otherwise. It ain't easy, but it is possible."

This talk is not lifting my spirits, that's sure. I feel really

147

doomed. It is this clunker, or move out. What bigger rock and hard place could I squeeze between?

Next day Casey asks if I feel OK, and if I have gotten over the accident. I spell "BIG FEER."

"I imagined so. Part of me says ask this, and part says, don't get into it. So here goes. Do you feel your bad experience will get in the way of coming out again?"

I point to yes, then point again to no, then I shrug and look baffled.

I spell "BIG SKAR," and then, "BIG WANT."

"Yeah, new things are like that, really scary, but you want them badly."

In the afternoon Marie crab walks me back to our window. We listen to the birthday tapes and watch the light wash a brown gray shadow over the faithful roof. So daily, yet different. I feel like I am back to square one. But I know that I know much more than before. Like when people say, "Oh, I wish I was 16 again knowing what I know now." I just don't know if I have the energy to get back to where I had gotten to.

Next visit, Casey and I call the van for a ride to the meeting next week. Jerry takes me out like before and I am shaking and sweating like a prizefighter. By the time the driver has me up on the lift, my teeth are doing drum rolls. During the entire, much calmer, ride, my body shakes so that the chair rattles continuously.

The driver takes me to the door of the A.L. Center. I wonder if she can hear my stomach rumbling and grumbling. A woman comes out and they chat.

"Bye, Mary. I hope your ride was a lot less eventful this time, Ms. Mason. I am Leslie; welcome to the Center."

I wonder how she knows who I am. I am on time, and we roll down the wide hall past desks and some doors. We turn into a large, heavily populated room. About twelve people gather around several pushed-together tables, most chatting from chairs they brought with them. There are two quiet dogs under the tables. Some folks glance in our direction, then continue on with their conversations.

Wayne comes in and takes a seat, stowing his crutches under it. The group settle and turn attention to Wayne.

"Well, as you can see we have some new members today, so as per usual we will go around the table for introductions."

"I'm Cecily Deeb, mother and dog lover, and this is Seymour."

"Ray Sutter, student, advocate, etc."

"Rachel Santini, mother, wheeler, and dealer."

"Hi, I'm Jenny Fanish, student of life. I'm checking out the impossibilities."

"Sandor Scott, and Peaches here." A large orange dog rustles and tailwags just beneath the tall man's chair.

"Hiya, Mary Settles here. I am a student, and volunteer, and I want to leave my parent's home, just like my brothers and sister have."

A person pushes a button on a gooseneck switch over her chair.

"Hi, I am Clare Porter," a robot voice comes out of the large boxy letter board over her chair tray.

A man reclining in his chair takes a sip on a straw and his chair sits up with him. "Fred Swift here, used to be swifter, but I still get around."

Quiet chuckles, probably a real old joke.

"Nancy Green here," says a little voice of a person sitting way atop a pillow on an office chair.

The next person is possibly smaller than I am and sits in a little blue motor chair that fits her like a glove and puts her right up where the action is. I want her chair, badly.

"I am Tracey Eggert and I like my place and my cat named Spacey. Yes, we are Spacey and Tracey."

Micky Kruze is next, and Casey. Everybody in the room has some sort of noticeable difference, Casey's being that she is different from everyone else. As people talk I am struck by how different their lives are. Some live alone, some with friends or family, some at their parents' homes, and one other lives in a nursing home, two in a group home.

149

One lady is a chair user raising two kids alone. Another guy works in a library doing computer programming. A student wants to show her parents she can live out on her own. There is a real sense that they all share ideas that could improve things for each of us.

This seems a bit overwhelming. All of their success and struggle makes my dreams feel even more distant. The bus ride home is scary. Their talk was more so.

As Marie and I sun monitor around 8:30 p.m. I wish that I could just talk out my fears with her. I feel like a coke bottle being shaken on a warm day. Any second the fizz could pop out and hit the nearest passerby. But the cap is still securely screwed on. There will be no relief.

Chapter 18

When Casey arrives this week, I have a question for her which I have practiced all week.

"INY WAY TO RITE?" I point out on my board.

"Mind another bus ride?"

Three days later we board the van for a ride to the public library. I've never been to a library before. This one has a room, Casey says, full of computers set up especially to teach people with disabilities how to use the special features available.

"You haven't heard of this room?"

"No," I blink and point. "NEVER," I spell.

We roll up several ramps to a big row of doors. Casey turns my cumbersome chair and we back in the heavy door.

"They could put in an automatic, it would help a lot," she grumbles. Not like Casey to grouch. She must have a reason.

Inside I am stunned. It is like the dream of the man with the shiny eyes. So many books, in rows and stacks everywhere. We wheel over to an elevator and then down to a room full of interesting-looking machines. The man in charge knows Casey. She introduces us.

"Emily Mason, this is Bill Brost."

He immediately begins to talk to me with my board. We go to a table with a typewriter thing and a little TV and a big pad.

"Can we trade beanies?"

Bill takes my hat and puts it on. He puts a beanie with a pointer on it onto my head. He switches on the little TV. He puts a little square thing in a drawer and stuff begins to happen on the TV. He pokes two keys and a typewriter board comes up on the screen. Under it is a space which he fills with words by touching the light onto the letters on the screen. I am excited.

"This is one way that you can write what you want, Emily." It says this below the board. Bill checks that I have been able to read it. "YES," I point with the stick beanie which he gave me in trade.

He gets up and moves another box near this one and puts some flat wires in the backs. He puts paper in the box. Then he hits a picture of a little box with paper coming out up in the corner of the letter screen with his light. I jump a foot as the real box rips alive with a racket. The machine stops and Bill pulls out the paper so we can see the line of letters.

This all takes a couple of minutes to sink in, but when it does I let out a yelp of sheer joy and amazement. Bill and Casey laugh right along with me. I claim my beanie light back and begin to hunt and peck at the TV screen.

"TANK U BIL AN KC I CAN NOW TAK TO MINY PEPUL MISEF."

I nod to Bill and he adds paper and I hit the little printer picture with the light and out it comes. I cannot believe it. It is the dream of the shiny man and I can tell people how I feel from now on.

Well, maybe. There is always the transportation problem. But I have made up my mind to use my monthly allowance to get the hell out of South Pines whenever I can. I can go to the A.L. Center, or come to this library and tell my stories to this machine as long as I can get someone to shove this monster chair around.

Casey explains that she has research to do, and if Bill doesn't mind and I want to, this time could be practice time for me. I mind? Hah.

I write for about an hour and at the end of my paper I write, "KC WIN CAN I CUM BAK."

"You can come any time you want. You could come with Marie, or George, or Ted. Just call Bill and let him know when you want to come, and he'll make a keyboard available to you. You can count on me for a few more weeks because I have a lot of research to do for my thesis. We'll come together."

Bill gives me my story and I feel I could light up the room with pride. I show it to several people that come by us in the library. Some just ignore us. A few stop and share our fun and read my story.

At home I rush out to see if I can find George. More than anyone else, I want to share this with George. I find him in the Lounge reading his magazine. They had published a couple of his stories about being young and in a nursing home. I wonder if I could get a story published in such a magazine.

"Nyawg, ooo, ooog!!"

He takes the paper out of my beanie strap where Casey had folded it for safekeeping.

"Watcha got there, Em, a bill?"

I laugh and spell, "KLOS."

George looks at me funny and carefully maneuvers the paper open with his splints and pencil eraser. He reads out loud.

"HI I M EMILY MASON
I WANT TAK TO PEPUL
TIS TV GIV ME TAK
I LUV IT
I CAN TAK MINY WUDS ON TV
I BE TO HAPY NOW TO TAK MOR
I LUV KC AN BIL AN JAWG AN MINY PEPUL
KC WIN CAN I CUM BAK"

George reads it out loud and then reads it to himself and then to me again. I am so proud a pin scratch would cause an explosion. George looks up at me and I think there are tears in his eyes, but maybe it is just the angle of light from the window.

"God, that's really beautiful, Em. I am so proud of you and happy for you. The world will have a treat when they can realize your ideas and thoughts. You and Teddy and Casey and Wayne have worked hard to achieve this and you deserve all the praise you can get."

I figure it isn't the light cause the lights are now caught in bright pearls dripping down his dark face, and I guess mine is wet, too.

"Please, Em," he sniffs, "don't let the aides throw this out when they clean. No, wait. Can I borrow this? I'll get it right back to you, OK?"

About two days later I run into George in the hall near my room.

"Ah, Em, just the girl I was seeking. I have something for you. Hey, Judy, can you lend me your fingers?"

"What now, Danton, ain't you out of your water up here?"

He grimaces at her and asks her to get a package from his backpack. She reluctantly obliges him and digs in the bag on the back of his high-backed seat. She fetches out a brown parcel and he wheels over and slides it close to me on his tray.

"May I take the liberty of unwrapping your parcel?"

"On ure anh yuh," I laugh and blink and mock his foreign TV accent. He gingerly pulls the paper aside with his splint edges, and there in the wrap is my story in a beautiful picture frame.

"Judy, could you wheel Ms. Emily to her quarters?"

Judy harumphs and pushes me down to my room with George close behind, his visor tipped jauntily. Then he asks Judy to get a picture hanger from his pack. He instructs her on the way to remove the tab and how to hang the sticky onto the wall. Then he asks me my preference of place. I laugh and watch Judy do what he says. That is surprising enough, but to have my own story on the wall, that is the best surprise of all.

A few days later and I am back to the library with Casey. Bill gets me set up at a keyboard and boots my disk. I am getting the lingo down. And I can write down just what I am thinking. Which means that someone else can really know what I am thinking for the first time. Well, as much as anyone can know what others are thinking. I write to the group at the A.L. Center.

"I WANT TO NO SUM MOR TO LIV ON OWT IN THE WURLD. KAN IT BE FER ME."

I write to Casey to let her know things that I am interested in.

"I LIK TO WATCH LIT AN MUSIK I LIK BUKS OF PIJERS OF RT NAT HAD PIJERS OF RT DIS PLAC HAV RT BUKS I LIK TO C."

Casey comes over when she finishes working on her paper and reads what I have written. She calls my spelling creative, but certainly adequate to our needs for now.

"Emily, do I get the idea that you would like to take books home to look at and do some practicing with? But help me here. What are pijers?"

"PIJERS ON WALS TO LUK AT."

"Ah, like paintings?"

Yes.

"C'mon."

After detaching me from the light switch, we roll out to the elevator, down to the main floor, and over to the big main room. The stoney floor is lumpy under my wheels. There is a big long high table with more TVs and keyboards. This place is just full of computers. A lady and a man are standing behind the high table, but the man is talking with a boy who has a big stack of books.

We go to the lady and Casey asks, "This is where we apply for a library card?"

"Yes, you can do that here."

"My friend would like an application."

The lady looks over at me and asks, "Are you also interested in application for the Talking Book Library?"

I slosh my head in Casey's direction.

"I don't believe that Ms. Mason is vision impaired."

"Talking Books is available now for anyone with a disability who might have problems with handling printed material. While Ms. Mason may be able to read there may be times when hearing a book would be more convenient. It is just another option."

They are doing this talking back and forth and I am just sitting here reveling in the very idea of being able to take a book home and look at it. I could get somebody to help me. Maybe Judy. No. Maybe Grandma Sample. She would turn the pages for me. Yes!

Tapes, too. But I haven't got a tape player. I noise at Casey, and beam at my letter board.

"NO PLAER."

"You won't want tapes?"

"WANT TAPS HAV NO PLAER."

"Oh, they send a player with their tapes. The biggest problem will be setting it up for you and finding a way to switch it on and off."

We work on the application. I spell out answers, and Casey writes them in on the cards. After a short wait we get a nice plastic-coated card with little lines and my name on it.

"We've got twenty minutes before the bus. Want to check out the art books you asked about?"

We head over to the far side of the room where a number of very big shelves are lined up. We tootle tightly down the narrow space between two shelves like deep tunnels, with books like tall shadows hanging over my head way up high. Casey dries my occasional chin leaks off my board and face. Then she pulls several big books off the shelves and lays them on my letter board. She opens one volume with a crack and a new smell. Shiny pages jump out at me.

Adjusting my head, I focus on the page as large as my letter board. The light from the window down the aisle catches on shimmering colors and I recognize all through me the water lilies that Nate used to share with me. I can smell the colors. Nate would try to put those colors on the old shades stretched on scrap boards. He would daub and dip, rub and stroke the colors back and forth, up and down. He'd talk to the canvas as if to beg it to give in and set up what he saw in his mind's eye. I liked what he did, but he could never be satisfied and once even laid down his brush and sat by the window and cried.

I nudge my hand over the page to prevent Casey from turning it.

"You really love this one?"

She doesn't need my board to know the answer.

After we check out the big book of prints and a smaller book on the man called Monet who made the lilies, according to Casey, it's on the dreaded van for us. Casey leans back from the front seat so we can talk. So we can talk. That's rich. I'd have never believed such a thing. A ride on a van with a friend and we can talk. Anyway.

"I have a friend you might like to meet."

I blink a reply.

"She teaches art in a school not very far from South Pines. In fact, I think at least one of your residents attends classes there. Bill Givens?"

Bill is a new kid. Has C.P. like me and I can't figure why he is at South Pines, except there are rumors that his Mom died. He does leave during the day.

"We could really walk over there some nice day that you're in the mood."

A week later Casey comes in dressed for a walk in jeans and sneaks. We roll out after a brief wrestle with my sweater against the breeze that has blown up and may carry rain.

"Jody Donovan has been teaching art here for several years. I think you may be surprised at her work. A lot of it hangs around the school building."

The still ungainly chair leapfrogs over big cracks in the sidewalk. I have never taken a walk in this neighborhood, yet I've lived here over fifteen years. No one has ever offered to push me about in the clunkers I've rolled in over the years. Funny, the only part of the neighborhood I know is those roofs near our wing.

The school is across a busy street. Two small van-like buses sit in the oval driveway. Swings and toys lurk to one side of the building. Windows are decorated with colored leaves and other early autumn symbols. We roll into the front door and past the office into a large open room.

"Let me check us in." Casey pauses my chair in the big room and goes back to the office window to sign in. Doors off the room emit children noises. Two little tow-heads scurry out of a restroom pushing a third in a mini-chair seated up high. Back to their classroom they go.

"This used to be a school just for kids who used chairs and needed equipment. Now all the schools are integrated, but this one still has a higher population of kids with disabilities."

I know Casey is baffled by my jerk smash move after she says that. I try to pull my head into spell mode.

"THES GIMP KIDS GO SKOL?"

"There is a law now, Em, that says all children can go to school."

I have to shove something. I am furious.

"Yeah, it wasn't fair. And a lot of parents had to fight a long time to get it changed, and a lot more will have to fight to get it enforced. Let's meet Jody. She can tell you a little about her experiences."

We roll to a room on the right of the great room. It is rather large and has high tables attached to the walls with low shelves above covered with paper and jars and brushes and other art supplies. A long low sink is on the far wall and towel rolls above it. There are several sets of odd paddle-shaped faucet handles on the sink top. The next wall is mostly cabinets with a counter, and more cabinets above. Over the top cabinets windows let in a lot of light. Near the cabinets are several easys, or whatever. That's what Nate called them. On one stands a very beautiful sunset painting. A lady in a motor chair wheels in from a different door. Casey goes and takes her rather limp right hand.

"Jody, I'd like you to meet a new friend of mine. This is Emily Mason who has been living over at South Pines for, what, Em, fifteen, seventeen years?"

I light touch the Yes on my board.

"Emily has told me of her interest in art, and she seems to like the French Impressionists the best."

Casey never ceases to amaze me. I don't even know what a French impersonator is, so how could she think I like them best? I grunt and catch her eye to spell, "A FRECH WAT?"

They both laugh.

"You like Monet, and Cezanne, and Renoir especially well. Their art is called French Impressionism."

The other lady starts to talk and while her soft voice is hard to hear I can catch much of it, like with Andrew.

"Do you paint, Ms. Mason?"

I blurt out an explosive laugh.

"Here is one I am working on."

We move over to the set-up easy and the lady asks Casey to hand her the brush in the can on the easy, and to set the board with the paint on it on a clip to the left of the canvas. I want to laugh. This is too goofy. She can't even move her arm. Casey puts an odd rubbery thing on the end of the brush and into the lady's mouth. She deftly adds color to the brush and begins moving it over the canvas right where she wants it.

I smell the colors and it takes me to my sofa spot where I watch Nate work the paints and make the magic. This lady is magic, too. I can almost roll into the meadow she is filling with sunset colors. Long evening yellows and oranges tint the green grasses into near bronze and copper hues. The sky fills with all those luscious unspeakable peach and apricot colors. There is a softness which makes it all dreamlike.

"I like the Impressionists, too." She manages to wiggle this skillfully through her teeth as she never misses a dab.

I wish I could try. But she can control much of her head movement. Even with my spelling practice, my head still tends to wobble between letters.

"You want to try, don't you?"

She also reads minds.

"What do you feel most control over?"

I shoot my right foot out over the rest. It is out of shape since I haven't gotten to exercise it with my shuffle shove walking. This hulky chair precludes that.

"Christy Brown," she laughs at Casey, who laughs right back.

"It's a movie you should see, and a book to read, too." Casey fills in.

Jody directs Casey to pull out a sheet of paper and prop it onto a strange easy leaning on the floor.

"The floor easel will make this much easier for you."

Easel. Easel, easy. Hmm. Casey brings out a small rack of paint pots. She shows them to me. They smell different. Red, yellow, blue, black, white, and three empties.

"These are temperas. They are not like the oils I am using here. They are easier to move, a better choice for a first try."

Casey asks to take off my shoe and brace. I light Yes, Thank you.

"Go ahead. Don't think of a picture, just let yourself play with the colors. Let them make any picture they want."

I squeeze the rubber grip on the long-handled brush between my toes. It feels funny and I want to just waggle it a while. Casey adjusts my chair so I can reach the paint pots and the eas . . . easel. I shakily dip into the red paint. It drips back into the pot in little blops. I love the feeling and dip again. Blop, blop. Dip, blop. Dip, waggle waggle, blop, blop. Then the paper. First the brush skims over leaving a tiny red track. Then I lower, smusch, shmusch. The track is widened in two places. I dip into yellow. It leaves a red streak in the yellow pot. I watch blops. A red-yellow streak then a good scmusch near the end. I dip into blue. Purply green schmusches at the bottom of the page. I like the greenish and daub it at the tops of the big red schmusches. It is good. I am through.

"Does it have a name?", Casey asks as she rinses the brush.

I light sign, "PIKED TOMATOS."

"Yes, of course. I do like that, yes, very much! I am surprised at how very much at home you seem to feel with the brush and paints!"

Jody Donovan seems honestly pleased with my first effort. Of course she can't know how many paintings I have made in my soul as I watched Nate. This was ecstacy. It was everything I ever dreamed and better. I know I will have to practice for years to do anything like Jody, but this was sheer pleasure. I know I have a looney grin on my face as my head travels its own course of joy on its way back to the letter board.

"THAK U JODE. MOS FUN EVER."

It took a while to get it said, but it was worth the time and effort.

Chapter 19

Marie and I are in the Lounge set up at the table with the art book. She can turn the pages for me and has the patience to sit with her jam box while I stare at each page until I can see it in my head. Marie likes the odd clothes and giggles at naked women. Mostly I love the colors that roll across the pages in waves. I can almost dance the strokes made over the canvas. My foot moves in slow satisfying arcs over imagined canvases as I linger over the lights. I have found the cathedrals in the back of the book. I watch as the day moves over each one. Then there are elaborate piles of hay that also change colors with the light. Marie wants to turn now.

Marie is particularly fond of page turning with fashion magazines. I only look with her as a time passer. I can't see much connection between my life and those ladies'. Like the people on the soaps. They all look rather alike to me. I have a startling thought. What might I look like to them? Would they sit and watch a show in which I was the star? What about them makes the aides take their breaks in the TV room watching the shiny people in the soaps doing nasty things to each other? Would they watch unshiny folk like me on such shows? Would they watch my wavering head trying to make words with a light on a board? Would they watch my occasional chin drips and wonder why? They could see right off that I am not shiny or rich. No, I don't think they'd watch.

One night I remember George called me into his room to watch a lady on TV. She was kind of like Fred Swift at the Center. She used a puff switch to get around and she told funny stories.

George explained that she was not like Fred and only pretended to be a quad. I can't even imagine why anyone would want to pretend such a thing. But she told such funny stories about living in a chair. She had a funny long face and straight dark hair, and eyes that laughed even when she didn't. How could she know the funny part of being crippled? She's not.

Next day I go see George who is in bed with his bad behind. I finagle my board against the bars on Larry's bed and by careful shoving and a miracle get it tilted just at an angle where he can see.

"KAN U C?"

"Yeah, kid, you are doing great!"

"?"

"You got a question?"

"YES. KRIPL TV LAYDE – Y?"

"Why, what, Em?"

"Y B KRIPL 2 LAF?"

"Well, you've got to admit that she is right on with those stories about being a gimp. Why don't you write and ask her?"

At the library I wrote a letter to the TV lady.

"I M WEELCHAR UZER. WHY U HAV LAYDE IN WEELCHR TEL FUNY JOKS, LIK ME AN FRENZ TO ME. UR LAYDE NOS OUR LIVS AND LAFS. I LIK HER. I LIK HER STOREZ. THANK AND LUV. EMILY MASON."

Casey found her address in a big directory and mailed the letter for me. I never heard from the lady. I guess a lot of people write to her about such things and she can never answer all of them. I just wish I knew why she would use a wheelchair person when most people don't want to see us.

I would like to write a letter to Mr. Monet, but Casey says that if I notice the dates in the book where his churches are, I will know that he is probably dead now.

Chapter 20

The bigwigs have called a meeting. The people in charge here at South Pines have called in Sarah and Wayne and Sherry Kemper and even Dr. West. It is pretty easy to imagine what the meeting is about, even if they didn't bother to ask me. One plus one says it ain't about Mr. Kneble or Larry.

Sarah told me about the meeting. She said that she had protested that I was not included, but was overruled. She told me that she would be registering a complaint with the ombudsman for long-term care. Then she said she'd fill me in on anything that happens, and let them know that any future meetings would include me.

"Emily, they are all concerned about your safety. They are alarmed that we might influence you to move out of here against their better judgment. They feel your safety is their responsibility."

Funny they should be so concerned about my safety. I have never felt very safe here with the opportunities I've had to be abused, forced to eat slop, unnecessarily drugged, shoved into closets, have my things stolen and destroyed, have my leg broken, and be raped in the basement. No, I cannot say that I have felt very safe. The question is, what safety is there in any other living situation?

"Emily, I have given this a lot of thought. Nothing in life guarantees safety. In fact there is an inherent oxymoron here. It's just contradictory. Being alive is unsafe."

I blink agreement, I think.

"All we are trying to offer at the Center are choices: chances to choose varied ways to live. Many people think institutions are the only places there are for people who use chairs. The whole damn society is so handicapped they can't see or hear the barriers we've put up to block people with disabilities from getting along like anyone.

"Ellen West said when she met you she knew in her gut that you ought to have more. She felt that you should at least have a chance to choose. Yet there have been so many who never have, and never will have, any sort of chance"

Sarah seems angry, but I know it is not at me. So I get her attention to the board.

"U R MAD."

"Yeah. Maybe in both senses. Angry and crazy. I am angry at the assumptions. For so many years people have had knee-jerk reactions to people who are different. Anyone who looks, acts, moves differently is practically intolerable. There is something about depending on anyone for anything that is so repulsive to our culture. But no one lives without depending. Markets depend on trucks, students on teachers, teachers on students, sick people on doctors, doctors on sick people. It is always reciprocal, and invariable. There's no such thing as independence.

"I guess the bad connotation comes from how we are raised. So much time and effort is spent on our becoming less physically dependent on our parents that we get a message that to be dependent like a baby is bad."

Yeah, like Jo and the potty perching. That was important to her.

"And what follows is that anyone who has any personal dependence is considered by many to be like a child. Consequently, anyone who needs any physical care is infantalized, I mean made to feel they are a baby. But there isn't anyone who isn't somewhat personally dependent.

"In the best of possible situations, interdependence can work. For example, Fred Swift, with a wife, two kids, and parents all still alive, and six siblings and in-laws. After his injury they all pulled together to make his life work for him again. With workers' comp, insurance, and his benefits and part pension, financial problems aren't a big worry. His whole family acts interdependently to keep Fred mobile, healthy, and busy. It is all working well.

"But you, Emily, don't have family that staff here know of. Out on your own you'd be your only resource."

I could feel another "it's a jungle out there" talk. Sarah's on her soap box and I'm not sure why. It's kinda like she's worried and is thinking out loud, defending her own ideas to herself. Maybe she's dealing with her own fears of being on her own. Maybe she does this kinda work to answer her own questions.

"You could live here all your life, Emily, and have a rich life that you'd choose. Look at the changes you've already made; it's been a hell of a year for you."

Yeah, but Sarah has a voice and an education. She can influence others. She'd do OK on her own. I don't know about all this.

There's one thing I want to think about now as I reflect on Sarah's tirade, in my window, with the slow drone of the jam box in the air. Can life work out there for a veg like me? Do I have to hurry this process of change? Can't I just take my time? It is like the sun. It changes the roof colors differently every day; the cathedral paintings on each page are completely different in each light. But no one is telling the sun when to make these changes.

Casey asks if I'd ever had my hair done. That's a word the older women say. Grandma Sample loves to have her hair done, and it is a pretty wreath of white curls when she's done. But aides just hack my hair off in the shower when they get tired of it. What do I care.

But I say yes to Casey's idea. Couldn't hurt. Aunt Jo used to sit my chair at the bottom of the back walk. I wondered what I looked like after. Nate always had a nice comment. But most mirrors have been way over my head. So who cared? Casey and I board the bus. The ride is mercifully uneventful, and we roll easily up a little ramp into the salon. Casey's cased the joint before hand for access, bless her. The pungent ammonia smells snap into my nose and my eyes close.

165

"This is my treat, Emily. I thought it'd be a nice change from the lady at your home."

"CANT FORD HOME LADY."

"You mean you don't get your hair cut there?"

"ADES CUT IT."

"Yeesh. A 10:30 for Ms. Mason. I called Tuesday."

'Yes, we have her. Would you like to use your chair or transfer?"

She is all in pink and has a great halo of yellow hair. She's very brisk but nice, and she asks about my chair, like a regular or something.

"What do you want, Em?" Casey says.

"STAY SUPPOT."

"Hmmm. Oh, stay in for support, your velcros?"

I blink. And we cruise back to an open area with four funny-shaped sinks. There are three chairs and one sink with no chair. I get a plastic poncho and a couple of pillows.

"I hope you won't mind, but I think you will see better."

And there I am in that mirror. I have to look at that face jutting a bit crookedly above me as I sit at a slant. Over we go for a shampoo. Casey helps tip my chair at rinse times. It feels heavenly with soft finger rubs all over my head. I could fall asleep if I weren't so aslant.

Back to the mirror. As the lady combs and snips I try to be objective. A skinny triangle topped by carroty colored wet rings. Longish nose, thin mouth, and too big sea-green eyes. I don't remember my parents. Who do I look like? Jo had a pointy face and big washy eyes. I don't know what color hair she had. It was too many different colors. When she got sick near the end, light brown and gray-specked roots grew up to meet the platinum ends. It looked sad.

Well, it's not a bad face. Good as any. I gotta laugh. This is Emily Mason. Howdya do!"

"I'm not pulling, am I, Ms. Mason?"

I blink no, and Casey says I must have a private joke.

My hair is short and breezy all over. Nice. My beanie back on makes the curls pop through the mesh. Not so bad, Mason. I beam a Thank you to the lady. I mean it.

Chapter 21

I'm trying the P.A.I.L. group on a regular basis. It's been good to get to know about these folks and how different all of our lives are. The differences are good, because I know it is possible to live all kinds of ways and that is OK. Knowing all the different ways also makes choices easier.

Today we all get settled in and the door opens and in jerks Andrew Duncan. He's come to tell us activist stuff. It's been a while since I've seen him and as he rolls in he glances at me and raises his brows and smiles. Then he wheels around the table, not taking his eyes away. Mine go down and I notice I feel hot and strange. Must be from the bus ride.

Andrew starts his history lecture. Wayne sits by to translate the spelled bits.

"How many of you are using Publicare Vans?"

Four people stick up hands or noise, one shilly-shallies.

"How many take Publitrans on regular routes?"

Two chair users and two dog owners raise their hands.

"How many drive?"

Casey, Wayne, Ray Semple, and Jenny Fanish raise their hands.

"Ah, the missing four. You all are an unusual group. Most folks I talk to in chairs don't know about public transportation. It is now the law that people be able to use buses that are accessible. Just a few years ago we couldn't go public. There were ambulances and a few private van services for doctor appointments or church, or group activities. In those days able people thought we only traveled in groups. We had to keep to our own kind. I rarely got anywhere, and only if my uncles would load me into their pick-up. I preach to the choir here.

"I was fed up when I got out, but couldn't get anywhere. I got wind of the West Coast activist group ABRUPT (Activists Bringing Radical Utilization of Public Transportation) and hopped a plane. Another transportation snafu saga, for later. I learned in Oakland that change doesn't just happen, people make it happen."

"More detail, Duncan, but nothing boring," Fred Swift drawls and there are chuckles.

But Andrew keeps on and tells horror stories of stopped buses and chained chairs, and jail cells, and police vans with no tie downs, strip searches, no food, people missing their meds. Sounds a little like nursing home life. Why would he want to choose this? I catch Casey's eye with my beam and spell, "Y ANDRU CHUS MESS IN LIFE?"

"Emily, you'd better ask him," she whispers to me. After more stories and discussion, people file out or stay to chat. Casey gets Andrew's attention. He wheels over and smiles. I am getting hot again like a rush of a morning shower. I try to ask with my beam light, but it's tricky 'cause I keep shaking. Can't tell why.

"ANDRU, Y U MESS WITH COPS & BUS, 2 MUCH TRUBL!"

"Emily, why don't you and Casey come grab a bite with me, if you've got the time?"

I freeze. Casey looks at me for assent. I think. I blink, she nods.

"I have time, Andy, it is really up to Emily."

What can I say. I've never been asked to eat out, in a restaurant. It's like TV. I'm scared. Shaky. I blink yes.

We wheel out, I'm Casey powered, Andrew jump bumping his motor chair. Casey lowers my chair over a not cut curb and Andrew takes it in a furious jump.

"Shit, gonna lose a wheel that way one of these days. I wish to hell they'd cut the rest of these curbs. The A.L. Center staff oughta raise hell with the city on this one. Shit"

We wheel into a Burgerbar and head to the counter. It's busy

169

and looks like ads on TV. Andrew and Casey order. The lady seems to understand him fine. I guess he's a regular.

"And you, M'am?"

Oh, god, she's talking to me! What do I do? Andrew's flashing all those damn teeth at me and the lady is waiting, with lines behind us. I get panicky.

"I can see your board, M'am," the cashier nudges.

I begin to spell what Casey ordered, but a cold pit opens up in my stomach. How am I going to eat this food, and in public? So I beam a no, and blink no at Casey.

"Emily, you gotta be hungry by now. Besides this is your big chance to gouge Duncan and eat whatever you please. Don't blow it!"

She smiles, and then I realize that she plans to be by me and help me with the food.

"BERGER FRYS CHOC SHAK, PLEEZ," I spell out, and the woman rings up each item.

"Do you want sauce, tomato, onion?"

"KACHUP TAMATO, PLEEZ."

"OK," she mutters and mumbles burgerfriesshakechoc into a microphone and takes Andrew's money. I picture the ordered foods appearing magically from behind the microphone. It is too high to see over the counter in this horrible chair. We look for relatively accessible seats and then Casey goes back for the trays.

I look across the table at Andrew smiling back.

"You are looking great!"

What is this heat, menopause? I'm only 35. Jeez, it is stifling in here.

"You OK, Em? You look like you are burning up."

Casey puts down the trays and feels my head.

"You feeling all right?"

"Hell, she's OK, just excited. I remember when I ordered my first meal out, I was a nervous wreck. You're just freaked, right, Em?"

Excited. I gotta think about this. Every time lately I am around Duncan I get the heebies. Haven't seen him in a while and I've been pretty calm in public situations.

"You wanna know more about ABRUPT?"

I blink while suck-gulping at the throat-freezing shake.

"You can work with the system till you are blue in the face, but the wheels turn too damn slow, 'cause everybody is carefully guarding their own little territory and won't change come hell. Or you can move outside the system and shake it up enough to get people outside of themselves long enough to look around and see what's wrong beyond their little territories. It's an education process. It's rough."

Casey is carefully cutting bite-size bits off the burger with a plastic knife. I munch one bit as Andrew continues his description of life on the lines. Can't figure out why the obvious ain't. He goes on about buses and some lady named Rosa Parks, and why can't we use the buses, and it seems to me that it's getting to be a big damn deal. I beam between bites.

"Yeah, it's a big damn deal! Why shouldn't you be able to get on a bus anytime just like anyone, if the technology is available to do it? Why can they air condition a bus, which is an extra cost, and is prone to repeated failures, yet benefits the public? But they can't lift a bus, which costs not much more and is no more prone to fail, and benefits the public, potentially all the public."

He's pissed. I chase a fry with a swinging hand while the tirade moves on.

"With ADA, access is supposed to be the law. But it is going to take some heavy-duty watch-dogging and testing to see that the law is enforced. It's gonna take people like you sitting at bus stops and waiting for the accessible bus before it makes sense."

"How are the Emilys of this country supposed to find out that they have a law that says they can get on a bus? Didn't you see where that Public Radio guy got thrown out of a theater for being in his chair, post ADA!"

Casey's pissed.

"I mean, if a newsman isn't even aware that he has a right in a theater, how is someone as sheltered – excuse me, Em – as Em gonna know that she has a legal right to be seated in a movie!?"

They go on ranting, letting off steam, I suppose. I'm enjoying my shake even with a touch of nervous stomach. As I sit between their rages I gotta marvel that I am sitting here having lunch like anybody. The tomato on the sandwich sits tartly in my mouth and plays against my teeth, calling up fond memories. Does Duncan really think he can change the world by sitting around with signs? Does going to jail matter? I notice the way his eyes flash like blue darts when he tells the hard stories about sitting up for three days, peeing in a cup, in a cold cell. Weird.

Chapter 22

At our next P.A.I.L. meeting, Andrew makes an appearance again. The group seem glad to see him and ask lots of questions about his current activities.

"Look, Andy, some of us still live in nursing homes. What about the possibility of retaliation? If a bunch of you came to, say South Pines, where Emily lives, and you whipped up the residents and got them to picket, what happens to them after you radicals leave?"

Jenny Fanish is grilling Duncan about the plans to picket at local nursing homes when the head of Health and Human Services comes to town for a big conference. Andrew says that ABRUPT is now trying to make the point that nursing homes suck up federal money that could be better used for effective home health care.

"Things are already changing. One of the first things the folks in DC did after '96 was to broaden state waiver possibilities so that states can make changes in how Medicaid money is used to provide care. We have to keep on this now so that they know we are serious. We want home care funded so people can choose to live where they damn well please."

"Duncan, you still haven't said what's gonna happen to somebody like Emily if she rolls on a picket line at her place. Is she gonna get to go back in? Will they put her to bed, or will she have to sit up all night?"

I like Jenny. She always gets in and scraps. She seems to have no fear.

"I really don't know. Sometimes you have to take chances

to make changes." Andrew glares at Jenny. She's just being devil's advocate. I mean, it's my choice whether I sit out with a sign or watch from the upstairs window. I haven't yet made the choice. I haven't really given it any thought until right this minute.

"Look, Duncan, I deal with retaliation in my own parents' home. When I had my own place I didn't have to kowtow to any time limits or restrictions on where I went. But now I am at home, Dad will restrict my use of the car if I do something he doesn't like. For Emily, what might they restrict? It could be downright dangerous! And it won't be just a curfew!"

Jenny pushes him angrily.

"If she wants to join the protest, Jenny, I feel that is her choice. It's not really my problem."

"Well you ought to make it your problem, if something does happen to her or others like her, because of your instigation. Think about it, Duncan!"

❖❖❖

Its nippy in the autumn air. We are all out on the sidewalk: four P.A.I.L. folks; Marie, who wouldn't miss an opportunity to hang around Duncan; Ted; Madge. Am I surprised! Sherry and Duncan are supposedly on their way because they are going from site to site. There are ten nursing homes being targeted. The biggest bunch of sign carriers will be at Community Health Care, the big multiservice complex down near the convention center. The bigwigs' cars will have to drive that way from the airport. They'll get an eyeful there.

My beanie is perched on top of a nice wool scarf Grandma Sample tied on my head.

"It's too cold for me to go out there and protest, Em, but I want you to stay warm if this is what you are determined to do. I really admire your spunk. Tell 'em like it is!"

I guess I'm a little surprised at how adamant she was.

It's now the second hour of what you might call picketing. No Andrew yet, and my sign has wilted a bit in the fierce fall wind which is frankly gnawing at my uninsulated bones. Marie's old jacket I borrowed is better than my sole windbreaker, but no great shakes. Lots of shivering.

Madge is down the walk a ways and Ted is lighting umpteen smokes for her. Her sign says, "Freedom Now." Marie carries one that says, "Redirect Funds, Provide Home Services Now." Mine says, "We Want A Life." Cars slow down. I notice strange looks from the people in them. But one woman raises her fist out of her rapidly-opened car window and yells, "Right on." A man hollers, "Parasites," angrily. It is rather entertaining to watch the reactions, and also depressing.

Micky Kruze rounds the corner from the bus stop where she just got off a Publitrans van.

"Well, they ain't gonna make the visit to you guys and the others."

She wheels past us with her head high and anger all over her body.

"Duncan, Kemper, a couple of the out-a-town dudes, and a few others I don't know were arrested and canned at Community Health."

"What did they do?" Madge growled.

"Chained themselves together and rolled across the road from the airport, blocking the way for the HHS convoy. There was a twenty-minute standoff blocking Broad Street for miles. It was great."

That was the closest thing to a chuckle I've ever heard out of Mick.

"Then the cops moved in and began popping clutches on people's chairs and rolling them all off. Duncan dug in his heels, but he hardly weighs a jot, so off he goes, via three cops, with his chair in tow. They'll be in the can all night till an arraignment in the morning."

Marie looks stricken. I don't feel so good. The wind seems to be taking a toll. What are we supposed to do now?

At suppertime Mira makes me take some kind of pill. I try to spit it out. What the hell does she think this is? She shoves it in with food and holds my mouth with a napkin.

I don't have my board. They've taken it off same time as my coat. I blink, no, repeatedly, to no avail. Now this pill shit. What is going on. I look at Marie's table. Now she's arguing with Mira. Another pill?

She comes over and pad-pads me out of the dining room in a hurry.

"Onnee, gonna fina TV, news, now."

In the quiet of the hall, "Miwa gih you a peow?"

I blink a quick yes.

"Shumpns gon on. Deya ge in bah a us!"

We shuffle into the lounge and Marie uses her stick to get the overhead tube going. She deftly switches channels with the wavering stick. She finds news. We watch through gang wars, street assaults, and a silly piece on a dog show. Then we take notice.

"A gang of radical cripples blocked Broad Street today in an apparent effort to get the attention of HHS officials in town for a conference on long-term-care facilities. Wheelchair-bound instigators from out of town led local nursing home residents and independent living center patients in an attempt to chain themselves into a living wall to disrupt traffic near the convention center. After twenty minutes police arrested the leaders and removed the remaining chairs from the street. Around town similar protests took place in front of nursing facilities.

"HHS officials declined comment on the action."

Marie is transfixed by the camera shots of the "radical cripples" being dragged off the street, some out of their chairs, some sort of half in them. I feel really sick as I watch Sherry being jerked around as they pull her chair to the side. Then Andrew is hauled up by three big guys and carried struggling away. It must be the pill. Without warning my dinner lifts, and takes wing.

Marie looks back at me barfing uncontrollably.

"Wuh kinna mecin Miwa gih you?"

She looks back quickly at the TV where the weatherman is now waving his hand at maps. She looks at me again and shoves her chair back sharply, then pads briskly out of the lounge. I continue to heave and shake as tears are streaming everywhere.

Gina comes striding in with towels.

"What's gotten into you, girl. Sitting out in the cold like some damn hippie then coming in here sick as a dog. I believe you've lost your mind, what's left of it."

She's super pissed. I just keep shaking and coughing in between dry retches that tear through me. What was that pill? Could they have gotten an order from Pescy that quick? Why? I wasn't sick. When I am sick and need a pill it takes forever to get an order. I am sick now.

Gina shushes Marie away. Marie is demanding to know what the pill was and how it made me so sick; why did they give it to me; they tried to give her one, and she refused and told Mira she'd call the doctor and the ombudsman and . . . Gina shoves her chair out the door.

I am cold all night. After a quick and cold bath and a tuck-in three hours early, I stay cold. Shaking. During the little sleep I catch I have terrible dreams. It's like I wake up and hear screams. Faceless men in black have come through the doors and pulled us all into the hall. Doctor types in white come through and look at us as we all lie on the hall floors. I can see where I am; I can see everyone in the home. A doctor flips his hand over and down, as he leaves the hall door. The black masked figures pull out guns and begin shooting us all. I scream, "Stop, stop!"

"You'd better pipe that down, Emily. You'll wake Edna and upset her. Here take this pill, it will calm you down."

"Noh, nah nah, noh mo. Ay ick, noh!"

"Quit fussing and take this."

I can see it is the same thing. Looks like the old Valium stuff they gave me to keep me quiet when I was a teenager. But its a little different color. It made me sick. "Noh ay, noh noh!"

My arms flailing as best as I can make them go, I still can't thwart the circling force of Mavis. She shoves the pill in my mouth. I spit. She finds it and shoves again pouring water from the pitcher in my face. I have to swallow or drown. She holds my jaw until she's satisfied.

"You're gonna feel much better if you get some sleep. So cool it and rest."

She flips off the bed light and pulls the door to. It's still cold. My sheet and pillow are wet.

❖❖❖

I guess I've slept late. Edna is gone. No Judy. My door opens and in sluffs Marie. She shuts the door, glances at me, and then turns on Edna's tube with her stick.

"Onnee, news."

"It's 8:00 a.m. and here are local headlines. Health and Human Services officials left this morning after a successful meeting outlining the future role of Federal and State funding for long-term health care.

"Protesters who attempted to disrupt the meeting have been arraigned in County Court this morning."

"Onnee, wuh kin we doh?"

I want to turn my head away from her piercing plea. Like there would be something we could do. Sure.

Chapter 23

The reporter is a smallish woman with thick dark hair and thick dark glasses and a thick little notepad. Marie and Ted and I sit with several of the P.A.I.L. folk in the lounge. Jenny, Sandor, and Mary have come, and Denia Blane. Aides walk slowly down the hall and some come in to have their break. Getting an earful. Andrew Duncan and Micky Kruze roll in from a late bus, apologizing for their delay. Duncan immediately turns it into a sermon for the reporter about bus access.

Micky translates the sticky parts in Andrew's diatribe.

"Yes, it is good to be able to be as late as the average person taking public transportation. Other people feel that the lifts slow the bus schedule down, but in the real world the buses are timed to deal with regular large loads, and they will be timed to deal with regular lift users. There is no difference in the amount of time needed for say ten passengers loading, or for a lift load."

"Well, I'd really prefer to talk about your nursing home protest, Mr. Duncan, if we may?"

After the arraignment, Andrew and Sherry and the others were fined $100 each for disrupting a right-of-way and causing a safety hazard and a public nuisance and warned never to do it again. Fat chance. They are already gearing up for a big action in Atlanta which really ought to turn heads. Denia and Sherry are organizing a fund-raiser to get some money for future fines, and to pay off the ones who had to take out loans from Center funds to pay theirs.

"What do you think is accomplished by getting people out with signs?"

Andrew doesn't look too happy to be talking to this lady. They ain't hitting it off. Not a lot of smiles and jokes today.

"Where have you been for the last thirty or forty years? Oh, excuse me, you couldn't even have been around that long."

The reporter looks puzzled at his response. Micky's translation is hesitant.

"Do you really think people like these should be living out like anyone else? How can they get around? Who will take care of them?"

Them. THEM. Shit. Who are THEM? I am getting as pissed as Duncan. She waves her arm indifferently in our direction as she discusses the anonymous them. She could ask us.

"Do you really think people like you should be living out like anyone else?" Jenny crabs.

Jenny Fanish is deviling again, and this could really sour our little talk. The reporter seems to have the cool to ignore that jibe and moves on with Duncan.

"Seriously, Mr. Duncan, who will be expected to care for people like these who are confined to wheelchairs and incapable of much of anything?"

The room seems to be getting darker, maybe a passing cloud. Micky wheels around to face the reporter.

"You imply that people are only worthy if they can dress and toilet and feed themselves. It is your attitude that keeps worthy people in places like this where they are ignored and left to vegetate, or even be hurt and further damaged. You are confined to mental barriers which exclude many people from consideration by you and people like you."

Micky is really steamed and her face is as red as her hair. The reporter is sitting stiffly, defended behind her dark-tinted glasses. I decide that the air is getting too thick.

Marie has noticed my light, flashed into her eyes, then onto my board.

"IF U CUD LIV HEAR 1 WEK UD NO Y WE HOLD SINES"

"But if you lived here one week thinking you would never live anywhere else again, you'd really know what the protest is about.

What if we dared you to?" Duncan is grinning wickedly again.

"You mean that you think I should live in a place like this for a week?"

"Yeah, why not?" Jenny is grinning right along with Andrew. "You're a reporter, you do undercover stories and stuff like that. If you don't think you can pass as a gimp, why don't you just arrange to stay here? Tell 'em you are writing a book about nursing home care and how wonderful it is, and you want first-hand experience. It oughta fly!"

"No, she has to be in a chair and, like Emily, need total care, otherwise she won't know what it is to never be able to get around and express yourself or any of that." Duncan is challenging her flat. It's all or nothing for him.

"I just wouldn't know how to go about it. I can't imagine how I'd convince the people here that I should do it." The reporter is edgy and confused.

"You want a good story? One that'll sell? Try this. See if it won't be a major feature."

"Mr. Duncan, can we continue this interview? I'd like to concentrate on this story."

I can tell that this meeting is a bust. The reporter keeps asking the same kind of questions about how people like THEM could expect the world to accept THEM. It goes nowhere and she eventually gets up to leave, obviously frustrated.

❖❖❖

On wrestling night, George has invited me up for the fights. I finally convince Leena to give me the necessary shove.

"Hi, kid. What is all this shit about your friends protesting living in a nursing home? Don't be fooled, baby. None of them live in a nursing home. Why is a bright girl like you listening to their garbage, and going along with it, when you'd be the only one screwed by the outcome?"

'LETS WACH FITES, OK?'

"No, man, I wanna know if you are crazy enough to let these sons-a-bitches mess with you. 'Cause if you are then I guess I am going to have to take action here. I'm gonna have to see that they can't come back to hurt you. I'm just gonna have to raise some sand about this, and protect you since you won't take care of yourself."

"NOT U BIZNES. WACH FITES, NOT HAV 1."

❖❖❖

A few weeks later I am parked, kindness of Marie, at my window. I still can't get this chair moved around. I'm going stir crazy. I put in a request for a smaller chair in the social worker's office. She smiled an "I'll see what I can do" smile and went back to the phone. My hopes are not high.

A new lady moved in about a week ago. I feel sad for her, coming in to such a place around holiday time. We will have our usual Thanksgiving bash next week. Construction paper turkeys, and ground mess on my plate. Yum.

Mira moves the woman's chair near mine, so she can vegetate and mull over the light as it moves over the roof. She must not speak either. I glance in her direction, in my slow, head-going-the-wrong-way manner. She looks up and around at me. I blink and noise a hi. She blinks back and sorta smiles. She has a tape player like Marie, but smaller, and it plays very quietly.

I bring my head back around and catch her eye with my light.

"CAN U READ?" I spell slowly, looking repeatedly at her for a yes.

She seems to smile and blink.

Over the next month, I find out that her name is Millie Goulding and that, on top of C.P., she is recovering from a stroke, which makes it harder for her to talk or to move her right side at all. We talk on my board, and she asks me more questions than I do her. She asks a lot about my life and how I feel about South Pines. She has a letter card and her left hand moves enough that she can ask a lot. She is not shy and I am really enjoying talking with her. I notice she is chummy with Marie and George, and even Madge will read her card. I remember when Mattie Breen had her stroke it made her paralyzed on the right side. She couldn't talk either, but she also couldn't understand a lot. Yet Millie is getting along really well.

The P.A.I.L.s are planning a big Christmas Party at the Center. They are excited because Nancy Greene and Clare Porter are getting ready to make the break. Nancy is a little person who still lives at home with her parents. She and Clare have become great friends since they have begun the P.A.I.L. process. Sherry and Denia discovered a nice little house that the ladies believe they could make into home. Clare has been living in a place like South Pines for about six years and is eager to leave. Because she has no speech, her family nixed her living independently. She has really fought to achieve this.

The Christmas party will be a celebration and sort of house-warming. They need everything. An arrangement with the folks at the Goodwill lets them go pick out a lot that they need, basic furniture and kitchen stuff. A fund at the Center pays a minimal sum to cover the costs to Goodwill. But they need some new stuff, too, things that anyone moving out on their own would like.

Clare will need an attendant to do baths and dressing, but Nancy hopes to adapt the kitchen to her size, because she loves to cook. They feel that Clare's cleverness and business sense and Nancy's hands and practicality will make for a great team.

I find it all really exciting and scary. I dream about finding a hands person like Nancy, who really wants to share with me and would like to make a home. I could be smart and learn to do the bills. Yeesh, the whole idea is too frightening.

It is December 18. I have asked Marie, Millie, Ted, and George to come with me to the party. Everyone but George says yes. He tells me that he doesn't think that he could deal with that level of foolishness without saying something nasty to someone, so better not go and be a pain in the butt.

"PANE IN BUT TO WHO?"

"I just don't want to go, Em. I don't trust what these people are doing. Too many times I have seen people like them get the shaft out there."

❖❖❖

It's a great party. Lots of people bring every kind of goodie and snack, sparkly colored Christmas cookies, and gooey brownies. There is thin turkey and ham for sandwiches. The hands people throw together plates for the non-hands crew and everybody sits down to pickles, potato salad, bean salad. A picnic in winter.

After the gorge, there is a game. Everyone is dealt cards until they are all gone. Many have brought little gifts and there is a pile of these under the tree near the big window. As Sherry calls out the card numbers from a deck that Sarah is dealing onto the table, the holder of the same card gets to choose a gift, from the tree, or they can swipe another person's prize. This gets really wild as walkies and wheelies vie for the tree pile, and for the laps of friends.

"That's mine!"

Duncan rolls past me with my blue package belapped, and snatches the gift away. My protests go unheeded. I plan my vengeance.

"Ace of hearts!"

I flail at Casey. She moves fast, glancing at the heart on my board, and the beam pointing out A and D and she gleeps the biggest parcel from Duncan's lap. He feigns horror, and yelps, "No fair sending your hitperson to do your dirty deeds, Mason."

Casey and I laugh conspiratorially, and plan our next attack.

When everyone has a package or more, each opens the gifts. There are mostly food goodies or household things. Several exchanges take place. Fred relinquishes an iridescent head scarf to Mary Settles in exchange for a baseball statistics book. Casey and Leslie start a trend by donating their gifts to Nancy and Clare. Denia offers Nancy a nice set of measuring cups and spoons.

Casey and I have opened a very nice can opener, which Nancy can twist with her hands. I have Sarah put it on Nancy's pile. Then I open a pack of chocolate cookies. I fear that Nancy won't be getting these.

"We will be moving in next Saturday and Sunday, and want you all to know that you will be coming to our place soon for a do. Thank you so much for all this great stuff. The spice rack is going to be super, and I'll think of you, Em, everytime I fix a can of food."

Nancy and Clare thank each of us for the gifts. I have brought a ceramic candlestick which Nate loved. Marie helped wrap it. It does me no good on my cramped dresser top which I share with Edna's children, grandchildren, and million nieces and nephews. In one way it's hard to part with. It's all I have of Nate. The hard part is hoping one day I would have a room of my own to display it. I just can't get my head around that idea, especially now not even being able to get around the halls of South Pines.

Chapter 24

"Tell me more of your life."

Millie can spell like in the books. We are heading home from the party. Marie couldn't catch our bus. Only two lockdowns. She seemed put out, but we had to leave when we could.

"NOT MUCH TO TELL." My spelling is improving. "NO SKUL, NO FAMILY SINS 17, ONLY HOM SOUTH PINES."

"Awful. Do you have friends to go out with?"

"ONES AT P.A.I.L. ONLY, AND HERE. GO P.A.I.L. ON BUS NOW."

"Nobody but the Center visits you?"

"WHO WUD? Y? NO FUN HERE. I STUK IN 2 BIG CHER NOW."

We reach home and jerkily sink to the sidewalk and Millie moves through the patio doors. She hustles up Jerry to come out and get me to shove me in. It is nearly dinner time and we get pushed into the dining room where Mira wrestles with our coats before trough time.

Millie can maneuver food fairly well with her left hand. She is very slow but usually successful. Mira will likely feed me, with growing disinterest. She was such a nice person when she first came here a couple years ago. Now she is kinda zombie-like.

Jerk. Like the good old days.

"Here, Em, your bib. Take off that damn beanie thing. Now eat."

Mira's headed to a fire. The muck comes at me hard and fast. Mercifully I can't taste it much, and I have my delicious lunch to tide me over. But if she keeps shoving peanut butter at me, I'll lose both meals.

"EEMH! EEMH!"

Millie noises in Mira's direction.

"Slow down," she spells,"She is not a machine!"

"Look, Millie, I'm in a hurry. We are two short on 2-C and I pulled dining duty, too. I am just doing my job, OK!"

I bring up a foody burp.

"Shit, Em, don't start on me, and Millie, don't you encourage her."

Mira napkins me unmercifully and continues to shove the spoons. I try to signal her to stop. I am more than full. Please stop.

"EEMH!"

"Leave off, Millie!"

Millie desperately spells out my plight. Too late.

"Damn it, Em, you just did that to get back. Shit."

I sit in technicolor puke while Mira storms off to get reinforcements.

"This happen lots?"

I blink no at Millie's question and hang my head in whatever direction it wants to go while folk at nearby tables wheel or walk quietly away. Luckily most had finished their peanut butter sandwich and tomato soup. I look at Millie again and blink yes.

"I thought so. Looks routine."

The place is cleared save for Millie and me when Mira comes back with a bucket and paper towels. Martine from housekeeping follows her with a mop. With the worst of it up, Martine makes short work of the mess, shorter than I did bringing up the issue. Mira jerks me out fast; her huff is audible.

Millie's chair whine fades as we zip like bats around the corner and onto the elevator. Another early night, after an unbearable cold bed-bath. At least I have a splendid day to meditate on.

❖❖❖

"Tracey has an offer for you, Em."

I am Leslied carefully into the room where the P.A.I.L. gang are congregating. Sherry catches my attention before I get to my place.

"An offer you may not be able to refuse." She puffs her cheeks and says this in an odd gravelly whisper which I barely understand. Not the usual Sherry.

Tracey, Clare, Jenny, and Nancy are all clustered at the head of the table talking. Leslie puts me there at Sherry's suggestion.

"Em, I am going to be getting a new chair in February. There are a few minor glitches in this one that make it replaceable for me, especially for outdoor use long range. But, since you are still mostly using a chair indoors, we thought that you might like to think about getting this one."

I don't think I am yet awake. I remember the bus, and Jerry pushing me out to the stop. But I'm not hearing right since Sherry did that take-off voice.

"Medicaid will cover my new chair. They don't like to junk usable equipment, but they won't allow trade-ins. So the chair is mine to deal with. I need $110 to pay a pharmacy bill and get a new cushion like I like. Sherry said she'd foot me the $110, if you could pay her $10 a month for the next eleven until you pay it off."

What is happening here? I'd try to pinch myself, but that would take too long. I beam at my board.

"NEED SUM TIME THINK THIS OVER. WOW!"

The meeting continues, but I am not really into it. I am watching Tracey and her blue machine. She rides so high and comfortably. She has a head support. That would keep me from lolling south at every possible moment. I would have better beam control with that support. But ten bucks a month is a chunk from my $34.00 cash. But what do I buy? Shampoo? Overpriced at best in the gift shop. I could get a P.A.I.L. person to get me enough to last forever at a discount place, and toothpaste and soap. I just gotta get Judy to quit leaving my soap in the basin where it melts away. Bus fare. That is my current big chunk of change. It is $1.20 a trip, at about six trips a month. Well that is only $7.20. I am getting good at my multiplication. Since I've only been using about $15 a month for spend money, I ought to have a bit saved up for a down payment. This is all too unreal. Wouldn't George just crap! Good for him.

I really am not paying attention when Sarah asks how things are going for Nancy and Clare.

"Other than some timing problems with Clare's PCA's, we are really doing great. My mom has had a tendency to want to hang around the place. But I was very careful to give our extra key to my sister, not to Mom. Janice will keep to herself, and doesn't drop in unannounced, like Mom would. I know it's got Mom's nose out of joint, but I really believe Clare and I have our right to privacy."

"That must have been a hard decision," Sarah mused.

Clare's printer is clicking. "Easy decision, harder to enforce."

After the meeting Tracey and Sarah, Denia and Sherry circle my chair.

"I THINK I CAN SWIG IT!"

"Swig it?" Sherry looks baffled.

On her way by us, Clare clicks, "Swing it."

"Right!"

"Wanna test ride, Em?"

I don't know if I am ready for this. I realize that every molecule in me just started to shake. But I am going to go for it. Shit, no point in holding up progress.

Leslie is cornered as she heads down the hall. Denia will give a hand.

"Need some transfer nudges, here," calls Sherry.

Leslie unbelts Tracey, who is giggling massively. She pivots and settles into one of the soft office chairs. Sarah has unvelcroed me and I get the swing-your-partner ride from Denia, now. The big blue is cushy soft, easy on the bones. I sit up like a queen, able to see all around me. I can look Nancy in the eye, if not slightly downward. I can see Denia's upper arm without cranking my neck around. The blue head support makes neck cranks easier and Clare, who stayed to watch, clicks, "Don't forget test drive."

Since I am boardless, I can't tell the gang about my last test drive, in which I nearly killed hapless bystanders. I am at a disadvantage too, Tracey's joy stick is not on my best side.

"Something not kosher, Em? Where's her board?"

"JOY STIK BAD SID."

"Well, this one has an easily movable box. Some of them are hard to change, but this one is a snap. Maybe Leslie, the wrench wizard, could lend a finger."

Leslie laughs and heads out for tools. A few turns and snaps and the power box is moved around the back to the other arm and installed.

Here goes. Look out, world. I concentrate everything in me to not focus on that arm and stiffen it. Then I take deep breaths and gently nudge the stick. Unlike Andrew's chair, there is no jerky fast start. The motor makes a gradual move and I am very slowly off. I am not sure if I can steer this, but I've seen Micky maneuver her buggy and she has even stiffer arms than I do. I see that a slow nudge in the direction I want to go gets me going just that way. This is unreal. It is better than toes, where I have to back up everywhere I go. I manage a circle all around the whole table. The action is as smooth as my spasmy arm will allow. Incredible. I turn the chair to look at the gang and their grins hit a switch in me and the splendid freedom of this chair hits me and sobs and guffaws start rolling out of me at once.

Sarah comes over with the board and lets me finish watering my slacks. After a good wipe I beam at the board.

Chapter 25

*I*t may be another week before the chair can be delivered. The Medicaid process is so slow and tedious. Clare said that her last chair took six months for delivery. No matter how long, it is a long wait. I feel stunningly stuck in this piece of junk here alone in the hall. I am even impatient with my sunshine. Which is better, to have been teased by the freedom of such a chair, or never to have loved at all?

Am I taking on too much? I fear getting the chair, and having to face it breaking down on me. George's fix-it contract with his church has run out of time. I worry that his chair will run out too. And I don't even have a fix-it arrangement to look forward to. If I didn't live here the Medicaid would cover my chair repairs. Clare says that she simply rides over to Markham's Hospital Supply for repairs, if her chair is still running. If it's not, they will come to her. What would she do without it? What would George do without his chair? It is really scary to depend so much on something so unknown. But this clunker has a lot more disadvantages. What am I bitching about?

❖❖❖

I want to catch a ride to George's room. Maybe Judy will pass this way after break.

I finally hitch a ride with a hurried Ms. Neeley. We briskly spin into George's room. I perch near the bottom of his bed.

"Yo, Em! What you want, kid?"

George is in bed nursing a break on his permanent pressure sore scar.

"KNO BOUT CHER?"

191

"The actor on TV? Cher?"

"NO SILY CHER TO RID."

"What about it?"

"BRAK? TO MUSH?"

"No I never broke it to mush. Oh, I should stop griping. The buggy has been remarkably reliable. Just about five major repairs in ten years. The usual belts replaced and once a clutch. You do have to replace the battery periodically. I don't get out on the streets much so I replace fewer tires than your rowdy P.A.I.L. people. Why the hell you wanna know?"

"I GET NU CHER"

" No shit!"

"NO SHIT."

"Where are you going to get a chair? They cost a fortune."

"FREND GET NU CHER, GIV ME OLD."

"Is this another one of those damned independent people's tricks?"

"I WANT CHER DONT CARE MOV OUT WANT CHER NOW!"

"Never trust a gift horse, kid, they are always full of Greeks."

"WAT?"

"Forget it. When do you get it?"

"DONT NO SOON I HOP."

"Oh, so they won't tell you? Just lead you on. Get your hopes up? Em, they are going to set you up and then dump you. Those types always do."

"U HAV NO FATH."

"Not in the church of the independent crazies. Anyway, you wanna watch math with me?"

We watch math and social studies for an hour before lunch. I love the history stuff. Imagine living in the Middle Ages. Well I probably wouldn't have. Not long anyway. The aide comes by to shove me to lunch. Almost on time. But she has to make room to feed Larry and help George with his stuff.

❖❖❖

Millie is here at the P.A.I.L. meeting with me. She seems to enjoy it and is actively talking to Sandor, Clare, and others who live out on their own. I sense she'd like to move out as soon as she can. She asks Sandy where he's come from to get to this point.

"Lived with my grandmother, but since she hadn't been well for a long time, I figured it was only a matter of time before I would have to go into a 'home' of some kind. None of my cousins would have me and certainly not my brother in Omaha. With their attitudes, I didn't really want to have to live with any of them.

"I was taking a math and an English course at the Community College and the counselor there asked if I knew anything about an independent living center. After three years here, I took the plunge, and I have a great little place in Briarhills with the Peachman and I'm working on finishing my courses."

Peaches snores appreciatively during Sandor's chat. I wonder how guide dogs are so perfectly trained.

Millie listens intently to each person's story. I notice that her boom box is working. She must go back and relisten to these tales on her own. That seems funny, like she can't remember.

❖❖❖

I got a message last night that Tracey has her chair now and will have mine delivered here today. I could hardly sleep all night for thinking of that blue magic carpet and what it might be like to make it mine. I can't run around and tell Marie and George and Millie and Ted to be there when it comes, because I am still stuck in this rattletrap. Maybe they will announce it and that way George and the others will come. If I could just get to the switchboard to tell Donna that. But everyone is running around crazy since four aides called in sick. Holiday weekend, the schools are going on spring break so aides go out of town with their kids to see grandma and such, and we get caught short.

"Visitors for Emily Mason in front lobby."

As the P.A. blares, I cast about in hopes of hitching some feet for the trip down. I'll be so glad to get the hell outa this chair. I wave at a fast-moving Judy.

"Not now, Em, I have to change Genney quick."

Jerry tears past with someone I don't recognize on a gurney. I know there is no hope for a ride there. Mira rushes by.

"You had a P.A., Em, ain't you heading down?"

She disappears around the corner. How am I supposed to head down? How in god's name did I survive for fourteen years sitting immobile like this? Everything in me is straining to go and no one notices that I can't get there. Jerry is heading back by now zooming toward the elevator, empty handed. I shriek at him.

"Bweth?!"

"I gotta hurry, Em."

"Owth, ow!"

"Well, I'll run you down on the elevator on my way down."

We rip for the elevator door and pile on with a late breakfaster. First floor and Jerry slides me out and runs in the opposite direction. The new social worker, Ms. Butler, is heading this way.

"Bweth?"

"What?"

I try to point my beanie light toward the direction of the lobby. This lady doesn't know me, but maybe she'll get the idea.

"I'm sorry, do you need something?"

I catch her eye with my light and bring it to the board.

"PLEEZ, GO TO LOBY NOW."

"You want me to go to the lobby?"

"NO, ME GO LOBY, PLEEZ."

"You want me to take you to the lobby?"

"YES."

Finally we push off for the lobby and after a twenty-minute struggle I reach my desired destination. Sarah greets me coming through the door. She is alone.

"Emily, we thought maybe you caught the wrong train!"

"NO WAY GET DOWN IN THIS CHER. STUK."

"Well, those days are over!"

As she says that the whole lobby fills with people, P.A.I.L. people, and all of my friends at the Home. Everyone wheels and

194

files in and Casey, who I haven't seen since Christmas, pushes in the Blue Magic Carpet.

"Ehyeeh!!"

They all start laughing as I let out several shrieks. Sarah and Casey move the blue next to this thing and begin de-velcroing me with a vengeance. With a whoosh Casey pivot transfers me into the chair. Wow, I am on top! This is too much. The control box is on my better side and I focus my hand onto the stick with joy. I manage a leftward nudge, and ease around the table slowly.

Sarah backs toward the door and gestures me into the hall.

"Let's see what she's got, Scotty!"

❖❖❖

I can't stop feeling like I am moving. I know I am in my bed and it is dark, but in my head my body keeps moving down halls and around corners. I never liked being drunk, when Aunt Jo would force foul-tasting cheap wine down me to keep her company. But when I hear someone describe, like, drunk with pleasure, they must mean how I am feeling. Perhaps I had to lose what little get-around skills I had for the past few months to really appreciate what being able to get around meant to me.

Can I ever tolerate being immobile again? After they've seen Payree? And yet I know that there will be more times when I will get stuck. I've lived a long time in my dreams, and I'm not sure if this running, moving life is all it's cracked up to be. But I feel that I know what I lost. And I want it back. Freedom.

Chapter 26

God, this is starting out to be a hell of a fine spring. I have always loved spring the best, but this one's a topper. I am on my way to my weekly art class. I just wheel myself out the door, down the patio, and out the gate. That is I do if no loony has locked it. They are supposed to have it open for me on Thursdays.

It is one of those days where the air has an intoxicating clarity. I can see for miles, it seems, and the hairs stand up on the back of my head for joy. The little side street behind South Pines is only a single long block before I get to the school where Jody teaches. But it is a block chock full of pleasure. Daffodils and tulips and forsythia color the yards, and babies play and dance. Fifteen years I sat in that building while this went on all around me and I never knew. Sometimes I tear up with the loss of those years, as I wheel up to the busy corner. I wait here for someone from the school to see me. There is no curb cut, and I am not fool enough to jayroll across this mayhem to get to the other side.

Jody's friend Carol sees me and plays dodgecars to get across.

"Yo, Em!"

"OO Ewoh!"

We watch for a break and make a dash for it. She gives me a boost to power over the inch of curb on the driveway.

Jody's high windows all around let in the intense light and she sits at her easel, brush in mouth. She has a pot of clear stuff and is putting tiny dabs on the heavy paper.

"Carol, tell Em what I am doing, and I'll keep on to demonstrate for everyone."

Jody say this slowly through her teeth, continuing to dab the fluid on. There is a very faint pencil sketch that I can now see. It appears to be grain or grass of some kind with little pod-like heads. The dabs go above the heads, or down the side of stalks.

"Jody is putting mask on the paper to keep the paint from getting on those places. When it dries the water color washes go on and then the detail of the little grains is put in. When all the color is applied and dry then we will peel off the bits of frisket and the light seems to shine in from the back of the painting."

Carol sets up my easel on a small prop board on the floor. Off with the footrest and the sock. On with the brush with the nice rubber grip. I am trying to figure out colors as I mix in the center of the pot strip Carol has placed just below the prop easel. I wish I could get just the blue in the sky outside. I dab more white in to the gouache mix and still the cobalt refuses to yield to what I see coming in over the cabinets. But it is the search that is the pleasure. I could puddle in this stuff all day and be very content. I see the darkest part of the blue going on the very top of my paper and I move the lighter shades down to the rocks and stream I've tried to suggest below. It's no Renoir, but its mine.

"Your control continues to improve. But remember the looseness is also good. It is tricky to achieve a perfect balance between the two. Very relaxed control. Super, Em. You have found a true love in this, right?"

Jody is wise and sees the sheer pleasure seeping out of my face. If only Nate could have had a bit of this. He would have been so happy.

When our two hours are done, all of us wheelies get ready to go. I can feel by myself in this class but there are really three others spending this studio time with Jody. She demonstrates techniques, and we either do along with her or continue with whatever we are doing on our own. She gives each of us time for questions and critiquing. Jody has said that I should get a prop board and paints for "home." I can't imagine anyone being Carol for me. Judy would complain if I made one drip and to have to spend time putting up my easel and taping on the paper, Oh, heaven forbid.

"Would you like me to call Anita, and get her to set you up a corner in the Activities Room? I know she has crafts and games going there for others."

"SKARD SHE WONT LIK MES"

"I think you might try asking, Em. You tend to hang back when it involves something important to you."

❖❖❖

Supper. A bad memory, but not important to me. But as I sit here in my window with Millie and Marie I study the gradually fading sky color and ponder what Jody meant. Without an acknowledged voice, I never felt I had the privilege of asking for anything, what I want, or what I felt I needed. Jo paid no attention, and Nate thought of it before I could. He nearly always anticipated my every real need. I never fathomed any need other than food, water, and a place to rest. I got those so erratically from Aunt Jo that when Nate did provide I considered what I got to be special, not routine.

And everything here is routine, no needs or wants. It fits into the schedule, or it doesn't exist.

This never put me in the frame of mind to consider what was important to me. I just needed and waited until that need was met. Never thought ahead much, or considered what I might want, or feel was important.

I catch Millie's eye with my beam.

"WAT IMPAWTENT TO U?"

"Beauty," she spells on her board. "And love, and health." She pauses and looks at the light with me. "And freedom."

Marie is involved now.

"Onnee, Ah naw hingk bouw inhpaw nt hings. Maybe heowf, yah, n' lyuov."

She turns quite red at the last word putting her hand near her face in a hiding gesture.

Millie spells out, "What about you, Em?"

I DONT NO. BIN THINKIN ABOUT. JODY ART TECHER SED I HANG BAK WEN IMPAWTENT TO ME."

"Meaning you tend not to speak up for yourself? For what you want or need?"

198

YAH, GES SO. HOW LERN TO DO?"

"It's not easy when you depend on others for those needs. You might talk about this at the next P.A.I.L. meeting."

❖❖❖

The room is crowded today. Lots of chairs arm to arm. On a pretty day in April people feel like talking independence stuff. Full of piss and vinegar, we all roll out to face a hostile world. I am thinking this, but I want to ask what these folk really want in their lives. I am hoping it will get me thinking about what it really is that I want.

Sarah speaks up in the first lull in the social time. Denia echoes her words with airsculpting signs.

"Let's get together for a while here and be a group and later we can all catch up with each other. Has anyone brought an idea or issue that needs poking at?"

I see my chance and flash my light in some eyes and at my board. Micky notices first and calls Sarah's attention.

"WANT TO NO WAT U ALL THINK IMPAWTENT?"

"In what sense? Important to the world; to each of us individually?

"ECH 1. ART TECHER SAY I HANG BAK NOT ASK FOR IMPAWTENT FOR ME. I NOT NO WAT IMPAWTENT TO ME."

"I would say, Em, that this is a good example of your not hanging back." Micky doesn't crack a smile as she says this, but everyone chuckles.

Before the group breaks up for social time and snacks, nearly everyone speaks about their sense of what is important to them. I am interested in the consistency of some things, like health and love and the stuff Millie and I talked about. Yet there are a number of things I'd never considered. On my trip home on the van, and the long wait before, I have time to think about Fred's concerns for his kids. They are most important to him, and he worries about whether he is a good enough father, since his fixed income is limited and he can't be a football Dad. Andrew is most concerned about what he calls "the movement," whose purpose is making changes in the society's view of people with disabilities.

Denia stresses the importance of recognizing people who have more than one societal strike against them. She believes it is very important that minority people with disabilities make their statements extra loud, so that the able-bodied white male "majority" wakes up to the real world. Micky feels that decent, honest, competent attendant care is most important to her, and to all gimps living out in the community. As she says that, I agree for gimps who are not out, like me.

What is important to me is really basic. I need to eat, sleep, be clean, and be around other people. I don't hang back about those things. Or do I? I guess I do. Because I never make waves if I don't have to. Like accepting the mushed-up muck I am force fed at South Pines. If I want to eat good food, like in the hospital, or at P.A.I.L., or out to eat, I'll have to ask to have this changed. It is important to me. This is important. To me!

❖❖❖

It's another really pretty April day. I want George to help me write a letter to the bigwigs to have my food like everyone else. I think I can catch him before he goes out to sun on the patio. Around the corner I see him heading toward the outside door. I gun it. Whew, what a rush.

He hears my chair and turns his to greet me.

"Well if it isn't Danny Sullivan, or is it Andretti?"

"HUH?"

He has my board in his sights.

"I was teasing. Those guys are race car champs. Shoot."

"PLEZ RIT LETER FOR ME."

"What's it about?"

"EKY FUD."

"Huh?"

"WANT ET GUD FUD. NO MOH MUCK."

"Hah, you want them to quit fucking with your food? Right? And you want me to write for you a letter to tell them to stop it? Uppity, aren't we?"

I flail at him randomly in mock rage, fueled by the real thing. We wheel up to his room where he manages to cadge Mira into getting out his best letter paper and envelopes. He splints his pen and says, "Shoot."

"HU TO RIT TO?"

"Well, you want to tell 'em all so we'll write one and then make copies to send to social services, dietary, nursing, administration, and hell, the board. Why not?"

"DER PEPUL, I BIN AT S.P. 17 YRS. I WANT ET GUD FUD NOW. SIK OF MASH UP STUF. I ET GUD FUD OWT. Y NOT HER? I NOT CHOK, I OK. WANT FIX NOW.

THANK U."

"Now that's what you want said. Shall I embellish it a bit? Would that be OK?"

"SHUR."

"To Mr. White, Administrator, Mr. Beavin, President of the Board, and Ms. Neeley, Director of Nursing, Ms. Pelvey, Dietetics, Mr. Kramer, Ombudsman, and others:

With assistance of my friend, Mr. Danton, I write to you to request that you make a change in the manner in which my food is prepared.

I have lived at South Pines for over 17 years and have received a ground and pureed diet since 1977 when during a bout with pneumonia I had trouble chewing and swallowing my food. I am a slow eater, and find it difficult to be fed so fast, especially when the food is cold and mashed beyond recognition. I can eat anything, and do so when visiting friends or out to eat. I just need time to chew and swallow at my pace.

Please remove the ground and bland diet restrictions at your earliest convenience. I would also appreciate if the aides would slow down the feeding pace.

Thank you
Emily Mason.

"THAT'S GUD, YES, THANK U SO MUSH GAWJ. HOW U REMEBER ALL THAT?"

We run around to the Activities Room and beg Anita to let us copy the letter seven times. She's grumpy about it, but says OK. Since it is easier for her to do, she reads it as she does it. I am not glad about that.

"Em, you are always trying to get yourself in a heap of trouble lately."

"Can it, Nita. Would you want to eat that shit she's been given for the past 17 years? I don't know why she hasn't yelled before this."

"Well, it's just that every time she stirs the waters, it gets ugly for a while."

"LET IT."

I roll out the door with George behind me carrying the offending sheets. We take them to reception and ask Pam to help fold and stuff our envelopes. George writes all the names on them for me, and puts them in the pony mail.

"Now we sit back and watch the fan," George grumbles.

Chapter 27

I wasn't too sure why we should watch the fan until later George explained to me about the shit that did hit it, what a mess. I am with Millie and Marie at our window with a peachy half light creeping into late evening mauve. Learning lots of colors with Jody.

"Onnee, Mihtah Why naw too haphy wi oo an Gawj."

"TUF SHIT. HIS PROBLUM."

Marie is still being very careful not to rock any close boats. It scares her that I sent the letters to the bigwigs. She fears that being my friend could cause problems for her. Of course she wasn't in on the meeting. It was pretty strange. When there had been enough time for them all to get their copies of the letter, Neeley cruised around to my room waving the letter in her hand.

"Need I ask what is the meaning of this? Emily, I don't mind that you are getting out and doing more. I think it is very nice for you. But our job is to protect your health and safety. You have this dangerous new chair, and god knows who you might kill in the hall. We don't know when you leave here whether you will get back in one piece. It is enough of a worry, just that. Now here you go and want to change your diet."

At this point in her diatribe, I thought I heard George's chair stop near my door. I figured he was eavesdropping.

"You have been eating these same foods all these years and I seriously doubt if you could acclimate yourself to regular foods again. It could be a real problem for the aides who feed you and you probably have lost any oral dexterity you may have . . ."

I had been flailing and grunting in rage since I'd heard George approach. At this point he popped in.

"I realize, Ms. Neeley, that I am totally out of place and order in this matter, but I think you should know that I have been sharing my family-provided snacks with Emily since she came here. She is very capable in the matter of oral dexterity. She can inhale a whole bag of cheetos before you can say junk. She loves to gnaw on beef jerky, and dried apples, and her real favorites, if I am not mistaken, are raisinets and tomatoes."

I flash a big grin at this, because George is right. He could pick out what I was really enjoying the most. Just 'cause my swallow reflex is more cumbersome than yours, Neeley, doesn't mean I don't enjoy those flavors and textures just as much.

"Surely you remember her birthday on the patio last year. Anybody who can eat cold pepperoni pizza can eat anything else. It just takes her more time. She is not Larry."

He sort of harrumphed and sat there seething in an out-of-character way.

"Yes, Mr. Danton, you are totally out of place and order."

She whirled in a hiss of white and was out before we could focus.

"How long has it been since you saw a dentist?"

Without my board, I just made a gradual headshake at George. I don't know that I have seen a dentist. Seems like when I moved in here someone looked in my mouth and poked with a stick. Maybe that was the dentist.

The next day, Ms. Neeley informed me that there was to be a meeting in the afternoon at three for all the people necessary to address my issue. I didn't think of it as an issue, just a simple request. They were making it into an issue.

"Come right in, Ms. Mason." Mr. White waved me into his very large office. Neeley was there, Pelvey from the kitchen, the assistant from social services, and some folk I'd never seen. George was absent, and no one else that I considered a friend was present. It was them versus me.

"This is Mr. Beavin, our Board President; this is the Long Term Care Ombudsman, Mr. Kramer; and I am sure you know everyone else."

Mr. White fairly oozed at the others, and especially the ombuds whatever. George said that if he came I should make nice with him because he can get things changed on a very high level, and can carry a little weight that even White can't.

Beavin starts. "Well, Ms. Mason, it seems that you have called the staff's attention to an issue that concerns you. You are not satisfied with your food?"

"17 YERS OF MUCK, WUD U BE?"

Ms. Neeley is obviously not enjoying translating my slowly spelled statements for this group. She is visibly offended by my muck reference. The others seem surprised by it, too. Funny.

"Now, Ms. Mason, I am sure you realize that the foods prescribed for you were in your best interest. And you've never mentioned a problem before."

They all seem very anxious and impatient as I beam at my board. Neeley reads again.

"WAS SIK 17 YERS AGO. NEVER NEW I CUD ASK. NOW I ASK."

"Ms. Mason was placed on restricted soft bland diet during a severe bout with pneumonia. It was considered safer since she was having breathing and swallowing problems." Pelvey seemed to be reading off a clip board.

"Did it not occur to anyone to see if her swallow reflexes had improved after she recovered?" Mr. Kramer looked a bit bemused, and made notes as he talked.

"ADES DON WANT TAKE TIME TO FEED ME GUD FUD. NEED TO CHU TO LONG."

That long sentence unnerves them. They shift in their seats as I spell out the real reason things weren't changed back.

"I assure you, Mr. Kramer, that nursing and dietary made the correct decision. It is unsafe for the patient . . ."

"Excuse me, Mr. White. Ms. Mason, when did you decide that you wanted your diet changed."

"WEN I GOT WEL DIDNT NO TO ASK. THOT IT WAS ALL I CUD GET. ID SNEK SNAKS FROM GAWJ FOR YERS. FUD WAS CRAP."

Mr. Kramer looks down at his notes fast and seems to suppress a smile. I like that. But Neeley shows sparks shooting out of her eyes, and Pelvey shrinks further into her clipboard.

"MY TECHER SED ASK WHAT U RELY WANT! I THING I RELY WANT GUD FUD!"

"Has Ms. Mason had adequate dental care? Are there any problems there?"

Mr. Kramer looks at Neeley. She's still hot.

"I am sure she has had adequate care, Mr. Kramer," Neeley grits her teeth in response.

"I would like to see a copy of her dental records from your file there."

After considerable shuffling through a big gray binder, Neeley and the social worker look a bit daunted. Finally a little scrap of paper is pulled out of the very back of the stack.

"This says she was examined upon entry into the facility, and her teeth were apparently fairly sound, with three small potentially carious spots, although molars worn from bruxism due to C.P. Could I see a more recent report? This one is 17 years old."

After the women make another attempt and come up dry, Beavin stands up and moves to the window. Kramer makes more notes, with no smile.

"Could I see Ms. Mason's most recent medical records?"

More shuffling. Ms. Neeley pulls a few sheets out and hands them to Kramer.

"This was recorded during a hospital stay last year? Why was Ms. Mason in the hospital last year?"

"She has joined some club at an Independence Center and on her way down the first time the van had an accident and her chair was destroyed."

Neeley's flustered. Beavin is still staring out the window. White studies his desktop.

"This is just a release form. You were apparently not badly hurt, Ms. Mason?"

"JUS XRAYS BRUS SORE PLAS CUTS. MOST SKARD."

"Yes, I can imagine."

"Mr. Kramer, I really can't see how any of this pertains to Ms. Mason's request for a dietary change. Can we return to the subject? Our time is short."

Mr. Beavin looks over his shoulder at this statement by Mr. White, then leans harder into the window frame.

"I'll be happy to save you some time. With Ms. Mason's permission, she and I could take her file to another room and review it together. That way I could get the information necessary for me to make an informed decision, and get to know Ms. Mason better. This would allow you to return to your work."

Ms. Neeley looks pale, and Mr. Beavin slumps even further against the window.

Kramer and I headed over to a staff lounge. He locks the door behind us.

"I hope you don't mind if I secure the door Ms. Mason. I think this is a private matter for you."

For a couple of hours we go over the notes in the file. Mr. Kramer asks me a lot of questions about my history, my health, my interests. It takes a while to fill him in, but he gets used to my creative spelling fast. He asks if anything had ever happened here that had hurt or scared me. I laugh. Gradually I spell out the basement and laundry room incidents, the closet activities, the bathroom abandonments. I let him know that these are not particularly unusual, nor exclusively my experiences.

Mr. Kramer makes a lot of notes on paper. He also uses a little tape recorder, so he reads everything that I write and then asks me to confirm what he read by voice.

When we leave the room Mr. Kramer asks if he could visit with me another time in order to confirm a few questions he still has. Of course I agree. I can't see this as any disadvantage.

But the whole situation could be a disadvantage and advantage both. I am definitely not the "in" resident. Marie's worries about Mr. White's displeasure make me laugh. Nobody seemed to care what happened to any of us before, so why should I worry that they are upset by what we've done now. But I have been watching carefully so no one slips me a mickey like they did after the protest.

Millie has been keeping close tabs on George and me and what's coming down. I tell her about Mr. Kramer, and the planned second meeting. When we meet again he asks me a lot about my interests and plans for the future. He wants to know about P.A.I.L. and if I really wanted to leave SP.

"I DONT NO. SCARY. SUM FRENDS HAV MUVD AND LUV THER NEW PLAC. IT ISNT PERFIK BUT THEY ARE HAPIR THAN AT NURSNG HOM. BUT THEY HAV ECH OTHER AND ECH CAN HELP OTHER. I HAV NO 1 LIK THAT. ID GO NOW IF I DID, I THINK."

He asked if things had been different since our big meeting.

"I BENG IGNORD. NEELY DONT TAK TO ME OR KICHEN PEPUL. OFIC PEPUL NEVER DID TAK TO ME. DONT MISS THAT. JUDY DONT TAK. ALL BIZNES. KWIK BATH, KWIK FUD. BIN GIVNG ME SUM REL FUD. NOT MUCH. STIL MOSLY GROWND STUF."

"Has your friend George had any problems?"

"BETER ASK GAWG. THINK THEY DONT TAK TO HIM. DAN-GERS IF HE IGNORD. BAD SORES, NEDS ATENSHUN. WORY ME."

Mr. Kramer thanks me for visiting with him. I thank him for listening to my problem. He says he will be talking again with Mr. White and Mr. Beavin about me and some other people he has talked to as well, if that was all right with me. He wishes me good luck and says he hopes that if I really want to move that I'll find the kind of place I want.

As he heads down the hall toward the lobby I see Millie wheel into step with him. They seem engaged in some conversation as I turn into the kitchen hall to go toward the Activity Room.

Millie later meets me at our window and mentions that she met Kramer and thought he was interesting. She asks if I would let her know if he came again to meet with me.

Chapter 28

I'm at breakfast early. Marie and Millie have joined me at a table. George trails in as the trays are beginning to roll in. He is not looking his best. Circles under his eyes go with a kind of ashy look about his face. I don't have my board, since it is time to eat, so I can't ask how he is. But Marie can.

"Gawg, oo no ook oo good. Oo OK?"

"Well, I've been better. Service at this hotel has not been the best the past couple weeks. I'm a tad off schedule in several areas. Hmmfh."

He shakes his head in a frustrated way, looking pained. I must talk to him later, when I have my board. This is all my fault and I can't let this go on. He may be getting sores from not being moved or bathed enough, or they are not getting his bowel program scheduled right. Any of those could make him quite sick.

Millie begins tapping out a message.

"I have some news. I may be able to move out in another month."

George looks shocked and a little hurt, but Marie and I just shriek for joy.

"Weh oo goin? Gon a yiv wif anyon we know?"

Marie seems delighted for Millie. I detect a new attitude about this moving out stuff for Marie. I can't ask anything, and add Millie to my list of people I want to catch with my board later. For now there is a banana and a bowl of rice crispies on my tray that need attention, crisp crunchy attention. At least as I wait for assistance, I know they won't get cold.

It is nearly eleven when I discover that George is in his room.

I watch for a time when the aides are out and tuck in his door, board at the ready.

"Nhawg? Oo a eeeh?"

"That you Em?"

"Yeehh."

"Can you get around to this side with your chair?"

I study the situation for a moment. Chair and I move out of the room and then back in. We back past Larry's bed, and past George's bed. With some tricky hand work I maneuver a turn and back up into the tight space between George's bed and the window and heater. Couldn't have done it with a standard size chair.

"Great job. Now I can see your board."

George nudges his power bed a tiny bit higher in order to see the board past my head. What a lot of work to say hi.

"I WORY YOU NOT WELL GAWG. BE MY FOT. I COZ TRUBL."

"No, Em, I just haven't been myself lately. Having some real problems with my back. I probably will have to go in for some grafting."

"YOU BIN GETN BATHS? WIRLPUL? HELP SORES?"

"Certainly not as often as I'd like, but I guess as often as they think they can do it."

"YOU BIN MUVD AT NITE? SHETS CLENED?"

"You sound like the nursing supervisor. This is a new Emily."

"Ms. Mason, I believe you are wanted at the front desk. You may leave now, I need to assist Mr. Danton."

She rushes in so fast with this line that she startles us both. I would have lost the chair if I weren't so well propped in. George jerks so hard I feel his bed shake. I don't think I recognize her as I endure her stare while maneuvering out of the tight spaces.

"Who, may I ask, sent you?" I hear George ask as I head out the door. He doesn't know her either. For that matter, Donna had no idea who might have wanted me at the front desk. What a snide trick.

I find Millie watching the end of a movie in the downstairs smoker. She doesn't smoke, but she knows that the aides are all dealing with beginning lunch duty so she can usually watch undisturbed. I watch with her as the man and woman talk about her going on the plane. She is crying. He is telling her she must go. She does. He watches the plane go away. He walks away talking with a policeman. I think I've seen this end before. I don't know what happens before this.

"CAN U TEL ME MOR ABUT LEVING?"

"Not a lot. I will be living with people I lived with before. Em, I want to tell you something. You will hear more about me after I leave. I hope it won't make you angry with me. I hope you will understand why I came here. I have grown to care a lot for you and George and Marie, and many of the others. You guys were my best friends here. You have taught me a lot, and I will be sharing some of that with many others."

It takes time to tick that all off on her new little machine. I am a bit befuddled by what she is saying. I think she can see that.

"I will be back sometime after I leave, to ask you all for a favor. My worst fear is that my leaving and what I will do might affect you and the others. This is why I wanted to get together with Mr. Kramer."

Then she laughs really hard.

"Besides you can take it all out on Duncan later on. In ways, it is really all his fault. Whatever you do, may all that's good go with you."

We head out to lunch and I puzzle a lot about all of this.

❖❖❖

Millie leaves us on a Saturday morning with very little commotion. The night before a bunch of us get together in the Dining Hall for ice cream and cake that Sarah has brought in. Some folks have little packages and cards to give, but the whole evening is very low key. Marie has brought some of her tapes, so we have musical entertainment, and we gather in a group to ask Millie about her future.

"I don't understand what the big attraction is out there, Millie. You have a safe place here and lots of friends. Why don't you stay?"

"I was only here to sort of rehabilitate. I am through with what I came here for, and I am moving back to what I was doing. It isn't that I don't care for my friends, but I think in the long run that you will be glad that I have left."

She says that with a laugh.

Mr. Kramer comes to visit again with a few of us. He is curious about our meetings with the P.A.I.L. folk and wants to know if we mind if he talks to the people at the Center and maybe joins us for a P.A.I.L. meeting.

"What's an ombudsman do?" Ted inquires

"I am a sort of watchdog. The state governor appoints me to keep an eye on private agencies that use state funds to serve people. I am particularly in touch with the nursing homes and state residences. If I see that people like you are not getting the services you are entitled to with state money, then I need to remind the owners of the facilities that they have to shape things up. And I can tell you that there may be some shaping up here at South Pines.

"Here is some good and bad news. Some of you need dental checks, since you haven't had family keeping up with such things. I have taken the liberty of recommending some dentists who take Medicaid who would be willing to see you. If you wish, I will advise your social worker here to help you set up appointments."

"WHAT BAD NEWS?"

"Well, Ms. Mason, some people don't like to go to the dentist. They have fears left over from their childhood of incompetent dentists, or their elders filled them with horror stories of dental problems. Most times a visit to the dentist is not a problem at all."

So here we are, Marie and I, having vanned over to the dentist for an early morning check. Early so we won't get too hungry. No breakfast in case of upchucking under any sleeping stuff the dentist might have to give us.

"Hi, ladies. You must be Ms. Mason and Ms. White. No relation to the administrator at South Pines?"

Marie chuckles at the tall thin lady who has popped her head out the door. Must be the nurse. She has on an Indian-looking skirt and a soft silk blouse. Not very nursy.

"Be right with you guys."

I wheel back first and find myself more nervous than I thought I'd be. Judy had given me a Flexoril at shift change, I guess to relax my jaw muscles. The tall lady nudges me into an empty space near a weird chair.

"How are you for transfers, Ms. Mason?"

I nod and blink and in another blink she's undone all my straps and done a perfect pivot onto the chair. I skootch back with some help from her and she adds my velcros to the new chair.

"Now for a little ride up and down instead of forward."

The chair moves further up and she slides a wheely stool next to me. She has on a mask, white jacket, and gloves. I guess she's the dentist.

"Your record shows no dental work for seventeen years. Let's see what we've got here."

I don't remember much of what happens next. She has this really soft voice and it got softer and softer. I think I open my mouth, and I don't know if I did my usual gag-choke thing, like when Neeley checks me for a sore throat. I really don't remember much of anything. I just know that she talks in that soft voice and tells me things about my teeth. Then she says, "Three, two, one, and a deep breath." I open my eyes and she's there with the airy suction thing, and she's kinda laughing, "Not too bad, huh?"

I feel a little woozy but good. My gums are achy but not bad.

"You have a few little spots that we'll want to work on in a few weeks. But other than a little tartar buildup and sore gums and some wearing on those back teeth from clenching so much," here she makes a silly face at me and grinds her teeth in mock tension, "you're in pretty good shape. So I'll see you back in about three weeks and then we'll mend some little holes. OK?"

She kinda reminds me of the doctor on Star Trek that I get to watch with George sometimes, but her hair is blonder. I like this dentist, Dr. Branson. She is like Dr. West, she treated me like a person from the get go.

Chapter 29

*T*wo months later Millie pops in with Casey, of all people, to visit us late one afternoon. She looks great. She is in a really shiny spiffy chair and is wearing a businessy-looking suit and swell hairdo. Wow, will I have that if I move out?

"Gee, you guys look great. I dropped by to see George at the hospital yesterday, and he seems to be getting better. He sends his love to each of you."

These words are crawling past us on a lighted strip which is right on the edge of Millie's board. Her board is neat and looks like a desktop in a classroom. She has a keyboard built right into it and she sees on a little fold-out screen just what we see on the front of the desk. Wow.

"Em, I see you admiring my adapted laptop. It is my chief tool. Well, I want to ask that favor. George has already said yes. But let me tell you what it is. I am a newswriter, a reporter. This is my computer which I use to speak, but also to write. I just plug it into the terminal at my office to send stories to the copy editor for the paper. I am writing a story, a long story, about life in a nursing home. You might remember that Andrew challenged one of my colleagues to do just that. She couldn't figure a way to do it, but when I heard about her dilemma, I volunteered. Who better than me, a full-time gimp, to play the role."

Casey is translating for the non-readers in our group. Even Ted and I appreciate some help with the words going so fast and so much to grasp. A lot of these words are really new.

"So, the favor is, may I write about you, each of you? I need to have you sign a paper, or have Casey witness your mark, in order to use your situation in the story. I want you to think about this, because some of what I say about this home, and others like it, may not seem too nice. I also need for you to mark the line where it asks if you want your name in the story. I will tell the story without your name, but if you wanted, it sometimes adds punch if people can connect the story with a real person. Also, Casey has a stack of photos which she will be asking you for permissions on."

Well, I think we are dumfounded by all this. I remember the challenge and the thickish reporter who came after the protest. Now I remember Millie's ever-present tape player with two tapes going most of the time. I guess one was playing and one recording. Weird. And she was quite the snapshooter. Often she'd just go around during the day shooting heaven knew what. Now we know.

"Why you crafty bitch. I admire your gall, sure do. You can smear this place to holy hell. Suits me."

Madge mutters this through her cigarette as she signs all the forms, with Casey's help. Ted then leans over Casey with some photos. He smiles his sunny smile and chuckles over the photos as Casey holds the ones he's through signing. Grandma Sample is poring over the stack of photos and laughing with Marie at some of the shots.

"It is not my intention to smear. I hope to put the situations of the residents and staff in some kind of perspective. Neither is very good. There ought to be better ways to offer people the care they need."

"What about the staff? Will you be asking their permission? Do they need to sign?"

"I will be going with Mr. Kramer to speak to Ms. Neeley and Mr. White and Mr. Beavin tomorrow. I want to interview them, too. A good news story is told from everyone's point of view. You want to be as objective as possible."

Ted and Madge are cracking up over a snap. I go see what it is and start to roar. It is Millie just waking up, startled by the flash.

"Yeah, Judy shot that one morning as a nasty wake-up joke. It is my better side, don't you think?"

❖❖❖

In a few weeks Marie and I head out to a P.A.I.L. meeting. There is a big crowd here for this one. Everyone is gathered as tightly as possible around the tables in the big meeting room.

"Have you guys seen these articles? Nothing is left to the imagination. It's incredible."

Fred has a copy of one page of an article set up on his board. Other copies are scattered over the table as readers peruse them, and non-readers hear the story from friends.

At the top of the paper just under the name is a big headline that Fred reads, "NURSING HOMES – A LIFE-OR-DEATH SITUATION." Under that it says, "Week-long series on conditions inside, funding for, and protests against the nursing home industry." There's an article on how nursing homes get their money. It is hard to read the small print. I wonder how I could get a copy to take home to read. I wonder also if that would be safe.

Fred starts to read out loud as folks ask if someone would do just that.

"As our population ages, there will be more and more concern about providing care for older people who need help with their daily activities and supervision for their safety. In the past, this service was provided by women in families caring for elders at home.

But there have always been, since medieval times, hospices, hospitals or asylums where the very old, ill, disabled or indigent were housed and possibly helped. In most cases they were just warehouses for the poor or workhouses. Many of the institutions were church-sponsored and charitably funded. Many were places of horrific conditions and abuse, with a thriving criminal sub-culture.

Some things have changed, especially since state and federal entitlement funding. Medicaid and Medicare, insurance for long-term care and Social Security have provided some means for elderly and severely disabled people to live in present-day charity-sponsored, or for-profit nursing facilities. Some things have not changed. Substandard conditions, understaffed facilities, poorly paid and managed staff all can contribute to a difficult and often intolerable way of life.

"Sr. Maureen O'Callahan, administrator of Bethlehem House, cited by the state as the best nursing facility, described her view of the difference in funding and how it affects the quality of care.

"'The for-profit facilities cropped up after there was some assurance of federal funding. No entrepreneur worth his or her salt will set up a for-profit business and not anticipate a good profit. The average private-pay charge for a month of nursing care in this area is about $2800.

"'Supplemental Security only pays $512 to an individual in this state. That money is sent directly to the facility, with a Medicaid bed subsidy of about $58 a day, which covers about $1740 of the cost of care. With two hundred residents, that draws an income of $348,000 a month.

"'You might staff a facility with two hundred beds very lightly, say, ten wings of twenty residents each, having per wing one R.N. and for each shift two aides. You put five in your kitchen, and ten in housekeeping and maintenance, with five or six doing administration and social services. Then you are paying out about $125,000, $130,000 if you have a small benefit package, and mostly full-time staff.

"'Add to that your ball-park figure of $8,000 for building, another $3,000 for utilities, a slim $30,000 for food, $4,000 for recreation, $4,000 for social services, $10,000 for laundry and medical supplies. It would run you about $186,000 per month. Now without unforeseen costs, you've ended the month with a fair profit of $162,000, and that doesn't include private pay.

"'Now, facilities sometimes will contract out for services, such as physical therapy, expressive therapy, speech and occupational therapy. Most of these are directly billable to state or federal funds. But even if you had these in-house, and few facilities do, that's only another $10,000 or $12,000. You still have a profit of nearly $150,000. Now, this is on the government funding level alone. If you base it on the $2800 per month average private-pay charge, then you are enjoying a considerably higher profit.

"'Granted, there are other costs involved such as insurance bonding for staff, facility insurance, costs for temporary staff, replacement costs for materials and equipment, grounds and landscaping, but those should not run you more than $50,000 more per month. It is not cheap to run such a facility, but the for-profits are doing just fine. I would imagine that my figures would be disputed by many other facility administrators, but they are based on our own estimates.'

"Sr. O'Callahan said that her facility does indeed house 200 residents; two-thirds of these are members of the Sisters of Mary.

"'These sisters receive the $990-per-month indigent bed money, but no Supplemental Security Income because they are considered ineligible for those public funds. Our diocese, which paid them maintenance stipends while they worked as teachers, nurses, social workers, etc., from the '40s until the mid-'70s, now provides a $200-per-month stipend. Our private pay residents pay $1800. We do slightly better than a Medicaid-only facility. We pay our staff on average 10% more, and we have more staff. We break even, with an occasional surplus which goes into our emergency fund.'"

Everyone looks a bit dazed after Fred's reading of the first article. It was kind of dull, but scary. I had no idea that people were passing around that much money just to keep me in a home. I wonder what I could do for myself if I had $1740 a month to use. Surely I could get a better place to live, even someone part-time to help me out. Naw, I'm used to baths every other day and someone to help me eat. Who'd do that?

"You guys ain't heard nothing yet."

Micky is gloating over another installment of the articles. Tracey is sitting on the table with her tiny legs curled up under the paper, getting ready to read more.

"Most seriously disabled people are haunted by the possibility of having to live in a nursing home. It is always imminent. The fine line depends on availability of money, decent attendent services, community access. If these things are not available then people are forced by circumstance into the nursing-home setting.

"Recently, people with disabilities who are at imminent risk of institutionalization have been protesting their circumstances nationwide. They are demonstrating to the powers-that-be that alternatives to institutionalization should be available to them under a national health-care policy.

"After a local demonstration last fall, activist Andrew Duncan challenged a reporter ,who questioned the need for alternatives, to live in a nursing home. He angrily dared the reporter, adding, 'Even if you did live in one, you'd know that some day you could leave. Our people are put in these places with no hope of reprieve or parole.'

"That reporter, a colleague of mine, discussed the situation with me. Since I have an obvious disability, and could be at risk of institutionalization at any time that my circumstances changed, I agreed to take on Mr. Duncan's challenge.

"I moved into South Pines just before Christmas."

Everyone looks at me questioningly since they were not aware of Millie's meeting with us.

"Shit, this is really interesting." Micky Kruze looks shocked and confused and somewhere between betrayed and triumphant.

"South Pines is a middle-sized, 126-bed facility. It is rated satisfactory by the state Board of Licensure. It is not-for-profit, regulated by a voluntary board loosely affiliated with the Methodist Church. It is relatively clean, usually understaffed, appallingly dull, and not where I would want to live for very long. The food is tedious and usually cold. The staff, when there, are a mix of everything from Mother Teresa to the Gestapo, and sometimes that is one person on a good or bad day.

"I made some great friends living there. My closest friends' names I have changed, for their sakes. Angela just recently got her first motor chair. She has lived in institutional care since her family all died. She was thought severely mentally retarded until a few years ago. During an emergency hospitalization she was tested by a physician and referred to the Access to Life Center, an independent living center for people with disabilities, for peer group support. She now goes out regularly to meetings and classes. These changes have been resisted by the staff and have caused Angela some trouble.

"Bonnie has also lived a long time at South Pines. She was placed there by family after what they considered a reckless marriage failed. Like Angela, Bonnie has congenital cerebral palsy, making movement and speech somewhat difficult. Bonnie has tagged along with Angela to her meetings, and talks dreamily of leaving the nursing home.

"Steve has lived there since an injury in his late teens. He is studious and thoughtful and supremely bored, but has set up a fairly rich inner life to sustain him despite his fears of the world outside. It would be some time before he considered moving out, if ever. As a double amputee and quadriplegic, his concerns about getting adequate care are very pressing.

"Boredom is the watchword of life in an institution. All the day is planned around the possibility of eating and socializing. Much of the residents' time is spent simply sitting and staring.

"Angela told me that she had spent sixteen years sitting and staring. Since her work with the independent living center she has had outside tutoring and classes to develop reading skills that have allowed her to speak using a letter board. This is most unusual. Many people who never learn to read as children have a very difficult time developing this skill as an adult. Yet Angela, and her friend Tom, who is mentally retarded, have worked intensively with their volunteer tutors to learn reading and writing. Angela says she is through sitting and is taking art classes and reading classes, regularly attends peer meetings, and visits the Computer Center for the Disabled at the public library.

"Bonnie says that she used to drag Angela's chair from place to place to give her a change of scene. Bonnie, being more mobile, has always been as social as one can be at South Pines. She volunteers to move people around for activities such as bingo, card games, visiting acts, and parties given once a month. Bonnie moves slowly backwards with another chair in tow, usually one of the older residents.

"Steve reads, writes occasionally, watches tons of TV, and meditates. He has regular contact with family. He enjoys a visit when he is out sunning. He is a quiet person. He is watchful and will not let an unkindness or an injustice go unnoticed. He knows how far he can push staff and is keenly aware of the sharp edge of retribution.

"What is so bad about a life where you are cared for and have time for bingo? Many many things.

"In a nursing home, if you are relatively immobile, your day begins with the aide coming in after shift change, around 6:30 a.m. She flips on the TV and the light and pulls out your clothes, her choice. Off come your covers, and if you are in luck you get a chilly bed bath. If staff are short you may wait in bed several hours and not have a bath for a day or more. More luck is a once-a-week whirlpool bath. These necessities are scheduled, but staffing problems foul up schedules regularly.

"If you make it out of bed, you are dressed and stuck in the hall for an hour. That is so your roommate can go through the same procedure, and the aide can change your bed without you underfoot. There are usually too few aides expected to care for too many people. They are pressured by other staff and by many residents. They are often angry about their lot and can take it out on the most vulnerable residents.

"If you can move yourself, you head for the elevator. There are only two in a three-story building containing over 100 non-ambulatory or semi-ambulatory people. It could take most of the hour to get down to breakfast. If you can't move, you hope for a Bonnie or a freed-up aide to take heed. The very ill or completely immobile are fed in bed, or in some cases require skilled care such as tube or IV feedings.

"Breakfast, like most meals, is dull to adequate: dry or hot cereal and milk, with occasionally scrambled egg or fruit. People who would need to be fed usually get hot cereal. You often have to ask several times before you might get hot cereal if you self-feed. There always seems to be an unexplainable gap between what people ask from dietary and what they get. While residents are regularly polled about their preferences, results of these surveys rarely reach the table.

"Very little happens between breakfast, which could occur any time between 8:30 and 9:30 a.m., and lunch, which could occur anytime from 11:30 a.m. to 1:30 p.m. This variance was also never explained. Often people gathered in the dining hall, after four hours of vegetating, and waited another hour for trays to arrive from 20 feet away. The same thing happens at dinner time. Between lunch and dinner there are opportunities for bingo, cards with friends, or sometimes someone will share a video with others. Steve will occasionally send out a relative for videos on a special long-lend basis if there are to be parties or outside entertainment.

"Dinner is the light meal. It is often soup and a sandwich. Peanut butter and bologna are not very appealing at 6:00 p.m. Many non-ambulatory people end up in bed promptly after dinner. One young friend often was in bed by 6:30. Imagine a 21-year -old man having to be in bed for over 12 hours a day. He didn't have to stay long, luckily. He is now thriving in a foster home.

"The residents do not have an ideal existence, but neither do the staff. The majority of staff are aides and housekeepers who are underpaid; thus, many of them do not have a serious feeling about their work. This is unfortunate, because those few who do are remarkable people that offer their charges a real sense of family. A man who can kick a football is paid millions a year; a woman who stays in the night holding the hands of desperately ill or dying people is paid the minimum wage or pennies over it.

"This disregard for the caregiving worker can lead to some serious abuses. Turnover is constant and rapid in many such facilities. Poor training and rare upgrading of skills leave both the worker and the resident in dangerous circumstances. Lack of communication abilities on the residents' and the workers' parts can make day-to-day needs requests real problems. Lack of affirmation leaves workers burnt out and exhausted.

"Sad to say, the poor pay scale and desperate need for staff not only contribute to high turnover, but also admit questionable workers. Several residents have described abuses by staff which were vicious, intentional, and in some cases permanently damaging. Residents have been beaten, unnecessarily restrained, locked in closets or storerooms, and inappropriately medicated. Nonverbal residents have been repeatedly raped, and threatened with secret retaliation if they managed to report the assault.

"This does not include the accidents which happen to residents due to staff rushing and being pressed for time, and the negligence of poorly-trained workers. Our culture throws together two groups of devalued people and expects them to help each other survive. Many people with disabilities are now saying it is the responsibility of these facilities to improve their internal culture massively, or go the way of the dinosaurs.

"TOMORROW: Disabled activists are angry. Can they alert the nation to make changes?

"FRIDAY: Alternatives to institutional care. What are they? Are they working? Who benefits?"

Chapter 30

The P.A.I.L. group asked that as many of us from South Pines that could, please come to the next meeting. It seems that some people who act as advocates of disabled people, mostly people considered retarded, will be there to ask us questions.

Marie and I board the usually late van with no problems and are on our way. She leans in her chair as we round the corner.

"Onnee, wah dey wanna tawk bout?"

I shrug as we arrive.

" Is George coming?" hollers Madge, an earlier arrival.

"No, Mawj, he feewin bah." Marie returns.

"Idn't he always?" she rips back, then wheels her chair back through the door.

We all ramp up, another van behind us with folks from another home.

The meeting room is crammed. We are chair to chair, three to four deep all around the tables. Near the door is a group of new faces, six walkers and two chair people. Other new faces are gathered round the table.

Sarah opens the meeting by announcing that six visitors in front are with Now People, an advocacy group who want first-hand accounts from people in Millie's article and others in similar circumstances. Three others are state representatives and a Congress member.

I notice Duncan sitting quietly and intently in one of the back rows. Micky and a guy I don't know are with him.

Sarah introduces Mr. Maloney, state representative; Mr. Krantz, state representative; and Ms. Rapier, Congressional representative. After introductions Sarah says, "Now Representative Maloney will ask some questions."

"Thank you for letting me come. Right to the point, how many of you consider yourselves "at risk of institutionalization"?

All but about three raise hands, including Fred even though his insurance and extended family provide major buffers against incarceration.

"This never occurred to me. You are just a few representing a big group of people. Several of us are working toward developing legislation which would provide support in your home if you have a developmental disability."

Madge is making noises. I crane in an attempt to see her, and catch a glimpse of Ted holding her cigaretted hand in the air.

"We would like to hold questions until the end."

Madge continues her assisted wavings, and blurts, "Why only developmental disability? Many of us at risk of institutionalization, like Fred and me, are people with injuries gotten after age 21. Are we getting stiffed by your law?"

Mr. Krantz notes, "There is a program offering attendant-care subsidies for people who want to live at home." He did his homework, now preaches to the choir.

"Yeah, and there is a two-year waiting list at best. I know, I've been on it two years and now I'm told that it could be two more. It is always two years. I want out, I am going nuts in that hellhole and I don't care who knows it."

Ted leans over her with tissues. She is pissed. "I live in that place described in the articles. You ought to try it. No privacy, no food, stuff stolen, no money, can't get anywhere. Driving me nuts!!"

"Ah wuh lah to ay sominh," Andrew pipes up from his corner. It is now obvious that Maloney and Krantz recognize him.

"Yes, Mr. Duncan?"

Andrew punches Micky who translates for him when the words get tough.

"Everyone in this town is at risk of institutionalization, as long as there are such institutions. I would suggest that you look at the root of this problem, the existence of such places. Start there."

"Mr. Duncan, do you have suggestions or alternatives to institutional care?" Ms. Rapier asks.

"Your attendant-care program and your proposed in-home support bill are a good start. If we ever achieve national health coverage, these issues must be included first, before the institutions get their chunk. The way that Medicaid was set up, it is obvious that the medicos, legislators, insurers, and business interests worked hand in glove to ensure that the institutions would always get the biggest bite of Medicaid money. That mechanizes the truly poor, as disabled people usually are, right into institutions with no recourse. Cut off that drainage and turn the money over to support people in their homes. For a quarter of the cost you will have accomplished the death knell for these types of institutions."

"Mr. Duncan, what about people, old people without family? These people often benefit from living in a community setting," Mr. Maloney asks Andrew.

"There are better ways to provide community. There are self-chosen and -governed communities. There are familial communities. There are group-living situations based on a home model, which could be more economical and healthier places to live. Few people thrive in the nursing-home setting. Often people do in self-chosen communities."

Mr. Krantz has been rapidly writing. He looks up.

"Mr. Duncan, I am sure you are aware of the strong long-term-care organization which lobbies for continued and increased Medicaid dollars in effective ways."

"Yeah, so?"

"How do you expect legislators like me to counter their very strong pull on state government? There is no counterforce from your quarter who can equally influence the legislature or governor."

"Down to the dollars, eh, Dick?"

"Excuse me, I didn't catch what you said."

227

"He said, 'Down to the dollars, eh, Dick?'" yelled Madge, who was continuing her steaming. "And that is what it is about. Those people suck the money off old people, and the government, and then they use their profits to come sucking up to people like you, so that they can keep the flow going. And that is what it is about! It's not about people and hurting and being scared, and wondering where your next meal will come from, or if your current aide hates you, or if you'll ever get a decent bath again! NO!!"

In a much cooler tone, Andrew continues, "It's about what you will get out of it, right? How can people stuck in prisons get out to lobby against the very people they depend on for food and care. Yes, the long-term-care people have both our groups over a very large barrel. What is each of us going to do?

"Well, we are going to get your ears, just like here today. And we are going to persist in telling you our side of the story, because we have no money to bribe you, nor contracts to award you or yours, nor ways to wine and dine you and win you over. But you will hear what we have to say!"

Ms. Rapier seems impatient with the somewhat slow progress of Duncan's impassioned speech, but Mr. Krantz hangs on every word.

"Do you speak for everyone here, Mr. Duncan?" Ms. Rapier asks.

"No, I speak for myself. All here are capable of speaking on their own behalf. For example, my friend Emily Mason may not be able to literally speak for herself, just as many people don't believe that I can, but that won't stop us any more. Emily, do you want always to live in an institution?"

There he is staring at me. His eyes are jabbing blue darts into me and he asks me the question I've always been afraid to ask me. Why does he put me on the spot this way? Why in front of all these people? I look at Krantz, Rapier, back at Andrew. I can't panic, no. He expects me to say something important, to show them I don't want to live like I have for seventeen years. How can I?

Ted comes next to me. My beanie light hits the board. He

reads as I beam at the letters.

"NO I WANT LIVE LIK ANY 1. NEVER HAVE. DONT NO HOW. WANT TO LERN. SCARD. WANT BE REDY." I look right into Rapier's eye with my beam pointer.

"Ms. Mason, if you learned how to live out of an institution, do you honestly think you could survive on your own?"

"NO 1 LIVES ON ON. EVEN PEPUL ALON DEEP END ON JOBS OR FRENS OR KIN OR HARD HELP. DO YOU DO ALL ON YER ON?"

"Well, of course not, Ms. Mason. But you need so much assistance. How can you justify obligating others to take care of that for you?"

"DO YOU FIX ON CAR? DO ALL HOUSE WERK? KEEP JOB? LAW WERK TOO? RAZ BABYS? GRO AND MAK ALL FOOD? YOU SPEC TO PAY OTHERS TO HELP YOU."

"Yes, but I earn my money to pay for those services!"

The crowd goes wild.

"PEPUL WITH NO JOB SHUD ALL LIVE INSTITUSHUN?"

"Yes, let us return to the poorhouses and debtors' prisons of the eighteenth and nineteenth centuries. Those are the direct ancestors of our current system," Andrew throws that one out as my head sinks in weariness.

"These points are well taken. I hope that everyone will give them consideration. There are some situations which people here are enjoying that we would like for you to hear about," Sarah quietly pulls the meeting to order and calls on Tracey and Clare and Nancy to describe their homes.

When they finish, five new people tell about their family-originated supported-living home, which is partially overseen by a local agency. They mention that three residents work outside the home and the other two work in the home. They have four constantly rotated support staff who handle any things that residents cannot accomplish. The residents point out that their living costs, to which they contribute, run only $12,000 per year, as opposed to up to $60,000 in certain institutions.

Well, Sarah saved me from really sounding like Duncan. But I realize that I have to look at this decision that I am too scared to think about. I would like to live out. I don't want to be alone. I am not equipped or cut out for it. But with no family, how could I get a group like that one to accept me?

There are more war and success stories told, as Mr. Krantz gets writer's cramp from notetaking. Then Sarah adjourns and reporters circle to ask individuals questions.

Duncan wheels over to my chair. He looks me in the eye and takes my left hand. No words. I feel he knows what I am thinking. I beam onto, "HOW, U TELL ME?" I know he feels my hand shaking.

"Could I come over to your place to talk one day? Maybe we could wheel over to that little café on Avonton Road for lunch. Wednesday, 11:30, OK?"

I beam Yes. He wheels away into the crush of chairs.

Did I accept what they call on TV a date? Or was this strictly business? I am doing a little in-chair jig. I feel ten times more nervous than usual.

"Onnee, wha you n Andwu tawkin bout?" Marie has come up beside me.

"NOT MUCH," I beam in return. She seems so edgy, matches my case of nerves.

"You tawkin bout levin? Bout levin ol Ma wee behin?"

If I leave, I would be leaving her, George, Ted. Friends. Does she want to leave? Could she be concerned that I was talking to Andrew?

Chapter 31

Wednesday. It is 11:30 a.m. The first-floor window overlooks the bus stop. I find that I am just rocking my chair slightly, revving to get going. I am in a pacing mode but would rather not use up the battery. With this energy buzz I was able to override Judy's clothing decisions. I got her to pull my blue-green sweater. The new lower mirror in the can backed up my decision. Right color with my hair. Makes it look redder, maybe even curlier. I snuck Edna's lighter lipstick. Judy didn't notice as she applied it grudgingly.

The bus. Jerry comes out of the elevator, great timing. I get in and down in no time flat. As I roll out Andrew rolls in the patio door.

"Yo, Em. You are looking hot."

He gives an appraising stare, and lightly limply shakes one hand. I am feeling distinctly hot.

"You have to sign out or something?"

"ALL DONE." I find my light beam quite hard to control. It wants to wander all over the board, like Tinkerbell.

"Lets skip."

Since I go out on my own to art class and reading class, I am used to going and signing out early and splitting. I have been taking little detours on the way to class. I recognize a few neighbors, and I am recognized. It feels great to roll down the streets in my mean blue machine. Sometimes I just throw her into high and sail. What a rip! I feel like that now.

But we single file down the narrow street lined with little shotgun houses, all trim and manicured. We turn onto the side street, and then down a smooth alley to Avonton Road. Up the curb cut onto the walk busy with lunchers seeking out the various restaurants. So am I. Our goal is the little café near the bookstore. The makeshift ramp makes do up the front step.

"Hey, Andrew, good to see you. You and your lady friend have a seating preference? The front table is free."

"Thanks, Bill. How's Evie?"

"Real good, in back slinging soup. She does her specialty on Wednesday."

Bill, the owner, I guess, takes the chairs from the front table, in the window. He gestures us there and we take our places near the plants looming in the window seat.

"What can I get you folks, drinks while you think?"

"A coke, Em? Tea or milk? Coke?"

I smile on the coke and its repetition. Don't get them much at home. Never at meals, and the machines are 75 cents and too far up to put it in when I have it.

"Cokes, please, and straws."

"Sure, be right back."

At this point I begin to panic. I am here, now how the hell am I going to eat? With just me and Andrew? Maybe I'll just drink the coke. I can't sit in this window and make a mess.

"You OK, Em? You are looking pale."

Tinkerbell, get it together. I struggle to beam, "HOW EAT?"

"No sweat, we'll manage what we can together."

"HOW IN WINDO, PEPUL SEE!?"

"So, people eat in this window every day, and people see them."

"NOT LIK ME. MESS."

"Lay off. People like you, with hands, heads, mouths. They all eat in this window. You know people with faces, noses, eyes. People with really pretty green eyes. Pretty green eyes. Every day. People like that eat. Here."

"Excuse me, folks, here are your menus."

"Oh, Bill, let us have your special burger plates, fancy cut with home fries and slaw."

232

Bill has no problem with Andrew's speech which he is boosting by using my board. He is sitting quite close in order to use my board. Quite close as we talk. He has on a dark blue sweater and his hand moves near mine as he uses my board.

"I have gotten the impression that you would like to move now?"

"NOT SHURE, MAYBE. NO WER TO GO."

"Yeah. Seemed at the meeting that you liked the shared living idea. Those folks said some nice things about how they live."

"U NO THEM? ANY OTHER U NO?"

"Not around here. Most are out west, and are self-supporting. These family and subsidized groups are new. You want to keep your eyes open for possibilities."

He takes my hand and squeezes as he exaggerates opening his eyes. Bill sets down our plates with the burgers cut into bite-size pieces and cut-up wedges of potato steaming beside. He puts down extra napkins, and spoons for the salad. We must be a sight as Andrew slowly and carefully puts burger pieces in my mouth, and gives the necessary wipes in between. The sandwich is delicious and tender and tomatoey. Oh, heavenly. Not much chat as we concentrate on the luscious food. Andrew focuses his arm movements to time with my head moves. We manage.

As I slowly chew a crisp but mealy potato bit, Andrew huffs and shakes his head.

"To think those damn fools at S.P. have been feeding you lousy pap for years when you could have been slipping down here for a BillBurger special. Damn, what a loss."

"DONT MAK ME LAFF. MAK BIG MESS. TO MUCH FUN HERE."

We do get some weird looks from passersby. By now I figure it's their problem. One couple did ask Bill to be moved to the back of the place. Andrew asked when Bill refilled our cokes.

"Their problem, Duncan. You bring in folks, and you send me business. I never saw that couple before. Maybe they'll get educated, huh?"

"Slow going."

233

I watch as Andrew grasps a burger bite with care in an angled gesture, moving to make sure the tomato and sauce are stable. He looks in my eyes and nods, I blink back my readiness and baby-bird the bite. He smiles and moves to his plate.

"Don't you think that this is a better way to live?" he says, offering me my straw.

As I sip, I take in a bit of caution. Is this lovely "date" just a sales job? Is he interested in me, or in my furthering his cause? The ideal succumbs to the real. My floating balloon seems to have lost a lot of its gas.

"Living out on your own is not just more cost-effective. On your own you could choose your own friends. You could do what you want."

My beam skips around the crumbs and juice bits as I gauge my answer with care.

"I DO WHAT WANT NOW."

"Oh, do you? Think more about that one."

His smile is gone and he is looking right into my eyes. Its a great effort to beam back to the board.

"HOW GET CARE? SCARS ME."

"I take it you mean personal care?" He frowns as he fingers a potato into lift-up position.

"With the Medicaid I can get an agency aid in sometimes twice daily, who does bathing and clothes and food for me. And now I hire my own under the Attendant Program."

"HOW YOU FIND?"

"Ads, word of mouth, theft. The pay ain't great. Good people are hard to find and keep. They get stolen. Besides, I'm a son-of bitch to work for."

I can believe that. He sees my agreement in my eyes. We both laugh.

"I guess I feel kinda responsible about friends making the decision to leave an institution. But I know its better. I am proof. Neither can I make or interfere in that decision for you or any-one. It is hard. It is frightening."

So here I am sitting in a café window, my hand held by a man with intense blue eyes. I am thinking things I could not have even conceived of two years ago. I am wondering what I want, what he wants. I am wondering what could really be.

"Are you cold in this window?"

Blink blink.

"Your eyes are great. I had the best cat once with such green eyes. She was the prettiest yellow cat and she'd sit in my lap and purr. I loved to just stroke her fur. Are you too warm?"

Blink.

"Bill, a couple more cokes, please?"

I knock a slurp out of my glass as I maneuver my head to the straw. Andrew reaches with a napkin, dabbing off my sweater, then my chin. His hand moves choppily, but with a studied grace. He leans back to check his work and moves close to dab my cheek, and closer to reach my left eye. When I open my eyes he is smiling, then looks away quickly.

"When do you have to be back?"

"SUPPER TIME," I spell around the coke. "NO LOSS."

As we head back to South Pines, I am wondering what this all means. Seemed like more than a pep talk about leaving home. I am certainly flustered. I don't want to believe what is lurking in the back of my mind. Does he think of me, or am I just being buttered up for his agenda? I would love to feel safe and wish I could trust him.

We reach the patio, just away from the view by the windows. Andrew turns his chair parallel to my right. He takes my hand in a way that implies it was my idea.

"I really enjoy your company, Em. I would like to spend some time with you. To help you if you want to move, but, well, just to be with you, too. What do you think?"

He leans very close toward me, lifts my hand, and kisses it.

He is gone.

Chapter 32

*I*t is dark in my room. The night light blew around eleven. I sure can't sleep. I have no box to fit this day in. No compartment to contain it. I am feeling too many different feelings at once. It is like there are several Emilys in the bed with me, all sitting crowded together, each one having a separate emotion to cope with, and none of the group can reach any consensus.

I can remember when years ago I would go into my dream place and pretend that I was like the normal girls and had lovers and they would take me places and we'd talk and we'd love like what I saw on TV.

It wasn't the stuff like Jo did. Not ugly and rough with fighting and screaming and hitting. And it had nothing to do with those horrible tearing, bone-jamming struggles in the kitchen on the floor with nasty old Sam. I'd be left bleeding with joints all askew and out of whack. Jo'd just say my period had come early, and never mentioned the cuts or bruises. Nor was it like the sickening sleazy wrestling with Rawly and the others in the basement. I'd be left in the hall in an inconspicuous place just hurting and full of hate.

No, this was another galaxy. So far away and so unrelated. It was something gentle, tender, soft, yet exciting. But I knew it was all pretend, and always would be.

So one of the Emilys says, forget it kid. That is not for you. It is just a dream. Watch out. It is just dangerous and you will get hurt.

Another Emily says, don't listen to her! You could have a lover, too. You could have that American dream, a lover, a husband, even a family, and a home. It would be different, but it would be yours.

The first Emily laughs a nasty laugh. When have you ever seen that really happen? It doesn't even happen for normates, so how could gimps have such a life. Look at the aides. Look at all the horror stories they tell about their lovers, their families. Do you want such messes? It is bad enough as it is. Forget it.

A third Emily cynically chimes in. Duncan is just a user. He is spreading on the sugar so you'll dance to his tune. He has to have guinea pigs to show off to the powers-that-be. You'd be a great show-and-tell. He doesn't care about you. Don't you believe it.

The second Emily wants so badly to believe the best. Andrew, she says, is a gentle caring man. When have you ever seen a man share a meal with a woman with such care and sensitivity? He has beautiful exciting eyes. They tell such fine things to me. I want to know more of the stories of his eyes. I want to know the textures of . . .

Will you just stop that shit, Emily-one shrieks. Don't let her slide into that dangerous muck. She will sink and can never be saved. This would just complicate any wish she might have to move out on her own.

Don't make me laugh, Emily-three pipes up, she will never move out on her own. She's satisfied here and knows she'd rather not take the risk. Like George says, it would be foolish to think that They would be willing to make life livable when life is only lived on Their terms.

The TV just went on. It must be 5:00 a.m. Edna is so regular. Above us an energetically square woman lifts her right heel and bends her knee as she leans like some automaton into the motion. "Three more, that's good, two, one, and switch." The music chunka chunkas on as she leans to the left to repeat. I realize that I fell asleep in the middle of a committee meeting. Apparently no resolution was reached in my absence, but I dreamed that it was. Or was it?

There was a big house near a lake. Most of the P.A.I.L. people and several from here all seemed to be living together in or near this great house. Inside it all looked like a big circle, with rooms all around the circle. Andrew and I were giving a cookout. Bill, the café man, was doing the grilling and people were sunning near the water. Some were swimming. Then there were suddenly ambulances everywhere and people being put on stretchers and taken away. I was scared and started rolling down the road as fast as I could, until the TV music started.

After breakfast, a nice slice of toast and some juice, Ted comes over to my table in his kitchen whites.

"Emy, can we talk for a bit in the Lounge after I am through with cleanup?"

"SURE," I beam, as he smiles and takes my empty dishes.

The Lounge isn't really crowded this morning, so I go as near the light from the windows as I can get. It feels warm as the very early spring sun pokes in. I find that my committee meeting is continuing anytime I have time to myself. The Emilys take seats all around me and begin their tirades again. But Ted comes in pretty quickly and practically skips over to my chair.

"Emy, I have news, and since none of this coulda been without you, I want you to hear about it first."

I beam a question, "WITH OUT ME?" as he smiles like the sunshine.

"Emy, I talked to the People Now group. A member of their group home moved out on his own in January. They asked me to think about moving in with them. I can get a real job, now that I can read a little. There is a job like mine, at the Oaken Pail Restaurant, which I am going to interview for Friday. I will have a job coach for three months and then if I do OK the job is mine alone. I will move next month, if I get the job and do OK. I am so excited."

I am amazed. Ted is one person who has completely changed from the way I that I had thought he was. People said he was stupid, and couldn't think and didn't care. But the Ted I have gotten to know is a careful planner, a hard studier, and always willing to lend a hand. How can the world be so stupid, and unthinking and uncaring?

"I AM PLEEZED 4 U. U ARE A GOOD GUY, A HARD WORKR. I WILL MISS U. VERY MUCH."

"I have to thank you and Casey. It was learning to read that made me believe I can do a job good. I am so excited. I am packing my stuff. But I will come back to visit my good friends here. Don't you worry."

Ted runs out with a wave. He will be going down to help with lunch now. His only real break is after 7:00 p.m. He has worked here from six in the morning till seven at night, with an hour at ten and at three, six days a week for over ten years. He never complained or questioned. He just did it and learned. He deserves the very best situation he can find. I am really pleased for him.

I am even a bit jealous. No, I am a lot jealous.

At lunch the word is out. Nancy resentfully cuts up my fried chicken as the talk heats up.

"Onnee, ah her Ted mowin ouh! Dat rih?"

"Oh, God, no, have the crazies even gotten to poor old looney Ted?"

Marie and I both look shocked daggers at George. I've never heard him say a cutting thing about any resident that was so untrue or unkind. He realizes his slip and apologizes.

"Yeah, I am sorry. It is just that you people are all losing your grip or something, just because you keep going to those damn meetings. And I am angry and worried, especially about you, Em. You are being taken in by that slimeball Duncan. Don't fall for his line. He is shifty and sly and full of tricks. Just you watch out. I saw him come for you yesterday. What kinda hanky panky is this about?"

I glance at Marie. She looks stricken. I realize that all her flirting and silliness aside, she must really feel something for Andrew, too. She looks back at me as if at a traitor, or a rival to be vanquished. I feel like cheese on a hot sandwich, stuck between two steaming slices and melting.

❖❖❖

My window is bright with the springtime sunset. But I am alone, since Marie has been avoiding me all day. Life was once so simple, sitting here measuring the pace of the shadow on the roof. Now it is getting really complicated. Ted is leaving. George and Marie are mad at me, and I am wondering what I am wanting.

It is Tuesday. It was a cold weekend. Blackberry winter, both outside and in. The prickles were in evidence everywhere, and the winds blew ill and chill. I spent a lot of time alone in my window with the Emilys arguing and debating. Marie spent time in another part of the building. George took to his bed, and had the door pushed to most of the weekend. Only Ted, Judy, and Leena said anything to me all weekend.

George comes down for breakfast Monday. While we each sit in our usual places, little is said, nothing is asked. I go back upstairs to my window. At 9:30 I see a bus stop up at the corner. Someone gets out. My heart skips a beat because it might be Andrew. As the figure wheels toward the patio gate, I zoom to the elevator. One is marked out of order. And the other is locked down for loads. Oh, crap. I begin the long and arduous journey all the way to the other end of the building. I know it will take forever to thread my way down the obstacle course of skilled wing. But I have no other alternative. Little by little, I wind my way around the sleeping or semi-conscious figures parked in the hallway as their rooms are cleaned. Meds carts, tray carts. It feels like climbing Mt. Everest must, as I desperately push forward. I wait for my page. Halfway down the hall, I still haven't been called. Hope there is nothing wrong. Maybe Andrew stopped to talk with someone. Please, would you move out of my way?

I have never gone on so long a journey, but two tray carts more and I'll be through to the north wing. The door swings open at the hands of an entering orderly. I am struck to discover that there are two gurneyed patients blanketed heavily and waiting for the elevator to take them down to a waiting ambulance. I am low priority. I am getting crazy.

I wait for the two trips to be made on the small north elevator. It seems like years. Oh, please hurry.

Finally. I get on the elevator and endure its astonishingly slow progression downward. Out the door, I head through the maze outside the kitchen area. Luckily most of the tray carts are at rest now, and I only have to dodge a few to get nearer the cafeteria. There is a terrible commotion going on down the hall near the patio door. Someone is really giving somebody a verbal pasting, and who knows what all else. I am shocked at the level of the raised voices. As I round the last tray cart, I am devastated to see through the cafeteria glass that it is George and Andrew. Even though I gun the blue machine on high, I don't reach the patio door before Andrew has taken a very hasty leave. I try to shout as the outer door shuts behind him. He's gone. No one will open the inner door for me, even though I bang my chair against it several times. I turn on George.

"Eeep ou, Eeep ou na ifh!" I try to scream out my rage. He *should* keep out of my life. I'll listen to his advice, but I'll make my decisions. I am too upset to spell anything. I try to bang his chair with mine. On my second try, Jerry comes running down the hall and pops the clutches on my chair. He manually pushes me back to the now usable elevators, and he takes me upstairs to my room.

"I am sorry, Emily, but you have no business trying to attack George like that. You will stay in here with your clutches disengaged for a while, until you can get your cool back. I can't figure out what has gotten into you. You used to be the sweetest girl here."

Shit, I'll sweetest girl you, you rat. Who should have been stuck in his room is that stuck-up snake George. Who the hell does he think he is, scaring my friends away? Of course, after I let out the steam in that outpouring of rage, Jerry hasn't understood a noise I made and is long since gone down the hall. I dance with hatred against my velcros. I flail and screech. I feel so stuck and helpless. A sweet girl is a stuck girl. All in the eye of the beholder.

So for the rest of Monday, except for meals, I sit in my room with my chair out of commission. Which is worse, this or Neeley's closet? Tomorrow is my P.A.I.L. day, and I have some serious questions to ask.

So Tuesday of blackberry winter, I board my bus for the Center. Of all people, Madge Stark boards with me. We try to chat as we jostle against the lock-downs.

"I know it ain't none of my business, Em, but rumor is all over the house that you and Duncan are an item. They also say that you are going to get yourself in a hell of a mess and won't be able to come back to S.P. cause they won't let you. Is any of that shit true?

"NO."

" Ah, c'mon, you can tell old Madge. You sweet on Duncan?"

"ANDRU IS FREND, OK?"

"Well, I heard more. And I heard that George was on the warpath and that he gave Duncan a really big piece of his mind. Now, you know George has been sweet on you for years, and yet you'd go shaft him for that crazy old hippie."

My face must be several shades of hot new designer colors. I am being tossed news that is news to me. I have always thought George was my friend. But he never said anything more than that. He's always been kind and generous with me. But I thought that was our friendship. I don't believe that he can see Andrew as a rival. Oh, brother. A rival for what?

As we wheel into the Center, I stop at the front desk and ask to speak with Sarah before she starts the group. She comes up to the front desk from the meeting room.

"CAN WE TALK WHILE TODAY ALONE?"

"I have a half hour break between groups. Will you share my lunch with me then?"

"YES THANK U."

The group is unusually small today. There are some of the usuals, especially Fred, Nancy and Clare, Jenny Fanish and Sandy Scott and, of course, Madge. There are two new people. One lives in a nursing home, and one at Community Health, where the big protest took place last year. Barry says that he really has wanted to come down to get to know the people that had the guts to get out and demand their rights. He had been on the sidelines and was very surprised when all the commotion occurred.

My own inside group is not letting me pay much attention to the topic, or to comments that are made. There is too much argument going on. I just want to get on to talk with Sarah. As soon as group breaks up I head down the hall to her office. She follows with two sodas, a paper bag, and a cup. I tuck up to her desk and she shuts the door and turns off the phone. I begin to spell as she pours soda into a cup with a straw and breaks up a half sandwich of pimiento cheese.

"GEORGE MAD AT ANDRU, MESS AT HOME. ALL MAD AT ME."

"Emy, help me here. Are you saying that George is mad at Andrew, and this is a mess at home because everyone is mad at you?"

"YES. I TALK TO A. ALL SP FREND MAD AT ME. G. YELL AT A. SAY A. JUST USE ME MOVE OUT. TELL HIM NEVER COME BACK"

"How do you feel about this? Do you like Andrew? Does he like you?"

"I NOT SURE. NEW FEELINGS, SCARY"

"Maybe you need to talk to Andrew a bit and clear this up for yourself."

She gives me some sandwich and takes a munch herself, knowing that our time is short.

"It sounds to me like George is jealous, but is afraid for your safety at the same time. I know Andrew pretty well, Emily. He is a bit showy, but unlike most people who have never gotten much attention, he uses his need to be noticed to call attention to things that other people need. I have never seen him use anyone just to further those aims. He is always careful about people's readiness for involvement. Personally I find Andrew to be rather shy and close with his feelings. He jokes a lot about politics and bureaucracies, but he is serious about what he considers important.

"I don't know George very well. But I recognize and I understand, as well as I am able, about the fears he has for himself, and for you. The one thing that is certain in life is change. Another real certainty is that no one likes change. Most of us will do all that we can to keep things going just about the same, even if that same is not so great. Change is too scary to take on. And yet it is inevitable. You know what I mean? It is bound to happen."

She tips the last of the soda into my cup and offers me the straw.

"Maybe George is very afraid of all the changes you have made. Maybe he is fearful of his own wishes for change. Maybe it is easy for him to blame all of this on Andrew, so he needed to attack Andrew with all of his anger about you and about himself."

"I CONFUSE. NEW FEELINGS. NOT KNOW G. GELUS. I STILL FEAR MOVE OUT. WANT TO MORE."

"You have grown so much in the past three years. If you want to move someday, I will bet that when you are really ready, you will know, and you will be the one to decide. No one will make that decision for you."

"MY FRENDS ALL MAD AT ME, NO TALK. NO SP STAF TALK MUCH. I MAK ALL MAD AT ME."

"You can't make people mad at you, Emily. If they are mad it is because they need to be mad. They don't understand the changes that are happening to you. As I said, even if things are not so hot, most people will resist changes even to make things better."

"I THINK MARIE GELUS, MAD AT ME."

"Here's a new wrinkle. Does Marie like George, or is she interested in Andrew ?"

"A."

"Is Marie considering moving from S.P.? Do you think that Andrew would use her to further his cause?"

"SHE NOT SAY WANT MOVE. SHE JUST WATCH A. MAD AT ME, MAD AT G. I NOT WANT HURT M."

"Well, Emily, this is a very old sad story when friends become rivals over another person's attention. You'll need to talk this out with Andrew and with Marie. There is bound to be some hurt. I am sorry. If you want to meet with me to talk about things like this again, I'll set aside time just for us. You have a lot of thinking to do, I realize. Oh . . . !"

A quick knock on the door. The door squeaks open. A hand, then Andrew's face, pokes around the knob.

"Oh, I am interrupting, sorry."

"Yes, you are, but I see it's time to get ready for the next group. Andrew, maybe you would meet here a bit with Emily. She has a lot of questions, and perhaps you can help her with some?"

She ought to get an Oscar.

"Well, I'll just run on down to the meeting room. I really didn't expect you today, Andrew. Good to see you."

She scoots out with her soda cans and cane and shuts the door behind. And here I sit with him.

"I tried to see you yesterday. Wanted to see you. I was really, uh, stunned by the welcoming committee. I am sorry I left so fast. I just couldn't listen to what he was saying."

"WHAT HE SAY? I SORRY TO."

Andrew's chair is still by the door. I am next to Sarah's desk. He is looking down during most of our conversation.

"Well, uh, he accused me of, uh, trying to take advantage of you. He was really screaming that too many people have hurt you, have used you, and, uh, that he'd see me dead first."

I don't remember telling George all that much about what has happened to me over the years, but I guess the rumor mill grinds fine, and maybe a lot of people at S.P. know my messy history.

"Have I hurt you, Emily? I haven't meant to."

"NO HURT. U R KIND TO ME."

"Do you feel like I am trying to make you do what you don't want to?"

"NO. ONLY ME MAKE ME DO WHAT I WANT."

"Emily, I am a big mouth who can't talk. I am a show-off with nothing to show. I do have a reputation for being a tease, and for chatting up girls. But, and I hate to admit this, I'm just a lot of hot air. I, uh, always wanted, uh, dreamed of having a friend, a lover, who was, you know, a normal girl. Even us gimps are susceptible to the cultural ideal. Right? I've slung a lot of lines at a lot of women, gimps and straights, in a lot of ports. Haven't been many bites. So I mostly just teased. I don't find myself teasing

245

with you. I really want to be your friend. I probably want much more than that, but maybe I am not ready to let myself wish for that."

I feel like I am watching this from far away, or from outside. I can almost hear the blood rushing through my ears. Maybe I haven't been ready to wish for this either. Or maybe I could never believe I could wish for such a thing to happen.

"If you also want me to go, and to stay away, like George does, please tell me now so that I can go away and try to forget again."

"PLEEZ DONT GO. G. DOES NOT HAVE RITE TO TELL U GO. I WANT U BE FREND, MUCH MORE THAN THAT. I DO."

Chapter 33

I t is Thursday morning. I'm so lucky to be up first. Judy is in top form and she got me out and dressed in no time. I am out here watching a sunrise which aches to be painted. I can almost see the special mixes of colors as I daub and move the brush to get just the shimmering corals and rich pinks below and the deep lavender and violet above. There are soft lilac streaks over a blue patch separating the two colors. I just want to become the colors and let them wash through me like brilliant energies.

Bump!

I blink at Marie, who has bumped the side of my chair. I think that lump under her bathrobe is the axe she has brought to grind. Nope, here it comes.

"Her iz yor ssampoo you gave me Christmas. Tak it back."

First thing she's said to me all week. This isn't going to go well.

"NO, YER GIFT. KEEP IT."

"Don wan no gift from a traitoh."

"NOT TRAYTOR. FREND."

"Andru ony lahk you cuz you thinkn of movin ou. He wount care bout you if you wan stay. Ah bet you! Gawj say so, too."

"U BOTH TO MAD TO MAK SENSE. I SORRY U HURT. NO MEAN TO. I STIL DONT NO MOVE OUT. NOT DESIDE."

Now Marie starts to cry, and I am very sad for her. I think of so many times she has helped me when I have been hurt or sad. Now I can't help her because I am why she is hurt and sad. I try to reach my tissue stash to offer her one, but my left hand has ideas of its own, and there is no convincing it. I try to reach to Marie's arm. She bumps back from my chair.

"No. Traitoh. Noh my fren."

She shuff shuffs away rapidly, sobbing angrily.

At breakfast my table is empty. George, Marie, and Madge are sitting at a new table on the window side of the room. I am alone until Leena asks if I need help with my juice and toast. Toast is cold now, but still tastes fair with a bit of strawberry jam.

"Since you been chewing, you've put on a little weight. No, it looks nice on you. It ain't enough for the floor aides to complain. You just look better lately."

Long pause, while I have a big swig of juice.

"Hear you have a sweetie."

I look daggers at her with my toast on hold.

"You don't have to look so mad. I seen him before. I think he's kinda cute with that curly gray hair. George tells me that he's no good for you. He wants you to go live with him and it would be dangerous."

"GEORGE FULL SHIT."

"Well, Emily. You don't have to get nasty. I was just telling you what he said."

"HE SHUD MIND OWN BIZNES."

"It is obvious that he is, now, since he has his back to you today. We all thought that George was your sweetie. So this came as a surprise."

"UNLOCK NOW."

"Well, be snippy. I don't care. But mind what you do. You could get yourself in a hell of a fix."

She unlocks my wheels and I make a fast exit. At least I have reading class to look forward to this evening.

Ted and I leave about 4:30 p.m. to take a leisurely walk over to school for our class. We have really been having fun on our own for these classes.

"I did good on my job interview, Emily. The man at the restaurant said that I knew all the equipment and how to use each pan. He told Mr. Brant from the Job Group that I probably could teach my job coach a lot of things. I am so proud."

At our class we have volunteer tutors who work with us after the big class finishes. We get to read from books that interest us. Ted loves to read the easy recipes in many cook books. He even slowly copies down his favorites on little cards and keeps them in a yellow plastic box. He says that's his special file.

I have been reading from books about painting technique. I am never bored to sound out the words around the pictures of paints and beautiful brushes. I am learning more about different painters, too. People have been painting since long before history was written. Ms. Corlett, who tutors me, and who studies art too, said that some of the pictures of animals in my book are thirty- or forty-thousand years old.

This is a good way for people to learn. Mr. Blake who sits near us, likes murder mysteries. He reads out of books by a lady named Christie and one named James. He said the James lady is harder to read, but her stories are very exciting.

Going to class has been my way of coping lately. I am eating alone, when I eat. Well, it is not really alone since Leena or Mira or whoever is usually shoving stuff at me. They aren't able to keep from spooning in opinions with the chow, so that ain't much fun.

But I look forward to my times with Ted, and my classes, and P.A.I.L. That is my social life now. I can't complain. It is a lot better than those years of window gazing. And maybe Sarah is right. I asked her last Tuesday about the continuing chill at S.P.

"You know what I said about change. With Ted getting ready to move, and all the changes you have made, it may be that this chill is your friends' way of preparing for all the hurt and loss that you are all bound to have. Micky told me that when she left B.H. there were more scuffles and feuds there than she had ever noticed before. Everyone was having to adjust for the changes and deal with the pain of letting go. It is sort of like the fussing that goes on in families with teenagers. When the chicks try their wings, all the nestlings are disturbed."

Well, that makes sense but it doesn't make it any easier to lose your best friends.

Today there is to be a big party for Ted. Mrs. Butler, the new social worker, called Sarah about arranging it with her since Ted has so many new friends at the Center. They are all invited, as are his new "family" and everyone here at South Pines.

They asked me to pick out the decorations, since they felt I would know best what Ted likes. We decorated the Dining Hall with green and yellow streamers and balloons. There are yellow flowers on the head table. Ted is not in today. He has been doing some shopping with his new friends, to get ready for his move, so he won't see all of this until he comes for the party.

I hope he won't see any ill feelings between the guests and the residents. I am holding my breath as I see the first buses arrive. I go down by the north wing route to avoid the crowds. As I pull in the north door of the Dining Hall, I see Nancy, Clare, Tracey, Jenny, Mary, and Fred already seated. I wheel in toward them and see Andrew and Casey coming across the patio. No George or Marie yet. I breathe easier.

Casey runs in the south door and rushes up to share a hug. Andrew wheels by me with a winning smile and before he turns he sticks out his tongue just a bit, and wrinkles his nose. I try to pull a face back and Casey laughs at my attempt. We take our places.

Fred pushes his sit-up switch with his chin. As he rises he quips, "Geez, Emily, you are looking really good. Tip top. You in love or something?"

Casey coughs real loud and glares at Fred. I glance quickly at Andrew, who, though nonchalantly looking at the head table, has turned a shade of hot peach. I know my cheeks are burning, too. This is ridiculous.

The tables near us are filling with residents. Mr. Halpern, Genevieve, Rose Maple and her sister-in-law Myrtle, talking without hearing each other, are to our left. Even Mr. Kneble has come down, though he may not know why.

I notice the south door open. Marie, George, and Madge wheel in and take the corner table. The big doors open and Ted comes in followed by Mr. White and the top staff, a surprise there. Also there are his new "family." I recognize one face, but I would like to get to know them all better. I look forward to an invitation to see Ted's new home.

After the head table is full, Mr. White asks Pastor Crane to offer a blessing.

"Let us pray. May the Lord lead each of us on our true path, show each of us our true home, and grant us the grace to give our best in whatever endeavor we are led to. May the Lord bless our brother Ted, and all who have supported him, and all who have shared and will share his home and his life. All by the power of the Holy Spirit, Amen."

I glance up and meet Andrew's eyes. But our connection breaks as the crowd calls, "Speech."

Ted rises hesitantly, but smiles. He knew about this and has been thinking and writing down things to say.

"I am not used to speeching, but I do want to be able to thank everyone here, and everyone who helped make today happen. If I don't say your name, please don't be mad. It is just there are so many to thank.

"Casey, Emily, Sarah, thank you for showing me my confidence. Like the Cowardly Lion with Dorothy in my Wizard movie, I needed 'da noive.'"

As the crowd laughs, Casey leans to Fred. "His favorite film. I bet he has watched it a million times."

"Thank you, Ms. Pelvey, and all you kitchen dudes. You have helped me a lot and taught me a trade."

I notice Ms. Pelvey has a tissue dabbing, up at the head table. Part of the kitchen staff are seated at tables and the rest are leaning out of the tray window and cheering.

"Thanks to all my special friends here, like Mr. Halpern who has books to share on third floor, Grandma Sample who let me read with her, Rose and Myrtle who asked what I had been learning. Special thanks to George, who helped me think, and Marie, who cheered, and dear Madge who is like a sister to me."

Even with Madge's back to me, I see she is feeling his words. I catch George's eyes and blink. He looks away quickly.

"To all my old family here, and to my new family, thank you

251

all for kindness and for a new home. I want you all to come visit me at 2567 Woodferry Road, 555-3265. Thank you."

As Ted sits the room roars with clapping, yelling, stomping, and the noisings of many. A group of the aides, with yellow flowers on their uniforms, wheel in a big cart heavy with gifts. No one minds as Ted takes his time opening and sharing each item. It is great entertainment as he rushes out to kiss or hug every donor, as all are included.

He gets soaps, shampoo, aftershave, socks, treats, and books. I give a cookbook which Sarah helped pick out. His favorite gift is from the kitchen staff. It is a heavy-duty cook's apron and hat. The apron is printed, "If you can't take the heat, stay out of the kitchen."

Ted announces dinner with a flourish, "It's gonna be good. I didn't have to cook it!"

After the unusually delicious meal, the kitchen dudes wheel in a big white cake with chocolate decorations which spell, "Best of Luck, Ted." Interesting that everyone now calls him Ted; Teddy just no longer suits.

There is a social time planned for after dinner. Everyone is welcome to linger in the Dining Hall or on the patio, where the lights are on. It is still light out with summer coming but the lights add a party mood. People have tied balloons on the fence and it looks like a celebration. But the lines are drawn. The P.A.I.L. people are all gathered around the patio tables. Inside the windows I see the old gang sticking together at their side table. Ted has been making the rounds with his new friends, introducing them to everyone. I see him heading out towards our group.

"Everyone, please meet Dan Abrams, Clark Spencer, Frank Smith, and Greg Boland. These are the guys I will be sharing home with. And this is Michael Kraft. He is our staff guy, along with Gary Wright, and Tom Pulaski."

We all do our intros and they pull up chairs to talk.

"You guys better be good to our buddy Ted, or you'll have to answer to me, and I can get really mean." Fred likes to razz people.

"What, no girls, Ted? What kinda place is that to live?"

"Andrew, I will have you know that we have a neighbor home where five very nice women live. We often have dances, and parties, or even video nights. A couple of the ladies work where Frank and Clark do. It is like family." Ted smiles at his new friends, as they nod agreement.

"In fact, Greg and Rita are even talking about getting married and getting a place of their own."

There was just a flicker of light as Andrew caught my eye, for just a second.

"You cold, Emily? I can run in and get your sweater."

I beam No thanks and reassure Casey about my comfort. She must have seen me shiver.

Gradually the guests take their leave of Ted and his friends. Buses come and go. People in the cafeteria wheel out to their destinations. The patio is shadowed where the building is blocking the sun's setting rays. Andrew and I are near the gate just watching the night remnants of Grandma Sample's birds.

"You see. Other gimps are comfortable in seeing each other. They even talk about commitment. Like Ted's new friends.

"U TALKING TO ME OR SELF?"

"Maybe both. Can you bear with me while I try to figure it all out?"

"NOT IN RUSH, GO NOWEAR."

"I am not so sure of that. I feel like things are changing for you."

"FOR SURE, NOT EXPECT!"

Our chairs parallel, we sit facing each other with hands and heads as close as can be, enjoying the cool evening and the waning reddish light on the red and beige roofs across the street.

Bang!!

We both startle and hit heads as the noise hits us. The patio door behind me has opened in a slam. As Andrew is facing that way, he can see the cause.

"I told you to get your ass out of here and never set wheel here again. You're just a mothah-fuckin' trouble-stirrin' radical out to raise sand. I won't have you near Emily. All you want is to get her in trouble and hurt her. I didn't ream you out before because this was Ted's day. But that's over now, so get the hell off this property or I'll call security."

Without a word, Andrew takes my hand and kisses it, then backs and turns toward the patio gate. I haven't looked at George. I hit my stick and follow Andrew to the opened gate, and out.

"Mason, you get the hell back in here. I warn you there's no end to hell out there, and you don't want to go to hell with a loser. Get back in here!"

"Let her go, George. I think she has made a choice."

Ted's quiet words float over the patio wall where we sit at the bus stop.

Chapter 34

*A*t the next P.A.I.L meeting, Micky has an invitation for me.

"I would like for you to spend a long weekend with me, Em. Susan said she would be glad to meet and to work with you, to help me show you the ropes of having an attendant do your personal care."

"SCARED TO LOSE ROOM."

"We know if you're out more than two nights in a row and not hospitalized they confiscate your space. Sarah and I talked with Mrs. Butler. She can't change that, but she suggested that you come to my place early on Friday, stay Friday night and Saturday night, and come back to SP Sunday night late. Three days, two nights, all expenses paid. Good deal? Huh?"

I am all packed. I am shaking like a leaf. I have remembered two sets of underthings, one nice outfit, shampoo, toothbrush. Micky said to pack light, 'cause she'd have anything I forgot. So my backpack is loaded and I have some money. The aides said, "Have a nice vacation, and don't forget to write." Snicker. Mrs. Graven, the older aide on One-South warned me of "things that can happen to girls out on their own for the first time." Maybe I wish I were the 16-year-old she sees in me.

The bus rounds the corner. It is the real bus, and this is my first time. I have my three quarters tight in my hand as the door opens and I back up to the lift. The lip deftly catches my front wheels and up the roller coaster I start. The driver takes my quarters, with a slip of paper, and slowly I maneuver my board down the aisle. I am glad for this junior-width chair. I back into the auto lockdown and pray that I fully engaged it.

The bus is off and I watch the passing traffic. Three stops down another lift request. The passenger pays and, as he heads down the aisle, I recognize Andrew. I can't help laughing. He has on a cap that says Cruise the Caribbean. He locks in next to me.

"Hey, lady. You are sharp today. I don't usually pick up girls on buses, but I spied you from the street and knew right then you were the girl for me. Got any plans for tonight, or – considering what a hot number you are, you may be heavily booked – tomorrow night? Or both?"

"I DONT TALK STRANG MEN. YOU REAL STRANG."

"Oh, c'mon ,cutie. You won't get an offer like this again."

"DID YOU SET THIS UP WITH MICKY?"

"No, suspicious. Micky is not aware that I am making this play for your evening hours. I cannot see you on your territory. I am banished by the king; therefore, I must make desperate attempts when you are freed from your tower. My lady, I wish to be chosen your champion. I will spend any time you choose. I will even play Monopoly with Micky and Susan, just to be in your company."

"RATHER SEE GOOD MOVIE."

"Well, there it is. Publitrans and I will bring coach and four to collect you at 6:00 p.m. for a light repast and an entertainment."

"PLAY MONOPLY OTHER NITE, OK?"

"I really wanted some time with you, Em, because I will be going to Atlanta for a month. We'll be planning strategy for the next actions, in plenty of time to get attention before the Health Care Bill is shaped. DC has to know about the long-term-care racket, and what to do to get it changed."

I hadn't realized what a racket it could be until Millie's articles came out. It made me think that maybe most business is a racket. How can people use others so? I'm thinking this so that I don't have to think about what he just said. He'll be gone a month. Where will I be without his eyes?

It is so sly of Andrew to come with me. I wouldn't have the foggiest idea where to stop. I handed the driver my destination, with my six bits, but that's no guarantee that she'd paid attention. Yet as we approach Springmill Road she calls out my name and stop. When the bus comes to a standstill she comes back and pops our lockdowns, and we roll for the lift, and down.

Micky's apartment is two blocks over, so we take the alley route, as there are no curb cuts on this part of Springmill. The Watchdoggers at the Center have surveyed most of our town and sent the mayor a list of all corners needing cutting. At the rate the changes happen, it will be a long haul.

Micky's building is nice with light bricks and white iron balconies on the upper floors. She is in what they call a "garden apartment," meaning you can see the grass around the patio out back. It is all flush with the ground. No wheel problem.

"Emily, you made it! Ah, I see you brought an escort."

"NO STRANG MAN PICK UP ON BUS. WANT TAK ME OUT NITE."

"You see, all the warnings were right. You get out of that safe place and wolves are everywhere hunting you down. C'mon in and meet Susan."

A tall graceful lady with long dark frizzy hair in thick locks comes over and high-fives with me.

"Great to meet you, Ms. Mason. Mick has told me about you.

"You guys come in and have some brunch with us. We usually have a big brunch, then Susan leaves for classes. She gets back about six."

"What are you studying?" Andrew asks.

"Physical therapy. It is a five-year course, six and a half for an MS. I hope to make the MS. Working with Mick has been great because she arranges our hours around my classes. I'm able to make full-time classes, and still make enough to live on, since I share space with Mick. Next year, my fourth, I'll begin clinical practica and my time will be a lot tighter, but Mick says she thinks we can still work around it."

Susan goes into the kitchen to get our drinks and lunch.

"I'm going to be lost when she graduates in a couple years. I can't believe I'll ever find another Susan. She says she is keeping an eye out for a replacement. She wants to find another PT six-year person, so that I won't have to keep shifting."

"You've got it made, Mick. The turnover for PCA's is like three months. Some folk last a year, but it is rare."

"Maybe so, Andrew. But this has been a deal for me, too," Susan says while arranging drinks and straws. "Where else could I live for six years as a student, study full time, and make a full wage? Besides I have a super place to stay and a really nice boss. She has taught me as much as many of my classes have about living with disability, orthopedic conditions, and practical PT."

After a nice lunch and quick clean-up, Andrew leaves, promising to be back at six, and Susan and Micky give me a tour of the place. The bathroom is neat with a freestanding commode and grab-bars, and a lipless roll-in shower. Micky backs out of the bath and leaves Susan and me.

"If you would like to and have a need, lets demonstrate this room before you guys head out."

"GREAT."

Susan deboards my chair, and with great grace and no hassle transfers me for an easy stop. After carefully positioning and supporting me, she leaves the room, waiting outside for me to call. On her return she shows me the bidet in the commode, and after a freshening up, we are back with Mick. Mick takes a turn.

Susan packs her books to go. "Mick, wish me luck; big exam today."

"I hate to tell you, Em. Susans are rarer than hen's teeth. If you get one, you do everything to keep her. PCA's come in the same assortment as nursing-home aides, and they can burn out just as fast. One thing most of us coming from homes, or very dependent family situations, forget is that we are employers, not children. I have seen so many people act like babies, and then get treated that way. Besides, there are a lot of people working in 'care' who are drawn to it because they like to make others do what they want.

"Let's split. We'll head for the Mall and then Nancy and Clare have invited us at three for tea. They want you to see their place, and it's just two more blocks from here."

The Bonnington Mall is a cavernous place with banners hung way up in huge skylights. We roll down easy carpeted halls poking into shops with everything from pets, to weight lifting stuff, to art supplies. There are department stores and a grocery with everything to sell.

"I love where I live. This place is so close and so accessible. I'd never really have to go anywhere else to shop. The grocery is at the far end. Susan and I get our stuff there on Saturday afternoon. Maybe we can do that tomorrow. Lets grab a coke and then look at what's on sale at Markie's."

Micky manages to buy a bulky sweater on a super season-end sale for only $8.00. I refrain since I have so little money and I want to have it for snacks and the movie tonight.

We head out the big doors at 2:30 on our way to Nancy and Clare's. It is a few blocks from the Mall but nothing difficult. After a leisurely cruise down side streets and alleys, all curb free, we reach their street. The houses are small narrow one-floor places, and little bungalows. Really cute and well groomed. We roll onto the walk of a gingerbread wonder with cream and rose trim. The side ramp leads straight into the door. Nancy opens it and welcomes us in. The house is just as cute in as out. It is all done in cream and rose and a pale blue, with dark wood furniture where needed. We enter into a big country-style kitchen, dining room, and sitting area.

"This is our everything room. We really live in here. Clare can even use the sink and stove because of the cutouts underneath and the front controls on all of it. It is where I study and write. It is where she does the book work and reads. We just love it."

We roll into the next room. It is a large bedroom with lots of space around the large bed. No other furniture except a big dresser and a bookcase. Clare waves at herself, showing off her room. We roll back further, to what is really the front of the house. There is a smaller bedroom with small bed and low dresser and chairs. It really suits Nancy. There is a very small room right in the front. It has just enough room for a pull-out sofa, a chest, and a bookshelf, and it is nicely lit from the front windows and door.

"This is where a PCA sleeps when I go on trips, or when we just indulge ourselves by having a student living in to do PCA stuff. We just love our house."

We return to the big room. There is a large roll-in bath off that room. Micky washes up and we have tea. It is iced since it is a very warm day. Micky has brought almond cookies from the Mall.

"Are you thinking of making the change, Emy?"

"MORE AND MORE. NOT QUITE SURE."

"We have never regretted it for a moment. But then in emergencies we have each other. It is bound to be harder alone, like Mick."

"I don't feel alone, though, with Susan, and good neighbors like you guys."

"Yeah, but we really have it good. There are a lot of people with disabilities living out on their own who have had awful experiences. Remember that time Andrew was attacked by that crazy with the knife?"

I feel suddenly cold. Must be too much tea.

"Yeah, this looney had been watching, because he identified himself as Andy's aide, so Andy buzzed the door and the guy got in. He went at him with a knife. Andy said he had nothing for him to steal. He gradually talked the guy into following him into the hall. Security had gotten a buzz from him while he looked 'round the apartment to prove to the guy that he had nothing. His wallet was in the fridge in the crisper. 'Isn't that where everyone keeps their lettuce?' Anyway the security guy grabbed this dude and Andrew escaped with only one little cut."

"Then there was Marissa Boley's aide who took her credit cards and used them repeatedly. When Marissa got the bills she told her to give her the money to pay the bills and the aide told her she wouldn't eat or breathe at night again unless she paid all her bills for her. Marissa kept it quiet until she could get out and talk to the advocacy people at the Center. They helped her get another aide lined up so she could fire this one. She then took her to small claims court through Legal Aid and the woman had to pay all the bills. She was not happy and threatened Marissa. Now Marissa has to worry about what the woman might do to retaliate."

We leave about 5:00 with these war stories hassling my head. They did tell a few good stories, and their own place is a great story. So, I guess it balances out.

Susan is home at 5:30 and she is nice to help me into my better outfit. I choose the special green sweater, but I didn't think of bringing it because of Andrew. I didn't know he was coming.

The door opens and there is Andrew in his khaki jeans and cream shirt with the khaki denim cowboy jacket and cream and blue bandanna.

"Your coach and four await, madame."

"You guys have fun. Don't worry when you come back."

"Right, I'll have your bed made up and be ready to pop you in whenever. Just you watch out for the midnight cowboy, there."

I know this is a real date. I believe that we are beyond the sales-job level. We wait at the bus stop.

"Italian, Chinese, Mexican, Korean?

"KOREAN? NEVER HAD."

We get off the bus near a storefront place with writing I can't make out on the window. I let Andrew order because I wouldn't know what there is to eat.

We sip delicious tea from cups with half straws in. Andrew is probably a regular here, too, because even with his thick C.P. accent and the lady's Korean accent they somehow manage to agree on what we'll have. The lady brings small dishes with vegetables in them. They smell spicy and strong. He gives me little bits to start. Whew! Wow. It is a shock at first. But I really like the taste. He laughs as I screw up my face to cope.

The lady brings him a dish of meat shreds and more vegetables and I get a bowl with pretty colorful vegetables in sections with an egg on top.

"You have a surprise underneath."

He took a fork and moved the egg, and showed me a layer of

meat bits under the vegetables. Then he cut the egg all in and the mix was really different and tasty. His was a kind of barbecue and we shared back and forth. Delicious. Never had this at S.P.

Jo used to bring home Chinese food in little white cartons. I liked it a lot too. I liked the way rice felt in my mouth and the crispy vegetables. It took a long time to eat it. Lots of chewing, and worth every bite. I especially liked the spicy dishes. At S.P. I had just about forgotten how good spicy food tastes. Funny how when you think you will never have something again, you find ways to forget, so that the hurt goes away.

We munch slowly in the little dark room with candles on our table. Everything doesn't end up in our mouths but what does is scrumptious. We watch other eaters use two sticks to put food in their mouths and marvel at such a feat.

Andrew pays the lady and she gives us cookies. It takes him quite a while to open the little plastic wrappers, using teeth, fingers, and muttered curses. He finally gets them out of their covers and takes the first one and pops it open. A little paper appears in the crack.

"Yours, Emily. 'You will be wooed by a handsome graying devil. There will be good fortune.'"

"LIAR, READ IT RITE."

With a smirk he reads, "'The current year will bring you much happiness.' Well, that one covers all the bases. Every year is the current year. So you will have much happiness from now on. Are you sure you don't like the one about the graying devil?"

"READ YOURS."

"You will be seduced by a green-eyed fox with hair like flames."

"YOU ARE STIL FUL OF SHIT."

"OK, 'A near journey will change many things.' I wonder what things."

He looks at me with real deep questions in his eyes. I sense that he is very uncomfortable about the upcoming trip. I light catch his eyes for a question.

"WHAT RONG ANDRU?"

"These trips haven't bothered me so much before. Once I got used to being out on my own, I've loved sailing out into the unknown to do who-knows-what to get things changed. I didn't care if I got arrested or killed or yelled at or clubbed. It was all the same. But it's so different for me now. I want you along with me. But I don't because I know how easily you could be hurt. I could never let that happen. So I have to leave you here. I have to go away, just as I've gotten to know you better. I've never felt so torn."

Somehow I suddenly remember the night Marie and I watched the police haul Andrew off the road on the news. I remember my stomach turning inside-out with pain. Now I understand. Funny how much we know before we know that we know.

It takes a while to get it back together, but we do. We head out to the movie place across the big parking lot.

"This is a second-run house. Good flicks for less money. You want something funny, or something really good?"

"GOOD, U PICK.

We get tickets for *My Left Foot* which I think that Casey mentioned once about an artist.

We roll down a hallway and into a dark large room full of chairs. There are spaces in the middle empty. We roll for those spaces and take our places. I have seen theaters on TV but never been in one.

The front of the room is a big curtain. We sit quietly awhile and listen to music. Then the curtain just pushes aside and the very big wall becomes a picture and the sound is all around us. Wham! It is fabulous.

The story is so real. Andrew says it is real, but actors are playing the real people. The guy playing Christy Brown is so real. Andrew says he's not a gimp, but he oughta be. I think he is beautiful. He is a little like Andrew, but not with bright blue eyes and iron gray curls.

When he becomes angry at his teacher I just cry. I can feel how hurt he is, I can see how sad she is to have hurt him. She was just dense thinking she wouldn't affect him that way. Dense.

It is so funny at the end when that dry witty nurse and he go off and fall in love. I just lean on Andrew and cry more. I have heard about people who cry in movies. Now I am one.

We take our time getting home. We go back to the Mall on the bus and have a drink in the little bar off the Mexican restaurant. I only take a margarita and hope it won't knock me, or I won't be able to drive home. It isn't like the nasty stuff Jo made me drink. But I remember too clearly what drinking did to her, and I won't make this a habit. But it is nice to sit here with Andrew and watch the people and pretend I've always had Friday nights like this.

We get to Micky's pretty late. I'll have to ring, but Andrew circles my chair first while we are a way down the path in a secluded little grove of trees and bushes. He is facing me and asks to move my board as he slides out his right arm rest. He touches my hair and face and I lean the best I can toward him. He undoes my velcros and lets me ease toward him till I am on the edge of my chair. We lean together in a delicate balance with Andrew supporting most of me.

It is a lot later when I get to Micky's door. Susan waves as Andrew takes off down the path. She easily undresses me and after the bathroom slips me into the comfortable pull-out bed. I fall asleep immediately.

Chapter 35

"I feel like the mother of a teenager this morning. Susan told me, under pressure, that you got here around 2:30 a.m.. Must have been a hell of a date." Micky is working with a piece of toast Susan just gave her.

"NO, OTHER PLACE."

"Ah, a heaven of a date?"

"NICE DINER, GREAT MOVIE. GREAT FREND."

I had no plans to go into detail. I'm not too sure of the details. I am still in a bit of a fog.

"I know he is planning to leave for Atlanta Monday. Will he be coming over tonight?"

"PLAY MONOPLY?"

"What? What do you mean? You want to play Monopoly?"

"ANDRU SAID."

"I would bet he was teasing you, Emily. He jokes that Micky and I just sit around and play games because she doesn't always approve of his 'actions,' and doesn't always participate when he wants her to."

Susan set a cup and straw down for me and sat by the window to drink her coffee before leaving for a Saturday class. The sun on her copper brown skin added depth to the twinkle in her bronze eyes. She leaned to replenish Micky's toast, as Micky straw-sipped tea. Then Micky looked at me.

"Andrew is a great guy and funny, but he and I just don't always see eye to eye on things. That's OK. If he comes we'll have a nice supper and chew the fat. Meanwhile, let's you and me, Em, do some serious talking about what you need to know to move into a place of your own. It is hard to get into this in the groups."

We have a great, if scary talk about what goes into living out. Susan has set out all of Micky's financial records. She shows me how she pays Susan, and the taxes on Susan's wages.

"Every three months I must pay Susan's withholding tax and Social Security. It is figured on what I will be paying her in the upcoming three months. If you have an agency aide, the agency does this, but frankly, to have a friend like Susan is worth much more to me than avoiding the red tape."

She shows me how to keep track of income and expense in her checkbook. She explains about bank accounts and how to handle them.

"At first you will need to open a checking account. Some of the locally-owned banks still have no-fee checking which allows you to use just a few checks a month and you need to keep $100 in the account at all times. That will be difficult on your exorbitant income, but it saves sometimes $10 a month. That can really add up."

The part about Medicaid and SSI restrictions is hard to understand, but I'll just have to keep up with them as they change, which they do all the time. Micky's only allowed to earn a tiny bit each month before they start cutting back her income. She has to keep track of every penny.

When Susan gets back from class we head for the Mall to do the week's shopping. Micky lets me watch how she plans the food and menus and keeps track of each price. She knows what she will spend before she gets to the store. Susan is pulling a wheeled cart and Micky has a nice wagon attached to her chair. We cruise around the store. After down-hall slalom at S.P. this is a breeze. It is crowded because it is Saturday.

It has been at least seventeen years since I was in a grocery and I am amazed at the variety. There are seven types of apples; six of potatoes. There are strange little green fuzzy fruit and star-shaped yellow ones, and soft oval ones, creamy yellow with a red blush, that Susan calls mangos. She tells us that they are delicious blended with ice into a summer shake. So many types of pepper.

I thought they came in hot and sweet. I'm appalled at the prices.

"Yeah, that stuff costs a lot. But we don't buy it. We use dried milk, bulk cheese and peanut butter, rice, beans, canned tomatoes and a few green vegetables, bread and potatoes. Fruit is for dessert. We get oranges and apples in season. You'll see what we can do with poor-folk fixin's. We are ovo-lacto vegetarians, too, so that makes things cheaper."

When we get home, Susan puts everything away in no time, and Micky lines up the ingredients for dinner. Sliced onions go in a big skillet with oil and they quickly wilt down. Then Micky carefully adds large spoons of a spicy-smelling powder. Susan fries it with the onions. My eyes water and I sneeze. Then the juice from the canned tomatoes goes in with chunks of cabbage, green beans, carrots, and potatoes. The rest of the tomatoes are added.

"And the extravagant part, since we have guests," Micky adds washed mushrooms on top.

The room has filled with the intense aroma of the spices, and it is a little dizzying.

"A curry like this is better with really fresh spices. But we make do. When we make a lot like this, we freeze it in single-serving portions and use it on days we don't cook. We can store a sizable backlog of instant dinners which I can even cook myself in the microwave, if Susan has meetings or late classes. They are probably ten times cheaper than the instant dinners in the store. And they taste better!"

Susan has filled a double boiler with rice and set it on to cook. There is a knock at the door. She pulls a face at me and goes to open it.

"Well, we were wondering if you were coming. Staying for a good hot curry, we hope?"

"Yo, Suse, I wouldn't turn down an invite from the kawean of da nile, or is that denial? But as stunning as you are, I am heavy into redheads lately. Any here?"

"I think you'll find two in the kitchen; that way you can pick."

Our dinner is again searingly spicy. I have a big serving of rice, veg, and a bit of yogurt on top. It feels warm all down to my toes. Susan spoons it up for me with bits of chopped raisins and peanuts. Just delicious.

Micky and I review for Andrew what we have covered, and we talk for a long time about further pros and cons of living out. Susan mentions a program they want to see, and they go to Micky's room to watch, giving us some private time.

"You want to come with me to Atlanta?"

"NOT NOW."

"What! You mean you wanted to yesterday, but now, forget it?"

"NOPE, DOPE. CANT COME LOSE ROOM."

"Well, why don't you just lose that room for good, and move in with me?"

"U NOT FUNNY. GEORGE WARN ME. YOU IN IT FOR WHAT YOU CAN GET?"

"Sorry. I realize how it must sound to you. I'm just having a really hard time figuring out how I can go down there without you."

"SAME AS ALWAYS."

"But you know it is not the same."

"DO I?"

"You really play hard to get, the hard way."

"EVERY THING I GET HARD WAY, GOOD AND BAD. YOU MAKE MY HART FLY. I IN NO RUSH TO SEE END. I WAIT. YOU COME BACK. WILL STILL CARE?"

"Will which of us still care? You or me?"

"EITHER. BOTH. WE'LL SEE WHEN YOU COME BACK."

"I have this sense that, no matter what, you will make it on your own. You are a very practical and determined person. That is one thing I find so fascinating about you. You have come back to life after being buried for sixteen years. Like a seventeen-year locust, you've reemerged to a new life. That comparison ends there. The rest of yours will be long and lively."

"I WANT IT TO BE. I WORK HARD FOR THAT."

We make our goodbyes. Mine are tearful; his, a bit, too. He

calls goodbye to Micky and Susan. They pop out to offer luck and success on his trip, and let him out.

"Come watch a funny show with us, kid. You need laughs to counteract the sads."

Chapter 36

*K*erching, chinga chinga, pop. The light is suddenly on and the curtain is being thrown around my bed area. There are footsteps and whispers, and a few louder voices requesting hurried assistance. Latrisha, the new night aide, pokes through the still-quivering curtain.

"Sorry, Emily. Edna isn't doing too well. She's being moved, and may have to go to the hospital."

I try to make my right hand touch my chin in the thank you sign. I think she figures out what I am doing.

"That's OK, I'll let you know in the morning how she doing."

While I wait for morning, which Edna's clock tells me is five hours away, since Edna won't be here to announce 5:00 a.m., I think about what I am wanting to do. Life here is cold. My real life is in my classes and my groups, and meeting with people at the Center and the library. George hasn't spoken to me since Ted moved in May. It is late June, and Andrew has been in Georgia nearly a month. Marie has spoken to me, but only for practical purposes. I guess she feels that I am less a pariah with Andrew out of town. She hasn't called attention to the postcards I have been getting and putting on my door. Every other day or so, one comes, and I read it over and over, then hang it. Stone Mountain, Peachtree Street, Carter Center, etc., all wish you were here.

But I am hearing from two friends at the Center that they would like to find a place to share with one other person, and two rotating live-in people. Mary Settles and Jenny Fanish are both eager to move. Jenny has lived out on her own, but is home now because of expenses. Mary has been a student and lived a short time in a care situation after her mother died. She didn't like it and was glad to go to school and live in a dorm. That has gotten old and she wants a new place. I think that we would make good roommates. We get along, but don't interfere. We like each other and appreciate similar humor. Jenny can drive, Mary likes to cook, and I could learn to do a lot of things to help out. We have been talking, and they have said that I might be just the person they are looking for. I suggested we ask Susan if she knew of any students looking for steady housing and paid work. We worked out how much we could afford in rent split three ways, and food, and utilities, and how much we could pay the people. We have talked about having one live in and one part time just to spell her. That might be more feasible cost-wise.

With Denia's help at the Center, they have looked at three locations. One older house is only partly accessible. A large apartment is very nice but teetering over the top range of what we can really afford. One newer house is all on one floor, except for a finished basement/laundry. We aren't sure that would work out unless the attendant wouldn't mind having the basement and doing the laundry.

I am still musing about all of this when Judy mutters in and yanks back my curtain. She turns on the TV to listen during the bathing process. I tune in as Judy puts on my bra and shirt.

"Also from Atlanta, a freak accident occurred during a staged sit-in by a crowd made up of nursing home patients and the disabled. It took place just outside of a meeting of the National Long Term Care Association, and Health and Human Services officials. Two men, Kirk Elbert and Andrew Duncan, were thrown from their wheelchairs as a truck skidded onto the sidewalk outside of the Peach Center Hotel. The hotel lobby window was damaged. Both men were hospitalized in serious cond . . ."

I guess I fainted. I don't remember anything more, and I don't remember finishing being dressed. The next thing I know, Marie is sitting next to my chair crying and holding my hand.

"Onnee, Ah so sohry. Ah been so mean. So sohry."

I work to lift my head off my board where Judy must have left me. I guess she thought I fell asleep. Nothing new. Marie pushes at me and secures my top velcros.

"WHAT RONG?"

"You don know?"

"HAD BAD DREAM, EDNA SICK, ANDRU HURT?"

"Noh a dwream. Andwru en hospal en Landa. Vary bad."

"WHAT U NO OFF NEWS?"

"Yeah."

"CALL SARAH."

I maneuver my chair around my curtained bed to the little chest. I am determined to get the drawer open and take out the address book I keep there. It takes a while, but I stick with it until I manage to pull it onto my board.

We head down to Mrs. Butler's room. Luckily she is in early. I hand her my book and the page and ask, "CUD U CALL PLEEZ, NOW. EMERGESE."

"Sure, Emily. Hang on. I am trying to reach Sarah Cohen, it is an emergency. This is Mrs. Butler at South Pines. Thank you.

"Sarah, this is Betty at South Pines. Emily Mason is here and needs to talk to you right away. Let me split the line so that you can talk to her, and I will read her questions to you."

She hands Marie a receiver to hold to my ear, and she picks up the other after punching a button.

"Emily, this is Sarah. I assume you need to know about Andrew. He is alive. He is not doing well now, but they believe that both he and Kirk will pull out of this. I just spoke to the doctor in charge and she said that Andrew just came out of surgery. His legs were badly hurt. One was almost crushed, the other a compound fracture. Kirk had a cracked pelvis and a damaged femur and some internal injuries. Andrew will be in Atlanta a long time. There will be more surgeries on his legs, and then he will be in Rehab there for several months. He rarely walks, but he uses his legs to transfer, and sometimes to stand to reach things. He will need to have them heal the best way possible."

"Do you have any questions, Emily? I'll be glad to relay them." Mrs. Butler takes my hand.

"WILL U TALK TO HIM, SARAH?"

"He won't be able to talk for a few days, Em, but as soon as he can I will call him. Sherry is down there. She saw the whole thing. She was nearer the door, and Andrew and Kirk were on the edge of the sidewalk with signs, trying to get people to stop or honk. The guy in the truck was dead drunk and was startled by the chair people apparently and swerved and lost control."

"PLEEZ TELL SHERY, TELL HIM, I SO SORRY, HOPE HE WELL SOON. SO SCARED FOR HIM. I CARE. I WRITE SOON. THANK U."

"As soon as he is conscious, and is feeling up to it, Sherry will have your message to give him. I know he would be so glad for your letters. Maybe he had a premonition about this or something. He wasn't the usual rush-out-and-make-them-do-right kinda Andrew that I know. I know he misses you, Em. He has asked after you every time he has spoken to anyone here, since he left."

I beam, "BY SARAH," at Mrs. Butler. I am feeling so weak and awful, I need to leave and put my head down.

"I believe Emily needs to leave now, Sarah. Call me anytime you get some word and I will make sure Emily gets it right away. Bye, from both of us."

I try to back out of her office and hit the wall. I try to turn and hit the chair. I'm a mess. My head sags toward the board and I sob. Mrs. Butler takes my clutches out and wheels me back to my room. Judy comes in behind her and they transfer me back in bed and throw a blanket over me. I can't sleep for crying, but I know that I'll eventually sleep. I think Marie is sitting at the bottom of my bed.

Marie is on the van with me for the next P.A.I.L. meeting. I am surprised when she comes to ask if she can tag along. I guess she is just as anxious to get details of Atlanta as I am. I think she will be more upset, though, when she realizes that I will be spending most of my time working with Jenny and Mary on our house plans. We head toward the big meeting room, but I detour into Denia Blane's office, where they have been meeting. Denia signs and says a big, "Hello, how are you?" Marie peers in.

"Marie, do you want to know more about our plans, too?" Jenny asks.

"Powans?"

"Hasn't Em told you what we have been working on since May?"

"Uh, noh, fwaih noh."

"Keeping to yourself, Em?"

I shoot Jenny a stern look. She knows what I have been dealing with, the cold shoulders and the silences. Why put this on me?

"Noh, Ah been busy. Dinn knoh." Marie covers, not wanting to get into the month's hassles.

Denia shows us another house. This one is a little larger, and there really are four bedrooms on one floor. Denia says the rooms are not big, but that there is space in each for a bed, a chest, a vanity or dresser, and each has its own ample closet. She describes a very nice galley kitchen with turning room, no cabinets under the sink and a stove on an island which has front controls and no cabinet underneath.

"The bath will need a little work. The handy guys are saying that it wouldn't be too hard to take out the current tub and to retile the floor with a new drain for a roll-in shower. The landlord said that that could be done, if you guys were planning very long-term occupancy. I told him that you probably were, and that if any of you decided to leave, that we could find new tenants in no time, since there are always new people looking for a nice place to live."

Denia says that the house is in the Bonnington neighborhood. That is just the other side of the Mall from Micky's place, and not a long roll from Clare's. I can't believe that all these accessible places are cropping up in the same area.

Denia answers my beamed question.

"Bonnington is an old area with new stuff going on. Some of the old houses are post-war tract houses which are well kept up. The one-floor plans lend themselves to adapting for chair users. We have been hassling developers looking at the area to adapt some of the properties because there is a market for this housing. There is a hitch. We can't arrange for any more than three residents, because there is a local ordinance which regulates what they call 'group homes.' We have been trying for years to get that one off the books. Something like, 'No household in a dwelling set for single family use shall house six or more unrelated persons.' So if you have three residents, and two or three staff living in they can stir up trouble."

Denia goes over income problems with us. I will receive SSI. Jenny is on Social Security Disability, which she draws on her parents' account. Mary will get SSI. Each of us will pay about one-third of our income into the rent. Then we split the other bills by thirds. Our utilities are in the rent, so that is a bonus. Phone, except for long distance, is divided. And we will pool by thirds to pay for the food, unless we find that one person eats a whole lot more.

"Yeah, I think we can count on Mason forking in more food money. She eats like a horse." Jenny like to throw in a barb or two at my expense.

At this time Mary and I together could have four hours a day of agency aide help on our Medicaid, and Jenny would be allowed six hours a week. If we use that time, and have a student live-in as well, we should be able to do OK. The student, or working live-in, would pay no rent or utilities. That would be an in-kind payment. And she would have to know, coming in, exactly what tasks she is expected to perform, and whether she will be paid beyond the in-kind payment.

"What you have to understand, really understand, is that you will be managers of employees. You will need to decide on all the tasks that must be done daily, and divide them fairly between yourselves and the aides or attendants that work with you. Here is a sample check-off sheet of tasks that most people need to have done in a week. Go through it together and determine, times three, what you will need. Be painfully specific. It will only save you trouble later.

"Say for example, your student or live-in assistant can do

breakfast and get Jenny up while the agency aide can help Emily up and assist Mary with her clothes. With a roll-in shower, only Emily would need bathing help. Or the live-in could get Jenny up and she could do breakfast, while Emily got a shower and then Mary got help with her clothes. But all of this would need a daily schedule, and you would have to stick to it. Jenny needs to get to classes on time. Mary needs to get to her volunteer position, and Emily will need to get to her classes and to the library tech center. And your live-in will have to get to classes or a job. It all needs to work together like clockwork."

"Souwn awfu hard," Marie says in a very small voice.

"It is, and it has to be worth it to you for you to want to do it all. There have been people who came out of institutional care, tried this way of life, and decided it was too hard. That is OK. They have a right to check out options. One man went back to his institution; one lady went to another nursing home. It is no disgrace. We all have to decide how we want to live."

After we go over the checklists a while and add things we agree on, we decide enough for today and break up. I have been getting more and more tense as the meeting continues. I hope Sarah is back in her office by now. But I bump into her as she comes down the hall from group.

"C'mon in my hole, Em."

We scoot in and she pushes the door behind us. I think that I heard Marie behind me, and I don't doubt that she will be waiting outside.

"I have a long letter from Sherry, and I spoke with her last night. She said that Kirk is doing really well and may get to fly back to Oakland in a couple weeks. I know, you don't want to know that. Andrew is not doing quite as well. He is mostly sleeping, but he's out of the coma. He hasn't really spoken yet, but like for you, speech is a big effort for him. Sherry has visited every day. She says that he looks better than he did over the weekend. The doctors say that he has to pull out of this slump before they can continue the surgery on his legs."

"CAN U HELP RITE LETTER?"

"Sure. You dictate, and I'll key it in."

She turns her computer screen so that I can see it, too.

"DEAR ANDRU"

"Would you like it sent with corrected spelling, or do you like the way you spell from your board?"

"MY SPELL. HE RECOGNIZ."

"Right."

"DEAR ANDRU, I GESS COOKIE RITE. MUCH CHANG FOR YOU. I NOT CHANG. I STIL CARE. YOU MUST GET WELL. I WAIT FOR GOOD NEWS. IM WORKIN HARD ON NEW PLANS. TELL YOU MORE LATER. MUCH MUCH LOVE, EMILY."

"Here is his address, to take with you. You may find someone at home to help you write letters by hand or on the typewriter. The more you send, the better I'll bet he'll feel."

As we leave Sarah's office, I run into Marie's chair just outside the door."

"Been waitin foh you, bus comin soon, Onnee."

Her eyes are sad and full of questions. Sarah immediately tells her that Andrew is improving very slowly and could use some encouragement and prayers.

When our bus gets to the corner, I pop off and head for Avonton Road. There is a bookstore not far from the café and I can get postcards and stamps there. Marie wheels up behind me.

"Where you thing you goen, Onnee?"

"GO GET CARDS."

"You beah noh, beah go in and sahn in."

"NO."

I head down the side street, make the turn and down the next street to the curb cut up Avonton. I pass Bill's and head to the newly-remodeled bookstore. Before, it had several steps up to it, and Andrew bitched enough that they looked into the law and realized that they needed to make it ramped. They put a lot of effort into the renovation, and now it is easy to get in and out and browse. I wheel in and go to the postcards.

" Hi, Emily, what can I get for you today?"

"ANDRU HURT IN AXIDENT IN GA. NEED FUNY CARDS."

"Let me put an assortment on your board, and you tell me which to pack for you."

We look through the cards a while. Luckily the store is quiet, and Terry has time to help. I pick the funniest I can find. I want to try to send one each day, like he did for me.

I purchase the cards as Terry helps me with my chained-on purse. I remember some stamps for them while she has my purse. Then I head back.

Marie is waiting at the patio door.

"They were mah. Wen Ah sahn in they wanna know wheah you are. Ah tol em ah the stoh. They goh mah at me. You goddah go polagish, say sorha."

"BULL."

"Onnee, come bah, do ih. Dey be mah ah me."

I head on down for the elevator and back to my room. After supper I am going to try to corner Grandma Sample and see if she would help me write these cards each evening.

Chapter 37

*E*dna is back from the hospital, but it seems that even less of her has come back. She has lost the roundness and the cheery lostness. She is thinner and drawn. She doesn't shuffle around in her chair and mostly sleeps. Judy tells me that it was a stroke on top of her Alzheimer's.

"I just don't think Edna will be with us much longer. You'll have to get a new roomie."

I don't bother to add that I won't be with her much longer either, and that I won't need a roommate where I am going. Jenny, Mary, and I have set September as our target date. Sarah and Denia said that the remodeling will be done then, and we can move in. I cannot believe I am thinking thoughts like this. I won't be telling the administration until mid-August. That is just a few weeks away. At times I feel that I am just making this up as part of my window dreams. Sometimes in my sleep dreams I am already living in another place and it is very different and comfortable. My sleep dreams have been less scary, except when they are about Andrew.

Our P.A.I.L. meeting is a 4th of July party. We are making a big deal of Independence day. There is cake and raspberry, vanilla, and blueberry ice cream. Jenny has brought in a big picture that she made. She calls it our declaration of Independence. It shows Jenny, Mary, and me sitting in front of our new house. There is writing.

"When in the course of human events it becomes necessary for people to dissolve the previous bonds which have connected them to others and to assume separate and equal status to which they are entitled, they should declare the causes which impel them to the separation – and you can ask any of us.

"We hold these truths to be self evident, all things being equal, that we, too, are entitled to life, liberty, and the pursuit of happiness, and we will derive our powers from mutual consent and governance. If a governance is destructive of these ends, it is the right of the people to abolish it, and to institute new Government, laying its foundation on such principles as to us shall seem most likely to effect our safety and happiness.

"All experience hath shown that people are more disposed to suffer, while evils are sufferable, than to right themselves by abolishing the forms to which they are accustomed. But when a long train of abuses and usurpations evinces a design to reduce them under absolute despotism, it is their right and duty to throw off such Government and to provide new, for their future security. (Apologies to Thomas Jefferson)"

We put our signatures on the bottom. Jenny does hers really big in the middle with a long square-topped J and a lot of curlicues at the base. Mary writes hers in, and I make my mark. They explain to me that it is like the American Declaration of Independence. Jenny promises to show me a copy of it so I can enjoy the joke. But it is really no joke.

The whole gang has brought gifts. There are practical things like paper towels and soaps and house-cleaning supplies. Nancy comes over and hands me a small box. Leslie helps me open it. It is Nate's ceramic candlestick. I am so touched.

"You should have this back now, Em, because we have enjoyed using it a lot, but Nate would want you to have it in your home."

I wonder who told them about the candlestick? How did they know about Nate?

"Marie told us a little about your life before South Pines, and she just mentioned the candlestick and your uncle. We felt you would really like to have it with you."

"THANK YOU VERY MUCH. I NEED REPLACE."

"No you don't. It served us well."

There are some very nice gifts. Each of us gets two sets of new sheets and two sets of towels. We each get bed lamps. We get certificates to go to Goodwill to pick out things we'll need.

"HOW WE REPAY ALL THIS?"

"You have been coming to these parties for three years, Emily, and you always gave things to people moving out. There will continue to be opportunities, don't worry." Leslie laughs as she continues sharing ice cream with me.

Jenny and Mary and I stay late and list all the things we each own, and add what we received today, and then list what we think we might need. One thing we don't have and would like is a microwave. Andrew swears by his, because he is able to do his cooking in between visits from his attendant, and Micky showed me how useful hers is. The front-opening door and easy-use controls are really appealing. They cost a whole lot.

"A lot less than they used to," Denia offers. "I got mine last year, and it wasn't too bad. I paid $125 for it. I know that feels like a whole lot, but if each of you puts $5.00 in a pot each week you could get one in nine weeks. It doesn't need a lot of bells and whistles, just power to heat up food."

"HOW CAN I GET PACK?"

"Well, we need to get a group of your buddies here to come 'round to your place the day before you move. They can help you get everything sorted and packed, and then some of us who are walkers can give you a hand loading it on the van Monday when you leave. There is always a bunch who will help move."

"NOT A LOT STUFF."

"Just as well; it won't be a hassle for you to pack and get it to your new place."

❖❖❖

I'm hanging around the kitchen this morning trying to see if anyone has a clean box or two that I can gleep. Marie said she would go through my drawers with me and my closet to see what I can already pack. Marie has been spending a lot more time with me since that P.A.I.L. party. I don't know if she is still angry with me.

"Onnee, whah yoh doon down ere?"

"WANT BOXS, YOU HELP?"

"Bahthes to puh yoh hingth in?"

"YES."

"Onnee, Ah hay to see yoh go."

"NOT FEW WEEK AGO."

"Ah know, Ah am sohry. You knoh Ah hah a crwush on Anru. Ah wahned him toh lah me. Ah wath jewous. Ah huht thahat yoh goin way. Ah verah sad."

"I SORY TO. NOT MEAN HURT U AT ALL. OLD FREND. COME VISIT ME?"

"Cuhd Ah? Lahk yoh vithit Mihkah?"

"YES."

"Here's your boxes, Emily."

Fred, one of the kitchen dudes, puts two clean boxes on my board. Marie and I start up to the elevators.

In my room, Marie pulls out the bed-table drawer onto my board. It is a task for both of us to yank and pull until it drops onto the board. She lifts items and watches for my blink as we sort through wants, don't wants, and tosses. I figure the more we get done, the less Denia's crew has to do on moving day. At the bottom of the drawer are some photos. I don't remember them being put in there. Maybe they are Edna's. Marie lifts each one for me to look at closely.

The first one is a crackled black and white of a young man in a uniform. It is Nate with light hair cut very short under his cap. Must have been in the war. I had heard so little about that. I never knew much about Uncle Nate at all. I am amazed at how young and nice he looks. I only remember the old care-worn hurting uncle who worried so for me. I was a teenager. He and Jo were only in their late fifties when they died; they'd seemed so old to me.

The next photo is of a bunch of girls. They are different ages. The one to the left of the four is probably Jo. Maybe those are her sisters. One of them may be my mom, Retta. I look very closely as the light comes in Edna's window. Do any of them look like me?

The next picture is one of the girls in the group, by herself. Marie turns it over. "Retta" is written on the back.

"S'dah yoh mah, Onnee?"

I blink the reply and wonder at this photo that I don't ever remember seeing. I guess someone, a social worker, put these in this drawer when I first moved in. I am not in the habit of cleaning out drawers; as I never could get down into any, I have never looked at any of this stuff on the bottom.

The girl in the photo is rather serious. She has a small triangular face, with light hair and gray-looking eyes. It is hard to tell in black and white. I wonder how old she is in the picture. Maybe sixteen. She's pretty in a quiet sort of way. What would she be like today if she hadn't gotten killed in the accident? Would I be living with her? Would she be helping me move away?

"Do yoh membah yoh mah?"

I blink a no, and wonder where those other two sisters are. I believe there were four other brothers, too. Might I ever find any of them? Would they even care that I exist?

Marie puts my soap, hairbrush, and toothbrush and paste back in the drawer where Judy likes to have them. The other items, including the photos, go into the smaller of the boxes. Marie goes out to get an aide to help unload the closet. She finds the temp, Bobbie, who doesn't seem to mind, and puts the stack of clothes from my side of the closet on my bed.

"Y'all doing heavy housekeeping today?"

"Yeh. Wih yoh come bah an hewp us puh it aw bah?"

"Sure, Marie, just come get me. I'll be doing beds down the hall."

We sort through the clothes and pack what I won't need in the next two weeks. It isn't much. I use everything. We pack my other sweater, a winter skirt, a jacket, and two pairs of winter slacks. Bobbie rehangs my green sweater, my two summer slacks, three summer shirts.

"You guys trying to get some room in Emily's closet. Gonna go on a buying binge?"

"Noh. Bowbie. Jush cuh leanin."

I realize it won't be any effort to get all this packed in about ten minutes on the day I leave. I will tell Denia so she won't send people early. Marie and I straighten up with Bobbie's help. We say a few words to Edna, which she may not be hearing now, and head for our window, then lunch.

❖❖❖

There is a dark and cloudy sunrise. I am out in an open place, maybe a desert, and the wind blows hard. I am on the ground and have no way to move other than to try to scoot by shifting my right foot forward. That doesn't help. In the distance I think I see a building, perhaps a safe place. I become aware that there may be something creeping toward me from behind where I cannot see. I hear soft foot sounds, and breathing even over the wind. I desperately want to run to safety, to get up and away from those animal sounds. I fight to move anything I can, hoping to frighten away whatever threatens me.

"C'mon now, stop this thrashing, girl. You just having another nightmare. Lord, you must have some real doozies."

I wake to see Mrs. Graven, who is subbing for Judy this week. Today is my day to give notice. Today I tell Mr. White that I will be leaving. I doubt he'll be very cut up to see me go. But I know that I must give him two weeks. I also know that others have run into discharge snags at this time, and I am getting up the courage to deal with those. Somehow Ted had no problems with that, but then Ted had no "medical" reason for being here. These guys can think up some medical excuse to try to keep me here. But I have troops for the other side of the battle if there is one.

After breakfast, I wheel over to administration. I ease into the door and wait for Mrs. Litovsky to notice me.

"Yes, Ms. Mason, may I help you."

"I WOULD LIKE SEE MR WHITE TODAY, PLEASE."

I practiced all the words with Grandma Sample. I wanted to be really right.

"I'll have to check his schedule."

She pops up and into his office, shutting the door behind her. I am sure he has big important meetings on his plate which

284

would rule out two minutes today with Emily Mason. What a crock.

"Mr. White has a lot of meetings this morning, but he said if you could make it really short, he will see you now before he leaves."

"FINE."

I roll into the inner sanctum. Haven't been here since the big change of food snit. He didn't like that one bit. Maybe this message will be a relief.

"Good morning, Ms. Mason. You are up and going early today."

"YES. I COME TO TELL YOU I WILL BE LEAVING SP AUG. 29."

"Well, I must say. This comes as a bit of a surprise. I cannot say that I am entirely shocked, because, since your friend Ted left, I thought you might be following him. However, Ms. Mason, you are not equipped the way Ted was for living out on your own. He has skills and he has the use of his body. He has a pleasant personality, and he has friends to move in with who will be watching for his safety. I can't recommend that you leave, because you have none of these things.

"WRONG, MR. WHITE. I HAVE SKILLS, I HAVE CHAIR, I HAVE 2 FRIENDS MOVE IN WITH. ALL SETTLED."

"I am afraid that Dr. Pescula will have to approve your discharge papers, and without his signature, I cannot allow you to leave."

"WRONG. ANY DR CAN SIGN. DR WEST WILL SIGN."

That is true. Denia called Ellen to see if she would sign my papers if SP gave us any flack. She said that she would consider it an honor, since she probably started this whole thing in the first place. She said that I could get medical care at the hospital clinic where she is now working whenever I needed it.

I think it is the rap about the pleasant personality that galls me the most. The other stuff is a formality. But who is this guy to tell me that I have been unpleasant. The king of the hellhole, the most unpleasant place to have to live.

"Well, you seem to have done your homework. Do you really believe that you can live out on your own like a normal person? It is not a safe world. You could be so easily hurt. I think you ought to reconsider."

"SAFE AS HERE. HERE I BE RAPED, BEAT, STARVE, DRUGGED, JAIL IN CLOSET, LEG BROKE. SAFER OUT THERE."

"Maybe it would be better for you out there. Your outrageous lies could get you into a lot more trouble here."

"GOOD BYE MR WHITE. THANKS."

I need to split now before I go into some kind of fit and give him more ammunition for making me stay. So I back out and nod at Ms. Litovsky as she jumps up to answer Mr. White's call. I guess he has to plan how he will hassle me for two weeks and tell Ms. L. how to go about doing the hassles. He wouldn't lower himself to do it.

Well, the process is finally under way. I gotta say that I cruise down the hall with a sense of deep relief. I want to try to get in to see George to let him know myself before the grapevine produces abundant fruit. He may still not want to see me. I head off the elevator and around the corner to skilled. I see that his door is open. I see that he is in bed and facing away. Can I squeeze the blue machine in that tiny crack next to the window? Let's try anyway.

"Oh, it's you. I'm not sure I want to talk to you. Don't know that I can see your board."

Jerry comes in with some laundry to put in George's drawer.

"Hi, Emily. How goes it?"

"PLEASE READ FOR GEORGE."

"Sure."

"I AM MOVING AUG. 29. I WANTED TO TELL YOU FIRST. I CARE ABOUT YOU AND WILL MISS YOU MOST."

"I can't believe you are doing this, Em. I think it is damn fool stupidity. Look at your asshole boyfriend. He goes to Atlanta to get himself killed and even blows that. What kind of stupid fucking world are you moving out to, and for what? You haven't got the foggiest idea what life out there will be like. I never thought a smart girl like you would be so stupid."

"MAYBE STUPID. BUT HAPPIER. YOU HURT ME BY YOUR WORDS. I SORRY. GOOD BYE."

I thank Jerry and leave. I wonder why I even bother but I know that my old friend deserves to know about me, even if he is terribly angry with me.

Chapter 38

When Marie and I get to P.A.I.L. Denia asks if we want to be part of the trek to our new house.

"We want to make a dry run, and to let you guys see what a nice place you will have. Go 'round the neighborhood and see what is available. OK?"

Marie is beside herself asking if she can come along. The van will hold four chairs, so Denia says sure, and we begin the load in. Sardines in the can, we start out for Bonnington. While I have known about this for a while, and have seen pictures of the house, and have been in Bonnington Mall with Micky, I have to say that this is one of the most exciting days of my life. I am really pumping in the old ticker area and sweating up a storm. Of course the sardine can is hot with us all packed into our lockdowns and the heat on the raised topper doesn't help. But it is August, what can we expect?

"I know most of you have been to Bonnington Mall, but here it is. There is the big Parker Grocery; Drug City; Park and Wok, Asian restaurant, good carry out; Cinemagic, movies, second run. There is Laundromart and Dailey's Discount, the big department store. I can't imagine what you'd need that you couldn't get at Bonnington Mall."

Marie's eyes are about to drop out of her head. Luckily her lockdown is facing the Mall so she can get a good look at the whole place. Even though she's been around a lot more than I have, it has been a long time and places like this Mall are really new. She looks like I must when I came here with Micky just last month. And then with Andrew. Oh.

We turn down Cargill Road and then up a cul-de-sac and round a loop. The van pulls into a drive in front of a cute white house with blue trim. We look at each other with screams on the edges of our mouths. The van stops and the screams start. What a thrill; what a great house. What a dream come true!

Marie is the last off the van and she looks still open-mouthed and agape. We roll up the sidewalk and right to the door, made flush with an added concrete ramp. I am shaking all over as Denia opens the door. The front room is pale blue with white drapes over the big window next to the door. There is a mantlepiece over a fake fireguard, and a mirror above that. There are bookshelves to either side. It is roomy and bright. The floors are covered with a blue tight-weave chair-friendly carpet. No drag as we roll in. There is a divider with cabinets below and shelves above that separates the dining area. To the right is the kitchen. We can all fit in the kitchen. Mary wheels over to the sink and stove. She tucks under in a most satisfied manner.

"Good fit, Denia. Just great."

Denia pulls out several drawers. They have easy access, and one has a lowered cutting board that pulls out. The cabinets have pull-out shelves, and one has a lazy susan.

"The contractor really outdid himself here. He was paying attention to the whole process of accessing the space. We may be asking you guys if we can show this place off to other contractors and builders. It is the best we've found yet."

We cross back to the other side and check out the bedrooms. Each one has two windows and a big spacious closet. The bathroom is at the end of the hall and it is nearly as big as a bedroom. The shower has been rebuilt, as Denia had said. It is a simple roll-in with a slight slope to a drain, a fold-down shower chair, and a hand-held shower attachment. Jenny and Mary will neither need any help in here. I will be the only one to need assistance. How convenient.

"Well, just a week and a half and this will be yours. You guys can move anything you want to in before that. In fact we will be bringing your bed in tomorrow, Emily."

"WHAT! HAVE NO BED!"

"Well, you do now. The gang found a really nice one that is wooden framed, but will change positions electrically as you need. It was used, but it was a great price and looks like brand new. A little gift from the folks at the Center. Hope you don't mind our going ahead with it? We figured that if you hated it, we'd save it for someone else."

Denia laughs and signs the last part with exaggerated grace. I note that I am thrilled and relieved. I was stewing about how I could get ahold of a bed, and not looking forward to sleeping on the floor.

Denia hands each of us a set of door keys.

"Welcome home, ladies."

I can say that there isn't a dry eye on the van as we head back to the Center.

Sarah gets my attention as I head up the Center ramp. I turn toward her office, and head down the hall.

"Do you have a minute? I have something for you."

I blink and she pushes the door closed.

"This came in the mail. Sherry told me to look for it. Andrew didn't want to send it to S.P. and stir any negative waters there."

Sarah notices my startle that I try in vain to control. I haven't yet heard from him, even though I send my silly postcards every other day, with help from Grandma Sample. She has been such a trouper. I will really miss her.

Sarah opens the letter for me and places it on my board.

"Dearest Em, I have a gorgeous blonde nurse here at my beck and call, and she agreed to keep this letter confidential, as long as I was available later. I guess some things haven't changed about me, have they?

"I am beginning to feel nearly human again. That will be shot down next week after the third surgery on this leg. They have been doing bone grafts, and sticking strange plastic or ceramic things in my leg to pretend it is bone. They assure me that after this is all over I'll be able to play piano. Right!

"I have really been living for your cards. I'll feel myself sinking into an oblivion of despair, then Flicka here appears with a wonderful funny treat from you. Your cards are better than all the Demerol on the planet.

"Before Sherry left yesterday, she said that she might see if she could swing a long weekend trip in September for a few Center folk to come down to cheer me in my sickbed. I was stunned when I finally woke from my trip to hell and found Sherry still here doing her Florence Nightingale thing. Anyway, I have heard rumors that a certain stubborn lady will be making the great escape soon. I have heard that it will happen last week in August. That's only a week away. Since that lady will no longer be enduring the auspices of S.P., perhaps she could see her way to tagging along on that van trip?

"I know I am asking a lot, and I can easily understand if you can't see your way clear, but I would give several damaged limbs to see a certain pair of emerald eyes.

"Nope, I'm stopping there, or I'll have to fight off this Nordic Nymph. Give my love to Sarah, who is a lovely go-between, and to all the other dear folk that I truly miss."

I look at Sarah. She smiles at my teary eyes.

"ANDREW WANT ME GO SEE HIM. YOU THINK I COULD?"

"Well I did hear rumors that Sherry wants to get a 'get-well' party up to go down after his next surgery and harass him into better health. I can't see any reason why you couldn't go. I think Sherry is planning to ask the ABRUPT people down there if this group might stay in their crash pad. There would be no expense other than pitching in a bit on food.

"Have you ever been on a trip?"

"NO NEVER ANYWHERE."

"Then this is the perfect opportunity for you to start your travel career. Sherry is at a meeting today, so I will tell her that you are interested in making the trip down. You should be well settled into the new house by mid-September, and then off you go!"

I have another bit of business to take care of with Sarah.

"DR. PESKY WONT SIGN PAPERS. CAN U CALL DR WEST TO COME SIGN?"

"Right. She should be able to do that before the end of the week. I'll call her now before you leave. That way I'll remember."

Sarah makes the call. She is surprised to actually talk to Dr. West. She figured to leave a message.

"Yeah, Pesky is doing his foot-dragging act. He has to make damn sure his butt cover hasn't slipped off, and I guess he has to appease White to continue on staff and get all that nice Medicaid kick-back money. Yeah, I know, he works hard. Ellen, you are always being too nice. You fizzes gotta stick together, right? Anyway, if you wouldn't mind checking out Emily and signing her papers, it would ease the process. Let me ask.

"Dr. West needs to do a brief physical on you before she signs the papers. Will you have time to meet with her at S.P. on Wednesday morning?"

Marie is waiting as we come out. She and I will wait for our bus in the lobby.

"Onnee, yoh heah how Anwru doon?"

"BETTER, MORE SURGURY, FEELS DOWN."

I won't tell her about the trip now, even though I am popping to tell someone. I don't think she could go, since she might lose her room in the four-day stretch. They were miffed enough when I went to Mick's for two. But I am sailing, to think that I will move into my own place in a week, and then in two more go to Atlanta. Sheesh!

Wednesday morning the sun is promising a scorcher. I head down to the clinic room on first floor. I've skipped breakfast, but not for the old reasons. I know Dr. West is going to do some bloodwork and had asked that I fast from the night before.

"Emily, you are looking dazzling. I hardly need to poke and push to tell that your health is a damn sight better than it was when I first met you, three years ago. Wow, three years. Where'd they go?"

Leena gives a hand as we go through all the poke and stick routines. The worst part is the pelvic. Its only been done to me a couple times, probably because it is such a bitch. My muscles want to draw up and push away. We all do deep breathing to get me to relax as much as possible. Leena helps with some leg muscle massage and finally it is all over.

As Leena helps me dress, Dr. West fills me in.

"It all appears to be in working order, and considerably better than before. I would be careful about your leg, since it will always be a bit fragile. You don't currently take any meds? Great. Keep it that way. But you will know to call me if you need a doc? Your file says that you took Ovral for a while in your twenties, and then stopped. Will you be wanting to talk about an alternative birth control method?

"SP PUT ME ON PILL THEN. NOT MY CHOICE. WAS RAPES IN BASEMENT HERE. THEY FEAR I HAVE BABY."

"Might I assume that they also did something about the rapist? Or were they more concerned that you might get pregnant.?"

"THEY BELEVE MY FALT. THEY FIRED 1 GUY, NO CHARGES. OTHER GUY DID AGAIN EVEN AFTER CAUT ONCE. NO ONE LISTEN ME THEN. MY FALT."

"How did it ever stop?"

"HE TRIED RAPE SUE. SHE TALKER. TOLD STORY. NOT HER FALT. HE FIRED, NO CHARGES."

"That is just awful. How have you stood this all this time?"

"THIS HAS ALWAYS BEEN HOME."

Ellen shrugs and says that she'll be in to sign the forms when all the blood work comes back. She says she wants to be sure to have all my files in order to transfer them out of here in the discharge package. She says that way she will have them all with her at the clinic, and can properly transfer them on if I need to switch doctors. She says most people come out of care with no history, no files. They just start from scratch. Ellen says that is dangerous for anyone, but especially non-verbal people.

"You know how prejudiced people are, Emily. Medical people aren't any more enlightened than the general population, believe me.

"I need to bring this up again. If you feel you may need some birth control, let me know and we will talk about what is available."

We finish just about right for me to get straightened up for a trip to the Computer Center at the library. I go almost every week now. I am getting faster with the pointer and can type fairly well. On the van I plan what I will write. Of course I want to answer Andrew's letter. I have it tucked in my pocket.

"DEAR ANDREW, SO GOOD TO HEAR FROM YOU. MISS YOU TOO MUCH. YES IM GOING TO TRY TO COME DOWN ON VAN. FIRST TRIP EVER, TO SEE YOU. WOW. MOVING NEXT SATURDAY. SCARY JOY GOT NEW BED AND DRESSER. ALL PAKED BUT A FEW THINGS. LOOK FORWARD TO SEE YOU SO SOON. MUCH LOVE."

It didn't take as long as I expected to get that done. Carol helps me print out and offers to put on the address and mail the letter for me. I show her where to fish out a stamp from my chained-on purse.

"Gee, this is a great idea. I ought to get a chain to put on my wallet and hang it on my belt. I bet it keeps it close at hand. Less likely to get lost."

I head out for my van and wait on the corner. The intense late afternoon sun is baking down making me drowsy. While I nod I am suddenly brought alert. Someone is behind me. I sense my pack being opened. I am glad that I am still on full power, and with almost no movement I throw the chair into reverse.

"Yow, bitch, watch what you doing."

I turn in an Andrew style jerk and face the thief. He is nursing a skinned knee and sore foot and has nothing that I can see of mine in his hands.

"You could hurt someone in that thing."

"Yesh!"

I noise my threat and start toward him again with daggers pouring out of my eyes. Two other guys pass us. One stops by the guy and says, "I saw what you was doin'. Think twice before you try it again."

"No, man, you got it wrong. I just minding my business and this bitch backs over me. She's a fuckin' movin' violation. She oughta be in the looney where geeks like her belong."

They move nearer to him and push him away from me.

"We saw what you was doin'. We got good eyes."

They stand near him until he takes off. The taller guy smiles at me and tips his ball cap a bit. I noise a grateful thanks.

I am on full alert until the van arrives, in spite of the boiling sun. When I feel safely on the van, I really get the shakes. He could have pulled a knife on me and I'd write no more. But I am amazed and proud that I held my own, and I am grateful for those two witnesses who weren't afraid to throw their weight at the guy ripping me off. I just wonder where they came from out of the blue, tall dark avenging angels in baggies and t-shirts. Was this a sign that I am being a fool for leaving .S.P, or that I can trust that I'll be OK if I leave? As OK as anyone can be.

I get back to S.P. in time for dinner. If it is like the last few nights, I will probably get Marie or Grandma Sample to help me eat. The ice is really thick here at S.P. I guess the aides figure that if I have the stupidity to move out, then I must be able to feed myself. Marie and Grandma and Mrs. Blestich and I are now sharing a table. George has taken to sitting with a bunch of the old guys.

"Onnee, cah Ah go wih yoh to awh class, amorroh?"

I blink yes, while chewing some nice cooked cauliflower offered by Grandma. Marie's never been interested in art before outside of looking at books with me, but maybe if she takes it up now, it will be a nice hobby, and a way for us to get together regularly.

We head out a little early since Marie is foot powered and it will take her some time to foot down the little street. She gets the idea to grab my hand grips on the chair back and get a free ride when we can safely move down the middle of the street. She has to make sure of her seating so as not to fall forward out of her chair. We get to the corner across from school and wait. I have been scooting on across when I see a chance, but I am not going to take a chance on Marie not being able to keep up with me.

One of the teacher's aides, Kelley, crosses and takes Marie's chair across as I follow. We go into the dark cool hall, a relief from the intense sun. As we pull through to the big common room the classroom doors open and people stream out singing.

"For she's a jolly good fellow . . ."

I wonder what the occasion is as I look around at the crowd. It is the usual art class people, and the kids in the school, but there is Judy, and Mrs. Neeley, and Leena and Jerry and Fred from the kitchen and Mrs. Butler, and Grandma Sample and bunches more from S.P. Marie is laughing and pointing at everyone. Ah, she was in on this.

Mrs. Neeley comes over and a group of the children wheel in a cart of drinks and one of chips and snacks and a third one with cake.

"Emily, all of us who know you pretty well at S.P. wanted to have a bon voyage party for you. I hate to say this, but the powers-that-be frowned on the whole thing. I know that they have not given their permission for you to leave and won't take responsibility. But I say to heck with them, and best of luck and fortune in all that you do from now on."

Everyone cheers. Mrs. Neeley then brings a big paper-box-like thing over on a wheeled platform.

"From all of us to you, something practical for your new life."

She lifts the big paper box and a big tree sort of bursts out with branches waving. All the branches have money hanging from them, like leaves.

"This stuff is easy to pack and carry and always can be used!"

Jody wheels over.

"I have a gift for Emily, too."

Kelley brings in a box and a large package. She helps me open the box. In it are large brushes with rubber grips, and eight jars of liquid acrylic paint. I whoop for joy. Paints to have at home, to work on my own. Then Kelley opens the package. It is a stunningly colored painting of my view on Two-South at sunset. I am amazed at the subtle cloud reds, maroons, peaches, pinks, and the richly-colored shadows on the tops of the houses below the red roofs. I can almost anticipate the gray sweep of night moving across the rooftops.

"I think it may be the first in a series," Jody quips, but she has that serious look in her eyes.

"I had Kelley come over a few evenings that I knew you'd be out. She took some terrific photos from that window. I hope you don't mind."

❖❖❖

It is Saturday. Judy got me up before dawn so she could strip my bed.

"Well, kid, I don't wanna say goodbye. I know you'll be back to see your friends. I mean, lookit Ted? He brings Grandma flowers every month since he's gone, and brings the kitchen folk some kinda treat. He's a really nice guy.

"I'm sorry for all the hard stuff that's happened between us, but I gotta think we've been pretty good friends in spite of the hard times, eh?"

While Judy talks I can't help looking at her and realizing who is it she's reminded me of lately. She is a rounder, less cheery Roseanne, like on the TV show reruns. That makes me chuckle, and I guess she figures I am agreeing with what she's saying. That's OK. No sweat. I guess she's been something of a friend.

There's a knock at the door. It is Sarah.

"Hi, ladies. I just came up to see if you needed any last-minute things packed. I brought two suitcases."

Judy kinda ducks out the door after grabbing a tissue out of my box on the stack of stuff I have ready to go. Sarah puts a suitcase on the stripped bed and greets the non-responsive Edna just behind her. I point out some things that need stashing and Sarah carefully puts them in the case.

"Mary said that your bed is in and ready, and your closet is open for business. Jenny moved in yesterday, so you will be the final entry. You guys have really lucked into a find. That house is just a treasure. I can't believe that there are places like that now. When I think of what Andrew first moved into with Bob, and that sewer that Melissa first lived in, I am just relieved that it has begun to change it for a few people."

"GONNA RUN DOWN HALL, BACK MINUT."

While Sarah puts the last few things in from my closet, I am going to tour about my old home one last time. I greet everyone I know and get lots of good luck wishes in return as I hurry around to Two-Skilled. I have a card for George. He won't hear me, but I can leave the card and he can choose.

"Ngawj," I try to noise, as I round Larry's bed. George's back is to me as he gazes out the window from his slightly raised bed. He can't be on his recently reconstructed behind.

"Goodbye, Emily Mason. May all your dreams come true, and none of my fears."

I try to get to the bottom of his bed, but the aides have shoved his dresser/TV stand right up to his bed. I can't see him to wish him well and he can't know what I am trying to say. I go up behind him and make a stab at tossing the card onto his bed. That way an aide will see it soon and read it to him.

"Bah, Ngawj. Uhv Uo."

I head back over to Two-South to watch the sun on the roof. It is up a ways now and I have missed the best color, but I am glad to see the sweep of light-chasing shadow cleaning the rooftops of their night drabness.

Sarah comes up the hall with two suitcases.

"It's all in here now. Ready?"

We step onto and off of the elevators and head down the kitchen hall to the administration offices. Sarah picks up the discharge papers from Ms. Butler. Marie is sitting with Donna at the reception desk.

"Onnee, don evah fuhgeh me."

"DON'T WORRY, I LOVE U MARIE."

Tissues and hugs later, Sarah hits the plate to the new automatic doors with her elbow and they swing open. The bright sun makes me blink, "YES!"

298

Afterword

Getting Life started out as a terrible burst of automatic writing which was likely an outpouring of grief. I had spent the mid-'80s as an independent-living counselor supporting people in their journey out of long-term care. During the same time I supported my own parents-in-law in their personal journeys through nursing care. The dichotomous state this put me in was wrenching and painful. But the circumstances of the people I knew in the nursing homes (both residents and staff) were considerably more dismal and painful. I was and am always struck by how little is known of these conditions by the general public, and consequently how little is done to change them. Understaffing, inappropriate placement, indifferent medical care, the obfuscation of the insurance-as-payment system, extreme poverty, and egregious levels of stress in inhumane conditions all contribute to an environment which Wolf Wolfensburger described as death-making. In the same places, heroic staff, generous advocates and volunteers, conscientious residents, and struggling family members engage in a Sysiphean battle to provide some semblance of decent quality of life for people living in long-term care. Independent living programs work to give younger disabled people the opportunity to live in the community away from the long-term-care system.

Emily created herself and her friends out of extraordinarily ordinary encounters I had with a number of remarkable people during those years. None of the book characters represents any individual I have known.

When I completed the writing, I was invited to read the book to the Mattingly Adult Education Program Book Club. The members of the club, like Emily, all live with severe disabling conditions, and many of them have moved into and out of the realm of long-term care. I would like to thank them first for their kindness in choosing *Getting Life* as a selection for their club, and second, but more important, for their validation of Emily's experiences, which they assured me were accurate. Thank you, Harold, who never gave up on Emily, Tony, Tara, Mike, Robert, Karen, James, Mary Ann, Jo Ann, Gwen, and Todd, who thought Andrew was a butt.

I must thank Mary Johnson who got me into this situation in the first place, Donna Herp who taught me much, Arthur Campbell who kept me laughing, and many friends along the way, including Stanley, Jackie, Georgia, Pat, Joe, Mike, Susie, Barbara, Buddy, Annie, Gerry, Lisa, Melissa, Nancy, Therese, Tom, Jewell, Sharon, Joey, and the folks at the Center for Accessible Living and at the Council for Retarded Citizens and Citizens Advocacy, and all the extraordinary people from all around the country whom I have met through the Advocado Press.

I thank my mother who listened, Hert and Corinne who taught me a lot about generosity, my brothers who encouraged me, Mike and Melanie who nudged, Bob and Rob who transferred text, Corie who held my hand, and most especially Barrett Shaw who edited meticulously and with feeling and had faith in Emily.

About the Author

*J*ulie Shaw Cole is an expressive arts therapist and former independent-living counseling program manager. She has contributed articles to *The Disability Rag* magazine and *The Ragged Edge* anthology and to gardening magazines. She lives in Louisville, Kentucky, with her husband Robert, a son and daughter, two cats, and a toad.